FICTION LAND

RR HAYWOOD

1899 INC LTD

PROLOGUE

'I made you tea. Do you drink tea? There's milk and sugar if you want it. Okay. Let's start with your name.'

'John Croker. Are you my handler?'

'Something like that.'

'I need to find my van.'

'We have a few things we need to do first, John. Is it okay if I call you John?'

'Sure.'

'That's great. My name is Rachel, and the most important thing for you to know is that everything will be okay.'

'No, you don't understand. The surgeon leaves at five.'

'It's fine. I promise. Now, what I need you to do is tell me everything. Okay? Can you do that? How's the tea?'

'The tea's good. Okay. I mean. Where do I start?'

'We find the best starting point is wherever it *feels right* to start from. Does that make sense?'

'No, sure, I got that. I think I know where to start, you know, so it's relevant.'

'Great. Well, begin whenever you're ready. And remember what I said, don't leave anything out. Got it?'

'Are you FBI?'

'Let's discuss all that at the end.'

'Okay. Er, so this morning then . . . I mean. I guess I should start there.'

'Sure. Start there.'

'Okay. So. I mean, everything seemed fine. You know? Like I was worried about Wendy, but everything else was okay. Anyway, so I get to work for around 7 a.m. and it's Monday and we always have a briefing on a Monday . . .'

FADE TO BLACK.

CHAPTER ONE

'It's Monday morning, people!' Mac called out to a chorus of groans in the briefing room. 'Okay, your assignments. Sandra, route one.'

'All day long,' Sandra said.

'Ishmael, you're on two.'

'Bring it in, baby,' Ishmael said, taking a high five from Sandra. 'Our routes cross over. Wanna do lunch?'

'Arrange your dates in your own time! Paulo, route three. Jacko, route four. Teddy's gone sick so route five gets shared between you two. Mikey, you're on eight, and John, you got nine again.'

'I appreciate that, Mac,' I said.

'Hey, it's no bother. The guys all agreed you get nine until Wendy's out of hospital.'

'We got your back, Croker,' Sandra said, and the others all voiced the same.

I nodded back at them, humbled by their kindness.

'What about the bonuses?' Hank asked.

'I'm coming to it!' Mac said, as the others laughed at Hank. 'The bosses said you get those vans back safe and sound today and they'll be depositing them into your accounts. Yeah, that cheered you all up, huh. Go on now! Saddle up.'

I headed out after the others.

'Hey, John?' Mac said, guiding me into his office. 'You wanna do me a favor today?'

'Sure, Mac. What's up?'

Mac produced a small package. 'Drop this off at the DA's office would ya. It's right next to the hospital. How's Wendy doing anyway?'

I slid it into my pocket. 'The docs said she needs the operation to survive. But my sister's maxed out and the bank's already loaned what it can. But with the bonus we can make it.'

'That's good, John. You get the van back today and that money gets paid. She's a trouper though, huh? Just like her big Uncle John!'

I had one day left to get that money for Wendy's life-saving operation.

A moment later I took my van up the ramp from the underground garage onto West Forty-second Street, Manhattan, New York City. The greatest city in the world.

It was a cold winter day with a vicious wind whipping in from the Atlantic. My coat was zipped up and the heater was on full.

I turned the radio on. Old-timey hits. Old rock. Old country. Nothing too modern.

A black SUV pulled out behind my van, and this weird feeling of déjà vu swept over me.

I shrugged it off. I had it in Afghan once. My SEAL team was covertly tracking an ISIS death squad to intercept and extract the hostages before they were beheaded. I had déjà vu then. It happens. It's nothing new.

I reached the intersection and stopped at the lights, my fingers tapping the wheel in time to Dolly Parton's 'Jolene'. A classic. They don't make songs like that anymore.

There was an ambulance behind me. The siren screamed loudly as it went by. I let it go past and went back to drumming my fingers on the wheel in time to Billy Joel's 'We Didn't Start the Fire'. A classic. They don't make songs like that anymore.

Wait.

What?

I stared at the stereo. It was playing Dolly Parton before.

I shook it off and got on with my route. I did a few drops then reached the NYC Free Hospital.

I pushed out into the kids' ward, the walls painted with bright murals. The staff smiled and nodded as I rushed by to Wendy's room.

A breathing tube in her nose. Tubes in her arm. But she smiled big and wide when I walked in. Eight years old and as Mac said, *she's a trouper.*

'Uncle John!' she said. My sister looked at me, exhaustion and stress clear on her face.

'How's my girl?' I bent over the bed to hug my niece. 'How you feeling?'

'I'm okay,' she said, with that big smile. Her blue eyes still twinkling with mischief.

I spent a few moments fussing over her. Plumping her pillows and ticking her ribs until she laughed, and I only stopped when she started coughing and grew suddenly tired.

'You're gonna get better,' I told her, staring into her eyes. 'You got this, kid. I know you do. You'll have that operation and be back to skating in no time.'

'You promise?' she whispered.

'I promise, and you know what? Army Rangers always keep their promises.'

'She needs to rest,' my sister said.

'She'll make it, sis. I swear she will.'

'But without the operation, John . . .' she trailed off with a haunted look.

'Mac said we get the bonuses today. They're wiring it into our accounts. Tell the docs to do the operation.'

'They won't, John. They need payment up front, and they need it by 5 p.m. or it's too late. The surgeon has to fly out of state to operate on another kid.'

'It's okay. I'll get it. I promise.'

I jogged out into the hot summer air of downtown LA. The greatest city in the world. That feeling hit me again, like something was weird, but I shook it off because I needed to get my round done and get that bonus. That was all that mattered.

That's when I saw the back doors to my UPS van were wide open, with a guy inside wearing a ski mask, and two more guys in ski masks on the road keeping watch.

'Hey! Get out of my van!' I yelled as I started running.

'I don't have it!' the guy in the back of the van shouted, as the other two guys turned towards me and let rip with submachine guns. I dove for cover behind the hospital sign as the windows behind me shattered and bullets hit the sidewalks.

'Take the van,' one of the shooters yelled, and the other one ran to the cab of my van. A second later it was pulling away with the guy still inside the back, reading labels on parcels and throwing them aside.

Then the black SUV I saw earlier pulled out behind it with a squeal of tires, but the driver went too fast and hit another car, smashing headlights and crumpling fenders. I heard a radiator pop, and steam poured from the front of the SUV.

The driver kicked the door open. But he saw me and brought a submachine gun up to let rip. Bullets were hitting everything. People were screaming. It was chaos.

My only thought was to get my van back. That was all that mattered. Just that, and I ran hard, but my van reached the intersection, turned a hard right and drove off faster than I could ever run. I stopped with a shout, but saw the shooter had been left behind too. He yelled out and ran off into an alleyway.

I went after him, but he could see me getting closer and panicked, throwing the submachine gun at me as he pulled a pistol from the back of his waistband and started taking shots.

I stayed on his six. Pounding after him. The only thought in my mind to get my van back.

Another wall ahead. A high one, and there was no way the guy could scale that. He tried anyway, and for a second I thought he'd make it, but he slipped and impaled himself on a shard of rusty metal dumped out the back of a hardware store. I thought he'd scream, but he was gurgling and spitting frothy blood and going into shock.

I bent down and took his ski mask off to see he was a white guy with a shaved head and tattoos on his neck.

'Hey! My van. Where is it?' I grabbed the shard of metal poking out of his chest and gave it a twist. 'You're bleeding out. You're gonna die. You want an ambulance? You want me to stop? My van. Where is it?'

'Huschech!' The shooter gasped with a spray of blood, and a

second later his head slumped to the side, his lifeless eyes staring at nothing while I remembered a life I once had.

A life I'd left behind.

But they'd taken my van, and I really needed it back.

So be it then, and a moment later the cops ran into the alley to find a dead guy impaled on a stick, with no sign of the guy who'd been chasing him.

CHAPTER TWO

'You've stopped. Is everything okay, John?'

'Sure. But, you know, I killed the guy. Or at least I didn't exactly help him.'

'Yep. Got all that. How's the tea? Do you want another one?'

'No, I'm good. So, that's okay then? I mean, you know, he fell on the spike. I didn't make him do that, and he did steal my van.'

'It's fine, John. Just keep going.'

'You want me to keep going?'

'Yes. Keep going.'

'Sure. . .'

FADE TO BLACK.

CHAPTER THREE

I walked into Huschech's scrapyard, past the wrecks stacked four and five high.

The office was ahead. A dilapidated prefab. Grime on the windows. Blinds inside all twisted and bent.

A girl was behind the counter, filing her nails and staring at a cell phone propped against the dust-covered landline.

'I'm looking for Huschech.'

She thumbed the door to the workshop.

I stepped through into a chop shop. A big guy inside working a grinder under the hood of an old Ford.

'You Huschech?' I asked as the guy looked at my uniform.

'Deliveries out the front! You gotta see Donna.'

'I'm not here to deliver. My van,' I said, taking a step closer. 'Give it back and I walk away.'

'What are you? Some kind of fucking moron? Get outta here!' he yelled with a rush of anger, ditching the grinder and snatching up a wrench.

'My van. I want it back.'

'Fuck you!' Huschech started turning away, then whipped back around to swing the wrench at my head.

It was obvious what he was going to do, and the weight was

already on my front foot to help me step inside the swing and pluck the wrench free. 'My van. Where is it?'

I twisted his wrist and dropped him to his knees with a gasp of pain as his other hand quickly drew a Glock from his waistband. I twisted to the side. The shot missed, and Huschech cried out as I snapped his wrist bone with a dull crack.

'My van.'

'You know who I am?' Huschech asked, glaring up as I remembered the life I once had. The things I once did. The people I once worked for.

'Yeah. I know who you are. You're Otto Huschech. The sleazebag running the grand theft auto racket for Mascaponi.'

'You know and you did all this? For a van? Who are you?'

'John Croker,' I said, watching the shock hit him.

'No,' Huschech whispered. 'No way. You died! You're dead! Mascaponi shot you!'

'The bullet missed my heart . . . but everyone *thought* I was dead. So I got out. I left this life . . . But you couldn't leave me alone,' I said, while aiming Huschech's pistol at his head.

'Croker! No! It was a mistake! We didn't know it was yours!'

'And now my niece is dying. So you tell Mascaponi John Croker is coming for him. And you tell him he'd better not miss my heart this time!'

A bang and Huschech fell dead, and I realized I failed to find out where my van was – but the second I thought that, the feeling swept over me again. That weird sensation. But it was more powerful this time, enough to make me rock back and rub my temples.

'You got a headache, UPS man?'

I looked up to see a big Mexican guy walking into the workshop with four more Hispanic guys behind him. All of them swinging tire irons and chains.

'I got no issue with the Mexicans,' I said.

'That's not the way I see it, *ese*. What? You didn't hear? Our cartel is working with Mascaponi now. So it turns out you *do* have an issue with the Mexicans.'

Five against one. An ordinary man wouldn't stand a chance. But I wasn't an ordinary man, and a second later five shots rang out in quick succession.

I ditched the empty gun and stepped over the bodies of five Mexican guys, who'd come to the US in search of better lives but got sucked into crime to send money home so their families could eat.

But wait.

What?

How did they know to say that about Mascaponi? How did they know I was here?

Donna.

She must have made a call.

Whatever. The van. I had to get it back, and damn! I didn't ask the Mexicans *or* Huschech where it was. But it was too late. They were all dead.

I HEADED OUTSIDE to an overcast sky of a fall day. Rain in the air and high-rise buildings on all sides in downtown Chicago. The greatest city in the world.

Chicago?

It was New York.

No. LA. I lived in LA.

It was just stress. My mind needed to rest. My sister always said I put in too many hours. But then I've always been driven like that. That's how I got so good in the military, and then after, when I left Special Forces and did that other work.

The bad work.

The bad work for Mascaponi.

'You look like you're in a hurry.'

Someone was ahead, blocking my exit from the scrapyard. A big guy standing in the gate. Tall, broad, and black. Four more black guys behind him. Born into the cycle of poverty and crime where gangs offered the only real means to get money, so you didn't starve to death.

That feeling came on again, making me shake my head and blink.

'I just need my van back.'

'We all need something,' the leader said. 'And I need to get paid, so you need to get dead.'

Five against one. An ordinary man wouldn't stand a chance. But I wasn't an ordinary man. Only problem was this time I didn't have the pistol.

I killed four easily. Bones crunched. Blood sprayed.

One left. The leader. The main guy. He circled me while throwing his knife from one hand to the other.

'I just want my van,' I told him.

'This ain't personal, brother. We all gotta do what we gotta do.'

He lunged in fast, but I'd fought people for a living once, so blocking and removing the knife to stab into his chest was not hard.

I took his weight and lowered him down as we clasped hands.

'Please. My van,' I said quietly. Looking him in the eye, man to man.

He looked up at me. One warrior to another, and in a different world we could have been buddies. 'Chinatown,' he whispered. 'Lin Lin. They . . . They just wanted the hard drive.'

My heart missed a beat as he choked on his own blood and died in my arms.

But I could only think about the name he said.

The name of someone I used to know.

CHAPTER FOUR

'Actually, can I get another tea?'

'Yeah, of course. Sit tight and I'll grab one.'

'THERE YOU ARE. It's nice tea, isn't it? Right. You okay to keep going?'

'Sure. But er, so? You know? The men I killed? And Huschech?'

'What about them?'

'You gonna send someone, right? For the bodies and whatnot. I mean. The girl. She must have called it in by now.'

'The girl?'

'At Huschech's. Donna. The receptionist.'

'Oh, that girl! Right. Got it.'

'You think she called Mascaponi direct? Yeah, that figures. She'd have a number to call in emergencies. You should seize her phone and see who she called.'

'Tell you what, John. Let's get all this down and make an assessment at the end. Yeah? Sound good?'

'Sure. I mean. You're the handler, right?'

'Something like that. Anyway. Where were you? Er . . . Lin Lin? I think you were going to Chinatown to see Lin Lin.'

'Yeah. So. Lin Lin. Let me tell you who Lin Lin is . . .'

FADE TO BLACK.

CHAPTER FIVE

Lin Lin was a tech wizard who hacked for the highest bidder, but why would my van be taken to Lin Lin?

And what did the guy mean about a hard drive?

I jogged on through the downtown streets and spotted a yellow cab ahead of me with the passenger leaning in towards the driver's window, and another guy on the other side staring in through the front passenger window.

'Hey, you done?' I asked, as the guy near the driver turned fast with a .38 snub nose revolver in his hand.

I stepped in fast, grabbing his gun hand and headbutting his nose to snatch the gun free, then ducked from the deafening bang of a close-quarters sawn-off shotgun firing from the other side of the car.

I spun fast and got two rounds into the other guy's chest with the .38, double-tapping his center of mass. He dropped back with a cry as the first guy got to his feet with a knife, so I put a round into his head for good measure.

'I said are you done,' I asked as the cab driver stared up at me with wide eyes, his hands still in the air. 'I need to get to Chinatown.'

The driver looked at me and nodded. 'Get in please,' he said in an accent I recognized.

I clocked his ID on the dash. Ibrahim Mustafa. Arabic skin tone. Jet black hair. Most likely a refugee from Iraq. 'As-salamu alaikum.'

'Wa-alaikum salam,' he said. 'You army? Iraq?'

'Three tours.'

'I was an interpreter for the US army. But you don't look like infantry.'

Ibrahim was right. I wasn't regular infantry. I was something else. I was Special Forces. Green Beret. No. I wasn't a Green Beret. I was Delta Force.

That feeling came on again. Strong as hell and making me feel dizzy. I clamped my eyes closed and rubbed my temples.

'You are troubled, my friend,' Ibrahim said. 'And if this van is important, and something tells me that it is, then maybe you should clear your head first.'

I knew Ibrahim was right. I needed to be on my A game if I was going in against Mascaponi.

'I tell you what, my new best friend John. We make a quick stop to clear your head.'

A moment later we pulled into a street and stopped outside a small house.

I followed him inside. A thick, patterned rug on the floor. Chairs pushed against the wall.

He started heating an iron kettle over a stove, and I looked at the pictures on the walls: 6x8 prints of Ibrahim in army bases, giving the thumbs-up alongside US marines and infantry.

The kettle boiled. He poured into a pot. Scent filled the air. Assam tea. He brought a tray over. We sat cross-legged on the rug as he went through the ritual of stirring and pouring into delicate cups then adding cinnamon sticks.

I bowed my head to show respect and took a cup. We drank in silence, and Ibrahim was right. The tea cleared my mind, and it made me realize just what I was up against.

'We need to make another stop,' I told Ibrahim when we set off.

'Okey dokey orange pokey . . . Did I say that right?'

'Close enough, buddy. Pull up here.'

'Is this your house? Can I come inside?'

I smiled and headed to my front door, then spotted the ground-out cigarette butt on the stoop.

There was someone already inside.

'Wait there,' I said to Ibrahim, and surged through the door with the .38 ready in my hand.

Two of them were inside, both drawing fast. One by the bedroom door. One in the kitchen. I got a shot into the one in the kitchen, sending him crashing back into my pan rack as the other guy fired at me. The rounds hit the walls and door frame as I dove to the side.

I was out of shots. The hood in the kitchen smiled, despite the gunshot wound in his chest, and raised his Glock to shoot me dead, but Ibrahim ran in and clubbed the guy over the head with a tire iron.

'He's out,' I said, rolling away to see the second attacker on the floor in the bedroom doorway with his skull caved in. Then I heard another clunk and looked back to Ibrahim, standing over the guy in the kitchen with the tire iron dripping fresh blood.

'He moved,' Ibrahim said.

'Sure. And thanks for the help, but next time I tell you to stay put then you need to stay put.'

'Sure thing, partner! Is this you?' he asked, walking over to the pictures on my walls. Old 6x8 prints of my military service.

'Who is this?' Ibrahim asked, staring at a picture of me standing next to a big guy in an expensive suit. 'This man. I know him. He owns half of LA.'

Ibrahim was right. Mascaponi does own half of LA. I should know. I helped him take most of it. There was a time I would have done anything for Mascaponi. Boosting high-end cars and dealing drugs. Enforcing debts and intimidating the witnesses to his crimes. I worked my way into his empire to stand at his side. Doing what he wanted. Killing who he needed dead.

I went into my bedroom and came back holding a small glass case. 'I've got to do something in Chinatown, Ibrahim. Something I don't want to do . . . And I might not make it out.'

'You want me to feed your pet spider?' he asked with a look to the tarantula sitting in the corner of the glass case.

'She's called Sally. She's a Mexican red-knee. She's twenty years old and my best friend.'

'I will take very good care of Sally, John Croker. And I promise if anything happens, I will make sure she gets to Wendy. Now we must go, John. The surgeon needs to be paid by 5 p.m.'

And that feeling came on again.

That feeling of déjà vu.

CHAPTER SIX

'Hang on. Your best friend is a spider?'

'Yeah. Sally.'

'Do you play frisbee with her?'

'What?'

'With Sally. Do you play frisbee, or ball? Or like, you know, like go for walks or something.'

'She's a spider. How she meant to catch a frisbee or a ball? And you ever tried putting a leash on a spider? They get mad as hell. They don't like it.'

'You've tried?'

'Yeah. I tried. She didn't like it.'

'You tried taking your spider for a walk?'

'It feels like you're judging me. I mean. I just killed about twenty-five guys and you're judging me on my pet?'

'Good point. Apologies. Do continue.'

'You know what. Maybe I should go.'

'No! Stay. Sorry, John. Just. You know. A spider? I was like, a spider spider? No! Sit down. Drink your tea. I'm not judging you. Right, so you and Ibrahim were back in the taxi.'

'Yeah. We were back in the taxi. With Sally. My spider.'

'I'm not judging you!'

'Whatever. Anyway, so I'm thinking, how did Ibrahim know that stuff about Wendy, right? I mean. I hadn't told him . . .'

FADE TO BLACK.

CHAPTER SEVEN

We stopped near the big red arches into Chinatown. I checked the Glock I'd taken from the bad guy in my house. 'Okay. I'm good. And listen, thank you, Ibrahim.'

'Roger that, four to the ten good buddy. Was that right?'

'Close enough, buddy.'

It was busy, with tourists everywhere and the smell of rich, aromatic food hanging in the air. I was hungry as hell, but I didn't have time to eat.

I just needed to find Lin Lin.

'Where's your van, UPS man?'

A deep voice from the side. A heavy accent. A Japanese guy in a sharp suit. His dark hair smoothed back. Four more Yakuza with him, all of them moving out to block my path.

They knew I was coming. Word spreads fast in the underworld.

'Listen, there's a lot of innocent people here. How about we take this fight somewhere quieter.'

He looked at me with a show of respect, then turned side-on to usher me past. I didn't try to run. I'd given my word, and that means something.

We headed into a warehouse and along aisles stacked with boxes.

'We heard you were dead, John Croker,' the lead Yakuza said.

'I was.'

'Then why come back?'

'Will it make a difference if I tell you?'

He didn't answer. He didn't need to.

We reached an open area, deep within the warehouse.

I stopped and looked around at each of them, waiting for them to circle me. The Yakuza aren't like other gangsters. They have honor and discipline, and in many ways they're more like military. They don't kill innocents, and they don't kill kids.

I respect that.

Which is why I gave them a chance.

'So,' I said, looking back at the lead guy. 'You wanna surrender here?'

His gaze hardened and I heard the rasp of a short-sword being pulled from a scabbard from behind. I ducked fast and the sword cut through the air where my neck should have been.

A back kick to a knee. The bone snapped. The guy fell. I took his sword and faced off against the other four Yakuza, now drawing their blades.

They all came for me at once.

Which was the thing I feared the most.

I parried one and dodged and heard a soft 'phut' as one of the Yakuza slammed back with a bullet-hole in his chest.

We all froze, as stunned as each other. Even the guy who was shot looked stunned, until another round took the back of his skull out.

'Ambush!' the lead guy said, as the sound of more suppressed shots rang out, taking them down one after the other.

I stood still. Waiting to be shot.

But that didn't happen and instead, I heard another sound.

A click. Then a clack.

A click. Then a clack.

It was a noise I knew well, and one that made my heart rate shoot up as my mouth went dry and she finally stepped into view like a ghost from my past in high heels and a tight red dress.

A ghost carrying a rifle fitted with a suppressor.

'You died, John Croker,' she said, her black eyes staring into mine. Her bosom heaving in the tight dress. 'You died and went to heaven.'

She took a step closer, her hips swaying, and my heart rate went into overdrive. 'Or was it hell?' she whispered.

I stared back at her. At the best hacker I ever met. 'Hey, Lin Lin.'

The sound of my voice seemed to cause a reaction. Like she was still ready to believe it wasn't me, and for a second I thought she'd pull the trigger and put a round through me. But instead, she stepped in close and slapped me hard across the face.

'You shit, John Croker! You die.'

'Hey. I'm back!' I say with a wan wave of my hands, but that just earned me another slap.

'Give me one reason why I don't shoot you.'

'Cos you still love me?'

She leaned in closer. So close I could smell her perfume. 'You got two minutes before I call Mascaponi, John.'

'You work for Mascaponi now, Lin?'

'Everyone works for Mascaponi now,' she said, as she walked off into one of the dark aisles. But I went after her.

'Lin. I know there's history between us, but I really need my van.'

'And I really needed something once, John.'

She headed inside an office.

'Lin! You don't understand. I need that van. Please. I need it back.' Something in my tone finally made her frown into my eyes.

'In all these years, I never heard John Croker beg.'

'This isn't for me, Lin.'

'Who? For a woman?'

'My niece. She's eight. She needs an operation. I gotta pay the surgeon by five or she dies. I need that van back to get my bonus. Please. I'll do anything.'

She exhaled slowly, warm breath blasting over my neck as I felt her body push against mine. 'Anything?'

'Anything.'

She glanced at the clock on the wall. A little past noon. 'Still got five hours,' she whispered, a smile touching the corners of her lips. And I shouldn't. I really shouldn't. But the scent of her and the history we had, and besides, she was right.

I did have five hours.

She slid back onto the desk, her legs wrapped around my waist, and I kissed her breasts as we moved together.

It was explosive and fast and we climaxed together. Both of us gasping out with the release, and it was that weird feeling of déjà vu that saved my life – because right at that moment I looked down at the large binary code tattoo wrapped around her right shoulder.

The tattoo that wasn't there a split second ago.

I rocked back, feeling suddenly dizzy as the door behind me slammed open and a big Russian guy in a tracksuit came in firing a pistol – but I was already diving behind the desk and grabbing a bottle of whiskey to throw at his head.

It smashed on impact, blinding him with broken glass and burning liquid. He cried out as Lin Lin scrabbled to get a revolver from her desk drawer. I kicked it shut on her wrist then aimed the revolver at Lin Lin.

'Darling . . . I didn't know they were coming.'

I twitched my aim and fired the gun, sending a round close enough to skim her thigh, drawing blood and making her gasp in shock. 'My van.'

'I don't have your stupid van! It's not here. I only needed the hard drive.'

I aimed at her head. Something in my eyes told her I'd pull the trigger.

'Mascaponi has it,' she finally said. 'He thinks the hard drive is inside. He's got guys opening every parcel to find it.'

'Where?'

'Where do you think.'

I knew where she meant.

The abandoned docks.

The same place Mascaponi shot me and left me for dead.

I turned for the door.

'See you around, Lin Lin.'

'Not if I see you first, John Croker!' she yelled out, defiant as hell, and it brought a smile to my lips as I walked back to the middle of the warehouse to see Ibrahim clubbing a dead Yakuza in the head with a tire iron.

'He moved,' Ibrahim said, as I looked around at the other dead Yakuza, all with tire iron dents in their heads. 'They all moved.'

'Whatever. Let's go.'

'Where to, John Croker?'

'To the place I died, Ibrahim.'

'Yippey the kay away! Was that right?'

'Close enough, buddy. Close enough.'

CHAPTER EIGHT

Freezing flakes of snow landed on my face as I approached the abandoned docks.

I'd left Ibrahim a few blocks back and made him promise he would take Sally to Wendy.

I got to the side of the warehouse and made my way in. Cars inside, more than I was expecting.

I spotted something else. My UPS van with the back doors wide open.

I looked for a way to reach it, edging closer until I spotted a stack of wooden crates.

Wooden crates used to hold military grade weapons.

I realized why the Mexicans, the Russians, the Yakuza and the other gangs had been sent after me.

Because they were all there buying military grade weapons from Mascaponi.

This couldn't be happening. Even Mascaponi couldn't be that stupid. If those gangs got that level of hardware, it'd be war.

I started to rise but someone had gotten the drop on me, a barrel jabbing into the back of my neck.

I stayed completely still, knowing in my heart who it was.

Lin Lin prodded the rifle into my back, sending me tumbling

forward, through the gap between the crates into the center of the deal going down.

Into the Yakuza and the Mexicans and every other goddamn gang, all pulling pistols to aim at me with a chorus of clicks, and right there in the middle, with a big cheese-eating grin on his face, was Mascaponi.

The man who'd killed me once already.

'Are you delivering, UPS man?' he asked as the gang members all sniggered. 'But you don't have a parcel.'

I slowly looked up at Lin Lin with a double take at the attractive black woman staring at me. 'Holy shit! When did you turn black?' I asked, as that feeling of déjà vu came over me again.

'I've always been black,' Lin said, giving me a weird look.

'You were Chinese!'

'He's lost it,' Mascaponi said, as I blinked stupidly at the attractive Italian woman smoking a fat Cuban cigar. 'You used to be smart, John. Now look at you.'

'Mascaponi is a man,' I whispered to myself, squeezing my eyes closed then opening them again to see that Mascaponi was most definitely not a man, and suddenly gaining a series of flashbacks of Mascaponi and I making love.

What the hell was going on?

'Please. I just need my van.'

'You were right,' Mascaponi said, with a smirk. 'John Croker does like begging.'

'I'm not begging. I'm giving you a chance.'

She roared with laughter. They all did, and I laughed right along with them. 'What's so funny, John?' Mascaponi demanded.

'Nothing,' I said, as I got to my knees then slowly rose to my feet. 'But it will be funny when you get life in a maximum-security federal prison . . .'

That got their attention. Mascaponi even started to smile. But something in my tone made her look at me closely.

'I got out, Mascaponi. You shot me and I got out. But you had to bring me back in. And for what? For a hard drive? A hard drive that contains all of your contacts and all of your murders and crimes and the bribes you paid to city officials. Yeah. That hard drive. You thought it was in my van. But it wasn't, Mascaponi. My boss gave it to me this morning and asked me to deliver it to the DA's office. But hey. You wanna know the weirdest thing? You wanna know who posted that hard drive to the DA? I did. Because I made that hard drive. I was the one who put all the evidence on it . . . Because guess what? I was an undercover FBI agent, Mascaponi. That's why I did all of your dirty work, and that's why I got close to you . . . And in the event of my death, or disappearance, that hard drive would get sent to the DA.'

She looked at me with a wry smile. 'Well done, John. You really are a UPS driver, aren't you.'

'What?'

'The hard drive. It's in your pocket. I can see it. Now be a good delivery boy, John, and hand it over.'

I threw it over. She caught it, smirking as she ripped the top off, then frowning as she turned the box upside down to show it was empty.

'UPS apologizes for losing your parcel. Oh. Wait. It isn't lost at all. It's with my friend in his taxi on the way to the DA's office.' I checked my watch. 'And hey. He should be there about now.'

'Except he isn't,' a voice said, as Ibrahim loomed out of the darkness holding the hard drive. 'And guess what? I was in the army too! In Iraq. Which is how I made contacts to steal all of these weapons!'

'Which he sold to me,' Mascaponi said, with a smile.

'Well, John. I think you are up the lake with a paddle. Was that right?' Ibrahim asked.

'Close enough, buddy. Close enough.'

'I'm sorry, John,' Mascaponi said, drawing a gun from her belt. 'For what it's worth, I really liked you.'

'Trust me, the feeling was not mutual. But say – didn't anyone else order a delivery?' I asked, hearing the sound of engines and wheels. 'Hey, guess what?' I called as the crates started shaking from the incoming rumble. 'UPS, motherfuckers!'

They hit from all sides.

Big brown vans ploughing through the old walls, showers of brick and debris flying out and Mac leaning out of Hank's UPS van firing an assault rifle single-handed.

Sandra came in fast behind them, slamming into the Mexican cartel trying to run for it. Ishmael at her side, driving his van into the Yakuza. Paulo and Jacko driving down the Russians. Louise and Mikey going after the others.

'John!' Mac shouted, throwing a shotgun over. I caught it one-handed and crunched a round into the chamber. 'We got this!' he yelled. 'You get Mascaponi . . . And John? Don't let him shoot you this time.'

I offered a salute as Hank jumped out of his van, turning an RPG on the Russian gang, who were falling back while firing pistols.

The explosion rocked the warehouse, sending flames shooting up to roll under the roof, while I set off after Lin and Mascaponi, running out into the cold grey day and that snow coming down thick and fast.

'Where are you going?' I yelled, and they both turned.

'Let us go, John! We're in love!' Lin shouted, her hand clasped in Mascaponi's.

'The night of the threesome, John,' Mascaponi said. 'Do you remember that night?'

Flashbacks filled my head. Images of Lin, Mascaponi and me all in bed together.

'It was your idea, John. But we fell in love!' Mascaponi shouted as I stared at them. 'That's why I missed your heart, John. I didn't want to kill you! I wanted to you have that new life.'

I stopped close to them, staring at the two women I once loved. But the only thing I needed was my van. 'Give me the keys,' I said, crunching the shotgun and aiming it at them.

'Sure, John,' Mascaponi said, and reached into her pocket and threw them at me. It was an old trick and I should have been prepared, but I flinched from the keys hitting my face, and that was enough for Lin Lin to rush in and grab the revolver from my waistband.

The revolver I took from her drawer.

The revolver with only one round left, and she lifted the gun to aim at my head. 'I'm sorry, John. It was never meant to be this way.' She thumbed the hammer back, tears falling down her cheeks, and I looked past her to see Mascaponi crying too.

'Please. Wendy. My van.'

'Begging never suited you, John. And I can't let you live. You're

John Croker. You'll keep coming back . . . See you in heaven, John.' She paused to offer a smile. 'Or maybe hell.'

The gun fired and everything turned black.

CHAPTER NINE

Monday morning.

'IS THAT IT?' Rachel asks, as a guy dressed like an extra from a science fiction movie in a hard red plastic space suit brushes past me.

'I'm still looking for the Killer Sun,' he says through his helmet to the woman behind the reception desk.

'John?'

I look back to Rachel at my table.

'Was that it?' she asks again.

'Yeah, but I gotta find my van.'

'No. Not the Death Star. I said the *Killer Sun*,' the Stormtrooper says from behind me.

'What is it with Stormtroopers?' Rachel mutters, closing her notepad.

'And I'm a *Thunder Soldier*, not a Stormtrooper,' the guy says with a scoff. 'Whatever that is.'

Another voice, coming from the other side. I twist around to see a tall, dark-haired guy in a black suit walking towards the desk. 'I've really gotta find Salvatori's place.'

'Yes. I know. You told me. And I said I'd be back in a moment,' Rachel says, guiding the guy back to his table.

'Hey, you know Salvatori?' he asks me.

'No. I'm looking for my van.'

'Maybe we can team up. We'll find Salvatori *and* your van.'

He seems like my kind of guy. I rise to my feet, stretching my hand out. 'John Croker.'

'John Candle,' he says.

'For fudge's sake – no no no!' Rachel says, pulling our hands apart. 'No joint missions and no teaming up . . . Sit down, John.'

'Which John?' we both ask.

'Both Johns!' Rachel says, pushing the other John back to his table.

'But I gotta find Salvatori.'

'And I gotta find my van.'

'I don't know what the Death Star is! My ship is called the Killer Sun,' the guy in the red plastic suit says to the woman behind the desk.

'Right. You two. Don't move!' Rachel says, as the door opens and a beautiful woman strides in with a sultry pout.

'I'm looking for Benjamin Brown. I'm Svetlana Graphite.'

'Oh god,' Rachel groans. 'You'll have to deal with her, Pat. I've got my hands full.'

'We still getting that *Fifty Shades* shit?' Pat mutters, walking out from behind the desk. 'Right. Come with me. I'll find you a table.'

'Great,' Svetlana says. 'But make sure it's private. Benjamin insists on it and I'm not wearing any panties.'

'Urgh! Why do they always say *panties*?' Pat asks Rachel with a disgusted look as she goes by.

'So gross,' Rachel says in her British accent, blowing a strand of hair from her face. She's pretty. Very pretty, but I'm not here for that.

I need to find my van and save Wendy. But that means going up against Mascaponi again. Which is a life I left behind. But where did Mascaponi go? Lin shot me with her revolver, but she missed and I blacked out.

I push off the table and head for the door.

'Whoa! Where are you going?' Rachel calls over to me, while still talking to the man in the red plastic suit.

'I gotta get to Wendy by five.'

'I gotta find Salvatori before he kills my cat,' John Candle says, and I realize he's also going for the door.

'Hey, you wanna help me with Wendy and I'll help save your cat?'

'That sounds good. I'm John Candle,' he says, holding his hand out.

'John Croker,' I say.

'Holy sugar plum fairies, the force is strong with you two!' Rachel says.

'The force?' the Thunder Soldier asks in in alarm. 'FEDIS!' he shouts, aiming his laser gun, as I throw a coffee mug at his head while diving away from the gunfire.

Except the laser gun doesn't fire, so the guy just curses with coffee dripping down his head, which seems to piss him off, so he runs at John Candle and the two of them slap at each other's hands.

'Stop it! STOP IT!' Rachel yells as she and Pat get between them to push them back. 'L132, you need to sit down,' Rachel tells the Thunder Soldier.

'Is Benjamin coming?' Svetlana asks.

'You got coffee in my helmet!' L132 shouts. 'It's all sticky inside.'

'I wish I was sticky inside,' Svetlana says.

'That's gross!' Pat says.

'Okay, enough!' Rachel calls, bringing us all to silence. 'Sit down. No! Sit down. Mr Candle. Mr Croker. Miss Graphite, and you, Mr 132 or whatever it is.'

'My friends call me L,' the Thunder Soldier says, giving me the middle finger. 'That's for the coffee.'

'I don't have time for this,' I say.

'Wendy won't die, John!' Rachel says, grabbing my arm. 'Please. Just sit down.'

She keeps hold of my arm, and I look down into her pretty eyes and that strand of hair hanging down.

'And you can stop that,' she tells me. 'Not every touch from a woman is a romantic gesture. I'm holding your arm to stop you going out until we finish. Not because I want to have sex with you.'

'I'll have sex with you if Benjamin watches,' Svetlana says.

'Really? Which one of you is Benjamin?' L132 asks, while working at the buckle on his red plastic trousers.

'Just sit down!' Rachel says, pushing him into a chair as a tall man in an old-fashioned suit strides in with a cane in his hand.

'Tell Moriarty that Holmes is here!' he announces in a deep, booming British voice.

'No!' Pat says, pushing him back out. 'Go down the street to Victorian Detectives. You'll find Moriarty in there . . . All of them,' she says, slamming the door shut and flipping the closed sign over. She's pretty too. She must be Rachel's best friend. 'And you can stop that as well,' she says, with a look at me and John Candle. 'Just because I'm black doesn't mean I'm a sidekick.'

'Benjamin watched me make love to a black guy once,' Svetlana says.

'I don't have time for this. I gotta find my van,' I say.

'My cat,' John Candle says, as we both start to rise. 'Hey, you wanna team up?'

'Sounds good. John Croker,' I say, offering my hand.

'John Candle,' he says.

'L132,' the Thunder Soldier says, and we both turn to look at him holding his hand out.

'No,' John Candle and I say at the same time.

'Er, racist,' L132 says.

'That's not racist!' Pat says. 'You are literally made of red plastic.'

'It's not plastic,' L132 says. 'It's like some hardened polymer shit or something.'

'Benjamin asked me to shit on him once.'

'What the fuck!' all of us say at the same time.

'I said no!' Svetlana says. 'I peed on him instead.'

I don't know what's going on here, or who these people are, but I do know I gotta get my van back. But that means going up against Mascaponi and going back into the life I left behind.

But maybe if I get that hard drive back, I can take Mascaponi down, stop the weapons deal, *and* get my van back and save Wendy.

'It's gotta be worth a shot,' John Candle says.

'What has?' I ask him.

'Taking Mascaponi down to stop the weapons deal and then getting the van back to save Wendy,' John Candle says.

'How do you know that?' I ask.

'You just said it,' John Candle says.

'I didn't.'

'You really did,' John Candle, L132, Svetlana, Rachel and Pat all say at the same time.

'This happens with the Johns,' Rachel tells me. 'The need to keep self-narrating is a strong force in them.'

'Force?' L132 asks. 'FEDIS!' he shouts, lifting his fists as John Candle and I do the same.

'They're not Fedis, or Jedis, or whatever rip-off fanfic thing you come from was about,' Rachel says, pulling L back as Pat pushes John Candle and me away.

'Whatever. I don't have time for this,' I say as I turn for the door.

'He's not going to sit down,' Pat says.

'I know,' Rachel says with a groan. 'Right. We'll field-trip it then.'

'What does that mean?' I ask.

'It means we're going to help John Croker find his van,' she tells us all.

'What about my cat?' John Candle asks, before looking into the distance to mutter at himself. 'If we find this guy's van, he can help me find Salvatori and save Jenkins, my cat which my dead wife gave to me, then we can save the cat sanctuary my wife built from scratch from being demolished for Salvatori's new nightclub. But that means going back into a life I left behind – but then I promised my wife I'd never let anyone hurt Jenkins. And that's a promise I intend to keep.'

'That's a good promise,' I say.

He looks at me. 'What is?'

'The promise to your wife.'

'I never said anything about my wife.'

'You did,' we all say, as he frowns like he's got déjà vu or something.

'Okay! Great,' Rachel says. 'Let's do that then! Find the van, the cat and L's Killer Moon.'

'Sun.'

'And yes, Svetlana! We'll find Benjamin too. But rules! Do not talk to anyone else. Got it? No! Because if you do then Wendy and the cat will get put in a blender while the Killer Meteorite –'

'Sun.'

'Whatever – gets blown up and Benjamin becomes a monk. I mean it. That will actually happen,' Rachel says. Pat nods earnestly while I figure I really don't want poor Wendy to get put into a blender, and definitely not with John Candle's cat. Although if I'm honest I'm not that bothered about the Killer Moon thing.

'It's a sun!' L snaps.

Or if Benjamin becomes a monk.

'Trust me. Benjamin will *never* become a monk,' Svetlana says.

'Do you all agree?' Rachel asks, with her hand on the door handle.

We all agree, and I for one know I will keep to my word, because things like that mean something to me.

'Okay! Then let's go,' Rachel says with an eye-roll to Pat, before opening the door and leading us out onto the streets of New York.

The greatest city in the world.

'It's not New York,' Rachel says.

Back to the abandoned docks.

'We're not going to the docks.'

And back to find my van and the life I once had.

'Whatever. Let's just get this done.'

CHAPTER TEN

I keep my eyes up as we cross the sidewalk.

'Expecting trouble?' John Candle asks as we lock eyes. One warrior to another.

'No!' Rachel says, stepping between us to try and stop our souls from bonding. But I'm wary after Ibrahim. The guy was like a brother to me and look what happened.

'I had the same thing with Mwangi,' John Candle says. 'My Uber driver. He was Kenyan. We were like brothers.'

'No. You weren't,' Rachel says, still trying to push us apart.

'And we need to keep an eye out for mobsters and hitmen,' John Candle adds over her head. 'Salvatori's put a price on my head.'

'How much?' I ask as I look at him.

'One million dollars,' he whispers as we lock eyes. One warrior to another.

'I said no!' Rachel takes John Candle's arm to pull him around. He looks down into her eyes and lifts a hand to tuck the stray strand of hair behind her ear. 'Stop it!' she says, slapping his hand away. 'Boundaries.'

'You could set a safe word,' Svetlana says. 'Benjamin and I use –'

'Okay!' Pat says, clapping her hands to cut Svetlana off. 'Let's cross the street.'

'Hey, what was that safe word?' L132 asks as we set off.

'Star Wars,' she says.

'What's that?' L132 asks, running along in his red plastic suit as John Candle and I stride ahead.

'Why do the Johns always walk so fast?' Pat asks.

'They're think they're still on a mission,' Rachel says. 'Honestly, I prefer the Reachers. I really do. They just stay put and let trouble find them.'

I don't know what that means, but maybe these Reacher people are working for Mascaponi too. I look at Rachel again and think maybe I made a mistake when I opened up to her. But she made me a coffee and looked deep into my eyes, and I thought we had a connection.

'We honestly didn't,' she tells me. I guess she's playing it coy. But whatever. It's too soon for me to try again. Not after Lin Lin double-crossed me for Mascaponi. I won't fall for that again. I'm just gonna get my van and get back to the depot for my bonus.

That's all that matters.

But I can't help but wonder if it was Lin and Mascaponi who saved me. Or was it Ibrahim?

I woke up after blacking out when Lin shot me with the revolver. And by rights, I should have died. Either from the gunshot, or from the cold after being knocked out in the freezing snow.

Except once again I cheated death. Somebody saved me and moved me to a park bench somewhere in this city, where a fat guy in a dressing gown woke me up by kicking my feet.

'That way,' he said, pointing out of the park as he thumbed his round glasses up his nose. 'Two blocks over. Look for Hard-Boiled and Erotica.'

He sounded British and looked like a tramp, but I figured he was an informant telling me where to make contact with my handler. I said thanks and set off, and soon found the place he told me about.

An average store on an average city street. A sign over the door.

HARD-BOILED & EROTICA
(& MISC. SCI-FI FANFIC OVERFLOW)

I DIDN'T KNOW what that meant but it looked like a good front for an agency. I went in and met Pat behind the desk. She asked my name. I looked her in the eye and said I was John Croker.

She seemed to recognize me and blew air out of her cheeks. 'Okey dokey, grab that table and Rach will be right with you.'

Rachel came over. She gave me a coffee and sat down with a notepad. She said it works best if I just tell her everything then we can go over it.

I knew then that she was my handler.

I told her everything. About Wendy. About my van. About Lin and Mascaponi and the weapons deal. I even told her about Ibrahim and how he was closer to me than a brother, but he'd double-crossed me. I'd even given him my pet spider.

'Hey! I know this place,' Svetlana says, as we cross another street two blocks from the agency storefront. 'I woke up here.'

I glance at her as we enter the park and think about the coincidence of two people waking up in the same park in the same part of New York.

'We're not in New York, John,' Rachel says to me.

'No. This is Vancouver,' Svetlana says. 'I was at home, bound and gagged and waiting for Benjamin.'

'He kidnapped you?' John Candle asks.

'No, silly! I gagged and cuffed myself. Benjamin said he was bringing a client home for a business meeting. I thought it would be a turn-on for him to find me in the dining room on my back. But I guess I fell asleep, and he moved me here. I know why too,' she adds with a sultry smile. 'He's watching me right now. He wants me to fuck a stranger for him.'

'I'm a stranger!' L132 says, lifting his hand up.

'I think Salvatori is behind this,' John Candle says as we all look at him. 'Because I woke up here too,' he adds in a whisper.

'And I did,' I tell him. Eye to eye. Man to man. 'Mascaponi must have teamed up with Salvatori.'

'We should find them together,' he says.

'Deal,' I say, holding my hand out. 'John Croker.'

'John Candle.'

'L132,' L says from our side, holding his hand out again. 'And hey!

Guess what? I woke up here as well. But then the Dark Lord does weird shit like that all the time. Even to us on the Killer Sun. I mean. Honestly, though. It's a good career and the perks are great. The healthcare is awesome, *and* it includes dental, and even mental health. Do the Fedis offer counselling? No! I don't think so. And the hours are okay. The training is intense though, and er, yeah, they do kill the guys that fail, or if you can like shoot a Fedi and you *don't?* Whoa. They'll bin you for that. My friend. D384. She totally got killed for helping this ugly little yellow alien thing get away. But she was a dick and like *always* avoided her cleaning duties when it was her turn. So yeah. We'll team up, find the cat. Save the van then find my ship.'

'No,' John Candle and I say together.

'They can't,' Svetlana tells L132. 'They will be busy making love to me so Benjamin can watch.'

'I don't have time for that,' I tell Svetlana. As attractive as she is, and especially in that low-cut dress. 'I gotta find my van. Which way to the docks?'

Rachel looks at me, and for the first time since I met her, she looks sad. Pat does too.

'Tell Croker where the docks are,' John Candle says. 'We gotta find his van so we can save Jenkins.'

'And find my ship,' L132 says.

'No,' John and I say, as an albino guy in a skintight flesh-colored onesie with a shock of pure white hair slowly peeks up from behind a bush a few feet away to stare at us through pale blue eyes.

'You can't see me,' he says.

'Oh god,' Pat groans softly. 'Griff, we're a bit busy right now.'

'You can't see me,' the albino guy says again.

'What the actual fuck,' Svetlana says.

'Okay. Fine. Nobody look at Griff,' Pat tells us, as the albino guy darts out from the bush to get behind a tree.

'What's he doing?' John Candle asks.

'You can't see me!' he whisper-shouts angrily.

'Seriously. Just ignore him,' Rachel says. 'He thinks he's invisible.'

I shake my head at the absurdity of whatever this is and focus back on my mission. 'Rachel. The docks?' I ask, as she looks at me with pain in her eyes.

'I'm sorry,' she says.

'For what?' I ask.

'Guys,' Pat says, making us turn to look at her. She looks the same as Rachel, with regret on her face. 'You need to listen. This is not New York.'

'Or Vancouver,' Rachel says.

'Or Chicago,' Pat tells John Candle.

'Or wherever the hell you're from,' Rachel tells L132.

'So originally, I'm like from the Andromeda system on a little planet called Exocrag, but I hardly remember it. I mean. They murdered my family and took me into service when I was like five.'

'Yeah. We're not in that place either,' Rachel says, as a drunk old man with wild hair jumps up from a bench nearby and runs towards us with a white lab coat flapping around his legs.

'Great shits! Have you seen my nephew? I lost him in the last dimension.'

'Down that way,' Pat says, waving him on. 'Building on the right side with a blue sign. Time Travel & Interdimensional.'

'I'll portal there!' the crazy old guys says, pulling some weird ray gun from his pocket that he shoots at the ground. 'Damn it! I'm outta juice. MATTY! HANG ON!' He sets off running across the street.

An average street in New York city.

Except I don't recognize which part. And there's no yellow cabs, or police sirens, or skyscrapers. Come to think of it, there's no cars either, and we all pause to watch a horse and carriage go by.

'John,' Rachel says. 'This isn't New York. Look at me. No. Look at me. This is not New York, and nobody moved you anywhere. Nobody moved anyone anywhere.'

'Where were you before here?' I ask John Candle.

'Tied up in the old meat processing plant near the docks. Salvatori had the drop on me, but I guess he changed his mind, or someone else saved me.'

'We'll find out who,' I tell him. Eye to eye. Man to man. A bond growing between us. He's becoming a friend. More than a friend. More like a brother. 'The docks? Where are they?'

'John!' Rachel says, looking at me. 'There are no docks.'

'Lady, I don't know your game, but I will save my niece.'

'There is no niece, John! Listen to me.'

'I'm done listening. I've gotta find my van.'

'And there's no van either.'

'I saw it in the old fish warehouse at the docks.'

'Must be near the meat processing plant,' John Candle says. 'Let's go.'

'Guys, just slow down for a minute,' Pat says.

'Benjamin took me to the docks once,' Svetlana says with a wry smile. 'Maybe that's where he wants to watch me making love to another man.'

'No. He doesn't, because there is no Benjamin,' Pat says.

'You shouldn't risk it. We should have sex,' L132 says.

'Er, not with you, weird plastic man,' Svetlana says.

'Lo! Strangers,' a voice says from the side, and we all turn to a tall handsome man with dark features in a weird old costume. 'I seek the one they call Graggor the Grey. A mission I am on. One of great secrecy that cannot be revealed.'

'Two blocks over. Main street. Go to the far end. Big sign saying Middle Earth,' Pat says.

'Graggor is in this place? Aye. It must be an inn. Graggor likes an ale, as do I! I thank you, strangers, and please, if the mutant soldiers of the Dark Ear ask, you have not seen Baragon.'

He strides past. We all watch him go, then turn back to facing each other.

'What is this place?' Svetlana asks, as we look over to a man in a black tuxedo waking up on a bench. He stands up, adjusts his cuff-links, and walks off. 'This doesn't look like Vancouver,' Svetlana adds.

'Or Chicago,' John Candle says. 'Or anywhere I've seen,' he adds, as Pat and Rachel share a look as though he said the right thing. 'Where are we?' he asks, looking from Rachel to Pat.

'Yeah. I've never seen this place either,' L132 admits. 'But, er. Beats cleaning the latrines.'

'One left,' Rachel says, as she and Pat look at me expectantly. 'It helps when you want to know, John. Acceptance is so much easier when you open your mind.'

I've got no idea what the hell they're both on about. All I know is I have to find my van and save Wendy before it's too late. I check my watch. It's 4 p.m. One hour left to pay the surgeon.

'He's deep in it,' Pat says quietly as Rachel nods.

'I like it deep,' Svetlana says, and Pat lifts a hand to say something then thinks better of it.

'I'll find the docks myself,' I say, and start walking off.

'There are no docks, John!' Rachel says as they all rush after me. But I pay no heed and walk on. 'John. There are no docks.'

'Hey!' I shout, seeing the fat tramp in the dressing gown ahead of me. He turns to look and blinks behind his round glasses.

'What?'

'Buddy. You saved me.'

'Did I?'

'On the bench. You woke me up to stop the drugs taking me down or whatever Mascaponi gave me.'

'Oh, it's you,' he says. 'And no. I just kicked your foot, mate. Anyway. Ta-da.'

'No, wait,' I say, grabbing his arm as he turns into a narrow alley filled with storefronts that seem to bulge out into the sidewalks. Orange lights behind them, and other weird people walking around in their dressing gowns.

'Harry!' a balding ginger guy shouts from a table outside a bar. A glass of beer in his hand and a middle-aged woman next to him smoking a pipe.

'Hang on, Ron! And don't let Fanny nick my pint. Mate, let go of my arm,' Harry says, trying to pull away.

'I gotta save Wendy!' I say, then reel back from a sharp pain in my eye as he jabs me with a weird stick. 'What the hell!'

'Touch me again and I'll poke your other eye,' Harry says, waggling his wand as I clock an old scar on his forehead. 'You seriously need to control your Johns,' he tells Rachel and Pat. 'And whatever that is,' he says, waving a thin brown stick to L132.

'Hey, touch my buddy again and I'll ram that stick up your ass!' L shouts.

'I don't have time for this,' I say, and stride off to find the docks and get my van, with Rachel and Pat and the others rushing behind me.

'John! There is no van. There are no docks,' Rachel says, striding behind me.

'Then where are we?' Svetlana asks.

'John needs to ask too,' Rachel says.

'Why? Stuff him. Let him find the docks and tell us,' Svetlana says as I walk on.

'Because curiosity is the first step to acceptance. It overrides the sense of denial . . . In most cases.'

'John?' John Candle calls. 'Maybe we should listen.'

Damn. They've gotten to John Candle. That hurts. He was like a brother to me. We had a bond. Especially after what Ibrahim did. He was like a brother too.

'John!' Rachel says, grabbing at my arm. 'Ask me where we are. Ask me, John.'

'We're in New York,' I reply.

'What part? What district?' she asks, still running behind me.

'Or someplace else then. Mascaponi drugged me. Or Ibrahim. Someone did. I'll find the docks and find my van and hunt them down.'

'There are no docks, and this isn't anywhere!' she says, pulling me around until I'm looking down into her eyes and that strand of hair hanging down. 'Damn it! This isn't a romantic gesture. You have to want to know.'

'I don't have time for this,' I say, and turn away as Rachel and Pat both groan and rush after me, with John Candle and L132 and Svetlana all telling me to stop and listen.

But I can't stop.

I have to find my van.

'There is no van!' Rachel says.

And I have to save Wendy.

'Fine,' Rachel mutters. 'We'll do it the hard way. This won't be pleasant, but we've got no choice.'

Something in her tone makes me stop and look back, detecting the change of energy between her and Pat. A finality about them that makes me even more guarded. 'Who are you?' I ask them both, as Rachel opens the notepad and flicks to a page.

'This is an awful way to do it,' she says, shaking her head.

'Do what?' John Candle asks.

'I said who are you?' I step closer to Rachel and Pat.

'Right,' Rachel says. 'First thing: why the hell were UPS drivers briefing like cops?'

'What?' I ask her.

'John! You need to ask me where we are and what's happening.'

'I know where I am, and I know what the hell is happening. You're trying to delay me so they can get the hard drive back before the DA makes a copy.'

'You were gaining sentience, John. You were already questioning your reality. That's why you kept feeling déjà vu. You were noticing the changes. Okay, let's talk about your sister then. What's her name?'

I stop and look at her. 'What?'

'What's your sister's name?'

I go to answer, but the answer won't come. 'I was drugged. My memory is shot.'

'What's Wendy's father's name?'

'He's . . . I . . .'

'Where does Wendy live?'

'She lives . . . It's on . . .'

'Why didn't Huschech recognize you?' she asks, throwing the questions at me one after the other while nodding as though expecting me to continue. 'When you went into the scrapyard. Why didn't Huschech recognize you? And why didn't Huschech say where the van was? Why did you shoot him before he could tell you? And why shoot him *after* telling him to pass a message to Mascaponi?'

I scowl and try and think, but again the answers just won't come.

Whatever.

I don't have time for this.

'Flipping hell, John! You have to want to know. Okay, fine, answer this one then. Why did you keep changing locations? You told me it felt like you were in New York, then LA, then Chicago, then back to LA.'

'Hey. That was happening to me,' John Candle says.

'I had that,' Svetlana says. 'I thought I was in Paris yesterday for about an hour.'

'I thought I was on this alien world to meet a Fedi for about ten minutes,' L adds.

'What about your military service,' Rachel asks me. 'You were military, right?'

I nod at her.

'Hey, me too,' John Candle says. 'Which unit?'

I go to answer, but my brain feels fogged.

'And the constant groups of men you had to fight,' Rachel adds. 'Always five guys knowing where you'd be. And none of them have guns? And they all attack one by one unless someone else is there to save you.'

'Whatever. I don't have time for this,' I say and walk on.

'And the tea ritual? What was that? People from Iraq don't have tea rituals. They just drink it like we do! And what was Ibrahim?'

'He was like a brother to me.'

'Mwango was like a brother to me,' John Candle says.

'I had Betty. She was my black friend,' Svetlana says.

'So racist,' Pat says.

'It's a trope, John,' Rachel says. 'The ethnic sidekick. The author feels the need to include a non-white character, so they come up with someone funny or sassy.'

'FYI, people. I am not a sidekick,' Pat says firmly. 'I am married. I have a husband. I have a life. I am friends with Rachel, but my existence is not here to support her endeavors. Are we clear on that?'

'I don't know what that means,' I tell them both. 'I just gotta find my van.'

'It means it wasn't real!' Rachel says as we keep walking. 'And the pet spider? Every John has a pet.'

'I've got a cat called Jenkins,' John Candle says. 'We need to save him. Hey, wanna team up?'

'No,' I say, rushing on, but Rachel grabs my arm to make me stop.

'Why don't you want to team up with John Candle? Huh? Go on. Why not? Cos you're starting to question it, John. So ask me. Ask me where this is. Open your mind and ask, John.'

'Go to hell. I need my van.'

'There is no van! And the reason you were getting déjà vu is because your story was unravelling – the writer had lost all sense of direction and focus and was desperately trying to salvage it with more awful ideas. And you keep repeating things back to yourself to remind the reader of the complicated plot!'

I feel my heart thudding hard and my head spinning. I feel weird and detached, but then I've been feeling that all day. But she's right about one thing. I do keep repeating things to myself.

'And how about the déjà vu?' she asks.

'I had it all day,' John Candle says.

'I've had it all week,' Svetlana says with a frown at Rachel and Pat.

'What's déjà vu?' L132 asks.

'When you do something, but you feel you've done the exact same thing before,' Pat explains.

'I get that! I had it like loads today and yesterday,' L132 says.

'See? It's common,' I say.

'Why did we feel that?' John Candle asks with a glance at Pat.

'We don't know,' Pat says with a shrug. 'But we think it's a sign the writer is losing the plot and changing things to try and recover it.'

'They do other things when it's going wrong too,' Rachel says, looking at me. 'They change locations, and they add a sudden love interest and a sex scene. Is that ringing bells, John? Lin Lin? The warehouse?'

'She double-crossed me.'

'And that!' Pat says, clicking her fingers at me. 'They throw in more double-crosses than twenty detectives could deal with – and trust me, this place has *lots* of detectives.'

'And that guy who poked you in the eye? Fat George? He was the original Harry Potter rip-off,' Rachel says. 'Some awful fanfiction probably. But they've been here since they were kids. And he's not even called Harry Potter. His name is George Wheeler.'

Whatever.

I don't have time for this.

'No!' she says, grabbing my arm. 'No no no . . . You are going to ask me.'

'I know where I am.'

'You don't! And your refusal to ask just means your writer was a stubborn sod who wouldn't give up until the very end, which is why you're so locked in and they're not,' she says, waving a hand at the others. 'They're probably only half developed. You must have been close to the end.'

'What end?'

'Yes! He's asking,' Pat says. 'See. An open mind is always better.'

I look at her. Then at Rachel. 'I don't have time for this.'

'Fudge!' Rachel says, grabbing my arm again and refusing to let go. 'Right. Time for the big guns. You won't like this, but what illness does Wendy have?'

'What?' I ask, growling the word out.

'What's wrong with your niece, John? You've killed dozens of people for her. You've gone up against the Yakuza and the cartels for a girl you obviously love . . . But you don't know her mom's name? So tell me what illness she has.'

'I –'

'What operation does she need?'

'I –'

'Which hobby does she like? Skating? Ballet? Soccer? What's her surname? What's your sister's name? Why did Mac and the other UPS drivers turn up to rescue you? How did Ibrahim know you'd walk into *that* alley and kill those two guys? And how did you only remember about the hard drive right at the very end? And was Mascaponi a man or a woman? Come on! Answer one of those. Just one . . .'

I flounder, while all the time the minutes tick away, getting closer to 5 p.m.

'John. What illness does Wendy have?' Rachel asks quietly, her eyes locked on mine.

'I . . . She's got . . . She has . . .'

'You don't know because the writer didn't plan for it. You only know what the writer knows. You have to ask me, John. You have to open your mind to that possibility, otherwise you will literally go mad. I've seen it happen.'

'It happens, John,' Pat says, looking at me while the others all stare at Rachel. All of them clearly wanting to know where this is, and what this is, and what we're doing here, and how we all woke up in the same park.

'That's it,' Rachel says, nodding at me. Urging me.

I close my eyes and exhale.

'Ask me,' she whispers.

But I shake my head and walk on. 'I don't have time for this.'

'You selfish prick!' Svetlana snaps, making me stop and turn. 'Jesus. I thought I was self-involved, but you're up your own ass.'

'Yeah. Worse than the Dark Lord,' L132 says.

'That was a shitty move, John,' John Candle says with a shake of his head, as I realize they all wanted to know.

And I guess maybe I want to know too. I feel my shoulders drop as that fog in my mind becomes too much. 'Okay,' I whisper, looking back at Rachel. 'Where are we?'

She smiles at me. But it's soft and gentle. 'We're all the same,' she tells me, then the others. 'We all woke up on the benches after our writers gave up on their novels. We're all characters from unfinished books . . . And this,' she says, holding her hands out. 'This is your new home. Welcome to Fiction Land.'

I look at her. Then at Pat and the others, and I think about everything she said. And she's pretty. Rachel is very pretty.

'Inappropriate, but thanks,' she says. I guess I was speaking out loud, or self-narrating as she called it.

I don't know.

I only know one thing.

'Oh god,' Pat says, as the others all groan.

I only know I gotta find my van.

I set off again, and this time, they don't follow me.

CHAPTER ELEVEN

Friday.

'. . . And then I found out Tom was gay. Do you know what that felt like? Finding out your husband is gay. I was so confused. I mean. Yeah, a person can't control their sexuality. I get that. And I'm fine with that. But Tom and I had three kids together and I literally had no idea. It meant our whole marriage was a sham and it was like everyone was laughing at me. Like they all knew, and I didn't.'

Man. That sucks. Poor Gretchen. No wonder she looks so broken.

'Okay. Thank you for sharing, Gretchen,' Kathy says, as we all murmur *thank you for sharing*.

'John, you're doing the thing again,' Kathy says with a look to me, while motioning her own mouth. *'Self-narrating,'* she whispers.

I make a mental note to self-narrate in my head and not out loud.

'So what do we all think about Gretchen's story?' Kathy asks.

'I think it's a miserable tear-jerking shitty romcom,' Alice says. 'But without the com.'

I snort a laugh as Alice smiles at me.

'Alice,' Kathy says, giving her a warning look.

'Well, it was! Literally who cares about her marriage? What a waste of a book. No wonder it wasn't finished.'

'Alice, if you keep going you will be asked to leave,' Kathy says.

'Okay! Fine,' Alice says. A young goth or emo teenager full of anger. 'Tom's gay. Three kids. Poor Gretchen.'

'Alice!' Kathy snaps.

'I meant that nicely! I can't help the sarcasm sometimes.'

'No, that's a fair point,' Kathy says to the group, while motioning at Alice. 'Alice was a teenage character full of angst and it's a good reminder that we all have traits we have to break if we want to experience rewarding lives.'

'I'm sorry, Gretchen,' Alice says, forcibly trying to soften her tone. 'I meant what I said about the book though. I mean. I wouldn't read it.'

'I would,' Thor 46 says, and we all turn to look at him. 'It sounds so sad,' he adds with a wistful sigh.

'Thank you, Thor 46,' Kathy says. 'Mr Darcy? What about you? You're normally an aloof romantic hero.'

'Yes, quite,' he says, looking all dashing. 'But I gather my story differed in that it contained vampires.'

'Vampires,' Kathy says.

'And sex,' he adds.

'Sex,' Kathy says.

'Apparently it was an erotic fanfic piece. But with vampires.'

'Still better than the Tom and Gretchen marriage book,' Alice says. 'No offence, Gretchy.'

'It's fine,' she says, weeping into her handkerchief.

'Did you have sex *with* the vampires?' Thor 46 asks.

'Yes. All of them,' Mr Darcy says as the room falls silent. 'There were a lot of orgies.'

'Gretchy should have gone,' Alice mutters, and I snort again.

'Alice!' Kathy says, trying to hide her smile. 'And don't humor her, John.'

'Yeah, John,' Alice says.

I like the kid. She's got spirit. Thor 46, however, despite being the god of thunder, seems to have no spirit. But then I guess finding out there are literally forty-five other characters with the same name as you already in Fiction Land is probably quite a shock. Mind you, apparently there are quite a few Mr Darcys too. Or at least there used to be back in the day. Kathy said nobody really writes about them anymore. Unless it's some weird niche thing with zombies, or vampires and orgies.

Alice is cool though. She's unique, and I wonder why her writer didn't finish the story.

'I reckon she died,' Alice tells me as I realize I was self-narrating out loud again. 'Yeah, you were,' she adds with a smile. 'Good job you're not some pervert thinking about Gretchy's boobs and Kathy's ass.'

'Alice!' Kathy snaps again, as even Thor 46 allows himself a smile. 'Well. Seeing as you're very chatty today, Alice, would you like to share your story?'

'Oh, gee! I'd love to, but dang! Can't remember it,' Alice says with an eye-roll. 'Maybe next time.'

'You've been here the longest, Alice,' Kathy points out.

'So? Let Silent John go next. So, Johnno,' she says, turning to me and crossing one torn-stockinged leg over the other with her unlaced Doc Martens hanging off. 'Would you like to share?' she asks in a good mimicry of Kathy, who rolls her eyes and tries to look cross, but it's hard to get angry at Alice. She's too quick-witted and smart.

'John?' Kathy asks with a sigh and a wave of her hand at me.

'Ooh, can I take a guess?' Alice asks.

'Alice. Enough,' Kathy says.

'Sure. Go for it,' I say to Alice.

'John. I know you're new, but you don't have to humor her,' Kathy says.

'By all means tell her to be quiet,' Mr Darcy says, as Alice flicks him the bird.

'Is it a sad story?' Thor 46 asks me.

'Oh god, it's not is it?' Alice asks. 'Nah, it can't be. He's a John Wick copy. It'll be fighting and stuff,' she says, clenching her fists and throwing weak punches. 'And vampires and orgies.'

Mr Darcy tuts while I smile, and Kathy just shakes her head.

'It's cool. It's Miss Gretchen's turn,' I say. Gretchen looks over at me with an expression that isn't all sad and weepy.

'The Johns are always polite. I'll say that,' Kathy says. 'You could learn a thing or two,' she adds, pointing at Alice.

'Yes, Miss Kathy,' Alice says in a deep voice. 'But Gretchy's just gotta get over it. I mean. We're not real. We're not here. This doesn't exist.'

'No. We *are* real, and we *do* exist,' Kathy says. 'The point is that we are *not* defined by who we *were*. That's why we're here. To try and learn *how* to overcome those memories and begin again. You're all different from the other people here. You're all *Enders*. You were close to the ends of your stories. Most books are abandoned long before the end, which means the "characters",' she says with air quotes, 'are not as locked into how they were written. Which is why others might find it easier to accept where they are.'

'Yeah. And none of it was real,' Alice adds.

'It was real, Alice. Gretchen experienced those things with Tom, and she still has the trauma to deal with. Which means she also feels intense separation anxiety from losing her children. Would you deny her that grief?'

'No,' Alice says quietly.

'To be honest,' Gretchen says, 'I think the writer focused on Tom because – and I feel so bad saying this – I can't really remember much about my kids. I know I had two boys and a girl and their names and ages, but . . .' she trails off with a shrug.

'It can be complicated,' Kathy says. 'And layered too, because at the same time as trying to process her emotions about Tom, Gretchen is also feeling guilty *for not* knowing her own children.'

'But that makes it easier,' Alice says. 'She doesn't remember them. How can you care about something you don't remember?'

'Because Gretchen *did care* for her children. She's spoken about it at length, Alice. About how the kids were traumatized by their father leaving, and then having to learn to accept his new relationship with another man. It was real to her, the same as Mr Darcy *really* dealt with vampires.'

'And orgies,' he says.

'And orgies,' Kathy says. 'And Thor 46 really did go on a very, very long emotional journey to find his roots, away from the fighting and world-saving and the other gods.'

'Worst origin story ever by the way.'

'Alice! Stop it or you will be expelled. Our experiences happened to us. They were real. We felt them. We felt loss and grief. We got hurt. And those are real emotions that need to be dealt with in order for us to move on.'

She falls silent. We all stay quiet, and I take the time to look around at the others. Thor is a big guy. Broad and muscular. Handsome too, but man, I never saw someone looking so sad. Mr Darcy just looks exhausted. But then the guy's had months of orgies and vampires to deal with. But he nods along as though grasping it all. Then I notice Gretchen looking at me.

I smile back and move my gaze on to Alice. Dressed in goth black. Ironic and anti-whatever she wants to be anti- about. Probably everything.

'How old are you?' I ask her.

She shrugs. 'Seventeen. But hey. It's not real, which means I'm not seventeen.' She flashes me a big fake smile.

'Alice. We are real,' Kathy says again.

'Whatever. We done?' Alice asks. 'It's karaoke night in Diagonal Alley. It's half price mead or dragon piss or whatever all the Potter people drink.'

Kathy checks her watch. I know we have time to go yet, but it's obvious that Alice will walk out if Kathy doesn't end the session now.

'Sure. We can end it a little early,' Kathy says, and Alice shoots to her feet. 'But we *will* be doing a full session on Monday,' she adds. 'And Alice, you *will* be taking your turn.'

'Sure. Next time,' she says, already heading for the door.

'Your allowance gets cut if you don't engage, Alice!' Kathy yells, but Alice is gone. I stand up and nod at the others as a woman in bright sports gear walks in.

'You done, Kath? Alright if I set up for Zumba?'

'Sure. You go ahead, Bridget. Joys of a multi-function room share eh?' Kathy says with a smile at me. 'You staying for Zumba, John?'

'No, ma'am.'

'Ooh, go on,' Bridget calls over. 'We had a Bond last week, but that was only so he could bang Mary Poppins. And honestly, you'd never think she was a kids' character. Dirty cow.'

'We're not characters, Bridget,' Kathy says. 'We're people.'

'People! Got it,' Bridget says, giving me a knowing wink as a very attractive woman walks in. 'Talk of the devil, here she is. Alright, Mary? Had a spoonful of sugar from Bond have you?'

'That's quite enough of that potty talk,' Mary tells her sternly. 'And my name is Mindy Pippins. But hello. You look new,' Mindy says, walking over with her hand held out.

'John Croker.'

'Pippins. Mindy. One of the many Mary Poppins copies, although I like to think I am unique. I was an Ender too. Had the most awful habit of thinking I could do magic. Exercise helps though. Join us for Zumba if you want.'

'No, ma'am. I have a prior meeting arranged.'

'Shame. Well. Maybe next time. Or perhaps we shall see you in Diagonal Alley later?'

'It's karaoke night,' Bridget adds, as she comes out of a closet with armfuls of exercise mats.

'Sure. I'll keep it in mind. Ladies,' I say with a nod as I head for the door. Zumba isn't my thing, and besides. I don't have time for that.

I gotta find my van.

I come to a stop in the corridor and tap my palm onto my forehead. 'There is no van. Focus, John. There is no van.'

'Kathy says there was a van.' I look up to see Gretchen waiting for me. She offers a shrug, but her energy is weird. Wounded and hurt. She tries to smile. 'Thank you for being kind in the session today.'

'Sure,' I say.

'Yeah, it was such a hard time for me. All that trauma with Tom and then waking up here. Mindfuck or what?'

She says fuck like a soccer mom trying to be cool.

'Yeah. So. New me though from now on,' she adds, staring at me as though she's pleading for something. 'And that means getting back into the saddle, buster!' She adds an air punch. 'Fancy a drink then?'

'What?' I ask, as I realize where this might be heading. 'Er, no. I can't. I gotta be somewhere.'

'Oh.' She looks like she might be ready to burst into tears again. 'Sure though. I mean. Who'd want a drink with a mom of three that was married to gay guy! Not me, that's for sure.'

'It's not that. I gotta be somewhere.'

'Sure. Whatever. See you Monday.'

'I'm terribly sorry to interrupt,' a British guy says. Charming and cool. 'Couldn't help but overhear that you fancy a drink?' He smiles at Gretchen like he's hungry and just scented blood. 'I was meant to be doing Zumba, but I'd go for a vodka martini over Zumba any day of the week. Shaken though. Not stirred,' he adds with a wry smile.

I leave them to it and head out of the community center, a block back from Main Street. A warm day. Spring, maybe. I heard someone say it's Spring anyway.

I set off past the ancillary buildings. One of them a fitness center filled with guys from Middle Earth on treadmills, spies lifting weights, and more detectives and coroners than you can shake a murder plot at.

A few minutes later I get back to my quarters. One main room with a bed. A small washroom. I share the kitchen with L132, Svetlana and John Candle.

They keep new arrivals together so they can absorb at the same time. Apparently, that helps the process. And on top of the orientation sessions with Pat and Rachel, I also have to attend the Enders therapy meetings.

That's because I'm an Ender. My story was almost finished. Or it might have been completely finished. I blacked out when Lin shot me with the revolver. Rachel and Pat told me that kinda suggests it was the end of book one, and maybe there would have been a book two.

I don't know about that.

I still can't get my head around it. That I was a character in a book, and that none of it was real. Lin wasn't real. Ibrahim wasn't real. Mascaponi. Wendy. My job. My former life.

None of it was real.

But Kathy said it *was* real. It happened, so that makes it real. And she said we have to deal with it as though it was real.

I open the closet and look at my UPS uniform hanging up. Bloodstains on the shirt from where I was cut by one of the Yakuza. I've still got the scar on my stomach. But then, it was only a few days ago.

Five days to be precise. I got here Monday. Today is Friday.

I still feel an urge to put the uniform on, but Rachel and Pat said not to do that. I asked if they had a black suit instead. They said absolutely not.

They gave me blue jeans and a plaid shirt.

I hate it.

I look like a lumberjack.

I went off on my own that first day, when Rachel, Pat, L132, Svetlana and John Candle were all behind, calling out my name.

I needed to be alone, and I needed to find my van and save Wendy – but I couldn't find the docks. I got lost, then this guy who said he used to be Superman walked me back to Hard-Boiled & Erotica. He seemed cool. He said he works for the city newspaper now.

Rachel and Pat were still inside with L132, Svetlana and John Candle. I thought they'd be cross with me. But Pat took me over to a table and gave me some tea. Then later, they took us to our shared digs and said to go back the next morning to continue orientation, so they could sort the admin out.

I thought it would be some sort of structured program, but orientation just means hanging out in our genre center, talking about this and that. Reliving what we did in our books. I guess it's kinda like a much less formal version of the Enders therapy, which apparently works fine for the characters that were only half written.

I didn't think it was real. Fiction Land. Orientation. Any of it. I'm not sure I do yet, but John Candle, despite being *like* me in some ways, isn't *like* me at all. He seems happy hanging out and chatting, whereas I still feel that urge inside to get moving and finish my mission.

We get a basic allowance, enough for food and necessities. But once orientation finishes, we're expected to find work and get jobs. Rachel said I could apply to the postal service, seeing as I have delivery worker experience.

I shut the closet and head out into a place that functions like a normal city, except it doesn't have any cars. What it has is lots of horses, pulling either carriages or delivery wagons. The horses look healthy and cared for too, and it makes me wonder why more cities don't do it. What a way to solve emissions problems and still get where you need to, and there's something cool about being near the animals. It's calming. They liked being stroked and patted, and some of the owners let you hand-feed them treats.

I don't know why they don't have cars or combustion engines because they do have electricity and modern appliances, and I've even seen a few computers. Rachel said they're all connected to a citywide intranet system that functions like the internet, but with less porn.

Another thing they don't have is cell phones. Which is weird, and even after five days, I keep reaching to pull mine out of my pocket only to find it's not there. I don't know why mine didn't come with me. Nor does anyone else. They just don't.

What I do have though, is that urge inside. That thing driving me on. And I can't just switch it off, so when we're not at orientation and when I'm not doing Enders therapy, I set out into the city.

To find the docks.

And to find my van.

CHAPTER TWELVE

This city is like a maze and the roads seem to loop back on each other, but I got a lock on the sun's direction to maintain a straight course. I wanted to find the boundary, or the edge, or whatever delineates this place.

That's how I found the ocean.

Which is how I found the docks, which means Rachel lied.

But I get why she said there aren't any docks here, because these are not docks in the way she knew I was thinking.

I meant old, abandoned docks filled with broken fish warehouses and meat processing plants.

These docks are not the same. But they are old. And I mean *old*. A harbor filled with old sailing ships, like something out of a movie. The wooden ones with the big masts and sails.

I head closer and look at the people moving around. I'm not good with history. Not enough to say what clothes or styles were worn at which times, but at a push I'd say there's everything from the sixteenth century right up until maybe the start of the twentieth century, and seven or eight big ships and a bunch of smaller ones.

It's busy, with people everywhere, walking around the harbor or lounging on benches and big barrels talking.

'Eh! Someone's wandered out the city,' a guy shouts in an old

English accent as a few more people laugh and look over at me. 'Alright, mate! Chopping down some trees, are ya?'

I told you I look like a lumberjack.

'Bonjour, monsieur. Did you awaken in the park?' a guy in a ruffled shirt with long hair and a big moustache calls out in a French accent from the highest deck on the closest ship.

'I been here since Monday,' I reply.

'Ah. He has been 'ere since Monday,' he repeats to whoever is around him. 'Then pray tell, monsieur, what the shit are you doin' 'ere?'

'Looking.'

'He is looking. Well go and look at something else! We are not a zoo!'

'Oi, Frenchie! That's no way to welcome someone, is it,' another man says, leaping deftly from a ship moored nearby. A good-looking guy with dark eyes and dark hair and a swagger in his walk. Then he spots me looking at the sword on his belt. 'The city lets us keep them, mate,' he says with a wink. 'Men like us feel naked without a sword, ain't that right, Frenchie.'

'Go fuck your mother, Jack!' a French accent shouts.

'Jack Blackbird at your pleasure,' the guy says with a charming smile, as he sidles in close. 'But a word to the wise, me old kipper. You do look like a lumberjack. Anyway. What you after? Let old Jack sort you out. Bit of rum is it? A bit of brandy?' he asks, tapping his nose and winking at me again. 'Eh. Jack's your man. Fancy a woman tonight? I know a good few Moll Flanders, if you get my meaning. Or would you prefer a Mike Flanders? Eh? Modern times. No judgement. We all dabble, I mean, how do you know what's it about unless you put a toe in.'

He looks me in the eye, and he seems a good man. Honest and reliable. The kind of guy that will stand at your side.

'One of the most important things to remember, John, is your propensity to seek a bond with other men. It's a John trait. Just be careful because it makes you kind of vulnerable.'

Rachel's words come back to me as I swallow and break the eye contact. 'Nothing. I er. I just wanted to find the edge of the city.'

'Oh. The edge,' he says with a knowing smile. 'Well. I'll tell you what, mate, you come on board and let me show you something.'

'I'm good.'

'Hey now. I don't know what you heard, but Jack Blackbird is as honest as they come. And my sword is blunter than a kipper,' he adds with another wink. 'The city doesn't let us keep them sharp. Which is fair enough. Half of 'em here don't know how to use one anyway. Writers aren't sword experts, are they? Go on. Feel that,' he says, drawing his sword.

He's right. An edge like that wouldn't get through soft butter.

'Mate, it's confusing here. I get it,' he says softly. 'Come on. I got something that might help.'

'What?'

'A map.'

That does it. A map is exactly what I need. I follow him up a rickety old plank onto his ship and marvel at the wooden spokes and how the ropes are fastened. A few people look over with frowns at my clothes.

'What's he doing here?' one of them asks. A handsome guy with dark eyes and dark hair and a swagger in his walk. 'Jack Finch, mate. Now get off my ship.'

'I said he come could on board,' Jack Blackbird says. 'And it's my ship today. It's your ship tomorrow.'

'No, mate. It's mine tomorrow,' another guy says from the side. Dark hair and eyes and a ready smile. 'Jack Robin, mate. What's your fancy?'

'I'm with him,' I say, pointing at the first Jack.

'Not me. Him,' Jack Finch says, moving my hand to point at Jack Blackbird.

'He was looking for the edge of the city, lads,' Jack Blackbird says.

'You gonna show him the map, mate?' Jack Robin asks.

'I am, mate!' Jack Blackbird says as he leads us all down a very steep set of stairs to the decks below.

'Who goes there?' a woman calls from ahead of us. Dark hair and dark eyes and very beautiful. She swaggers towards us with a ready smile and a wink. 'Jane Tit, mate. And don't look like that. A tit is still a bird. Anyway. Why are you dressed like a lumberjack?'

'He's looking for the edge,' one of the Jack's says.

'Edge of what?' Jane asks.

'Edge of the city,' one of the other Jack's says.

'Apparently you have a map, Miss Tit,' I say.

'Cor. Get them manners,' she says, fanning her face while winking at me. 'You trying to ruffle my skirts?'

I look down to see she's wearing trousers.

'Figure of speech, mate. This way,' she says, leading us to the back of the ship to what must be the captain's quarters, and a large map spread over a table. She puts a finger on one specific spot. 'This is where we are, and this is the city.'

I look at the spot she's marking and the drawings of the harbor. The streets marked in black winding lines. The landmass brown, and the surrounding sea a pastel blue.

'It's an island?' I ask.

'It is, mate,' Jack Blackbird says, his tone as soft as Jane's. But then they all seem that way now. Softer. Gentler.

'We get people down here now and then,' Jane says quietly. 'Normally Enders.'

'You an Ender?' Jack Finch asks me.

I nod at him.

'I was too,' Jane says. 'The therapy helped, but yeah, wow. I was convinced I was still in my plot and King James had taken me prisoner and drugged me to find out where I'd stashed the Spanish gold.'

'She came here looking for a ship,' Jack Blackbird says.

'What happened?' I ask.

'We tried talking to her, but she's a Jack Sparrow,' Jack Finch says with a shrug.

'So I stole one,' Jane says with a smile. 'And promptly realized I didn't have a clue how to sail and crashed straight into Frenchie's ship,' she adds as they laugh at the memory.

'Cor, he wasn't half angry,' Jack Finch says, wiping his eyes. 'Still the funniest thing I ever saw, though.'

'We brought her back in,' Jack Blackbird says. 'Then, once we'd gotten her calm, we took her back out so she could see for herself.'

I look at them all. Sensing there's more to come. 'What did you find?' I ask quietly.

She smiles sadly again. 'Nothing but ocean. What's your name?'

'John Croker.'

'This is real, John,' she tells me, as one of the other Jacks pours shots from a bottle into little glasses. She passes one to me and motions for me to drink it. 'Fiction Land!' She lifts her glass. The others repeat it. I do it too and knock the drink down, then immediately cough from the harsh burn.

'Rum, mate!' she says, back to the broad accent and the comical wink. 'You'll be okay, John. Go back to the therapy and see it through.'

'And don't put pressure on yourself,' Jack Blackbird says, pouring more shots.

'One day at a time,' Jack Finch says, raising his glass as we all do the same. 'TO THE ENGLISH!' he yells out.

'FUCK YOUR ENGLISH MOTHERS!' the French guy yells back as the Jacks and Jane all laugh. I smile too, the rum feeling nice in my belly as I look back down at the map and the large island surrounded by nothing but ocean.

'There's nothing hidden,' Jane says, pouring another round of shots. 'But be careful. Cos clinging to your story is a red flag to the city officials. Anyway. Your toast.'

I think about that one thing which is constantly driving me. 'There is no van,' I say, lifting my glass. I guess they don't know what that means, while at the same time knowing exactly what that means.

'There is no van!' they chorus.

'AND THE FRENCH ARE TWATS!' Jack Blackbird shouts.

'I WILL FUCK YOU ALL UP!' the French guy yells, as we all laugh and down our shots.

CHAPTER THIRTEEN

With a few rums in my belly, I wobble across the plank and back onto the harbor, while telling myself there is no van. Which means there's no Wendy or Lin or anything else.

I'm struggling with the concept of those things *not* being real, while also trying to remember that Kathy said they *were* real, and they happened.

I don't know about that. I don't know about anything.

I just know I gotta find my van.

'Focus, John. There is no van.'

It's dark by the time I get back to Hard-Boiled & Erotica and find it closed up. Then I look round and see that Main Street is also very quiet.

Too quiet.

I feel a rush inside at the idea that something else is going on. Where is everyone? Why have they all gone?

I set off with purpose in my stride and a head filling with the thought that Mascaponi's taken everyone as a way of getting to me.

Which is exactly what Mascaponi would do.

Which means there is a van.

And all I have to do is find it.

It feels good to think that. It feels right.

Then I hear an awful noise coming from the next block over. The sound of someone in pain and other people groaning, and in my head Mascaponi has everyone grouped together and is torturing them one by one to find out where I am.

That gets me sprinting as I realize I was right all along and this is all just part of some sick scheme – until I round the corner and realize it's karaoke night in Diagonal Alley, and the noise is someone singing.

I come to a stop, breathing hard and smacking a clenched fist into my forehead.

'There is no van, John. There is no van.'

'John!' a voice shouts from a table near the mouth of the alley. I catch sight of an arm in the air and Rachel appears, pushing through the crowd to wave me over. 'Hey! You made it.'

I don't tell her I ran here thinking they'd all been kidnapped and were being tortured.

'Come in, we saved you a space,' she says, grabbing my hand to pull me across the street. 'Johns are predisposed to seeking their own company. Most of the hard-boiled detective types are like that to be honest. They prefer a quiet bar to down shots in misery. You need to socialize and be around other people.'

'You look like the kind of a guy a man can drink with,' John Candle says, holding his hand out. 'John Candle.'

'John Croker,' I say, grasping his in a firm grip. Man to man. Warrior to warrior.

'Idiots,' Rachel says, rolling her eyes as the others laugh.

'I'll drink with you,' L132 says, holding his hand out next to us.

'No,' we both say, earning more laughs at the jokes which have grown within our group over the last week. A bond between us. But not the bond of brothers that Ibrahim and I had, because that wasn't real. This is a gentle bond that grows as we spend time together.

'So, have you found the docks yet, John?' Svetlana asks over the table.

'I did. And you lied,' I say with a smile to Rachel to show it's said in humor.

'He found the docks,' Pat says.

'He found the docks,' Rachel parrots.

'Wait. There's docks?' L asks.

'Relax,' Pat tells him. It's weird seeing L's chubby little face out of his helmet, even though he's still wearing the rest of the outfit.

'So?' John Candle asks. 'The docks?'

'Yes, mate. The docks,' I say, in a very poor mimicry of the Jacks. It makes John, Svetlana, and L frown but Rachel and Pat both burst out laughing.

'Love it!' Pat says, squeezing my arm, which I now know is just a friendly gesture.

'Did you meet Jane?' Rachel asks. 'How pretty is she?'

'She's very beautiful,' I admit.

'Who is?' L asks. 'Is she here? Introduce me!'

'You are one horny little man,' Pat tells him.

'I'm a virgin!' L says.

'You've never had sex?' Svetlana asks him.

'On the Killer Sun? No way. If the Dark Lord even thinks you touched your pee pee then it's blam blam laser time.'

We laugh at the way he says it, but a second later Svetlana is thinking and leaning in. 'Maybe we're all virgins.'

'Er, you're definitely not,' L says. '*So then Benjamin and I had sex on the table, then on the fridge, then with the hoover, then with some football guys, then with some fruit at a wedding . . .*' he mimics her voice and mannerisms, setting us all off as Svetlana swipes his arm.

'It was a funeral, not a wedding. And I don't sound like that.'

'You do,' we all say.

'Shush. I don't. My point is we could all be virgins because that wasn't real, right? We were just characters doing things in books.'

I think about what Kathy said. That our experiences were real, but they both seem right. It wasn't real. But it was.

'It's different for us,' Rachel says, shifting closer to be heard over the music.

'For us?' I ask. 'You were an Ender?'

She nods and takes a sip of her beer, leaving a frothy moustache on her upper lip.

'Froth,' I say, pointing at my own lip.

'I know. I'm leaving it for later,' she says as she pulls a cross-eyed look. She seems different. Less formal. But then we are at a bar, and I guess this isn't technically work. I wonder why she and Pat are with us, if this is still part of the orientation, and if other new arrivals are also with their genre reps. 'What are you thinking right now?' she asks with a look of genuine interest.

'If you're here for work or pleasure.'

'Both,' she replies quickly. 'But going back to what I said a minute ago. It's different for Enders. So like, Svetlana and John and L . . . they're what? Probably less than half written into their stories, so it's easier for them to process the change and accept it and say *hey, it wasn't real. I'm cool with that.*'

'Coping mechanism,' I say as she clicks her fingers and winks at me.

'You've been listening to Kathy. That's good. So yeah. Don't overthink it when you hear someone else say it wasn't real. Because to an Ender it was very real.'

'Did the Enders therapy help you?'

She shrugs. 'There's nothing to compare it to, is there? I mean, I don't know what I would have been like without it.'

'That makes sense,' I say, and take another drink of the rich, malty beer.

'People are people, John. Some cling to what they were, either because they like how it defines them, like the Jack Sparrows, or they are too scared to change. Which is why the city has ended up with zones for different eras. Like Little Victoria or Marvel Town. Or Middle Earth, way out in the countryside. The city doesn't tell anyone to go live in a certain area, but people gravitate to where they *feel* like they fit in. To what's familiar and comfortable for them. And then you get others who embrace the opportunity to change. Look at L for instance. Being a Thunder Soldier or whatever he was gave him instant attention, which is why he chooses to keep wearing his uniform, whereas Svetlana is already showing signs of change, and her saying it wasn't real is a way of distancing herself from her character. She's saying *I'm more than that. I'm not just a beautiful woman put on the Earth for the gratification of men,*' she says with a sudden hardness to her voice. 'The point is, we're all given a chance here, John. A chance to start over.' She looks at me over the rim of her glass as we both take another drink. 'The question is. Who will you be?'

I nod. Trying to take it all in.

'You know what I like about you though?' Rachel asks. I look at her and frown. 'You're very stubborn, and *very* determined, but you do listen. I can see it in your eyes.'

I nod, then frown again. 'Sorry, what?'

'You wally!' she says, bursting out laughing as she hits my arm.

'My writer had me making wisecracks,' I say in explanation.

'Is that right?' she asks. 'And that's something you don't do. You don't really talk about your story.'

I shrug. 'Not much to say. There is no van.'

She looks at me with that strand of hair hanging down on the left side of her face and I have to remind myself that she's a rep assigned to take care of new arrivals and it's not a romantic lingering gaze.

'Let's hear it for Gerry!' an amplified voice says as we all turn to look down the alley to a guy with long white hair getting onto the stage. He smiles and takes the microphone. 'This is for all of us,' he says, as the first simple chords of 'Yesterday' by the Beatles start coming from the speakers.

Then a second or two later the guy starts singing with this haunting voice that has us all rooted to the spot.

'The Witchers are so cool,' Pat says, shaking her head.

'What's a Witcher?' L132 asks, as Pat waves him to be quiet and promises to tell him later.

We listen to the song in silence. A few people are singing along to themselves, moving their lips and swaying.

'Yesterday . . . All my troubles seemed so far away . . . Suddenly . . . I'm not half the man I used to be. There's a shadow hanging over me . . .'

The words sink in and take root and I get that feeling again. That feeling that all things are connected, and this song is a message.

Luckily it's a short song, but I guess it gets everyone going, because after that more people start getting up to sing.

'Let's hear it for the DC Marvels!' the hostess says a bit later.

Applause breaks out as four people get on the stage. Two guys and two women.

'Oh, I love these!' Pat says. 'So the blond guy is Thor 26. The other guy is Superman 19, and then that woman is Black Widow 4 and that's one of the Harley Quinns but I don't know which one.'

'She was the thirty-eighth,' Rachel says.

'No!' Svetlana says in shock. 'There are thirty-seven other Harley Quinns here?'

Rachel shakes her head. 'There's more like seventy.'

'They all work together in the DC Coffee Shop in Marvel Town,' Pat says, meaning the four singers on the stage. 'I even heard they're working on some of their own material.'

They cover a few Abba songs, then some other classic hits that get the crowd going. I don't know much about music, but it's good enough to get my foot tapping, and with the beers flowing that urgency to fulfil my mission starts to ease off a little.

'Let's hear it for the DC Marvels!' the hostess says. We all applaud as they head off, then a sudden groan sounds out from the front.

'Oh god, no!' Pat suddenly says as the reaction spreads, and I look to the stage to see Fat George Wheeler getting up, flicking the Vs out in a show of defiance. 'Seriously. Cover your ears,' Pat says as the tune starts playing for 'You Ain't Seen Nothing Yet'.

'I love this!' Svetlana says.

'You won't,' Pat tells her as Fat George strikes a rock-god pose and starts screaming the words into the screeching microphone.

'I met a devil woman . . . She took my heart away . . .'

As one, the whole of Diagonal Alley seems to recoil, the groans and protests getting louder by the second, but Fat George just adds more power with the speakers distorting until people start flinging drinks at him. The guy just keeps going. The same guy who poked me in the eye with his little wand the first day I got here.

'He's such a prick!' Pat shouts with her hands over her ears. 'GET HIM OFF!'

'SCREW YOU!' the balding ginger guy and middle-aged woman who were with Harry the other day shout at everyone else from their table off to the side.

'FUCK YOU, RON!' Pat yells, as the drinks get flung and bouncers move in from the sides, and finally the music cuts off.

'You lot are wankers,' Fat George says, throwing the microphone aside as he storms off the stage.

'And this is our alley!' Ginger Ron shouts as the crowd all shout back at him, while a female wizard takes advantage of the distraction to pour Ron and Fat George's drinks into her tankard.

'Wow. Okay!' the hostess says, grabbing the microphone up as she waves at the crowd to settle. 'I think we need something special after that. What do you say, Fiction Land?'

'I think he needs a broomstick up his arse!' someone yells as the laughs spread out.

'Rach. You need to get up there,' Pat says, making us all blink and double take as Rachel shakes her head.

'Nooo! Not a chance.'

'Rachel! Rachel! Rachel!' Pat says, chanting her name and clapping along. A few others nearby take it up, and within seconds the whole alley is doing it.

'Alright!' Rachel says, pulling a face and rising to her feet as everyone starts applauding. She mounts the stage with a self-conscious smile and tucks the strand of hair back as she takes the microphone. 'This is for my department's new arrivals. Everyone say hi to John Candle, Svetlana Graphite, L132, who we call L, and John Croker. Stand up, guys. Say hi!'

L's the first on his feet. Svetlana and John Candle follow, while I just lift a hand and stay seated.

'We all remember what it's like being new here,' Rachel says as the crowd settle. 'It's all a bit weird.'

'I've been here seven damn years and it's still weird,' Pat says to a few laughs. 'COME ON, RACH! GET SINGING!'

'Okay okay,' Rachel says, rolling her eyes and nodding to the host to start the track. I look over and can't help but admire Rachel's bravery, being able to get up in front of so many people like that.

Then the track starts, and my heart misses a beat at the instantly recognizable guitar chords. It's a song I know well.

'Jolene, Jolene, Jolene, Joleeene . . . I'm begging of you please don't take my man . . .'

Monday morning in my UPS van. This song was playing until the ambulance went past, then it switched to Billy Joel.

Déjà vu hits me again. My vision narrows and it's like the stage moves closer until I only see Rachel smiling and turning to face me as she sings the lyrics while my mind latches onto the coincidence and seeks to find patterns and meanings.

'There is no van,' I mutter to myself as Rachel looks over, and I swear it's like she's staring straight at me. Right into my eyes, and such is the intensity of the moment that I have to look away until the song finishes, and the crowd applauds as she takes a comical bow and starts threading her way back to our table. 'You want another drink?' I ask, standing quickly to grab the empty glasses. 'Same again guys?'

'John, you don't have to get them,' Pat says.

'It's fine. I'd like to.'

'Take this then. We claim the first social event on expenses,' she says, pushing money into my hand. I don't look at it. I just need to be moving to shake off that feeling. I turn to leave and almost walk into Rachel as she smiles up me and again, I swear there's something in her eyes and expression.

'You okay?' she asks with a frown.

'Yeah. Drink?' I ask, holding the empties up, and it takes everything I have to remember it's just my mind searching for plot, and it was just a random song.

She nods. 'I'll give you a hand.'

'I'm good. I got it,' I say, and head off into the tavern, or inn, or pub, or whatever they call these places and thread a route to the bar until the albino guy in the tight, skin-colored spandex steps into my path with wild staring eyes.

'You can't see me,' he says.

'Whatever,' I say, and walk around him to the packed bar, to wait my turn in this messed-up town where random songs aren't random and albinos wear Lycra.

I'm jostled again, an elbow digging into my side. I grunt and ignore it, catching the eye of a server who smiles apologetically and goes by, as I get pushed hard enough to slam into the bar.

'Hey, I can't go anywhere.' I twist around to see Fat George Wheeler grinning at me.

'Stop doing that,' I tell him.

'Doing what?' he asks innocently as another elbow drives into my side and I twist again to see balding Ginger Ron glaring at me.

'What?' he asks angrily.

'Your elbow,' I say and turn back to the bar, only to get a few more digs until I twist back to see more Potters and Ginger Rons. 'Guys. Quit it.'

'Guys. Quit it,' an Asian wizard mimics as the others laugh.

'You're in the way,' angry, balding Ginger Ron says, as the others murmur and tell me to move and, truth be told, I don't know how to handle it or what to say.

'You're a John, aren't you?' one of the Ginger Rons asks me. 'One of the Wick wankers.'

'Wick wankers,' Fat George snorts with a laugh.

I turn back to the bar as the server goes by with another apologetic smile.

'We want to get served,' balding Ron says. 'Get out the way. This is our bar.'

'It's our alley,' another one says.

'You need to fuck off,' another one says, as I turn back to see more weird wizard dudes gathering around me.

'Wick wanker!' Fat George laughs again. 'He's a Wick wanker.'

'You just gonna keep saying that?' I ask him.

'You just gonna keep saying that,' the Asian wizard mimics.

'Wick wanker,' Fat George says.

'We need to get served,' Ron says, pushing my shoulder.

'Don't do that,' I tell him.

'Or what?' he asks, squaring up as the others all surge in and start tugging their wands out. 'This is our boozer, mate.'

'And our alley,' Fat George says, trying to look menacing.

Eight of them and only one of me. I figure an ordinary man wouldn't stand a chance. But then I'm not an ordinary man.

They all blink as I realize, with a terrible sinking feeling, that I said it out loud. A second later, they're roaring with laughter.

'You bloody diamond,' balding Ron says. 'Best Wick ever right here. Seriously! HEY GUYS! BEST WICK WANKER RIGHT HERE!'

'I'm not an ordinary man,' the Asian wizard mimics, setting them all off again while my cheeks burn with humiliation.

'He doesn't know,' Fat George says, still laughing hard. 'Ron! He doesn't know.'

'Know what?' I ask.

'Know what?' the Asian wizard mimics.

'He thinks he can fight,' Fat George laughs.

'He thinks he's a real John Wick,' another one says.

I can't fight?

It didn't even occur me that I wouldn't be able to fight.

'You need to piss off, mate,' balding Ron says, as the rest squeeze in and force me away from the bar. I think to stand my ground, because that's what I would have done before.

But I was character in a book. And not even a unique character, but a knock-off of another famous character, and besides, I can't fight. Which means I have no skills at all.

The realization hits me harder than anything else since I've been here and I drop my head and head back into the alley, feeling humiliated.

'Come on, buddy. Watch it.' A big guy tells me off for getting in his way and shoulder-barges me aside as I spot the white-haired Witcher man who was singing earlier.

'Hey, is there another bar here?'

He nods to the other side. 'The Potters being pricks again?'

'Something like that.'

'There's too many of them. They gang up on everyone else. Fat George thinks he's a mob boss. But hey, don't sweat it. I don't think we'll do karaoke here again. This place is toxic. We'll put it back in Middle Earth. You seen it yet? You should come over. We're really friendly.'

I say thanks and head off into the other place. As I get to the bar to wait my turn I feel an elbow in my side. I tense inwardly, turning to see Gretchen staring up at me.

'Surprise!' she says with a forced smile.

'How's it going?' I ask, relieved that it's not the weird wizard people again.

'Great! Just great! Honestly. Really great,' she says, while looking like things aren't great at all.

'Get you?' a server calls over the noise. I place my order and ask Gretchen if she wants one.

'No! I think I'm going to head home after this,' she says, holding her half-empty glass of wine. I can see she's made an effort tonight, in a tight sparkly top and tight jeans and her hair all pinned up and makeup on.

'You here with your group?' I ask.

She frowns at me. 'Oh, you mean my arrivals group? No! I've been here for two months, and we didn't really connect that well. They were all young. You know. In their twenties and hip and cool,' she says with a sing-song head-dip to both sides. 'They didn't want Old Gretchy clinging on.'

I nod and wait for the beers, not quite knowing what to say.

'Yeah. So. I had a date!' she says brightly.

'That's great,' I say.

'Bond. James Bond,' she says in a deep voice, followed by a laugh that veers a bit too close to crying.

'Oh, the guy. From the Zumba class? Hey, that was only today. Like a few hours ago.'

'Yep! Speed dating, anyone?' she asks with another laugh.

'You're here with him tonight? With the Bond guy?'

'Er. I mean. You know. I saw him and . . . Yeah. No.' She trails off as I try and decipher what she's trying to say, or not say. 'But I was married for a long time. You know. And I don't know how these things work. But we had the drink, and he was all lovely and he said *hey, come and see my place,* so I was like, *aw, he's being so nice,* and I told him about Tom being gay and we had another drink at his . . .'

I tense inside at where it's going, willing the drinks to get here, feeling guilty as hell that I don't want to hear it.

'Yeah. But hey. I said I needed to get right on that saddle, buster!' She gives another air-punch while her face displays way too many emotions. Pain and regret. Trauma. Suffering. Confusion. 'I mean. Tom was fucking someone else so why shouldn't I? And it was James Bond. Ha! Beat that, Tom.'

I look over to see the server pouring the beers.

'And then he said I should go because he needed to work out, seeing as he'd missed Zumba.'

Ouch. I wince and look at her.

'But. You know. I said about meeting here and he said yeah maybe, and I took that like he was playing it cool. I mean. Duh. He is James

Bond. Anyway.' She falls silent with a wretched look then downs the rest of her wine. 'And you know what he asked me?'

I wait for her to continue.

'Right in the middle of fucking me he asks who the hot little goth girl was in our therapy group,' she says, as the server places the beers on a tray and I hand the money over.

'Hey. Come sit with us,' I tell her, not knowing what else to say.

'No. I should go home,' she says, leaning past me to put the empty glass on the bar. 'I'm too old for bars.'

'You're not too old.'

'My body has given birth to three children,' she says, glaring at me. 'I'm covered in birthing scars and my stomach muscles are like jelly. But I don't have the kids. Or the marriage. How is that fair? What the fuck am I supposed to do here?'

I don't know what to say, so I say nothing at all.

'I said I was thinking about joining Zumba. You know what he said to me? He said *you'll need more than Zumba, sweetheart*. Whatever. I sound like a bitter old hag. See you Monday.'

'Hey!' I call out, but she strides off and disappears into the crowd, leaving me holding the tray of beers and not knowing what to think, or say, or do. I've got no skills for this. No life history to draw from, and hey, apparently I can't fight either.

I head back out into the alley, towards our table and Rachel looking for me. 'There you are! I thought you'd left or something.'

'Yeah. Sorry. There was a queue.'

'In there?' she asks, looking behind me to the bar I came from.

'I tried the other one first.'

She winces at my expression. 'Oh, poop. Sorry! I should have said. My bad. The wizard bar is super toxic. I even heard they're not doing karaoke here anymore. Anyway. Beer! I'm thirsty after singing. And you haven't said if you liked it.'

'It was great.'

'Really? Did you like it?' she asks, as we pass Fat George and balding Ginger Ron and their dressing gown-clad guys all laughing at me.

'HE'S JUST AN ORDINARY GUY!' one of them yells to more laughing.

'What's all that about?' Rachel asks, as I spot two people at another table just down from the Potter bar.

'What's the drinking age here?' I ask.

'What? Er, eighteen, I think. Yeah, it's eighteen. Why? John! Where are you going?'

I pass her the tray of drinks and walk off towards the two people I just saw.

To the table with the James Bond guy I met earlier.

The same one Gretchen went home with.

The same guy now pouring liquor from a hip flask into a glass held by a seventeen-year-old goth chick in torn tights and DM boots.

'Hey,' I say, coming to a stop.

'Go away,' he says in that clipped British accent, without looking up.

Alice snorts a laugh into her glass.

'Alice?'

She finally looks up. 'John!' she says with a huge grin.

'Hi, John. Bye, John,' James Bond says.

'She's seventeen,' I tell him.

He looks at me coldly. 'Your concern is noted.'

'It's just a drink, John,' Alice says with an eye-roll. 'Bit of rim . . . Rom . . . Bugger. Ha! I said bugger. I'm turning British. I say old chap! What what! Hey, so, John is a John. You know, *a John*. And you're a James Bond,' she tells him. 'Woohoo!'

'That's great, Alice. You had a few?' I ask.

'A couple. But er, whatever! It's not real, is it.'

'It is real, Alice.'

'Sorry. Who are you again?' Bond asks.

'Nobody. Alice, you wanna come over to my table with my buddies and –'

'Well, why don't you go and mind your own business, Mr Nobody,' James says, cutting over me. 'The young lady is quite happy here.'

'Hey, John? You coming?' Rachel asks, rushing over after delivering the tray to the table. 'Ooh, atmosphere. What's going on? Oh, it's you,' she says with a look at Bond, before noticing Alice with a sudden frown. 'How old is she? How old are you?'

'Eighteen!' Alice says.

'She's seventeen,' I say.

'John!' Alice says, swiping my arm.

'Honey, you're a little young to be drinking here,' Rachel says.

'You are absolutely right. I shall deliver the young woman back to her quarters immediately,' Bond says, instantly charming as he stands up and makes a weird motion as though adjusting cufflinks.

'You're not taking her anywhere,' Rachel says. 'Do you even know her?'

'Of course. She's Alice and I'm Bond. James Bond,' he says with a smile and a wink.

'You're not Bond. He's not Bond. His name is Jimmy and he's a creep,' Rachel says, giving him a withering look.

'Wow. This isn't deeply embarrassing at all,' Alice says, giving me her sarcastic smile. 'And I thought you were my friend.'

'I am.'

'Well. Alice and I are now the best of friends,' Jimmy says, still holding his arm out for her. 'Shall we, my dear?'

'We shall!' Alice says in her British accent as she takes his hand. 'Cos I fucking hate it here and he's got booze and that makes you forget,' she finishes, with an angry glare at me.

'You know what?' Rachel says. 'I think I'd be happier if I walked the girl back.'

'Don't call me *the girl*. My name is Alice.'

'Alice. I'm one of the genre reps. Did you want to come with me?'

'What the fuck, John!' Alice says. 'Did you snitch on me?'

'That is very uncool, John,' Jimmy says, giving me a mocking look. 'And Rachel. Good to see you again,' he adds with that nasty smile.

'WATCH OUT, JIMMY. HE'S NOT JUST AN ORDINARY MAN!' Fat George calls out, to more laughs.

'Eight of them. One of me. But I'm not an ordinary man,' the Asian wizard says, as the laughs roll all the way over to Jimmy, who offers a delighted chuckle.

'He still thinks he can fight!' Fat George says, laughing hard.

Alice snorts a laugh, then looks at me and seems to spot the discomfort in my expression. 'Oh god, did that really happen? Jesus, John.'

'I forget to stop speaking out loud.'

'Idiot!' Jimmy laughs.

'Fuck you!' Alice says, wiping the smirk off his face. 'John's really nice, you creepy old man. What are you? Fifty? I'm seventeen!'

'Exactly,' Rachel says. 'He is a creepy old man.'

'I didn't hear you complaining,' Jimmy says, viciously.

'HE'S JUST AN ORDINARY MAN!' a few of the wizards call out in chorus.

'Enough,' Rachel snaps at them.

'Aw, he's got his rep telling us off,' Fat George says, laughing even harder.

'You sad fat cunts,' Alice says, shaking her head at the tables of wizards. 'You're worse than sleazy Bond.'

'Hey!' Jimmy says.

'Oi!' Fat George says.

'Blow me!' Alice says, giving them both the bird. 'John's my pal, so fuck you. Sad wizards with your bits of wood. *Ooh I'm a wizard on a broomstick.* No one cares. Get over it – oh, and FYI . . . Worst karaoke night ever,' she adds as more people start looking over. I spot another guy pushing off from a wall, adjusting cufflinks as he starts heading our way. Then another one a bit further down doing the same thing. Then another further up. All of them solitary men of a certain age. And all of them moving their hands to their wrists as they start walking.

'Okay. We need to go,' Rachel says, clocking the guys approaching as she takes hold of Alice's wrist.

'I said I would walk her home,' Jimmy says, reaching out to remove Rachel's hand.

'What is wrong with you? She's seventeen!' Rachel says.

'And?' Jimmy asks. 'The age of consent is sixteen here.'

'Do not touch me!' Rachel snaps, pushing his arm off and sending him into the table, spilling drinks and bottles. He surges off with a look of wrath and I step in fast to block him from going at Rachel as the angry, balding Ginger Ron springs up from his seat.

'Don't push him you twat! He's British,' he yells, driving me back from Jimmy as more wizards start coming in towards us.

'Hey! Enough,' Rachel says, trying to push balding Ginger Ron back from me while Jimmy reaches to take hold of Alice.

'Get off me, you pervert!' Alice snaps, wrenching her arm back and slamming into one of the Ginger Rons.

'Don't hit me, you emo bitch,' he yells, pushing her away.

'Do not touch her,' I say.

'COS HE'S JUST AN ORDINARY MAN!' the Asian wizard says.

'You Wick wanker,' Fat George says, pulling his wand out. 'Do him, Jimmy. He can't fight.'

'I'll bloody do him!' balding Ginger Ron says, pushing at my chest.

'Jesus. This place is toxic!' Rachel says. 'John, let's just go. Alice . . . Stop calling them names.'

'No! They're fucking freaks and John's my friend.'

'Alice, just go,' I say, trying to usher her away.

'Hey. What's going on?' John Candle asks, walking into the mess as a few bouncers start rushing over with the other Bond-looking guys.

'You alright, Jimmy?' one of them calls in a British accent.

'Oh. Look at that. Backup,' Jimmy says, with that nasty smile.

'We're going,' Rachel says. 'Alice! I said we are going.'

'Yeah. Get out of my alley!' Fat George yells. 'GET THEM OUT OF MY ALLEY!' he shouts at the bouncers. 'That John was giving alcohol to that young girl.'

'He didn't!' Rachel says, as several bouncers start coming for me.

'I told him she was only seventeen,' Jimmy says, holding his hands up with a disgusted look. 'He said he didn't care. He said she's over sixteen so he can fuck her.'

'YOU SLEAZY CREEP!' Alice yells, lunging at him as he smirks and steps back to let her fall over the table.

A bouncer grabs my arm. 'Don't do that,' I say, trying to step away.

'Watch out! He's an ordinary man,' the Asian wizard says.

'Get that Wick wanker out of here!' Fat George shouts as balding Ginger Ron pushes me again.

'Hey!' John Candle says, trying to push him back as Ron takes a swing and clocks him on the jaw.

'What the hell!' John Candle says, as the look of violence creeps into his eyes and I tense, expecting him the go full-on *John* and lay them all out, except he just rushes at Ron and starts slapping out, all weird and feeble, looking confused as the wizards laugh and balding Ginger Ron darts back in to punch him again.

'I said that's enough!' Rachel says, getting between them to push Ron back. 'Stop it. Stop it right now.'

'Sod off, *Lana Love*!' Ron shouts at her.

She slaps his face, and he lashes out to push her hard as Alice grabs a glass to throw at his head, but misses and hits Fat George instead.

'Out,' the bouncer says in my ear, twisting my arm up my back and pushing me on.

'Don't worry. I'll look after Alice,' Jimmy says with a wink as I'm pushed past, and I'm not sure what happens next. Only that one second the huge bouncer has my arm pinned up my back and I've got a voice in my head telling me I can't fight so I shouldn't try, then I see Jimmy grabbing Alice's wrist and Rachel on the floor with balding Ron looking ready to kick her – and the next second, I'm dropping to a knee and twisting on the spot to break the bouncer's lock, then rising fast to palm him back with a center-of-mass open-handed strike that sends him flying off his feet. Then I'm sliding back a step to grab and pivot and throw the other bouncer over my hip before getting upright and turning fast towards the *other* Bond who's coming in fast and throwing a punch aimed at my head.

And I catch his fist mid-air.

That happens.

And the whole damn place seems to freeze for one second as I realize they were wrong, and that I can still fight.

'Yes!' Alice says as I twist hard and snap his wrist then drive a knee into the guy's stomach, following up with an elbow to his jaw. Sending him off his feet, and while everyone else is still staring, I'm already taking the step needed to slam a fist into balding Ron's nose with a nice big crunch of bone. He drops like a bald ginger sack of shit as all the other wizards start rushing at me.

'GETOFFMYBUDDY!' a yell comes, as L132 sprints over, tugging his helmet on to give a brutal headbutt to the bouncer trying to grab me from behind.

The bouncer goes down as L sticks his arms in the air with a whoop – 'LET'S BRAWL, BITCHES!' – then he's wading into the toxic weirdos, swinging wild punches and having the time of his life while Alice jumps on the back of Fat George and starts punching his right ear.

'Get off! I've got an ear infection!'

I spot another Bond-type guy weaving through the brawl with his eyes locked on me, and another one coming in fast behind him as the first Bond goes for a leg-sweeping kick to take me down. I block it with a kick to his ankle that sends him spinning off, then I'm blocking punches thrown by the next Bond while turning away from the third.

I dance back a step and make it look like I'm ready to flee so I can switch and go in fast to drive a hard fist into a kneecap, making the guy grunt and drop while I'm pivoting to flip the last Bond and take him down before slamming a fist into his head. Two down. One left and I go for Jimmy, who dances back and tries to punch me, but I move in fast, grabbing the front of his nice fitted black shirt and driving him down to pin him against the table.

'You go near Alice again and I'll come for you.'

'Fuck you!' he hisses, and I'll give him this – he's either brave and defiant, or the most arrogant man I've ever met, and I can see in his eyes he already wants revenge. So I grab his hand and snap his thumb to get his attention real good.

'You want me to keep going?'

'No,' he gasps, and I push him off to let him fall on the booze-soaked floor as more people rush over to break us up.

A minute or two later we're out on the street, with L132 and Alice trying to get back in to fight everyone while Rachel and I, along with Pat, John Candle and Svetlana, pull them away and finally get out of the alley.

'FUCK YOU! HE'S JOHN CROKER, BITCHES!' Alice yells, while hanging over my shoulder as I carry her off.

'AND I'M L132, MOTHERFUCKERS!' L shouts with a whoop as he reaches up to high-five Alice.

'I love this guy!' Alice says, as I lower her down so she can jump up to hug L. 'That was so much fun! Honestly, I was so bored here. And oh my god. Did you see Bald Ron's face when John grabbed that guy's fist and everyone was like . . . uh-oh, this John can fight! Then bammo and whammo and then L was there and –'

'Did that happen?' Pat asks, looking at me then back to Rachel.

'I saw it,' John Candle says, looking at his hands. 'But how did you remember? I couldn't. I mean . . . I was ready in my head but . . .'

'I don't know,' I say.

'We normally don't have the skills of our characters,' Rachel says, looking at me again. 'Supermans can't fly here. Spidermans can't climb walls. I mean. There's theories about why some people retain *some* of their characters traits but . . .' she blasts air and looks at me again. 'I knew you'd be trouble,' she says with a laugh. 'Jesus. How are we gonna explain that?' she asks as Pat holds her hands out.

'Just say it was me,' Alice says. 'My allowance has already been cut in half. What they gonna do?'

'Why are you on half allowance?' Pat asks her.

'Alice is an Ender,' I say.

'And I won't go over my boring, sad backstory or whatever,' Alice says. 'They said I'm not engaging . . . And I keep running out of Juvie Hall . . . And I keep getting drunk . . . And getting into fights . . . And swearing . . . And I might have told the matron in the dorms she was a fat twisted Nurse Ratched.'

'Alice!' Rachel says with a wince.

'She is! She's horrible,' Alice says.

'And that's why you're on half allowance,' Pat tells her. 'But! Fat George had that coming. I'll say that,' she adds with a smile. 'And Jimmy.'

'Anyway. Whatever. It's done,' Rachel says. 'We need to get Alice back to Juvie Hall before this gets any worse.'

'Are you being serious? No! I can't sleep after that,' Alice says with a sudden pleading look. 'Let's go to the diner in Fifties Street. I'm starving. Please!'

'Fifties Street?' I ask.

'All night diner,' Pat says.

'I could eat,' I say, as I look at John Candle. Man to man. Warrior to warrior.

'I could eat,' he says with a nod.

'I could eat,' L132 says from our side as he mimics a deep voice. We both look at him.

'No,' we both say, leaving Alice frowning and the rest laughing.

'Pat, your call?' Rachel says.

'Don't put this on me,' Pat says, as Alice turns on the puppy dog eyes. 'But they do serve the best dogs in the city.'

'Yes!' Alice says, throwing her arms around Pat.

'Quick stop then we get you home. Deal?'

'Deal!' Alice says as we set off. 'And honestly. The hot dogs are literally to die for . . .'

We walk on through the park. The park we all woke up in after leaving our characters behind.

But I guess maybe I didn't leave *all* of mine behind, and as we walk on and as Rachel casts another look at me, I wonder why that is.

CHAPTER FOURTEEN

A knock at the door wakes me.

I sit up feeling a little disorientated and start thinking maybe it was a dream, but the knock comes again. Three sharp taps.

My room isn't big and I'm there within a few steps, turning the latch to see a black guy in a hat staring at me.

'Mr Croker?'

I nod and clock how he's standing, with his right hand in his trouser pocket, pulling one side of his suit jacket back to show the badge on his belt and the .38 snub nose holstered next to it.

Then I look up to see John Candle, Svetlana, and L staring down the hall from inside the communal kitchen.

'Mind if I come in?' the guy asks. Medium build with sharp eyes.

'Sure,' I say, and step back. He passes through. Unhurried. Unbothered. But I see how his eyes sweep the room, glancing back to me and down to my empty hands. I even bring them up to show I'm unarmed.

'Relax, kid,' he says. 'Just a routine call, is all.'

'Routine?'

'Routine,' he says, showing his teeth by way of a smile. 'Say, mind if I sit down?' He walks over to the small table and the single chair. 'You can sit down too, Mr Croker. Like I said. Routine is all. My name is Sam Shovel. I'm a detective with FLPD.'

I go over and sit down on the bed, wondering what's going on.

'Is Alice okay?' I ask.

'Why wouldn't she be?' he asks, cocking his head over. His hat still on. He waits for me to reply. 'Alice is fine. Or at least she was an hour ago when I spoke to her, but then she wasn't best pleased to see me either. I take it she had a wild night.'

The fight in the alley.

He nods, seeing the realization in my eyes. 'Wanna tell me about it?'

'Yeah, it got messy.'

'Messy,' Detective Shovel says with a smile as he looks around the room. 'I remember these digs. I was down the hall. Room 4. But that was what? Twenty years ago now. Time passes when you're having fun.' He falls silent and crosses one leg over the other before gently drumming his fingers on the table, letting that silence stretch on. 'Kid. I've had a long morning and I'm busting a gut for a cup of joe, so how about you spill. Will ya do that for me?'

I outline the events, right up until we walked Alice back to Juvie Hall, where we all split and headed home.

'That it?' he asks when I finish.

'Yes, sir.'

'You sure about that, Mr Croker? Cos it ain't the way Mr Wheeler says it.'

I frown. Unsure of the name until I remember Pat saying *he wasn't even called Harry Potter. He was George Wheeler or something.*

'Fat George.'

'Fat George by another name. But, Mr Croker, Jimmy had the same tale to tell, and his story matched that of a few others who turned up at the FLPD station last night, and what with their busted noses and black eyes and swollen lips they sure looked a sorry sight. Oh, and say, I seem to recall Jimmy had a broken thumb.'

'I broke it.'

He lifts his eyebrows at me and pauses for a second.

'And why would you go and break Jimmy's thumb, Mr Croker?'

I open my mouth to speak but his expression says he isn't done talking so I stay quiet.

'Because I'm sure what you meant to say was *Jimmy's thumb got broken in the fight,* rather than *I broke it on purpose*. Cos you see, Mr

Croker, one is a premediated action that has inflicted serious bodily harm by way of a broken bone, whereas the other is nothing more than an accident during a scuffle.'

I don't like lying, but I get what he's trying to do and so I accept the olive branch by staying quiet.

'That's good, kid,' he says, like he's straight out of an old movie. Even the suit matches the gumshoe persona, and I would put money on him wearing suspenders under that jacket. 'My boss, see. She wanted you brought in and charged, but I figure it's just first week nerves is all. You arrived on Monday, didn't you?'

I nod.

'Just Monday,' he says to himself. 'You meet Jimmy before?'

'Briefly. At Enders therapy. He was coming in as I was leaving.'

'What about Mr Wheeler? You meet him before?'

'He woke me up in the park.'

'Fat George woke you up in the park when you first arrived. You meet him any other time?'

'Same day. I ran off from our genre offices and asked him to help me, but I think I freaked him out.'

'Fat George says you attacked him. He says you were wild with anger. He says you were like a crazy man, and he had his wand up and you walked into it.'

'Something like that.'

'Something like that? Well okay, kid. I'm glad it's something like that. But see. Here's where I'm finding it hard.' He pushes his hat back on his head then rubs his jaw, the rasp of his stubble sounding out. 'See. We're all used to new folk getting freaked out on their first days. So that ain't nothing new. And you running up to the guy who woke you also ain't that surprising. But now maybe you can tell me why Fat George and his friends then decided to surround you last night?'

'I don't know. They said I was in their bar.'

He nods at me. 'They're telling me you were being abusive and cussing and whatnot. Said they asked you to leave to protect everyone else. So then you go out and start on young Alice. Giving her booze and trying to take her home to have sex with her. Easy now, Mr Croker. I'm only sayin' what they said. See? And Jimmy. Well. He intervened and tried to protect the young lady and you pushed him over a table.

So of course, Fat George and his friends tried to stop you . . . At which point it appears, Mr Croker, that you used *your skills* to bust them up while they were simply trying to ask you to calm down and leave.'

I stay quiet, but I guess my face says it all.

'Yeah. Horseshit, huh?'

I nod.

'That's what the others told me too. That it was horseshit. Mr Candle, Miss Graphite and Mr 132 out there.'

I stay quiet.

'And your genre reps too,' he adds with a level look. 'Rachel and Pat said the same. As did Alice . . . And a few more witnesses. Gerry was one of them. You know Gerry?'

'The Witcher guy?'

Shovel nods at me. 'And everyone loves the Witcher guy,' he says quietly. 'But let's get back to what I'm finding hard. Cos I can understand why you and Jimmy had the need to scuffle. Jimmy being the predatory sexual deviant that he is. And I can see why the other two or three Bonds would come over to help him. That's how they operate. You touch one Bond and they all start coming for you. Which is dangerous enough as it is. But, kid. See. What I'm wondering is why Fat George would come looking for you in his bar and cause that trouble, and then why would he back Jimmy up when that second issue started? Because as far as I know, there is no love between Jimmy and the wizards. None at all. So you tell me, Mr Croker. Why did the man who woke you up and helped you on your way cause you such an issue later?'

I feel my brain lighting up at the possibility of there being a conspiracy or a plot, but tell myself there is no such thing. It was a bar brawl and nothing more, and Rachel only sang 'Jolene' because it's a good song that everyone knows.

'I think I just pissed them off,' I say, looking back at Shovel. 'I was in their bar. They asked me to go, and I didn't. And someone else said they hated their alley being used for karaoke so maybe it was a way to stop it happening again.'

'Which is a very reasonable explanation,' Shovel says, still drumming his fingers on my table, before smiling and looking away. 'Anyway. Glad we cleared that up. Like I said. Routine, is all.' His tone changes instantly, becoming lighter and friendlier. 'How you finding it anyway?'

'Here?' I ask with a shrug. 'Hard,' I reply honestly.

'I was an Ender,' he tells me, then motions his clothes and hat. 'Could you tell?'

I smile for the first time and nod.

'Enders are different, Mr Croker. Sometimes, now and then, we keep the skills we had when we arrived. Now, you take me for instance. I walked in with a head full of notions about hunting down the Nazi gold the mob had hidden in Chicago. Heck, my whole police department said I was a fool. But see, I knew the mob had that gold. And I was right. I caught them red-handed,' he says with a loud slap of his hand on the table. 'And then this broad. Well now, you can't say broad here. It's not correct. But this broad, she finds me in this bar and we're drinking, but she slips a little something in my bourbon and the next thing I know I'm waking up on a bench and it ain't the 1950s, and it ain't Chicago, and there sure as anything ain't no mobs hiding Nazi gold. But see, Mr Croker. Somehow, or for some reason, I kept my skills. I was still a detective, and I still knew how to read people. And here I am. On a bright Saturday morning, chasing down leads to clear up the brawl from some singing contest. Which seems to me is now all cleared up.'

He pushes to his feet. I get to mine and walk with him to the door, feeling stupid in my boxers. 'But say, kid. Would ya do me a favor?'

'Sure.'

'Would you not break any more thumbs. We got cops here. Let them deal with it.'

'How would you have dealt with it?' I ask. He stops to look at me. 'Alice is seventeen. Someone said the age of consent here is sixteen.'

'It is, Mr Croker. Which means it's for Alice to call us. Not for you to break thumbs.'

That doesn't feel right. It didn't last night, and it doesn't now.

'I know I know,' he says with a sigh, patting me on the shoulder. 'I don't agree with every law either. But what I'm saying is don't break the guy's thumb next time. You get time for that here. Are you hearing me, Mr Croker?'

'I am, sir.'

He stands back and opens the door to stare out into the hallway as though remembering what it was like twenty years ago.

'Has it changed much?'

'The city has,' he says wistfully. 'But people? No, they don't change. Anyway, you got work lined up yet?'

'Rachel and Pat are contacting the postal service.'

'The postal service?' he asks me with a look. 'If it pays the bills. I'd suggest the police to you, but you're not a cop, Mr Croker. Cops show restraint. You take care now, kid, and maybe avoid Fat George and the alley for a while. They don't forgive, and they sure as hell don't forget.'

He walks off with a lingering look to the door of Room 4 and a nod to the others still inside the communal kitchen.

CHAPTER FIFTEEN

After a coffee and a chat with the others, I head out to see what the city is like on a Saturday morning, but within a few steps I get the sensation that I'm being watched.

I keep going until the end of my road, then stop and turn back as though I've forgotten something, and catch glimpse of someone darting out of sight.

After patting my pockets and nodding as though I did have the key with me all along, I turn back around and keep walking to the junction, making as though I'm going to go straight over, then at the last second turning a sharp left to disappear behind the building line.

The instinct here would be to run and find a location to undertake counter surveillance, but instead I jog across the road and stop outside a clothing store as though I'm looking at the goods inside, while really I'm using the window reflection as a mirror to observe behind me. I catch sight as the tail runs into the junction, and watch as he flounders for a second, before finally spotting my back across the street. Then he darts behind the broadside of a horse and carriage to keep obs on me.

I smile to myself at the amateur skills and go back to walking north, figuring I'll explore that area of the city before lunch. Just for something to do, and I've found walking helps clear my head.

It's definitely not to try and find my van.

Because there is no van.

But whatever the cause, I realize my tail seems to be tagging along with me. Darting from cover to cover and peeking through bushes and over hedges.

He's not exactly easy to miss. Not with that shock of white hair and his pure white albino skin tone in that flesh-colored bodysuit or whatever it is. It's like having an oversized ballerina chasing after you.

Then I figure it's a good time to brush up on my countersurveillance skills, so I start deploying measures to disrupt his pursuit.

I take the next right then run fast to the next junction, only slowing enough to let him see me turning right again. Then I sprint to the next block and again take the next right, and before you know we've done a full loop.

Then I walk on for a couple of blocks and repeat the block-running thing again. He follows suit. But this time, on the next block, I go to ground and hide so he runs right by me to reach the junction and try and see where I've gone – at which point I stroll out behind him, whistling a jaunty tune.

'Hi, Griff,' I say with a smile. He turns with a horrified look, but with something else too. Something like panic. 'Why are you following me?' I ask as he runs over to crouch behind a trash can. 'I can see you.'

'You can't see me!' he says, that tone of panic getting worse.

'Griff?' a lady calls, running over with a glance at me as she gets to Griff's side.

'He can't see me!' Griff yells.

'It's okay. It's okay. He's new, Griff,' she says, as the guy seems to start having a panic attack or something. 'Give me the card, Griff. Griff! Show me the card.'

He pulls a battered card from a pocket and hands it to her. She takes it then motions me over to read it, waving it at me while trying to calm the weird guy down.

My name is Griff
please ignore me
Thank you

. . .

'HE'S AUTISTIC,' the woman says, 'it's how he deals with things. Leave him alone.'

'I didn't touch him!' I say, as I back off and get across the next block. Then I use some real counter-surveillance drills, just in case Griff decides to follow me again.

I take an alley, then go over a wall and out onto another street, then run over a few blocks with a couple more lefts and rights until he's gone for good and I can carry on enjoying my walk.

A FEW STREETS on from the city center and I spy a little coffee shop and bakery next to a playground. A perfect place for moms and dads to grab a coffee and a pastry while their kids exhaust their energy on the slides and swings and whatnot.

I slow my pace to absorb it, glimpsing the lives of other people. A woman in a beanie looks over from a table at the café. I smile. She smiles back and looks away.

A guy and a woman walk past with their kid running ahead. The guy's in slacks and trainers and a casual shirt with a sweater over his shoulders, the woman in jeans and tennis shoes and a loose shirt.

Then I spot two guys walking hand in hand ahead of me, one of them carrying a kid on his back. It's all so normal. But nice though.

'Queers,' a low, rasping voice says from another guy walking past, dressed in faded denim jeans. Scuffed brown boots with spurs that make noise with each step. An old flannel shirt with a vest over and a wide-brimmed hat on the back of his head. He spits to the side as he goes by, with a nasty glare at the two men holding hands.

'Homophobia is against the law here,' the man with the kid on his back says, turning to look at the cowboy striding past.

'Get fucked. It ain't moral.'

'Just leave it,' the other guy says, pulling his partner on. 'Simon!'

'Why should we?' Simon asks, looking ready to remonstrate as the cowboy glances back with a sneer. 'Whatever. Go and eat horse shit,' Simon says, turning away.

'Better than eating man shit!' the cowboy calls as he walks on.

'How dare you!' Simon shouts as his partner yanks his hand, and I start to gain the sense that Fiction Land isn't the utopia it first appeared.

I walk on, absorbed in my thoughts, and spot another man and woman walking towards me, the guy pushing a stroller and making faces at a gurgling kid inside. The woman smiles at me. I nod in greeting and realize that babies must also get born here, which means some of these people were never characters at all, and must have lived here all their lives.

What are they called? Fiction Landers?

I file it away and figure to ask Rachel or Pat when I see them later.

THEY WERE cool last night when we went to the diner. They were good company. I was expecting to be bawled out because of the fight, but they seemed okay with it.

'It happens more than it should,' Pat said when we reached the diner which, as Alice said, was straight out of a fifties movie, with a red and white interior, retro booths and a retro counter and stools.

L loved it, and Alice was made up that we were there.

'I've literally only been here on my own before,' she told us. That made me feel sad, and I don't think I was the only one.

'Where do you live, Alice?' Svetlana asked as we slid into a booth.

'Juvie Hall,' Alice replied.

'It's where the kids go,' Pat said, before waving over at the counter. 'You all want dogs and coffee?'

'I hate coffee,' Alice said. 'But they do the best floats here.'

'Floats?' L asked.

'Oh, you gotta try one!' Alice told him. 'Have one with me. Can L and I have floats please, Pat?'

She was so polite and well mannered right there. We all saw it, and I think we all saw her vulnerability too.

'Sure,' Pat said, giving her a smile. 'Hey! Seven dogs and two coffees and two ice cream floats, please.'

'Coming up!' someone shouted from the counter.

'Hang on!' Alice called, reaching out to touch my hand. 'John, try a float.'

'Okay,' I said, with a shrug.

'Can I try one?' Svetlana asked.

'You know what, stuff it,' Rachel said. 'Seven dogs and seven ice cream floats.'

'Hey! Make your mind up, lady! I'm kidding. It's all good. I'll bring them over,' the voice shouted.

'So. Going back to this Juvie Hall place,' Svetlana said. 'You said kids live there? You mean kids turn up here like we did?'

'I never thought about that,' John Candle admitted.

'And they live in that Juvie Place?' Svetlana asked.

'Until they're eighteen,' Pat said.

'What. Like an orphanage?' John Candle asked, leaning forward to look at Alice. 'Where do you sleep? Do you have your own room?'

Alice shook her head. 'I share with two other girls. One was in this dystopian-place story thing and had to go through these trials to stay alive, like hunting pigs or whatever. She's seriously messed up. And the other was from a horror novel. She got trapped in a haunted house with evil spirits.'

'Oh my god,' Svetlana said, covering her mouth with her hand.

'She's actually really nice,' Alice said. 'Like, the most girlie girl ever. I mean. She wears pink,' she added with a grimace.

'Damn. That must be so hard for you,' I said, earning a sudden grin of delight from Alice at my wisecrack, followed swiftly by a middle finger, which Rachel told her to put away with a mild tut.

'Is it nice though?' Svetlana asked her.

'Juvie Hall? No! It's fucking awful,' Alice said.

'Language,' Rachel said.

'Sorry!' Alice said, with a wince. 'No, but it's horrible. I'm a young woman. I've got periods and hormones and shit like that going on. John's face!' she added with a laugh at my expression. 'And L!' she said at seeing him looked grossed out. 'But yeah. Zero privacy and the staff are total fascists.'

'Do you go to school?' John Candle asked her.

'Er, kinda.'

'I take it that means no,' Rachel said. 'You need to go to school.'

'Why? This isn't real. None of this matters.'

'It is real,' Rachel said. 'You're an Ender, right? That's how you know John? From Enders therapy?'

'John's my man!' she said, reaching over to fist-bump me. 'He laughs at my terrible jokes and gets in trouble with Kathy for encouraging me.'

'You shouldn't encourage her,' Pat told me. 'And school does matter.'

'Aw, come on. Don't nag me,' Alice said, with a groan. 'This is the first time I've had any real fun here.'

'Okay, okay,' Rachel said, holding her hands up as the guy from the counter started ferrying trays over filled with hot dogs in buns and big glasses of cola with floating ice cream.

'What about babies and young children?' John Candle asked. 'Are they sent to this Juvie Hall?'

Alice nodded as John looked at Pat and Rachel tucking into their dogs and floaters.

'Babies always get adopted quickly,' Pat said, covering her mouth. 'The older kids though . . .' she trailed off.

'Yeah, nobody wanted to adopt me. I wonder why?' Alice said, with a screwy expression.

'And what happens when you get to eighteen?' John Candle asked.

'I'm free!' Alice said. 'How nice are these, though?'

'Don't speak with your mouth full,' Rachel told her, before turning to John Candle. 'They have to leave and find a place.'

'What if they're not ready for adult life?' John asked. 'Not all eighteen-year-olds are equipped to be alone. Please tell me they have a caregiver, or a case worker helping them. And what about further education?'

'I'll introduce you to social services next week,' Pat told John. 'You can ask them.'

We ate the dogs. Then I remembered what Pat said when we first sat down.

'You said it happens more than it should,' I said to her. 'You mean fights?'

She nodded and swallowed her ice cream. 'And crime. Drugs. Robberies. Same as anywhere else really. They say Fat George has a finger in some of it. You know, cos he's been here for years and the wizards run a closed shop. They don't like strangers, and they try and get to new arrivals first too. That's probably why Fat George was in the park when he saw you, John. He must have been looking for new wizards.'

I thought about that for a moment. 'What about the Bonds?'

'Let's just say it's best to stay out of their way,' Pat said.

'Most of the people are okay,' Rachel added. 'But you know, some find it hard to let go, or move on, or accept new things. I mean. You take someone from the seventeenth century walking into the city and seeing two women kissing on a bench. He'd probably think they need to be hung.'

'And some white folk sure get freaked out seeing so many people of color walking free,' Pat added.

'I don't get that sort of stuff,' Alice said, as she harpooned her last bit of ice cream. 'Why can't people just get along?'

'Said the goth in the torn tights with a bad attitude,' Rachel said with a raised eyebrow, but she smiled, and Alice took it in good humor.

'Whatever. I mean, people should be more accepting,' Alice added as she finally got the chunk of ice cream on her spoon and started lifting it out. But it dropped at the last second to a collective groan. 'Story of my life,' Alice said, with a sigh.

'What is your story?' Pat asked her.

Alice shrugged and looked at L. 'How's your first float?'

'Don't even talk to me. I'm having my first orgasm,' L said, and it should have been wrong, and it was, but it was also funny.

'Anyway. Don't avoid the question,' Pat said.

'Don't ask then,' Alice fired back, a bit too harsh and a bit too fast, but Pat only softened her gaze as Rachel frowned gently. 'Sorry,' Alice said quietly, avoiding their eyes.

'How long have you been here, Alice?' Rachel asked.

'Few months.'

'Months? And you're still in therapy? What about your allowance?'

Alice shrugged again. Clearly uncomfortable, but with no place to go, being wedged between L and Svetlana.

'Damn!' L said, making us all startle as he pushed his empty glass away. 'Man. I could eat that again. You want another one?' he asked Alice.

'Yeah, alright. I'm game.'

'How about you talk, and I get you another one?' Rachel asked.

'How about you don't patronize me,' Alice snapped.

'Hey! She's being nice,' Svetlana said.

'No. It's okay. That was patronizing. I apologize,' Rachel said, then shouted over for two more floats and a round of coffees for the rest of us.

I looked over at Alice, who must have sensed my gaze and stared back. I didn't say anything, but maybe she got the hint because she pulled that cynical face she does sometimes and rolled her eyes. 'I'm on half allowance,' she said to Rachel and Pat. 'And that gets cut Monday if I don't go blah blah sad backstory or whatever. I mean. I could just say anything though. How would anyone even know? It's not like they can check.'

Rachel shared a look with Pat, but they didn't say anything else.

Then a bit later Alice piped up with a shy grin. 'I really want to ask what all your stories were now, but I don't want to say what mine was.'

'That's honest,' Pat said, with a snort of laughter.

'I'm a John that can't fight. John Candle,' John said, holding his hand out to her. 'I think I had to find Salvatori, but honestly? I'm already forgetting why.'

'He took your cat,' I said.

'My cat!' John said, then pulled a face as Alice grinned. She shook his hand then looked at Svetlana.

'Ask me when you're eighteen,' she said, with a wink to Alice.

'Oh! Hard-Boiled *and* Erotica,' Alice said, with a delighted grin. 'That's so cool.'

'Actually, I thought it was,' Svetlana said. 'But now I don't know. I'm not so sure.'

'L132,' L said, when Alice turned to her other side to look at him. 'Thunder Soldier. Saved a yellow alien thing. Shut up. This is nice. Shut up.'

Alice laughed again then looked over at Pat. 'Ooh, let me guess. Can I guess?'

'Sure,' Pat said.

'You were like a cop or something. But not a cop cop. Not like a shooting black people cop.'

'Alice!' Rachel said.

'Er, they do!' Alice said. 'But whatever. You know what I mean. Like . . .'

'Inquisitor,' L said, without looking up from his second float. 'We had them on the Killer Sun. They were the ones that kept checks on us, but they were really friendly, so you'd open up and they'd totally rat you out and get you whammed by the lasers.'

Pat laughed. 'I was a crime scene investigator.'

'Knew it!' Alice said, reaching over to fist-bump her.

'Knew it,' L said at the same time, still without looking up.

'Ooh, so what was the crime you were investigating?' Svetlana asked.

'Some serial killer nonsense. Honestly, I can hardly remember,' Pat said. 'I think my writer spent time on my character but not on the plot. I mean, I'm calm, studious, methodical, and thorough, but I am next to useless at solving crimes! Don't laugh at me. I am! I joined the FLPD and lasted less than a month. Then I jumped over to this as a stopgap and been doing it ever since.'

'Cool,' Alice said, before looking at Rachel. I noticed how Pat shifted in her seat a little and Rachel tensed a little.

'Tell you what,' Rachel said. 'We'll make a deal. You come and find me and tell me yours and I'll tell you mine . . . *and,*' she added as she leaned over to smile at Alice, 'I can guarantee mine is way weirder than yours.'

'Oh, I really wanna know now,' Alice said.

'Me too!' Svetlana said, as I thought the same.

'Come and find me then,' Rachel said to Alice, as Pat shot her an uncertain look. 'In fact, I'll be in the office from midday Saturday if you want to hang out.'

I FOLLOW the cowboy as he heads north and west away from the city center. Not for any reason than it's the direction I was already heading, plus it gives me something to do, and I'm curious to where he's going.

I watch how he lifts his hat at passing women and adds a swagger when he passes any man of fighting age. A walking figure of toxic masculinity that brings a fresh perspective to my mind, as I'd always thought of main characters as the heroes of their stories. But maybe that's not the case. In a lot of instances the main character might not be heroic, or even decent at all.

That then makes me wonder if I was a hero. In my head I was. But then people are programmed to think like that.

Was I the bad guy?

Another aspect comes to mind. I had also committed crimes. I'd beaten people up for Mascaponi. Intimidated witnesses and made people disappear.

I'd killed people.

But then I was an undercover FBI agent. Wasn't I?

Except I don't remember ever joining the FBI. I do remember being in the military and serving in Afghan as part of a Special Forces unit. But I don't remember which part of the Special Forces I was in.

I mean. I've got flashbacks of being in a hot dry desert, dug into hidey-holes and feeling the weird dual sensation of crushing boredom coupled with intense threat, while waiting for nightfall so we could cross a town and find the ISIS death squad to rescue Western journalists who were going to be beheaded.

I remember that. I remember the fire fights and the feeling of terror mixed with exhilaration.

But I don't remember ever joining the FBI, or becoming an agent, or going undercover.

What does that mean?

I don't know. I just know I gotta find my van.

I wince at myself and realize it's a fallback point. That whenever I'm faced with something I don't know, I simply revert to type and recall the mission as a way of resetting my head.

How do I stop that?

'Ladies! Beautiful mornin'! the cowboy says from a short way ahead of me, turning to lift his hat and leer at the backsides of two women jogging past. 'Woohee, now you didn't see that in Kansas.'

He gives me a hard look for a second then walks on with that swagger of his and a few minutes later I notice how he turns to sneer at me again as another man comes out of a store to his side.

'Morning,' the man says, holding position to let the cowboy go by instead of stepping out into his path.

'Mighty good of you,' the cowboy starts to say as he turns from glaring at me to the black man that just gave way to him. 'Fuck you, nigga!'

'What the hell!' the guy says, clearly shocked. 'You can't say that!'

'Say anything I damn want,' the cowboy says loudly, turning on the other man. 'Not a goddamn thing you can do, boy!'

'Whoa. I'm not your enemy. We can talk calmly,' the man says holding his hands up to placate the situation.

'I ain't discoursing shit with no negro!'

'Well. We kind of already are,' the man says with a gentle smile. 'And nothing bad has happened, has it?'

'You pokin' fun at me? Fuck you!' the cowboy says, stepping in with his right fist clenching and pulling back. I move fast to grab his elbow and yank him back and around, while sidestepping to avoid his other fist lashing out from instinct. A palm to his solar plexus instantly winds him, then a throat jab makes him stagger back to cough and retch.

'Hey!' the black guy says, stepping in to push me back. 'What was that for?' he asks as the cowboy drops to a knee, still coughing and gagging while casting me filthy looks through teary eyes.

'I was just gunna scare him,' he croaks.

'See. He was just trying to scare me. That was too much. What was that?' the black man asks.

I look from the cowboy back to the black man. 'His signals were solid. He was about to strike you.'

'Oh. So you saved me. Is that right? *Oh lordy lord, thankee massa. I gone needed a white savior to help me today, massa.*'

'What!? No! I just saw . . .'

'Whatever, Caveman,' he says, tutting at me as he rushes over to help the cowboy up. 'You okay?'

'Get yer damn hands off me.'

'He's a racist!' I say, pointing at him.

'He's a cowboy from the nineteenth century! And beating people up doesn't stop the cycle of violence. You need *tolerance* to live in this city, Mr Lumberjack.'

'Ha! Lumberjack,' the cowboy snorts, before coughing again and rubbing his throat. 'It's funny cos he's dressed like one.'

'Fuck me. Whatever,' I say, walking on, confused as hell.

'And don't use that Chinese fightin' shit on American soil,' the cowboy mutters, as I do an Alice and flick him the bird, then feel instantly stupid.

'Okay. And just on that point, we're not on American soil,' the black man says.

'Don't lecture me!'

I leave them to it and turn a corner, feeling humiliated and jarred for trying to help someone and getting chastised, but as I rush on I do notice how the city gives way to what feels like a passage through time, the houses changing from modern to older.

But not British older, like twee and cottagey and built close – more like New York older, with people in clothing that looks like it comes from the late 1800s or early 1900s.

Then I spot the large metal arch over the road.

LITTLE VICTORIA

INSIDE THE ARCH, another sign points eastwards to LONDON. I stay ahead, marvelling at the clothing and fashions, and how people here have clung to an old way of living simply because they didn't want to change, and I can't help but wonder what happens to children born in these areas. Surely they must mingle with kids from other eras and zones?

Again, I feel that thing inside as I shrug the questions off and tell myself to focus on finding my van.

Except there is no van.

Eventually, I leave that zone and step out into the countryside. Deep and lush and very green. I pass a few farmsteads, with people tending crops and animals pulling ploughs or whatever they are, and more people doing the work that machines would do in my world.

It's nice to be out of the city though, and I'm pleased to have found this area. I even scale a long sloping hill and stop at the top to look back over the fields and meadows and beyond, to Little Victoria and the city spread out in a haze of streets.

I spot a road sign giving direction to a place called Western World and figure that's where the cowboy was heading. I feel an urge to go there myself, but I can't see it, which means it must be a distance away.

I turn back, thinking I'll bump into the cowboy heading this way, but luckily I don't.

CHAPTER SIXTEEN

Saturday.

I REACH HARD-BOILED & Erotica an hour or so after midday and walk in to see John Candle, Svetlana and L laughing at Alice and Rachel having a face-off with their arms folded.

'Just tell me!' Alice says.

'You tell me first,' Rachel replies, before looking over at me. 'Found your van yet?'

'Nope,' I say, heading over to the water cooler to get a drink.

'Which way did you go today?'

'North then west.'

'Did you go through Little Victoria?'

I nod.

'Which bit? The London bit?'

I shake my head.

'Great chat, John,' she says, flapping her hands out. 'Try verbalizing.'

'Sorry. No. I went straight through then out to some farms and a big hill then saw a sign for some Western place and turned back.'

'Western World,' Rachel says. 'Apparently it used to be called West World, but then some people started arriving saying they were from *Westworld*, which had become a story thing with tons of fan fiction and, yeah, they changed it.'

'Great story,' I say, and she throws an empty water cup at me.

'Victorian London is cool though,' Rachel adds.

'Wouldn't know. I'm an orphan who isn't allowed to go anywhere,' Alice says with big doe eyes.

'You're a stubborn little madam who wants everything her own way,' Rachel tells her.

'Don't all women?' Svetlana asks.

'Sexist,' L says. 'You know, the Dark Lord was actually pretty good at equal rights. No, honestly. Boys and girls. All the same. Didn't matter.'

'I was waiting for the *but* then,' Rachel says.

'Me too,' Alice says. 'And for you to tell me your story.'

'Love to!' Rachel says with a bright smile. 'Straight after yours. Anyway. We're heading into the Village for a stroll. Who knows? We might find your van there, John.'

She laughs when I throw the empty cup back, as the others all get up and start heading for the door, leaving Alice sitting at the table. 'What about you?' Rachel asks her.

'What about me?'

'Have you eaten today?'

'I had a bowl of air at the evil orphanage.'

'Idiot. Come on. I'll buy some gruel or something.'

'Yay. I love gruel!'

'WHERE'S PAT?' I ask as we cross the road in the warm afternoon sunshine.

'Home with her husband, probably,' Rachel says. 'I said I'd do today.'

'Are you married?' Alice asks her.

'Married! Me? Nooo!' Rachel says with a laugh. 'God, I can't even remember the last time I had a date.'

'What about that Jimmy guy?' Alice asks as Rachel blinks at her. 'Didn't he say you'd dated or something.'

'You dated James Bond?' Svetlana asks.

'No! God no. Seriously, no. We didn't *date.* Not like. Urgh. Just no. Change the subject, and he's not James Bond. None of them are. They're just crappy fanfiction half-finished rip-offs who get turned on by everyone knowing who they were meant to be.'

We walk on and I shoot a look at the bitterness in her tone, figuring there's more to that story, but whatever it is, she clearly doesn't want to share.

'Were you married in your book?' Alice asks, with another look at Rachel.

'Nope.'

'No kids or anything then.'

'No!'

'Sorry! I get a bit direct sometimes,' Alice says with a worried expression.

'It's fine. You're fine. Don't worry.'

'No. I'm not worried. Not like, you know, *worried*. I'm like totally whatever. But some people get offended easily and . . . You know.'

'I know,' Rachel says.

'I don't know,' L says. 'Does anyone else know?'

'I know,' Svetlana says.

'I have no clue,' I admit.

'I think I know,' John Candle says with a thoughtful look. 'I think Alice is lonely and has now found Rachel, and us, and she's worried she'll annoy us by being overly direct and we'll tell her to go away.'

'Wow. That's so great you voiced it like that,' Alice says. 'Thanks, John! I don't feel humiliated at all.'

'Come back!' Rachel says, grabbing Alice's arm as she starts to storm off. 'John's new here too and we're all just learning about each other. It's fine. Relax.'

'Sorry. I didn't mean to embarrass you,' John Candle says, as Alice falls back in step with us, but with her head down and her cheeks burning.

'Sooo?' L asks. 'Was he right or what? Cos I have literally no idea what's going on.'

'Idiot,' Alice says, giving him a sheepish smile.

'Honestly. Social interactions were not encouraged on the Killer Sun,' L says. 'The only time we could really chat was over meals or when we were in the latrines.'

'Benjamin wanted to watch me on the toilet once.'

'Svetlana!' Rachel says. 'And er, young ears, thank you.'

'I'm seventeen!' Alice says. 'And who was Benjamin?'

'Oh god. Seriously. Don't ask,' L says. *'So like, Ben and I were lovers, but in secret and it was sooo sordid and sooo sexy and sooo sticky.'*

'Stop mimicking me!' Svetlana says, swiping at L's arm. 'But yes. Benjamin was my lover.'

'Er. Seriously not appropriate,' Rachel says.

'She's seventeen. She's fine,' Svetlana says. 'And it's natural. We've all had sex.'

'I haven't,' L says.

'We've nearly all had sex,' Svetlana adds. 'Apart from you. I hope you haven't had sex, young lady.'

'Urgh. I hate being called young lady. No, but go back, did he want to watch you having a poo?'

'Alice!' Rachel snaps as I burst out laughing. 'That's not funny.'

'No, honey. Just a number one,' Svetlana says.

'Eww,' Alice says, pulling a yucky face.

'We were going through an intense phase and people sometimes want to explore different things,' Svetlana says with a shrug. 'Which is fine if it's in a safe and loving relationship,' she adds, after clocking the look on Rachel's face.

'I'm seriously never letting anyone see me pee,' Alice says.

'Okay! Enough,' Rachel says. 'Changing the subject.'

'Or poo.'

'Alice!'

'Okay. Sorry. I was just saying. Can I ask another question?'

'Is it about sex?'

'No. Yes. Whatever. Svetlana, did you ever have a threesome?'

'Alice!' Rachel snaps again. 'Don't answer that.'

'Why not? She's not a child. She can read about things online,' Svetlana says. 'And yes. I did, Alice.'

'That's so gross,' Alice says with another yucky face. 'I mean. How do you all know what to do? Like, does one of you take charge and give directions or something?'

'Oh my god. Can we change the subject, please!' Rachel says. 'John. How was your walk?'

'And what if it's two guys and one woman and one of the guys touches the other guy's junk and the guy is like *dude! Don't touch my junk!* And the first guy is like *but it's waggling around all over the place.*'

'I mean it. That's enough,' Rachel says, as the rest of us laugh at Alice's impressions. Albeit with varying degrees of discomfort.

'That actually happens,' Svetlana whispers to Alice. 'But I think we should stop before Rachel sends me home.'

'It's fine. I'll look at some porn and find out,' Alice says.

'Don't look at porn,' Rachel snaps. 'It's absurdly unrealistic.'

'How else am I supposed to know things?' Alice asks.

'I don't know! Maybe go to school and get sex education?'

'Seriously? *Dear class. When a mummy and a daddy love each other they make a baby, and if you touch yourself you'll go blind.*'

'Right. Stop,' Rachel says, coming to a standstill. 'Boundaries. Okay? Alice, I mean it. I like you. You're lovely. But you're in the company of adult men that you don't know. So enough, okay?'

'It's John!' she says, waving a hand at me. 'And L . . . And the other John!'

'She's right. You don't know us,' John Candle says. 'And not everyone is comfortable talking about sex openly. Maybe you and Svetlana can schedule some time to talk together?'

'Do that,' Rachel says, nodding from John Candle to Alice. 'And are you sure you're not a social worker or something, John? You've got a natural aptitude for this stuff.'

'I don't know what I am,' John Candle admits as we walk on around a corner and find ourselves in the Village.

I was expecting somewhere with thatched cottages and streams and watermills or whatever. Like olde worlde England, or somewhere in Europe maybe. But this is more like an upstate New York village. Urban and chic with lots of places to sit and eat, bushes and trees growing everywhere, and boutique stores and organic grocers lining the road.

'Oh, wow. I wasn't expecting this,' Svetlana says.

'Lovely, isn't it,' Rachel says, strolling on as we take in the surroundings, admiring the way the trees and bushes grow to complement the flow of the walking areas and how every dozen meters there's another stall selling food, with tables and chairs laid out.

It's busy too, with people doing the same as us and strolling through, or already eating and drinking and listening to music being played over speakers.

We aim for the middle, Rachel motioning at a seating area alongside people playing chess at concrete tables.

'Hi guys!' a woman says, walking over to hand menus out. 'My name is Bella. Short for Bellatrix. I was a dystopian teen. Any of you from my genre? No? Gee. That's *so* interesting, and I love that suit,' she says to L. 'Were you like a puppet or something?'

'What? No!'

'Great. Just great. And hey, love the whole emo thing. Totally rad.'

'It's goth,' Alice says.

'Great. So anyway. There's your menus and I'll be right back for your orders.'

'Sorry, miss, can we just –' Rachel starts to say as Bella walks off, leaving us staring after her.

'I'm guessing she didn't last very long in her dystopian world then,' Alice says as we chuckle. 'I mean. She had to be the airhead sidekick, right? You know. The one with the big boobs who gets eaten or killed first so the jock can get angry and try to fight the baddies and end up getting killed next?'

'She did have big boobs,' Rachel remarks quietly while looking over the menu.

'She's got amazing boobs,' L says wistfully as we all look at him. 'Don't judge me. I'm a virgin.'

'No sex talk at the table,' Rachel says quickly as Alice starts to speak.

'I thought we were all main characters,' John Candle says.

'We were,' Rachel replies.

'So she couldn't have been the airhead sidekick then,' he adds with a look to Alice.

'Ah, no, so I've got a theory about this,' Alice says, as we all look at her. 'So, most of our stories are unfinished, right? And a lot of people here really aren't like main character types. Do you know what I mean?'

'No,' John Candle says.

'Yeah, I think I know what you're getting at,' Rachel says.

'I mean. So like, Johnsy is a main character, right?' Alice says, as I realize she means me.

'Johnsy?' I ask her.

'Well you can't be John C cos you're both John C and in my head you're like Silent John so that then ends up being John Silent which then becomes Johnsy,' Alice explains as Svetlana nods.

'I'm so glad I'm just called L,' L says.

'Or you could just call me Croker,' I say.

'Yeah. Why didn't I think of that?' Alice says with that comical screwy look. 'So, anyway, Croker is a main character, right? But a lot of people here aren't like him. Oooh, or like that woman there,' she says, and we all turn to see a very attractive woman walking by. 'She's *clearly* a main character.'

'That's Mindy Pippins,' I say. She looks over with a big smile as she hears her name.

'John! How lovely,' she says, veering over to stop with her hand on my shoulder. 'First time in the Village?'

'Er, yeah. First time. Nice to see you.'

'Still a lumberjack then?' she asks, with a wink and a nod at my plaid shirt. 'Black would suit you better. Give me a shout sometime. I'd be happy to take you shopping. Right. Well. Enjoy your lunch, and nice to meet you all. Toodles!'

I say bye and go back to the menu, and only after a few seconds do I become acutely aware of the silence and the others all staring at me. 'What?'

'See. Now she was a main character,' Alice says.

'Definitely,' Rachel says.

'Totally,' Svetlana says.

'I'm in love,' L says.

'And there's nothing wrong with your shirt,' Rachel says.

'I look like a lumberjack.'

'It's lovely,' Rachel says. 'How do you know her anyway? You've only been here a few days.'

'She's in the Zumba class after our therapy.'

'What's Zumba?' L asks.

'Like a dance fitness thing,' Svetlana says.

'I love dance fitness things!' he says.

'Yeah? Did the Dark Lord do a lot of it on the Killer Sun?' I ask, as the others shoot me a surprised look.

'Careful, you're wisecracking again,' Rachel says.

'Sorry. It just happens,' I say with a shrug. 'Like an involuntary reflex or when Alice says something inappropriate.'

'Boom,' Rachel says with a smile. 'Anyway. I want to hear your theory,' she says to Alice.

'Right. Main characters. So my theory is a lot of us were written as fanfiction, right? You know. So somebody reads an awesome book, and then they're like *hey, I can write a book like this*, but then, instead of writing about the main character, they think *I know, I'll write about one of the other characters*. But then they realize it's actually dull as shit and they give up. Which is why we end up with so many people like Booby Bella.'

'Booby Bella,' L snorts.

'Hi guys! Are you ready to order?' Bella asks, as I hear a snort of laughter from behind and turn to see two guys playing chess. One of them bearded and the other with a huge moustache growing across his cheeks.

'Garden salad and a coffee for me please,' Rachel says.

'Great!'

'Make that two, please,' Svetlana says.

'Great!'

'Three,' John Candle says.

'Great!'

'Gruel for me, please,' Alice says.

'Great!' Bella says, and I hear another chuckle from behind.

'Wow. Have you actually got gruel?' Alice asks.

'Sorry, what?' Bella asks.

'Sorry, what?' Alice asks as Bella flutters her eyelashes in confusion.

'Alice. Pack it in,' Rachel says.

'Sorry, what?' Alice says, as I laugh and hear the guys behind me still chuckling.

'Do you want a garden salad?' Rachel asks her.

'Do I look like I eat salad. My name isn't Bella.'

'Hey! That's my name. Twinsies,' Bella says, waggling her fingers at Alice.

'Sorry, what?' Alice asks.

'Sorry, what?' Bella asks.

'Alice!' Rachel says, trying to sound cross while smiling. 'Last chance or you'll get a salad.'

'Okay, fine. I was thinking me and L could share a pizza? Is that too much though?' Alice asks.

'I love pizza!' L says. 'We did pizza night every Thursday. What? I told you. We had good perks.'

'Okay. And a pizza to share,' Rachel says. 'Croker? Quickly, before Alice starts again.'

'Sorry, what?' Alice asks.

'Sorry, what?' Bella asks, blinking in confusion.

'Try the club sandwich,' one of the guys playing chess behind me says in an accented voice.

'I guess I'll try the club sandwich,' I say.

'Great!' Bella says.

'Great!' Alice says. 'Twinsies!' she adds, waggling her fingers.

'Twinsies!' Bella says automatically, before frowning lightly. 'Wait. What?'

'What?' Alice asks.

'What are we twinsies for again?'

'What?' Alice asks.

'Sorry, what?' Bella asks.

'Enough! It's fine. Our order is complete,' Rachel says, plucking the menu from Alice to pass back to a now very confused-looking Bella.

'Sorry. I was just being silly,' Alice says to her. 'But hey, quick question. So, in your story, did you have a boyfriend that got killed?'

'You mean Brad?' Bella asks with a sudden stricken look. 'Oh my god, he was just like so hot.'

'So hot,' Alice says.

'I know, right,' Bella says earnestly. 'And he was like the star quarterback.'

'Who for?' Alice asks.

'What?' Bella asks.

'Which team?'

'What team?' Bella asks.

'No. Brad. Which team did he play for?'

'Yeah. Totally. He was the star quarterback and like, so hot.'

'So hot,' Alice says.

'Oh my god. Enough. Bella, you can go.'

'Excuse me?' Bella says with a frosty look at Rachel, before walking off.

'What the . . . ?' Rachel asks as even Alice bursts out laughing.

'Very spirited young lady,' one of the guys behind me tells the other one.

'I was right though,' Alice says. 'She had a Brad, and he was like *so hot.*'

'So hot,' L says.

'Sooo hot,' Svetlana says, as I twist around to look at the two men playing chess again.

'You must be Mr Croker,' the one with the moustache says, as I give him a questioning look. 'The breaker of the thumbs.'

'Rumors spread fast in the city,' the bearded one says. 'Especially if you sit in the Village playing chess all day.'

'And we do love a good gossip,' the one with the moustache says. 'But well done, though. Jimmy isn't a nice man. Even Sigmund would agree with that,' he says while motioning to his bearded friend.

'I do try to see the good in people, or at least establish the reasons why they might not be good,' Sigmund says. 'But alas, yes. Not a pleasant man. Neither is Fat George by all accounts.'

'It's not something I'm proud of,' I say.

'Why not?' the one with the moustache asks me. 'Be proud of your abilities. To be otherwise is simply how you've been programmed to think.'

'At least introduce yourself before you start lecturing, Friedrich,' the bearded one says. 'Sigmund Freud,' he adds, nodding his head.

'Friedrich Nietzsche,' the other one says.

'John Croker.' I get to my feet to shake their hands.

'Good firm grip!' Freud says. 'Which means absolutely nothing,' he adds with a wink at me.

'Pleasure,' Nietzsche says, with his moustache bristling.

'Tell me. Do you play?' Freud asks.

'Chess? I don't know. I don't think so,' I say and look at the board, and I know some basic rules, but other than that the knowledge isn't there. 'No. I don't know it.'

'Shame. I'm getting bored playing with him,' Freud says with a nod at his friend.

'Bored?' Nietzsche asks. 'Isn't boredom another sign of repressed sexuality?'

'Not everything relates back to repressed sexuality.'

'You seem to think it does,' Nietzsche mutters. 'How about your spirited young friend?' he asks me. 'Does she play chess?'

'Alice?' I ask, getting her attention.

'What?' she asks, twisting around with a startled look. 'Moustache!' she says at the sight of his enormous handlebar whiskers.

'Alice!' Rachel whispers at her.

'Sorry! I didn't mean to be rude,' Alice says with a wince.

'Not rude at all,' Nietzsche says. '*See it – say it* is a very honest approach to life.'

'Unless it's done with intent to cause offence, of course,' Freud says.

'But how can honesty offend?' Nietzsche asks. 'Honesty is purity.'

'Because we live in a cooperative society, Friedrich. Within which, and by degrees of evolved and often changing traditions, we attach rules and norms. Some of which dictate that an overuse of honesty can be highly offensive. Would you openly call an obese person fat?'

'If they are fat, then yes,' Nietzsche replies. 'To not mention such a thing would be hiding the obvious and plain truth.'

'What if the person had no choice in the matter?'

'How would he have no choice, Sigmund? He needs to stop bloody eating,' Friedrich says. 'Unless he is happy to eat and accept the consequences. In which case, be fat! Be fat and be happy with it.'

'Eating disorders are indicators of unbalanced mental health, Friedrich.'

'You think everything is an indicator of unbalanced mental health, Sigmund. My point is that if someone is fat you should not be banned from saying so. Whatever next? Shall we be reduced to denying that the sky is blue or the night is dark, simply for fear of offending a blind person? Life is fleeting, Sigmund. Grasp it! Live it! Embrace what you can.'

'I'm with him,' Alice says, pointing at the man with the moustache.

'Are you?' Freud asks.

'Yeah! Definitely. Why shouldn't you state the obvious?'

'Because people are complex beings and sometimes a gentle approach yields far greater results,' Freud says.

'That's just pussyfooting around and treading on eggshells,' Alice says.

'Why don't you open up in therapy then?' Rachel asks her.

'I knew you were going to ask me that,' Alice says.

'But you just said honesty is the best policy,' Rachel says.

'Yeah. It is. But honesty and openness aren't the same thing.'

'Hear, hear!' Nietzsche says.

'That's what pisses me off,' Alice says. 'Like people keep asking me and then they get offended when I don't tell them, so they say I'm being dishonest.'

'I never said you were dishonest,' Rachel says.

'Not you, but others have said it. The evil matrons in the orphanage say it all the time. They call me a lying little bitch.'

'That needs to be reported,' John Candle says quickly.

'I am definitely introducing you to the recruitment officer at social services,' Rachel tells him. 'But going back to your point, Alice. A refusal to be open can be perceived as a form of dishonesty.'

'No. No!' Alice says, speaking louder as Rachel goes to say something else. 'They don't get what *they* want so they say the other person is being dishonest. Why should I have to open up? It was my experience. Not someone else's, and if I choose not to tell anyone then I'm not being dishonest. That's the stupid thinking of stupid people telling me I have to be grateful and humble and polite and not say what I think.'

'It's more than stupid thinking,' Nietzsche remarks as Freud studies the board for his next move. 'It's called the slave morality.'

'I'm not a slave!' Alice snaps.

'I never said you were. But in terms of our morality and how we think and act, we are all either slaves or masters,' Nietzsche says, as Freud mutters *here we go again*. 'It's how we are told to think from the moment we're brought into this world. We're either masters, and taught the values of courage and pride and how to be powerful and rule over others. Or we are slaves, and we are taught to be meek, and that kindness and empathy are the true virtues. And while the masters feast and copulate and enjoy what they've taken, the slaves are told to be humble and adhere to God's law, with a thousand empty promises that everything they could ever want will be delivered in the afterlife.'

I frown at what he says, initially thinking it's nonsense but then realizing it makes sense.

'And the most dangerous thing is that, because of repressed jealousy and spite, the slaves want everyone else to be slaves. They insist that the only goodness is what is best for the whole community, but to achieve that means bringing everyone down, because only when we are *all* miserable and starving and denying every pleasure can we be truly happy.

'But a master! Well, now. The masters take what they want from religion and use it to their own ends. They manipulate it. They corrupt it and they see no sin in doing that. They take what they want with courage and fortitude. Masters are bold and progressive. They seek more. They want more. But slaves, well. They are the inverse, and because they lack the strength, or the resources, or the sheer wherewithal to oppose the masters, they seek to undermine them by being subversive. They become cynical and pessimistic. They become petty and cruel. The slaves make the masters feel guilty for being outspoken and bold.

'They say *you can't say we are fat anymore. You can't say anything without causing offence*, and when enough slaves get together, they can weaken the masters by corrupting the strong into thinking the causes of slavery are evil, whereas denial and humility are good and right. And then we can no longer say to someone they are fat, but rather we have to watch silently as they gorge, while we convince ourselves that we and they are all victims. Which, to coin a modern phrase, is utter bullshit. One should seek not to be a victim, but simply to grasp their own existence and not be cowed into mediocrity. Seek pleasure. Don't hide from it, and don't leave the responsibility for your own happiness to a God that makes fake promises. Are you taking your turn this century, Freud?'

'I was waiting for your monologue to finish,' Freud mutters, moving a piece on the board that makes Nietzsche first scoff then blink and scowl, as Freud sits back with a smug look.

'People are certainly very complex,' Freud says with a smile at Alice. 'And Nietzsche's observations certainly have merit. I can't help but believe he is correct, but while, yes, it may be a condition of the *slave morality* to be kind and polite, there is also such a thing as being spiteful and mean simply for the sake of it. Which, by any measure, is not a pleasant trait.'

'I'm not spiteful,' Alice says quickly.

'But you are defensive,' he adds calmly, giving her a look. 'Take young Bella there. An attractive woman with a very pleasant countenance, yet you chose to mock her.'

'Cos she was thick as shit and not listening,' Alice says.

'Would you listen after working in a café every day for years on end, hearing the lives of other people and their incessant chatter, while still trying to accept that your life is not what you thought it was?'

Alice goes to retort but stops and pulls her head back. 'I feel really shitty now.'

'And now you are personalizing your own emotional reaction about how Bella might have felt, while still demanding that everyone around you understands exactly how you feel at all times.'

'Sigmund. Leave the girl alone,' Nietzsche says.

'But I thought honesty was the best trait we could have?' Freud asks with an innocent air. 'Was that not the case? Or have I caused offence by stating *my* observations?'

'I'm not offended,' Alice says quickly.

'But you are wounded,' Freud says. 'Such reactions show in our faces . . . Unless, of course, we are trained not to show anything,' he says, with a glance to me.

'Here we are, guys!' Bella says, sliding a tray onto the table. 'Salad for you. And you. And you. And there's your club sandwich, Mr

Lumberjack,' she says, with a chuckle at her own humor, and this time I notice Alice makes an effort to respond and smile.

'Thank you, that's really nice,' Alice says.

'Oh, you're welcome!' Bella says, offering her a warm smile. 'And I love your eyeliner. That black really suits you. I tried it one time, but it just didn't sit right on me, but you've got the right complexion for dark colors. They really pop on you, and great skin too. Anyways. Holler if you want me. Enjoy!'

She heads off, and all eyes turn to Alice, who sits back with a sigh. 'Fine. I was out of order. She's lovely and I apologize.'

'It's not a question of being lovely,' Nietzsche says. 'Bella is locked into her belief in the slave morality without ever knowing it exists, whereas you, on the other hand, are intuitively challenging it, which is why you are in conflict with everyone around you.'

'It's not everyone,' Alice scoffs. 'I haven't fallen out with Croker yet . . . Or like . . . loads of people!'

'Classic case of transference,' Freud adds, as Nietzsche studies the board. 'I'd suggest there's also a great deal of projection and resistance going on from childhood trauma, but then you are also still a child.'

'I'm seventeen!'

'Indeed, you are, and you are absolutely on the cusp of womanhood, but your body and mind, and more importantly *your emotions*, are still developing. And while all of those things are happening, and you are dealing with whatever trauma it is that you refuse to discuss, you suddenly find yourself here, in the most strange of places, without family or friends or any sense of familiarity at all. Which is what happens to everyone here, and some find comfort by locking into whatever system is in place and getting on with living. They become waitresses in outdoor eateries serving smart-mouthed young women. Oh, good move, Nietzsche. Good play.'

I pull my head back at Freud's sharp comment, and from the look on Alice's face I can see he scored a hit.

'No need to bristle, Mr Croker. I was not attacking Alice,' Freud adds without any sign that he even looked at me. 'Sorry, Nietzsche, but you've left yourself wide open,' he says, moving one of his pieces.

'So, are you saying that for Alice to remove the conflict she should open up?' Rachel asks.

'Not at all,' Freud says, sitting back with a wry smile at Nietzsche muttering under his breath while studying the pieces. 'It may be that opening up does nothing at all for someone as obviously intelligent as Alice. She'll find a way to think around it, or find other ways to project and transfer and ultimately resist any offers of help. And going back to your comment that Mr Croker has yet to annoy you, Alice. Mr Croker has only just arrived.'

'What difference does that make?' Rachel asks.

'He doesn't know who he is yet,' Nietzsche says. 'Is that right, Sigmund?'

'Quite right, old friend. Mr Croker and, I would suggest to a degree, your other companions, are new arrivals and have yet to assert any dominant character traits, while at the same time displaying good morals and friendly mannerisms. Mr Croker's underlying sense of ethics protected you last night, Alice, but what happens when he gathers his thoughts and questions you over your past?'

'Croker wouldn't do that,' Alice replies quickly.

'You don't yet know who Mr Croker will be. None of you do, or each other. And that, I'm afraid, Alice, is a classic case of projecting your own defense mechanism onto another person by verbally placing rules on them that they must not breach. Mr Croker must not ask you about your past, and if he should then you'd feel betrayed and hurt and no doubt lash out, which only serves to continue the conflict you'll face.'

'Damn you, Freud. You've got me again. Ah no! I can move. Ha!' Nietzsche shifts a piece with a satisfied nod.

'Oh, good move,' Freud says earnestly, studying the board as we all eat our food.

'But being in conflict all the time is draining,' Rachel says after swallowing a mouthful, and I get the impression she's not just talking about Alice.

'Absolutely,' Freud says. 'And again, while I see great merit in everything Nietzsche says, I tend to look at the individual, to see how we can be better as a person and remove that need for conflict.'

'What? By becoming stupid and dumbing down?' Alice asks.

'On the contrary,' Freud says. 'By removing the causes of the conflict and seeking ways to communicate with others on a calm level, we can invest less energy in defending ourselves and more into shaping the world to be better. I can't imagine any situation in which telling someone they are stupid would ever be beneficial. The best advice I can give you, Alice, not that you want it, is not to question why everyone else *wants* to know your story but ask yourself why you *don't want* to share it.'

'Cos it's mine,' Alice says. 'I don't want to share it with Kathy and Thor 46 and Gretchy. I don't want to share it with anyone.'

'Of course,' Freud says with a gentle smile, as he makes another move on the board. 'In which case, perhaps group therapy is not the best method for you. I'd personally recommend one-on-one therapy with free association to let you talk about anything you wish, to help prevent you transferring your feelings to other people.'

'Free association isn't always a reliable method,' John Candle says, then frowns as he obviously wonders how he knew that. 'I think maybe my writer really was a social worker, or a psychologist, because I know that using free association can elicit fake memories and attach meanings to things that aren't relevant. But I do agree with one-on-one therapy. Do they have that here?'

'Nope. They're barely coping with the Enders sessions as they are,' Rachel says. 'That's why they introduced the threat of cutting people's allowances if they don't comply.'

'Alas. A sad and sorry state as more people become lost in our ever-growing city,' Freud says sadly. 'Which also explains why we have so much crime now.'

'Send Croker around to break some more thumbs. That's what I say. Ah, dammit! Curse you and your blasted beard!' Nietzsche snaps, sitting back with his arms folded.

'Checkmate?' John Candle asks, as Freud smiles and Alice falls silent in deep thought.

'Eat some pizza before L finishes it,' Rachel prompts her, while I realize something and look back at the two guys.

'You guys are real. I mean, you existed. You're not fictional.'

'Debatable, my friend,' Freud says with a waggle of his hand.

'It happens quite a bit actually,' Rachel says. 'We had a Queen Victoria that refused to believe she wasn't the ruling monarch. And we had a JFK once, but he got killed. Then the guy who killed him got killed. Anyway. Yeah, so it does happen.'

I finish my sandwich, while figuring that whoever wrote Freud and Nietzsche must have known their stuff to transfer that knowledge into the characters. Which then makes me think about what they said about none of us knowing ourselves yet.

Which is because we were characters in books. We were not real.

'John,' Rachel says quietly, making me look over to see her pointing to her own mouth, the signal that I was self-narrating out loud again.

'We are not characters now though, Mr Croker,' Nietzsche says as I turn once more to see him staring at me. 'We have life. We have existence. The question is, what will you do with yours? Hmmm? And you, Alice? What will you do? Whatever it is, make it big. Seek an affirmation of life by grasping your existence. Seek experiences. Make it count.'

'But not too wild though, right? I mean. She's seventeen,' Rachel says.

'The wilder the better!' Nietzsche says.

'Friedrich,' Freud says gently but with a warning tone to his voice. 'Don't get carried away.'

'I shall get carried away. Alice should too, and Mr Croker, and that funny little man in his red suit. And you too,' he tells Rachel. 'Why are we here?'

'Nietzsche,' Freud says with a harder tone.

'Why are we here? What for? To what purpose?' Nietzsche demands, his eyes growing wilder. 'Just to live? To exist? If so, then let there be no constraints. But if there is a reason, then seek it. Seek it, Mr Croker,' he says, his eyes locking on mine. 'Seek it, Mr Croker.'

'Nietzsche. Enough now. You know how you get,' Freud says, leaning over to pat his friend's arm. 'Come on now. Take your turn and let them eat in peace. I'll call Bella for some more tea, shall I?'

A moment later and Nietzsche finally breaks his eye contact with me to smile at Freud. 'Yes. More tea would be nice.'

I turn back to my club sandwich, feeling there's something unsaid hanging in the air. Something they're not telling me or talking about openly. Then I realize my urges have been triggered by Nietzsche telling me to *seek it,* and once again I'm looking for plots and conspiracies, and even though it really does feel like there is something going on, I remind myself to focus on the now and remember my therapy.

'There is no van,' I whisper, and Rachel looks over with a sad smile.

'I will add one more observation,' Nietzsche says, as we all turn to look at him. 'Miss Pippin was right. You do look like a lumberjack. Another game, Freud?'

CHAPTER SEVENTEEN

Sunday morning.

EARLY. Still dark.

I turn the corner onto a deserted Main Street with L at my side, still holding his red plastic helmet, although he has at least changed out of the weird suit into red pants and a red top.

'It's closed up,' I whisper.

L looks ahead to Hard-Boiled & Erotica and nods. I'm surprised he's here, but I'm starting to learn that friendship and loyalty mean something to L.

'Who's that?' he asks, his voice low and gruff and sleepy. He motions to the doorway and the huddled mass of a person sleeping under a denim jacket. 'Damn. You think she's been here all night?'

I shrug and look down at Alice fast asleep, before another sound draws our attention and we both turn to see Rachel driving two horses pulling a modern carriage.

'Tell me again why I'm doing this?' she asks, as she brings it to a stop.

'Adventure. Woohoo,' L says, in a flat voice that makes Rachel snort a laugh and roll her eyes.

'Just us then yeah?' Rachel asks.

'Nope,' I say as L and I step apart to let Rachel see the sleeping form of Alice in the doorway.

She tuts sadly and drops down. 'How long she been there?'

'We just arrived,' I say.

'Bless her.' Rachel goes forward to lay a hand on Alice's knee. 'It's me,' she says as Alice blinks awake and stares up. 'How long have you been here?'

'I didn't want to miss it,' Alice whispers. I pass Rachel my new tan jacket with the sheepskin collar and step back as she ushers Alice into the jacket then into the carriage, and finds a blanket to pull up over her body. 'Don't go without me,' Alice says sleepily.

'You're already in the buggy. L, you get in the other side. There're more blankets if you want to sleep.'

He clambers inside to sink into the deep soft seat opposite Alice, and a few seconds later he's nearly hidden under a blanket and already snoring.

'Looks cozy,' I say, as Rachel gets back up onto the front and pats the seat beside her.

'I'll show you how to drive.'

'Don't you need a license or something?'

'It's fine. No one cares outside of the city,' she says as I climb up. 'That's the brake. Pull it back to go. Push it forward to stop.'

'Got it.'

'Well, go on then. Pull it back, Mr *I gotta see the north shore.*'

I release the brake. She takes the reins and flicks them, and a second later we're moving along the street, and I can't help the grin.

'What's that smile for?' she asks with a slow smile of her own.

'Nothing. I mean, I've never done this before. It's cool.'

She nods as we trundle along. 'It *is* cool, actually. And you were right, the backs of these are very cozy.'

I look behind me to L and Alice fast asleep under their blankets. There's a rigid canopy overhead, but I spot the hinged brackets and figure it must either detach or swing back for the roof to come off. It's quiet too. Really quiet, with only the sound of the horses and the faint motion from the large, rubberized wheels rolling smoothly on the road.

'Wait wait wait!' we hear Svetlana's voice calling out and catch sight of her rushing along a side street as Rachel slows the horses. 'I'm coming, I'm coming,' she adds breathlessly and reaches the buggy, looking somewhere between harassed and asleep. 'I haven't said that in a while,' she gasps with a wink.

'I did knock for you,' I tell her. 'You said you wanted to sleep.'

'But then I thought, you know, a day out, and FOMO kicked in and anyway, shush, how do I get in? Up here? Oh! Alice looks so cozy.'

She gets up onto the deep leather seat next to L and leans back into the corner with her feet up and a blanket pulled high.

'What about John?' I ask, but Svetlana waves us on and closes her eyes.

'Okay. So it's honestly not that hard. There's two lines. See?' Rachel says as I look over and trace the lines in her hands stretching out to the horses' heads. 'Wanna try?'

'We're still in the city.'

'Yeah, what will all these people say?' she asks with a comical look around at the deserted streets. Then she shifts in close to my side and hands the reins over. I hold them like they're fragile eggs or something. 'Okay. We need to take that left. Wait until we're closer to the junction . . . And start pulling on the left line. Gently, John!'

'Sorry,' I say with a wince, when the horse snorts and lifts its head. 'Sorry, horse!'

'Mark,' she tells me. 'And that one is Twain. Don't look at me like that. You had a daddy longlegs called Sissy.'

'She was a Mexican red-knee and she was called Sally.'

'Sally. Sissy. Whatever. Okay, now ease off, and see – the horses know to pull straight down the road now. Do you miss her?'

'Who?'

'Sally!'

'I don't know. I mean. I guess I do.' I trail off, focusing on the feel of the reins and the motion in my body and that rich, earthy smell from the horses. Then Rachel leans down between her legs and brings up a flask and two cups, pouring hot chocolate into both before handing one out to me, taking care not to spill any. 'What do I do with these?' I ask, lifting the reins.

'Hold them with one hand, you idiot. So what about Wendy?'

I shrug, not sure of anything. 'Of course. She's my niece.'

She stares at me for a long second. 'It's okay if you don't miss them, John.'

'No. I do. I mean. She's my family.'

'No. Sure. Of course. I'm just saying if you didn't. You know. That would be okay too. Take the next right, here, give me your cup.'

'You want the reins?'

'No. You get the hang of it so I can sleep. Okay, pull back now on the right . . . That's better. I still can't believe you're making me do this.'

'You could have said no.'

'Not after you got L and Alice going. *I'm going to the north shore, Rachel, and there's not a damn thing you can do to stop me,'* she adds in a deep growling voice. *'You can stay or come. I don't care. I'm John Croker.'*

'I really don't sound like that.'

'I'm John Croker and I'm a buying a black shirt.'

I tut and drink my hot chocolate as she strikes a manly pose, pushing her jaw out. *'And a new tan jacket with a sheepskin collar.'*

'You said it looked nice.'

'It does actually,' she says.

'So why are you coming?'

'Cos you lot nagged me into it.'

'You don't seem the type to be nagged into anything.'

She shrugs and drinks the hot chocolate.

'It got into you too,' I say.

'It didn't,' she says.

'It did. What he said got into you too.'

'It didn't!' she says, with a sudden smile. 'I don't know! I mean. He wasn't even Nietzsche. The real Nietzsche died in 1900. He's a Nietzsche written by someone who obviously read some real Nietzsche. Why are you looking at me like that?'

'Cos you said Nietzsche way too many times.'

She rolls her eyes and we drink hot chocolate while the horses pretty much drive themselves.

'Yes. Maybe,' she finally admits as she holds her thumb and finger a fraction apart. 'Maybe a teeny bit. And not all the mad shit when he was telling you to seek it. *Seek it, Mr Croker. Seek it!* Honestly. I wanted to throw my salad at him. I was like *hey, do you know what saying something like that does to a John?'*

I nod. Knowing exactly what something like that does to a John, because that thing in my brain was lighting up like crazy at the prospect of being tasked with a mission to seek something.

'But what he said about experiences?' Rachel says as she stares ahead. 'And, you know. I thought about Alice and L and how Alice has had a shit time here and, I don't know. I thought why not?'

I nod and think back to yesterday and how I set off looking for a clothing store after Nietzsche said I looked like a lumberjack.

'WHERE YOU STRIDING OFF TO?' Rachel asked me.

'To buy a new shirt.'

'John! He was joking.'

But I'd had enough and after everything Freud and Nietzsche said. I just wanted to make a decision and not have the slave morality thing. And I thought buying a shirt would be a good place to start so I walked through the Village until I spotted an outdoor clothing store called Fiction Island.

It caught my eye because the sign had a picture of an island surrounded by ocean and it made me think of the map Jane Tit had shown me. So I went inside and then L and Alice and Rachel came in with me. I thought maybe John Candle and Svetlana would come too, but they had walked into another store, and I figured maybe what Nietzsche said had gotten into them too and made them choose their own path instead of blindly following the group.

Whatever. I don't know. But I did try to buy a black shirt.

'Okay, okay. Fine. Plaid isn't for you, but black? Really?' Rachel asked me.

'What's wrong with black?'

'It's just very John. Ooh, try this one,' she said, pulling out a darker blue shirt to hold against my chest. 'That really suits you. And this dark green one. But the black ones? I don't know. They're just really clichéd.'

'Hi guys! Sorry. I was grabbing a quick drink,' a pretty young woman said, rushing onto the shop floor. 'So. My name is Trixi. Short for Trixibella, and I'll be your assistant today. Teen dystopian if you wanna twinsie my genre.'

We looked at Alice and waited for the comments.

'Hello,' Alice said nicely. 'We're looking for a shirt for our friend John.'

Turned out that the things Freud and Nietzsche said got to all of us.

'Do you have anything in red?' L then asked.

Trixi went to help L and Alice while Rachel looked at more shirts and I stared up at the signage inside and the painted picture of the island. 'Was it called Fiction Island?' I asked.

'Long time ago apparently,' Rachel said.

I looked at the island again, towards the southern edge where I knew the old docks were filled with sailing ships. And I could see that the city area wasn't really in the middle, but more towards the south, so I looked all the way up to the northern edge. 'What's it like up there?'

'Where?' Rachel asked as she held another shirt up against my chest and shook her head.

'The north shore.'

'It's really wild.'

'You've been there?'

'No. It's really far. Blue is definitely your color.'

'How far?'

'Very far. Why?'

'They sell boots here?'

'Boots? What do you want boots for? You've got shoes on.'

'I need boots for walking.'

'Walking where?'

'To the north shore. You said it was far.'

'You want to walk to the north shore?'

'Yes.'

'It'd take days.'

I shrugged. 'I'll get good boots then. And a bag. Miss? Do you sell tents?'

'You can't walk to the north shore, John,' Rachel said.

'Why not?'

'Cos you can't!'

'What?' Alice called over while the assistant passed L some red pants.

'Nothing,' Rachel said quickly.

'I'm gonna walk to the north shore,' I said.

Alice blinked, then grinned. 'I'm in! L? You up for it?'

'Yes. What? Whatever. I'm in. So hey, you fancy a drink maybe sometime?'

'Aw, sorry! I don't date puppets,' the assistant said, with a sad face.

'I'm not a puppet!'

'You're not walking to the north shore,' Rachel said. 'And you're definitely not walking to the north shore with Alice.'

'Er. I've already got boots?' Alice said, pointing at her unlaced DMs.

'Seriously. I'm not a puppet.'

'But you look like one!' the assistant said. 'All cutesy in your red puppet outfit.'

'Miss! Do you sell tents?' I called.

'You don't need a tent!' Rachel said. 'Don't let Nietzsche get in your head. You know he went mad, right?'

'Excuse me. We don't say the *M.A.D.* word here,' the assistant said, with a look to Rachel. 'Mental health is a spectrum.'

'What? John, I mean it. You can't walk that far. You've got Enders therapy and we need to start looking for a job for you, and Alice has got therapy and school and . . .'

'I really wasn't a puppet.'

'Screw therapy. Let's do the north shore,' Alice said.

'Oh god. No!' Rachel groaned. 'You'd need to hire a horse and carriage and have a ridiculously early start to make it there and back.'

'Cool,' I said.

'Brilliant!' Alice said.

'Seriously. Not a puppet.'

But a little while later, and after a lot of arguing, Rachel said, 'Stuff it then. Fine! I'll hire a horse and carriage.'

Then she gave a note to Alice and told her to show it to the matrons at Juvie Hall and we made the plan.

We invited John Candle and Svetlana.

Svetlana said there wasn't a chance in hell she'd get up that early but asked me to knock for her, and obviously decided to join us. John Candle declined outright. He seemed thoughtful and distant after lunch. But like I said, I think Nietzsche and Freud got under all our skins.

WE DRINK the hot chocolate and navigate the streets, deserted save for a few quiet people out walking and a few drinkers still singing songs outside an old pub when we pass through Little Victoria.

But the city soon gives way to the countryside, and we plunge into the darkness away from streetlights. That's when Rachel lights two lanterns at the front of the carriage.

'Right. You good then?' she asks as she climbs into the back.

'You're going?' I ask in alarm.

'You'll be fine. Just stay on this road. Shout me if you need anything, but try not to because I get seriously grouchy when I'm overtired.'

'What the fuck,' I mutter, twisting around to see her gently push Alice over so she can sink into the big soft seats and pull a blanket up.

I grip the reins and focus hard, but the horses seem pretty content to trot along on the road, and from the way they ignore the turnings into farmsteads and the roads leading off into the darkness, I reckon they know the route too.

I start to relax into it and enjoy the experience of driving the horses. It's peaceful. Calming even, and I'm in motion and doing something. Going somewhere.

Is that my brain treating it like a mission? Am I only making things worse? Or is it healthy to be out, exploring and seeking experiences? It certainly seems healthy for Alice. I don't know what she did with her time before now, but I think she got into a lot of trouble for causing scenes and whatnot.

But then it's a shitty thing for anyone to just suddenly appear here, let alone a kid. I'm amazed more people aren't jumping off bridges, or whatever they do in a city without bridges.

It stays dark for another hour, then I start to see the first lighter shades in the sky and realize that the sun rises in the east here too.

But how?

How can they have a sun in a place that isn't real?

But then I had a sun in my world, and that wasn't real.

I don't know, and thinking about it doesn't solve anything. I don't know where *here* is. Or how this works. Or anything at all.

I just know I am here. And as Nietzsche said, I am alive and I have existence.

Seek it, Mr Croker. Seek it!

What did that mean? Did it mean anything?

Why did Rachel sing 'Jolene'?

Why did Fat George pick a fight with me?

I shake my head to rid that desperate search for conspiracy and catch a glimpse of the eastern horizon through the bushes.

I ease the reins back until Mark and Twain come to a stop, then I sit and stare at the sunrise.

'Hey,' I say softly and reach back to nudge Alice. She wakes and blinks at me. 'Sunrise,' I say, nodding east.

'Oh wow. L . . . L!' she whispers.

'What?' he says from under his blanket.

'Look.'

'At what?' he asks, with a grunt and a shrug and one eye open. 'You should see the suns rise on Glaxon 6. One's purple.'

'Glaxon 6? Who wrote your book? The least original writer ever?' she asks, as I smile and watch the sun peeking over the horizon, sending amazing rays of oranges and reds streaming over land, bringing life and color, chasing the shadows away.

'Okay. Glad I came now,' Svetlana murmurs, and I glance back to see they're all awake, watching the sun come up in silence.

A moment later and it slides free of the land to start soaring up into the sky, and again I give thought to a planet turning on its axis while held in orbit within a solar system and how any of that can be happening in a place that doesn't exist.

But it does exist. And I exist.

Why are we here? What for? To what purpose? Just to live? To exist? If so then let there be no constraints. But if there is a reason, then seek it. Seek it, Mr Croker.

I look at the reins in my hands, worn smooth from years of use. I look at the horses and how they stand and twitch and move their heads. I look to the hairs on their bodies and smell the earthy scent coming from them. They seem real.

This is real. I am real. But, like Freud said, I don't know who I am, and I think that's where the uncertainty lies. Because everything else *feels* real and like it belongs, but I don't because I'm still locked into my story.

I feel motion beside me and think it to be Rachel, but the size and shape of the person tells me it's someone smaller and lighter. Which can only be Alice.

I glance over. She glances back. Sleep lines on her face, and I realize she hasn't put the dark eyeliner on, which makes her look so much younger.

'Don't say I look younger,' she says.

'Okay.'

I flick the reins. The horses ignore me. I flick them again. But Mark and Twain carry on ignoring me. I frown, not getting it.

'Can I try?' Alice asks. I glance back to Rachel who shrugs, and I hand the reins over. She rolls her wrists to flick the reins while making a click in her mouth and the horses snort and pull away.

'You done that before?' I ask. 'Looked natural.'

'Guess so,' she says, holding the reins with one hand while reaching down to unscrew the flask and pour herself a hot chocolate. I lean over to help but she waves me off and does it with ease as though she's been driving carriages her whole life.

But I don't ask.

I think about the rules she's set on us. Freud said it's projecting a defense mechanism and that she feels safe with us *so long as* we don't ask about her past. But he also said that only serves to continue the conflict.

Is that right?

Or is it okay to just simply respect the wishes of another person and not pry? Maybe she's got a reason? Maybe we're all thinking something awful happened to her, but maybe she did something awful to someone else. Main characters aren't always heroes, nor are they always kind.

'I keep thinking about what Freud said,' she says after a while, sipping from her cup while holding the reins in that easy way.

'Which bit?' I ask.

'All of it.'

I grunt and listen to the clip-clop and watch the hypnotic sway of Mark and Twain's backsides.

'Do you?' she asks.

I nod and watch the world go by.

'I said do you?' she asks, glancing at me.

'I nodded.'

'He does that,' Rachel says from the back. 'Verbalize, John.'

I nod and hear the snort of laughter from L, followed by Rachel tutting, but when I glance back she's smiling.

'He wasn't Freud though,' Alice says. 'And the other guy wasn't Nietzsche. And you're not John Wick. And Fat George isn't Harry Potter. And none of the Bonds are real . . . And I'm not Alice from Wonderland, whatever the hell that was meant to be,' she adds with a dark frown. 'We're not even carbon copies either.'

'Then what are we?' Rachel asks from the back.

'We're fanfic, aren't we. We're just, like, interpretations of famous characters that someone else tried to write, that never got finished. But I think that makes us more like our writers. I mean. We can only know what they know, right?'

'Superman can't fly,' Rachel says.

Alice nods. 'Superman can't fly. But John Croker *can* fight. Which I reckon means his writer could fight.'

'That's the accepted theory,' Rachel says.

'Is it?' Alice asks, looking a bit crestfallen. 'I thought I was being all smart then.'

'You were,' Rachel says. 'Just because someone else knew something before you doesn't diminish your intelligence.'

We ride on through the rolling countryside that slowly gives way to prairies and a small range of snow-topped mountains in the far distance off to the west.

'How's that for attention to detail?' Alice asks with a snort as we trundle past a herd of bison grazing peacefully. 'We're ticking the tropes off here. Snow-capped mountains, check. Prairie scrubland, check. Herd of buffalo or whatever they are, check.'

I smile at her commentary, and how her jokes lack the normal level of effort because it's just too beautiful to criticize, and we bounce along as Western World comes into view in the distance.

'Are we going there?' Alice asks, twisting around to see Rachel nodding sleepily.

'We'll change the horses and get some breakfast,' she says with a yawn, and shuffles down a bit further. 'Wake me when we get there . . . Honestly, I don't think I've ever been this cozy before.'

I know what she means because even up front the smell of the land and the rocking motion make me feel relaxed, and for a minute I think how nice it would be to get in the back and fall asleep.

Except I don't.

I guess Rachel would say it's because I'm a John.

But honestly.

I don't know what I am.

CHAPTER EIGHTEEN

I realize why Rachel went back to sleep, because although the town looked close, it isn't until mid-morning that we pass under a big arched sign.

WESTERN WORLD
PLEASE RIDE SLOWLY!

WE ROLL onto Main Street and trundle past the high-fronted timber-framed stores and shops, all with hand-painted signs advertising their services or goods.

Horses everywhere. Either tethered to hitching posts, or drinking water from troughs, or being ridden by men in dark suits or men in cowboy clothing, while women in gowns walk on raised wooden sidewalks under parasols giving shade from the hot morning sun.

Rachel comes up front and squeezes between Alice and me on the bench just big enough for three.

'Keep driving,' Rachel says, when Alice offers her the reins. 'You're obviously experienced at it.'

Alice doesn't take the bait and focuses on the road ahead, slowing the horses to let a woman and her two kids go past. A little boy in shorts and a blazer and the girl in a white frock, both smart with neatly brushed hair.

'Thank you, ma'am,' the woman calls with a nod. 'Most kind of you.'

'Anytime,' Alice says, and we trundle on, Rachel guiding Alice right at an intersection to a sprawl of big barns and buildings and a sign outside.

OLD COBB'S
LIVERY YARD & HORSE EXCHANGE

'WELL, HOWDY THERE!' a woman calls, striding out of a barn as we come to a stop. 'You lookin' to exchange?'

'We are,' Rachel says, fishing a piece of paper from her pocket that she hands down to the woman, dressed in denim jeans covered in leather chaps, boots and a plaid shirt, with a big hat shielding her eyes from the sun.

'What's that?' I ask, as the woman takes it to read.

'Receipt for the carriage which includes horse exchanges. It's a system the main towns all use. They share the money so travellers can swap horses,' Rachel says.

'Folk drive 'em too hard otherwise,' the woman says, patting Twain on his flank. 'You pop down now and we'll get you some fresh. You waitin' to go straight on?'

'Can we see the town?' Alice asks quickly.

'Ah heck, I reckon your daughter is bustin' for a look-see,' the woman says with a grin.

'I'm not old enough to be her mom!' Rachel says with a laugh.

'Well, I don't mean no offence, and you sure do look pretty and young, ma'am,' the woman says with a smile, and I can't help but wonder if she really talks like that, or if it's put on for show. But then I realize my mind is still expecting this to be some kind of tourist place.

'Come on now, let's get you down. You need a hand, ma'am?' she asks, offering her arm to Svetlana.

'I could do with a hand,' L says with a cheesy smile.

'You can go and get. I see that glint in your eye,' the woman says with a laugh as we drop out and stretch.

'Is there a restroom?' Svetlana enquires.

'We got one here. It ain't pretty, mind. Or if the miss there wants a look-see, then head up to Blondie's Saloon, or try the Angel Eyes Diner next to it.'

'Hey, Annie. You ain't seen my Jedediah have you?' a woman calls, rushing over towards us.

'I have not,' Annie replies, leading the carriage away, the woman following.

'Only I ain't seen him and he was due back is all.'

We set off into Main Street, marvelling at the sights around us as I remember what Annie said.

'Best saloon and diner names ever,' I say with a smile as Alice, L and Svetlana all frown. 'It's from a movie. *The Good, The Bad, and The Ugly*. No?'

'Literally the most famous western movie ever made,' Rachel says. 'Clint Eastwood? The stand-off? The music? *Dang-a-dang-a-dang whoowarewooooo*.'

'That's really good,' I say, impressed at her vocal rendition, and remembering how she sang 'Jolene' at karaoke.

'Thank you! And I now feel super old seeing as they don't know it. And even more that she thought I was your mom.'

'It's cos I look young without my makeup on,' Alice says.

'And better without it,' Rachel says as we reach the center of town. 'Blondie's Saloon or the Angel Eyes Diner?'

'Saloon,' we all say. I guess we all want the same experience of walking in through the swinging doors.

Alice starts rushing ahead with L running out to get in front of her. The pair of them laughing and reaching the saloon doors at the same time.

We follow inside. Wooden floors. Wooden tables. A wooden bar. Men playing cards and drinking beer. Cowboys at the bar sipping from shot glasses. An old guy at a piano banging out an jaunty tune.

'No minors,' the barkeep calls as he clocks Alice. 'Go on now. Get out before I get fined for having underage on the premises. I ain't having no kids in here. We got whores upstairs.'

'Don't call them whores!' Alice says.

'It's a damn whorehouse!' the barkeep says as the cowboys look over.

'They're called sex workers, you neanderthal prick!' Alice yells as Rachel takes her arm and waves an apology.

'Watch yer damn mouth you little piss-ant,' someone says in a gruff voice, making me turn back with a glare.

'Okay! We're all fine here,' Rachel says, taking my arm too. 'But FYI. Calling them whores is also illegal,' she snaps at the barkeep as she ushers us outside. 'And you can stop puffing your chest up, L. We're not getting into a brawl. Jesus. We've only been here five minutes.'

We head back through the creaking doors and into the Angel Eyes Diner next door. Tables covered in white and red checked cloths and people in nicer clothes.

We freshen up in the restrooms, find a table big enough for our party and order eggs over easy with toast and coffee.

'Go on then,' Alice says with a look at Rachel, who doesn't say anything. 'Alright. I'm sorry. Filter back on,' she adds, pulling an invisible screen over her mouth.

Rachel just rolls her eyes, but I can see the humor in her expression. So can Alice, who smiles over with a silent and more sincere apology.

'But seriously? They have sex workers here?' Svetlana asks.

'Same as everywhere else in the world,' Rachel says, and I notice how she avoids eye contact. 'The bread smells nice, doesn't it? You hungry?' she asks us all.

'So what? You just pay for sex?' L asks. 'With money?'

'You didn't have sex workers in your world?' Svetlana asks him.

'I told you! They see you even touching your pee pee then blammo with the lasers,' L says. 'So what? I mean. Is that like a good thing? Are the women *made* to do it?'

'No!' Svetlana says then frowns. 'Rachel? They're not forced, are they?'

Rachel shakes her head. 'It's a recognized profession here.'

'In Western World?' L asks.

'In Fiction Land. They've even got a union,' Rachel adds, and carries on stirring her coffee. 'You tried the coffee yet?' she asks me.

'It's nice,' I say, remembering Freud and how he said we impose rules on each other not to ask certain things, and in a way it kind of feels like that now. But then maybe I'm the only one picking up the vibe, because the others keep going.

'I couldn't be a sex worker,' Alice says with a grimace. 'Urgh. Gross.'

'We all gotta eat,' Svetlana says.

'Yeah, but not that,' Alice says.

'Why not? Are you saying that a woman doesn't have the right to use her body to gain the means to pay for food or rent?'

'No! I mean. Okay. Right,' Alice says, clearly caught out. 'No. So. What I mean is of course they have the right, but if a woman *has* to sell her body to feed herself then that's fucked up.'

'Language,' Rachel says. 'And can we change the subject, please?'

'Sorry!' Alice says, lowering her voice with a wince.

'What if a woman *wants* to use her body?' Svetlana asks. 'Not for food or desperation, but say she likes money and having nice things. And say she's okay with having sex with people for money?'

'Why would she?' Alice asks. 'There's no dignity in that.'

'No dignity?' Svetlana asks her with a look. 'So you want to go next door and tell those women that they have no dignity, *after* you just defended them from being called whores?'

Alice stays silent, clearly struggling between her own views and her instinct to defend women.

'Or are you saying I've got no dignity for exploring my sexuality with Benjamin? We did some very wild things, but it was consensual – and this won't be a popular view, but part of Benjamin's appeal was that he was extremely wealthy. A girl like me could never afford to stay in the hotels we used or fly on private jets. So maybe I traded what I had for that lifestyle. Does that mean I've got no dignity?'

The food arrives and I see how relieved Rachel looks at the distraction as we start tucking in.

'Well, hey. My view,' L says.

'Can we move on!' Rachel says.

'No, hey, let me just say this,' L says. 'My view, not that I'm like consenting or giving my permission, or whatever, but I think a woman, or anyone, should do what they want so long as they don't hurt no one else, right? I mean. If they want to do that. Like with me. For free cos I don't have money, like even just once would be nice, but yeah, why not?'

'No, I get that,' Alice says, but she frowns like she's still unclear in her mind.

'Personally, I think you need to re-think the whole no-dignity view,' Svetlana says. 'Because that's how sex-workers got called whores in the first place, from the perception that a woman had no dignity and would do anything for anyone for the right price. I mean. That's more like porn stars doing gang bangs for cash something.'

'Okay, enough!' Rachel snaps, slamming her fork down as she storms off to the restroom.

'Something I said?' Svetlana asks.

'I don't think she likes talking about sex,' I say. 'Maybe we can stop for a while?'

'Sure. Yeah,' Svetlana says.

Rachel comes back a few minutes later and sits down with a tight smile at the others.

'Hey, I'm sorry,' Svetlana says, touching Rachel's hand.

'It's fine,' Rachel says, as the main door swings open and the woman we saw at the livery yard rushes in.

'Hey, Betty? Y'all seen my Jedediah now?' she calls over the diners.

'He ain't been in here,' the woman who served our food replies.

'Well, damn. He was due back and I ain't seen the damn fool,' the woman says, but she looks worried.

'Where'd he go?' Betty asks.

'Into the city. Teacher said our boy is getting too smart for the schoolhouse and Jed went to see about a new school for him and some scholarship grant or something. But he ain't come home.'

'Maybe he got to drinkin',' Betty suggests. 'You know Jed.'

'No, he swore he wouldn't. He ain't touched a drop for five month now. Heck. I'll get home, but you see him you tell him to get right on back.'

She heads out as we share looks and eat our eggs over easy and, thankfully for Rachel, we don't go back to talking about sex.

AN HOUR LATER, and with our fresh horses Agatha and Christie all fastened or buckled or whatever they do to attach horses to carriages, we set off out of Western World to continue our journey north.

'I think we spent too long there,' Rachel says from the front as Alice drives the horses again.

'It was only an hour,' Svetlana says.

Rachel nods and twists to look back at us. 'We have to go through Middle Earth to swap the horses *and then* go on to the north shore, and honestly, it's so far. I asked around and they said you can only just do it in a day.'

'It's fine,' Svetlana says, relaxing into the seat. 'I could do this all day easy.'

'You mean get there and back in a day?' I ask.

'Yeah,' Rachel says and turns away, but I see her frown and look back at me.

'You sure they didn't mean it takes a day to get there?' I ask, as she bites her bottom lip.

'No! They meant there and back. It can't be a whole day to get there, can it? Shoot! I don't know.'

'What's the big deal?' Alice asks. 'More time away from Juvie Hall and Matron Ratched.'

'Because I only booked you out for one day,' Rachel tells her.

'Booked me out? What am I? A horse?'

'Dunno. Try pulling the carriage and we'll see,' Rachel says, earning a smile. 'You know what I mean. I'll ask again at Middle Earth. But god, I can't believe I didn't plan it properly.'

'It's fine,' I tell her with a nod. 'If it takes longer, you can drop me at Middle Earth and I'll make my own way.'

'Us,' L says, holding his hands out. 'Drop *us* at Middle Earth.'

'Us,' I say with a nod at him.

'And me,' Alice says.

'And maybe me. Depending on the level of walking required,' Svetlana says. 'And if there's an option of maybe a spa or luxury resort to stay in while you lot go fishing or whatever you want to do.'

'Looking for the docks,' Alice and L say at the same time.

I laugh at the joke and the play of it, and close my eyes, feeling the sun on my face as we bounce gently along.

'But that defeats the point,' Rachel tells Alice.

'What does?'

'If I drop you all off and go back on my own. You're the only one that has to go back. We can stay longer.'

'Ha!' L says with a laugh. 'Alice can drive the carriage back on her own.'

'Er, piss off,' Alice says as I smile and feel my mind easing down into sleep. Breakfast in my belly. The sun on my face. No place to be. No place to go.

No van to find.

'Then how do we get back?' Svetlana asks.

'Oh. Yeah. I didn't think of that,' L admits, and I drift off to sleep with their laughter and voices joining the background sounds of the horses clip-clopping and wheels trundling along.

'NEWSHIRE?' Alice says, bringing me awake as I look out to a landscape so very different from the prairie scrubland. Rolling hills and meadows full of wildflowers stretching off to big hills, and mountains beyond them with jagged peaks covered in snow.

I hear the rush of water and sit up higher to see a fast-flowing river at the side of the road and notice the sign board we pass by.

WELCOME TO NEWSHIRE
A HAMLET OF MIDDLE EARTH

'WELL. Seeing as we're now in fantasy land I'm guessing we will very soon pass over either an old stone bridge, or a rickety old wooden thing,' Alice says, as I stretch and yawn and realize someone covered me with a blanket.

'Hello sleepy,' Svetlana says, making Rachel and Alice turn and smile and offer greetings.

I wave back and watch as Rachel pours a coffee from the flask we had refilled and hands it back. I take it gratefully, expecting it to be cold but finding it's still pleasantly warm.

'Yes!' Alice calls as we round a slow bend to a big old stone bridge ahead that takes us over the gurgling rushing waters below.

'It's so green here,' Svetlana says. 'The trees are beautiful.'

'Glamthorp had good trees,' L says in a rare serious tone. 'Huge red and yellow things with these branches that supported like whole houses, and they had paths running around like towns.'

'Sounds beautiful,' Rachel says.

'It was. Until we blew the planet apart with our Death Laser.'

'Oh god, why?' Svetlana asks.

'No idea. I was a grunt. No, but, then I did hear someone say it was because the little alien dude we'd saved and hidden had come from there . . . And there was like *this memo* that said if the dumb shits that stole the alien didn't hand it over then they'd blow the whole planet up or, you know, like whatever.'

'Was he called Yoda?' I ask.

'Who?'

'The little alien.'

'No.'

'Oh,' I say, as we wait in silence.

'Xoba,' L says.

We shrug and figure it's close enough.

'There's a gorgeous little inn here,' Rachel says.

'You've been here before?' Svetlana asks.

'Once. But we didn't stop. The guys I arrived with all planned this guided tour trip to Middle Earth, but we started drinking way too early and I don't remember a lot. But I do remember this place had a cool inn. Or at least I think it was here.'

Rachel was right. We trundle along an unmade but worn and well-grooved track leading into a small hamlet of thatched cottages all built around a large central green, with a lake fed from a river filled with graceful swans.

'The Waystone Inn.' Svetlana reads the sign outside and frowns. 'That sounds familiar.'

'From a famous fantasy book,' Rachel says with a squint. 'I can't remember which one, but isn't it pretty,' she adds.

It is, but it's not the only thing to see. We hear music coming from the green and look over to see old-fashioned wagons painted in bright colors off to one side, and people in bright clothes playing musical instruments while the villagers dance and drink from tankards.

'Are we stopping?' Alice asks as she slows the horses.

'We don't really have time,' Rachel says with a wince, then tuts. 'You know what. Stuff it. Five minutes won't hurt.'

A stable boy offers care to our horses, and we head inside to a cool shaded interior and a big guy behind the counter. Well-muscled with red hair.

'Ho! Passing through or here for the Edema?'

'Sorry, the what?' Rachel asks as I clock several quiet guys in dark clothing at a table at the back.

'The Edema Ruh,' the barkeep says, nodding outside. 'They tour Fiction Land giving shows.'

'Oh, I see. No, we're actually just passing through. We're heading for Middle Earth town but we thought maybe a quick drink and a break.'

'City folk on a day trip!' the man says with a smile. 'Take a seat outside in the sun and enjoy. We'll get the drinks out to you. Bast?' he calls. 'BAST?'

'What, Kote?' another man asks, coming in with his fingers looped through the handles of empty tankards.

'Honey mead for our guests.'

'Is that alcoholic?' Rachel asks quickly. 'Only we've got a minor.'

'Tell you what,' Kote says with a wink. 'I won't tell if you won't.'

'Yes!' Alice says. 'I love this guy.'

'Everybody does,' Bast says, rolling his eyes. 'But try getting him to finish a story.'

'Boom!' Kote says, giving him a high five. 'Honey mead isn't strong. She won't even taste the alcohol. Go on! Listen to the music. Enjoy your five-minute stay.'

I glance at the table of guys as we start heading out. One of them with dark stubble lifts a tankard in greeting. I nod back and head out to the sunshine.

The honey meads come quickly, served in metal tankards. Cool, rich and very tasty.

'Oh my god. Mouth orgasm,' Svetlana says, and I spot a flicker of irritation cross Rachel's face.

'Amazing,' Alice says, drinking hers down, and looking awesome in torn tights and DM boots with the sleeves of her faded black T-shirt rolled up and her jet-black hair, holding a tankard of ale in a fantasy book-cover setting.

'Dude,' L says, nodding at her slowly as he holds his tankard out to clunk hers.

The music is nice too. If you like lutes and flutes and other weird shit.

'Weird shit?' Rachel asks, as I realize I was self-narrating again. I roll my eyes. She smiles and clunks her tankard against mine. 'You're fine. You're doing it a lot less. Or, you're doing it all the time and I'm just used to it.'

I get an urge to ask her where she's from and what her story is. Or was. But I suppress it, figuring if she wanted to tell me she would.

She frowns at me, maybe detecting I was about to ask something. Then gives me a faint smile and turns back to watching the men and women in bright clothes and the villagers dancing around.

I hear noise behind me and turn to see the five guys from the back of the inn heading out. All of them in long dark cloaks. They head round the back to the stables, and a moment later, ride out and through the village on big horses. That's when I notice they're not all men, two are women. The big guy who nodded at me does it again as he rides by.

'Who are they?' I ask Rachel.

She shrugs. 'No idea. Fiction Land is huge, and Middle Earth covers like half of it or something crazy. There's loads of little hamlets and villages. God, I could just crash here and drink mead and listen to this all day.'

I tilt my head, figuring yes to the mead part, but not so much to the music.

'Yeah, it's not my cup of tea,' Alice says. 'Cool place though.'

We drink the mead and head around the back of the inn to see our horses watered and resting in the shade, and a few moments later, we head through the village and along a track, through forests dappled in sunlight. Birds sing out and we see squirrels leap from tree and tree and hear the calls of other creatures.

We stay in the forest for a long time, passing tracks that lead to cottages glimpsed further away.

The ground starts to rise and the forest thins, giving way to bracken-covered fields and thickets of trees. Lakes here and there. It's still pretty, but more barren, and with that comes the sense of being wilder and more remote.

It's nice though, and we lapse into silence broken by sudden bursts of chat. I sit next to L on one of the seats in the back, facing forward. Rachel sits opposite me with Svetlana taking a turn up front next to Alice, who's still happy to drive.

'Bliss,' Rachel says, lifting her legs to rest on the seat between me and L. Her booted foot rests against my thigh. I expect her to move it. She doesn't. But then she doesn't show any sign of the contact either and I figure the boots are too thick for her to realize.

That other aspect of my personality was hard to overcome too. That I would see a romantic gesture in the merest fleeting touch from a woman. Or if a woman looked into my eyes, I'd assume she was sending some form of signal.

But again, listening to Nietzsche and Freud really helped. Plus, I realized just how fucking sleazy that is, outside of my own story. It makes me think back to Lin Lin in the warehouse and the sex we had. It feels so messed-up now that we'd do that. But it felt completely normal at the time.

Thinking about her stirs strange memories. In a way I kind of loved Lin Lin, and I had deep feelings for Mascaponi too. The fact that Mascaponi was a guy who later became a woman doesn't change that. Rachel said that was the story being changed, and I was becoming aware of those changes.

I don't know.

I just know that neither of them ever existed. But I still have the memories of them. The smell of Lin Lin's perfume and the feel of her body. And I remember that threesome. The tangle of our limbs and the way we touched each other.

How is that memory so real if it never happened?

I feel a tap on my thigh and blink over to see Rachel. 'Earth to John!' she says with a smile. 'You went all broody and quiet again.'

I nod at her and offer a smile, and realize she did know her foot was against my thigh. Or maybe she shifted it when she wanted to nudge me.

Don't read into it.

There is no van.

'There's a caravan or something,' Alice calls from the front.

'Is it wide enough to pass?' Rachel asks.

'No, I mean, I think there's been an accident,' Alice says.

'It's on its side,' Svetlana adds.

We sit up and see an old-style colored wooden caravan on its side, blocking the track.

'Oh! Thank god,' a woman calls, rushing around from behind it. 'Please, my husband, he's trapped.'

'Oh god,' Rachel says, as Alice comes to a halt and we all start jumping down.

'I think his leg is broken!' the woman calls, rushing out of sight as we head towards them, and I look to the front, expecting to see horses on their sides, but there are no horses there. Nor are there are any standing nearby, and there are no reins or lines or harnesses that would have been used to attach the horses to the caravan, and for a second it looks like someone just tipped the thing over.

'Stop!' I shout loudly. L complies instantly. Svetlana takes another step with Alice, but stops and looks back as Rachel keeps going.

'My husband!' the woman cries out in a voice *too* full of anguish, and my mind relays her face and matches it to one of the women I saw coming out of the inn in Newshire.

'It's a trap!' I shout, running after Rachel as she reaches the back of the caravan.

'Fuck it,' someone mutters in a deep voice, and Rachel stops to look round at me with an expression of horror as a pair of arms surge out of the back of the caravan to try and grab her. I reach her first and wrench her past me, using the leverage gained to drive power into my right foot to kick hard. Sending the guy back with a grunt, and I follow through with a fist to the back of his head, driving him down onto the road as the others swarm out from behind the caravan, swinging swords and cudgels. The people from the inn. All with scarves pulled up to cover their faces, but the cloaks are unmistakable.

I see all of that as I drop the first guy and spot a cosh tucked into his belt. A length of dense, strengthened leather with a weighted end. A vicious weapon in a close-quarters fight, and I snatch it free to swing up into the throat of a guy lifting a cudgel over his head. He sags back with a choking gurgle and drops the weapon.

Two down. I expect there to be three left, and curse at seeing there's still five. Which means the whole gang didn't go to the inn.

'Come on, motherfuckers!' L shouts, snatching the fallen cudgel up to wield in both hands as a crossbow bolt slams into the caravan frame between us, making us all start.

'STAND STILL BY ORDER OF THE CONSTABLE'S OFFICE!' a loud voice roars, and we all turn to see uniformed people in dark red tunics surging out of the tree line holding crossbows.

'Run!' the leader of the highway gang yells, and as they turn to start fleeing I grab the cudgel from L to launch at his legs, taking him down with a cry of pain.

I run over to pin him down, but he thrashes and tries to draw a knife to stab into my side. I block it easily and throw it aside, then slam my fist into his nose, knocking him clean out, and it's when I bring my fist up to deliver the next blow into his windpipe that someone grabs my arm.

'Enough!' a strong voice orders. The voice of a cop or someone in authority, and so I let him pull me back and hold my hands up, as uniformed people run after those fleeing while more go to the ones I dropped by the caravan.

'Ha! That's what happens when you try and rob John Croker!' Alice says as the men are bound and dragged to their feet.

'Well done, sir!' a man in a dark red tunic says, thrusting a hand towards me. 'Captain Slackbladder, Constable's Office, Middle Earth. Been after these rogues for a while. But good on you! Getting three down. Saw it all I did. Damn fast as well too, eh Colour Sergeant Bourne?'

'Damn fast, sir,' a burly fellow with a big moustache says in a deep voice. 'We'll chase the others down. But we've got the leader, sir. Broke his leg he did, and his nose.'

'Good show!' the captain says, clapping his hand on my arm with a big grin. 'Take it you're from the city, are you?'

'We are,' Rachel says, coming over with the others. 'I'm a genre rep, we're kind of doing an orientation thing, but I mean, no, more like a day trip. Sorry. I'm gabbling. Did that just happen?'

'I'd say it rather did!' Captain Slackbladder says. 'Eh? We knew they were up to something. Knew it! What did I say, Colour Sergeant Bourne?'

'You said you knew, sir.'

'Eh. We knew. Now we've got three of them. And the leader. I'll reckon we'll chase another couple of them down too before the day is out.'

'I'm sorry,' Rachel says, holding a hand up as she looks at me. 'How did you know?'

'No horses,' I say, nodding to the front of the caravan. 'If it just tipped the horses would be trapped.'

'Oh god, it's obvious,' Rachel says.

'And I daresay you would have noticed too soon enough,' the captain says. 'But they only need a few seconds to get the element of surprise, then bang! They've got the drop. Well experienced at it. They've been doing it for months and causing hell on our back roads. Killed a few too, I might add. Still. You're all safe and sound now. Are you heading into Middle Earth? Wouldn't mind popping into the Constable's office would you and leaving your details? In case we need a statement later.'

'We can leave them now if you want,' Rachel says.

'No need! I want to run these other scoundrels down. Eh, Colour Sergeant Bourne. We want to run them down.'

'Run them down, sir. You men! Shift that caravan for the good folk so they can get past. COME ON! LOOK LIVELY!'

They drag the van aside and that's it. They're off, taking the prisoners with them and leaving us in stunned silence.

'Right. Okay,' Rachel says. 'Er, so, that was pretty shocking. Did you guys want to turn back?'

'What? No!' Alice says.

'Hell no!' L says.

'I'm okay,' Svetlana says with a shrug. 'I thought it was pretty cool actually.'

'So fucking cool!' Alice says, giving me a high five.

'Violence isn't cool, Alice,' Rachel tries to say.

'It is when John does it,' Svetlana says, giving me a certain look.

'Okay. Yes. I'll admit there is a coolness when John does it,' Rachel says. 'But it was still violence. But seriously, John. How did you move so blooming fast?'

I shrug because I don't know how I do it. Only that I can.

'So? You guys want to keep going then?' Rachel asks, and a within a few minutes we're back in the carriage with Rachel driving and me up front while Alice and L replay the whole thing second by second.

'. . . And I was like, *come on motherfuckers!*' L says, and I turn back to nod at him in thanks for backing me up again. He might be loud and a bit chubby but he's loyal, and that means something to me, and I realize the bond isn't forced this time, nor does it come from a story. He nods back, grinning from ear to ear, and we ride on for Middle Earth town.

CHAPTER NINETEEN

Middle Earth.

'IT'S like something out of a computer game,' Alice says when we reach Middle Earth town mid-afternoon. Or more like a city from the sight of it.

We passed snow-capped mountains and caught sight of sweeping valleys with castles and crenellated forts dotted here and there. We saw more hamlets too, and I wondered why anyone would choose to live such a simple and obviously hard life in the middle of nowhere.

'Do they all know?' I asked as we went through an area of houses with round doors built into hillsides.

'Know what?' Rachel asked.

'That they're characters from books.'

'They're not. And we're not either. We're people, John.'

'No. I mean. Do they *know*?'

She thought for a second. 'Yes, they know. There's a law about it. Everyone in Fiction Land *must* be made aware.'

'What about the kids born here?'

'They're told in school, but I should imagine they grow up knowing.'

'You're saying all the kids from these little villages go to school?'

'No. I'm saying they *should* go to school, where they *should* be told. They probably don't all get told, but then the city is getting so full that more and more people are moving out and finding other places, and I guess they're taking information with them and passing it on. It's become a real issue, actually.'

'What has?' I asked.

'Overcrowding. I mean apparently, Fiction Land was this small city with just a few other little places. They say it's because of the whole self-publishing thing, that anyone can write a book and release it, which meant more people were *trying* to write books and giving up, which caused our population to explode, but it also meant, and I say this respectfully, that we have a lot more people coming in without usable skills.'

I frowned at her, not getting what she meant.

'I mean, writing a book used to be an intellectual pursuit, right? It took time and energy, and it had to be good to get an agent then a publisher. And that took a certain mindset, which meant those skills were transferred into the characters. So say an experienced author writes a new book, but he or she abandons it – they'd probably still have researched the subject properly, which meant they had knowledge which the character then had when they arrived here, which the city can use. Say a doctor writes a book. Or a dentist. Or a lawyer. We need those skills. So those people were valued. But then along comes the self-publishing thing and *anyone* can write a book, which means people who don't really have usable skills are creating underdeveloped characters which arrive here and become . . . You know.'

'Like me?' Svetlana asked, making us both turn to see her listening intently.

'No. I didn't mean you,' Rachel said.

'But I don't have any skills. What about you? What skills do you have?'

'Me?' Rachel asked, and I saw that flicker of worry again. 'None I suppose. Yeah. Maybe that means me then. I'm one of them. One of the masses that take more than they give.'

I thought back to Sam Shovel, the detective who came to my room and questioned me about the fight with Bond 12. He had usable skills, which in turn made him valued when he arrived.

'Jesus. I'm fucked then,' Alice said. 'Unless they urgently need a slightly fat, ugly teen goth full of self-loathing? No?'

'You're not ugly or fat. Don't say that about yourself,' Svetlana said.

'You're really pretty,' L said, with a smile.

'You think everything is pretty,' Alice replied to deflect her awkwardness.

'True. I think John is pretty,' L said, taking the quip to break any tension still in the air after the robbery. 'So what about my skills? Do they need a grunt from a Killer Sun? I can fire a laser gun, and I look great in red.'

I chuckled at the way he said it, and thought. 'Skills are teachable.'

'They are,' Rachel conceded as we all turned to look at a sign for FAR FAR AWAY CASTLE, and past it to a big fairy-tale castle far away. 'But the city isn't equipped to house and train and deal with such a growing population. And there's only so many coffee shops we can open for the Trixies and Bellas to work in. Which is why Alice isn't getting the individual case therapy she needs.'

'Er. I'm not a nutjob, thank you!'

'I know you're not. And I didn't mean it like that,' Rachel said. 'Okay, sorry. Shitty thing to say. But my point is the more we struggle to cope then the more crime we get, and the more things like that robbery happen. That captain even said that gang were targeting back roads, and this isn't a back road. This is the main road. We've passed dozens of carriages and people on horses – and none of them have their own John to protect them.'

'Ahem,' L said.

'Or their own L132,' Rachel added.

I smiled along and wondered what skills I had. I could fight, but what else? Paranoia and an instinct to be alone aren't usable skills, and Sam Shovel said I couldn't be a cop because cops show restraint.

A bouncer then? But bouncers have to show restraint too. And I realized I'm not just trained to fight. I'm trained to kill. Which is why, even when that guy was knocked out, I was pulling my fist back ready to crush his windpipe.

'You know what?' L said, with a thoughtful expression. 'I don't want to work in a coffee shop.'

Svetlana shook her head, silently agreeing, and I could see Alice was thinking the same. That their, and possibly our, futures were already mapped out, because other than me knowing how to kill people, none of us had any skills.

ONE THING IS FOR SURE, Alice is right. Driving into Middle Earth is like entering a video game. We join a slow-moving queue to get over the wide drawbridge over the deep moat and through the high stone wall, which runs out on each side as far as the eye can see.

Which itself is impressive enough, but the sight of the city beyond the wall is incredible, with medieval Gothic structures complete with gargoyles poking up alongside Moorish and Arabic towers and dwellings, built in tiers that rise up like the layers of some weird cake.

'It's like Tolkien and Martin did acid with Pratchett and made a city,' Alice says, earning looks from the rest of us, but she's right. It's exactly like that, with a stunning mix of architectural styles. White-washed stucco and red-tiled rooftops alongside dark grey houses with stained glass windows in narrow slits, and the whole city seeming to rise in segments to form a ring around the base of the tower in the middle.

A tower that stretches up into the sky. Dark and foreboding and dominating the city around it.

'Damn. Who owns that?' Svetlana asks as we all look up in awe. 'Please tell me he's male and single. Joke!' she says, seeing Alice's expression.

'I'm kinda expecting the Eye of Sauron to be at the top,' I say.

'It is,' Rachel says, as we all lean forward trying to see it. 'It's a nightclub inside at the top, and it's actually called the Eye of Sauron, and it has a giant eye. Apparently. I've never been there,' she adds when we all look at her. 'Which you'd also know if you'd read the orientation folders I gave you.'

'Oh, I didn't reach that part,' Svetlana says.

'It's at the beginning,' Rachel says.

'I know, right!' Svetlana says with a big smile.

'I gave mine to Alice,' L says. 'She sold it for drugs.'

'Whatever,' Rachel says, with a comic eye-roll. 'But it's also got a conference center, casino, gymnasium and a hotel, and a big mall, and they've even got a snow kingdom. Which isn't a kingdom but this area with the temperature like really low and they pump it full of snow, so it stays all wintery.'

'Why does this feel like foreshadowing?' I ask as Rachel shrugs. 'You been inside of it?'

'Nope,' she says.

'How can you not visit somewhere like that?' Svetlana asks.

Rachel shrugs. 'You just get on with work and life. Did you visit every famous place where you lived?'

'No, but we were controlled by writers,' Svetlana replies, making Rachel think for a moment. 'It's fine. It just means another day trip,' Svetlana says with a wink to Alice. 'You okay? You've gone very quiet.'

'No, fine. Just like blown away. This place is insane,' Alice says.

'Middle Earth?' Rachel asks.

'No, the whole place. Western World. Here. Our city. I didn't realize it was like this. I literally only saw Juvie Hall and school and therapy, and that time I went into the Village and got detention.'

'That sucks,' L says, as we finally pass over the drawbridge and through the keep.

'Halt!' a liveried guard yells, stepping out in front of us holding a big pikestaff. 'State your business!'

'What the fuck. Are we in Disney World?' Alice mutters, leaning between me and Rachel on the front bench.

'Horse exchange,' Rachel says, passing her receipt down to the guard. 'And is this necessary? My understanding was the towns all had free movement. We don't do this in the city.'

'You're not in the city.'

'Excuse me?' Rachel asks at his blunt tone. 'Captain Slackbladder *told* us to come here to leave our details after we stopped a highway robbery.'

'Course he did, love.'

'He blooming did! How rude are you? Where's your supervisor?'

'Alright, Karen. Paperwork's in order. Proceed.'

'What the hell! Did you just call me Karen?'

'Proceed!' the guard yells, as people behind us start shouting.

'I am so reporting you,' Rachel says, flicking the reins to get Agatha and Christie moving. 'Honestly. What was all that about? And they can't put a border control on. That's against the rules.'

'I don't think they care,' Alice says, as we pass through onto a wide cobbled road bordered by all manner of buildings.

We pass open stalls selling everything from fruit to blankets, along with memorabilia marked with MIDDLE EARTH in varying ways. Signs saying TANKARDS FOR DADS. APRONS FOR MUMS. SMALL PIKESTAFFS FOR KIDS.

'Sexist much,' Alice mutters.

'Dude. I so want a pikestaff. You want an apron, Svetty?' L says.

'Dick,' Alice says, swiping his arm as we come to a stop some distance back from an intersection.

'What's the holdup?' Rachel mutters.

'Clean yer horses?' a man asks, popping up at the side with a bucket and starting to sponge the horses' flanks. 'Lovely day for it! New to Middle Earth are ya? From the city, yeah? Gotta keep those horses clean. Town Act, it is.'

'Oi, sod off!' Rachel says.

'What's that, my love?' he asks, running to do Agatha as we start moving slowly forward.

'I said get off.'

'You getting off soon, are ya? Great stuff, my love. There ya go. All done. One dollar please.'

'I didn't agree to that!'

'Eh? You let me do the work! That formed a contract. You shoulda expressed your intent at the outset if you didn't want me to apply my skilled labor to your endeavors.'

'Just pay the guy,' Svetlana says. 'Or he'll call his mates and they'll chuck water at you. They do it in every city.'

'But I didn't ask him,' Rachel says, fishing into a pocket. 'I haven't got a one dollar, only a five,' she says, handing it over.

'Cheers for the tip!' he says with a wink and disappears.

'OI!' Rachel yells, standing up as the road ahead clears and the people behind shout and holler for us to get moving.

Alice jumps over to take the reins as I stop Rachel from jumping out after the guy. 'He just blooming robbed us!'

I can't help but laugh, as I look at the clean patches on Agatha and Christie's flanks.

We get through the intersection and realize most travellers are heading into a vast market, surrounded by buildings and structures of a distinctly Moorish style. Sandstone walls and walkways under elaborate archways. It's packed too, and we soon smell the rich tang of cinnamon, saffron and other spices in the air.

We all look at it longingly, clearly wanting to stop and go in for a look-see and stretch our legs, but I know Rachel is worried about time.

I spot a fellow at a side stall selling oranges and make eye contact to nod at him. 'Hey, how far is it to the north shore?'

'The north shore? What you wanna go there for?'

'Hello!' Svetlana says sweetly, leaning over the side to smile at him. 'We're on a day trip.'

'From where? From the city? You can't reach the north shore and get back in a day!' He adds with a laugh, 'It'll take a day just to get there!'

'Don't say that,' Rachel groans.

'Is there anywhere to stay there?' Svetlana asks.

'What am I? Tourist information?'

'No, you're a handsome orange seller,' Svetlana says, giving him a smile and a wink as he throws his head back and laughs. 'So? Any hotels up there?'

'Yes! There's a few places,' he says, and throws an orange over to Svetlana.

'Aw, just one? What about my friends?' she asks, making him roar with laughter again. 'Tell you what. How about I swing by and say hi when we come back through.'

'I'll never see you again!' he says, throwing more oranges over. 'But best smile all day. By far. What a beauty! What a woman! Marry me!'

Alice clicks her tongue and flicks the reins, and Svetlana blows a kiss to the orange seller as we move on. 'How's that for no dignity,' she says, leaning over to kiss Alice's head as she passes her an orange. 'What's the plan then? I mean. We might as well swing by and have a look at the market if we're staying the night at the north shore.'

'Who said we're staying the night?' Rachel asks.

'Duh. The orange seller,' Svetlana says, passing her an orange. 'Come on, Rach. You look like you need a break.'

'It's Monday tomorrow. I've got work! And I promised to get Alice back by tonight.'

'Please!' Alice says.

'Please!' L parrots.

Rachel huffs and looks ready to say no but she glances at me, and I don't know. We share a smile and a look, and she tuts and shakes her head while laughing. 'I must be crazy. Fine! Quick stop here then we get on, but if we end up in some flea-infested dump I'm blaming you, Svetty.'

'Hey. You'll be in the shitty flea place. I'll be in the five-star resort after seducing the owner.'

We find a carriage park and hand over to a young woman who promises to water Agatha and Christie and rub them down in the shade in exchange for a new house. Which is what Rachel says she'll be able to buy with the *bloody price she just charged us.*

'Why is everyone holding hands?' Alice asks when we reach the edge of the market and see groups going by, all hand in hand in long lines. And others holding bits of string between them, or lengths of material.

'I've heard about this,' Rachel says. 'They recommend you do it, so you don't get separated and lost because it's so big. Right, er, so, John, you take my hand.'

'I wanna hold John's hand,' L says, making us all laugh.

'John's going at the front,' Rachel says. 'Then me, then Alice in the middle. Then Svetty.'

'Why am I at the back?' L asks. 'How to tell someone they're expendable, huh.'

'The strongest always gets the rear guard,' I say, and he grins, his chest swelling.

'I'll bring up the rear,' he tells Rachel, taking Svetlana's hand.

Rachel slips her hand in mine, then takes Alice's as we join up and stand awkwardly for a second before Alice snorts a laugh.

I set off in the lead feeling weird and silly, but it only takes a few steps to realize just how vast the place is, and how full of twisting lanes and confusing alleys and people. 'Good shout,' I say over my shoulder.

'What's that?' Rachel asks, stepping in close behind me with her chin almost touching my shoulder.

'I said good shout. The hands.'

'Thanks. It's not freaking you out then? You know, holding hands with me.'

'Oh, I'm totally seeing it as a romantic gesture,' I tell her with a smile. 'I'm figuring we're gonna start making out any second.'

'Yeah? On a stall or against a wall?' she asks with a laugh, pressing close to be heard over the noise. Her breath blasting over my ear.

I laugh and walk on, but many a true word is spoken in jest and truth be told, it *is* hard not to read anything into it. And I have to remind myself I'm programmed to think like that because of my character development. It's not sexual, and it's not romantic.

'There is no van,' I say, and I guess it came out too loud or Rachel was still close, because I feel her fingers squeezing mine.

'You're fine,' she says, before blurting, 'Oh my god!'

'What?' I ask, immediately tensing.

'Cinnamon buns. Go left. Go left!'

We go left to a stall selling freshly baked cinnamon rolls. The air heavy with the smell of them.

'Is John feeding us all?' Svetlana shouts from the back. 'He's the only one with a hand free.'

'I gotta hand free,' L says.

'You touch your pee pee too much,' Svetty says.

'Yeah. True. I do,' he says with a sigh. 'John, you're gonna have to feed me too.'

We gain space enough to separate and eat warm rolls, and honestly? They smelled great. But the taste? I'm not so sure.

'Whoa! What's that face for?' Rachel asks me. 'Do not tell me you don't like cinnamon buns.'

'Okay,' I say, and don't tell her I don't like cinnamon buns.

'John Croker!' she says as the others tuck in.

'Er, you got a trash can or something?' I ask the stallholder, who pretty much looks like I just offered to crap on his feet.

'Give me that,' Rachel says, plucking it from my hand. 'Trash can! I am so sorry for my friend, he clearly has no taste,' she tells the owner before tucking into my roll.

'Urgh. Gross. How can you do that?' Alice asks.

'What?' Rachel asks.

'Eat something someone's else's mouth touched.'

'It's John,' Rachel says, as though that explains it. 'I'd eat it if it was yours or Svetty's, and maybe L's if he'd washed his hands.'

'Nooo,' Alice says with a grimace, as a picture starts to form of a teenage girl who clearly hates the thought of sex or sharing fluids, even in a purely functional or platonic sense, but still wants to ask a million questions about it all. It makes me wonder what the hell happened to the poor kid in her story, and I realize she still hasn't put the harsh makeup on either. She looks young and fresh, and vulnerable because of it. Which is what makes me realize *why* she wears that makeup.

We join hands and amble on to admire pottery and hats and this and that. Trinkets and baubles. Foods and drink, and we stop again to drink small glasses of hot sweet tea, and it's cool to see it all. I'm glad we did it, but it's also not long before it becomes too packed and busy and chaotic, with too many noises coming from too many directions.

I feel Rachel squeezing my hand and turn back for her to come in close again. 'Svetty wants to go and I'm feeling a bit hemmed in.'

I nod to show I agree and look for a way out. It takes a while, and I realize they don't put exit signs up, to keep you inside in the hope you'll spend more money, or maybe just stay forever and set up a stall selling dates or shoes or whatever.

'Let me just get something for Pat,' Rachel says as we reach the exit, and she darts over to buy a small earthenware pot glazed with a gorgeous pattern. 'She collects them,' she tells us when she comes back, and we head off for the carriage park.

'Why didn't she come today?' Svetlana asks.

'Pat's got a busy life I guess,' Rachel says. 'Husband. Hobbies. And they just got a new place they're doing up.'

'Which is a polite way of saying it's just a job to Pat,' Svetlana says.

'No! It's a polite way of saying I've got nothing else to do,' Rachel says with a smile. 'No, but seriously. Pat's been here a lot longer than me.'

'How long you been here?' I ask as we set off and, true to her word, the girl did a good job because Agatha and Christie are in the shade and have both been watered and rubbed down.

'Three years,' Rachel says. 'I think Pat's been here for seven.'

'You like it?' I ask.

She shrugs. 'I guess so. I mean. I have a job. A little apartment.'

'What's your apartment like?' Svetlana asks. 'Do we all get apartments?'

'Mine's small, but I like it. And no, you stay in your rooms until you find jobs, then you're expected to find your own places, which will probably just be rooms in lodging houses until you can save for a deposit. Unless you join the police, or the militia, or something like that. They help you out if you sign on for a few years.'

'I'm trying to imagine what your apartment looks like,' Svetlana says, as Rachel smiles. 'I bet it's very neat and tidy . . . And I'm gonna say you've got a minimalist thing going on.'

'Totally!' Rachel says, turning to smile and nod at her. 'How did you work that out?'

'I don't know. You just strike me as that sort. Hey, maybe I have a secret skill like Croker! I could be an interior designer. No but guys, if we get jobs maybe we could rent a place together? I'd hate to live with some filthy slob. Even L is super clean. Have you seen his room? His bed is made to perfection.'

'Hey. I'm telling you. Growing up on the Killer Sun gives you discipline,' L says, as I notice Alice has gone quiet.

'And we could take turns babysitting Alice so she doesn't get in trouble,' Svetlana adds, noticing the same thing as Alice's face lights up. 'L can teach her how to be neat.'

'I am neat!'

'I bet you are so not neat,' Svetlana says with a laugh. 'We'll get a place in Rachel's block and bug the shit out of her every day.'

'Oh god,' Rachel says with a groan, playing her part in the joke as we get free of the market area and pass along streets of varying fantasy-world themes. Olde worlde of various fashions mostly, and I gain a sense that this city seems as big as ours. Which makes me realize I don't know what ours is called.

'It's just called the city,' Rachel says when I ask her.

'Least original name ever,' Alice says. 'Could you live here though? In Middle Earth?'

'Nope. Not a chance,' Rachel says as we pass into a distinctly different area. 'Actually, scrap that. I could live here,' she says, as we fall to silence in awe.

White marble buildings with smooth lines and clean curves, flecked with grey, and with roses and vines climbing over the grand houses. Each one set within grounds of willow trees and flowers, with streams and babbling brooks and curved wooden bridges.

Rachel brings the carriage to a stop next to a set of long marble steps leading to columns at the top, the sides bordered by dramatic gardens filled with shaped hedges.

'I know we're on a schedule, but honestly, I need to see the top,' Rachel says, putting the brake on and dropping out. Alice goes with her, swiftly followed by the rest of us figuring what the hell, and we climb the beautiful steps, getting higher with each one and marvelling at the serenity of the place.

We reach the top to see the columns lead to an open-sided marble pagoda with an ornately carved round roof. Benches inside with a few people doing the same as us and seeing the sights. Courting couples mostly, holding hands and snatching kisses.

'Way too romantic for me,' Alice says.

'Not my bag either,' Svetlana says. 'It's pretty, but give me champagne in a piano bar any day.'

'Urgh. Not that either,' Alice says.

'What's your romantic place then?' Svetlana asks her.

'I don't have one!'

'Everyone has one,' Svetlana says. 'And this is clearly Rachel's.'

Rachel smiles at them but doesn't deny it. She seems happy too, with a look of serene awe on her face and that strand of loose hair hanging down. We fall silent. Enjoying the peace until Rachel sighs.

'Come on then. We need to change horses again.'

WE HEAD NORTH and hit the edge of the city area, passing into a wide unmade track bordered by stone and wooden buildings. Horses tethered to posts and men and women in furs and high, laced boots. We spot long, low thatched buildings just beyond the main road, evocative of Scandinavian culture. Vikings and whatnot.

We aim for a set of sprawling corrals and pens near the end with a big sign over the top.

YOUNG OLAF'S
LIVERY YARD & HORSE EXCHANGE

A MAN GREETS US WARMLY. Calf-length laced boots and thick leggings. A leather waistcoat over a thick-weave shirt. 'Got a twenty-minute wait,' he says, nodding at the people ahead of us. 'Tavern's just there, or you can wait in the carriage.'

'I really need a pee,' Alice says, as Svetlana says the same and Rachel nods and says she can go.

'The Clever Clogs,' I say, with a laugh at the name on the sign outside the tavern.

'Is that from another movie?' Svetlana asks.

'Video game first, then a TV series,' I reply, wondering how I knew that.

'*The Witcher*,' Rachel says.

'Oh. I've heard of it. Never saw it though,' Svetlana says. 'Benjamin preferred these old black and white French movies.'

'Oh god. I can't think of anything worse,' Rachel says.

'No, they were pretty shit actually,' Svetlana says. 'This one movie this woman just smoked the whole time in a kitchen, then this guy walks in, and she says *non*, and he goes out. That was it. God it was so boring.'

We head inside to bare wooden tables and a stone floor. Stone walls and low ceilings. A few people here and there. We pass through to the toilets, L and I going into the men's, with a weird shift from a quasi-medieval inn to modern restrooms with modern plumbing and white subway tiles and ceramic sinks.

'Dude,' L says, blinking at the change.

'Yeah, right,' I say, heading to a urinal with L adhering to the unspoken social rule of not using the one immediately next to me, but the one after that.

'Great day though, man,' he says as we pee. 'I think it's helping too. You know what I mean? Like seeing everything is giving me perspective. Does that make sense?'

I nod because it does make sense.

'Great chat, Croker.'

'Sorry,' I say, and we chuckle and pee and wash our hands before heading back out.

'I've ordered some drinks,' Rachel says, as we find the table, Svetlana and Alice coming out of the toilets a moment later.

'So I was thinking,' Alice says, once we've gotten the drinks. 'What about the science fiction people like L?'

'What about them?' Rachel asks.

'So, the fantasy people have Middle Earth, and the Western people have that cowboy town, and the city has the Victorian area and whatever. But what about L?'

'They're still building the giant spaceship for them to all live on,' Rachel says.

'Wait. What? Seriously?' L asks.

'No! Of course not. They just get lumped in with everyone else. It's a thing that gets people riled up actually, with all the sci-fi people demanding their own land, but as everyone else points out, sci-fi is massive and covers everything from zombies to space operas. I think science fiction is *the* biggest genre in fiction now or something crazy like that. Look at it this way. Tolkien wrote *Lord of the Rings*, right? Like way back, so that created the need for Middle Earth, and Western novels were a massive genre all through the nineteen hundreds, so they got their own space. But with so many people coming in, and so many niche genres, I mean, how do you accommodate everyone? Do we have an apocalypse zone? Dinosaur land? Time Travel town? What about Steampunk? We've got hundreds of those characters in the city.'

'We've got a guy in therapy who was in a historical novel with vampires and orgies,' Alice says.

'Oh god. No more sex talk, please!' Rachel says.

'No! I just meant, where does he fit in?' Alice asks.

'Maybe there's an orgy group in the city,' Svetlana says. 'Erotica was a big genre.'

'I'm gonna go sit on my own,' Rachel says, standing up as Svetlana grabs her wrist.

'I'm sorry. No sex talk. You're very prudish. I get it.'

'I'm not prudish! I just don't want to, you know.'

'Okay, okay,' Svetlana says.

'So I have a question,' L says, as Rachel groans and sags.

'No seriously. What about my name? I can't just be L132, can I? Is that allowed? I mean, that's not a name.'

'Anyone can change their name when they arrive. It happens all the time,' Rachel says. 'Some find it a good way to create a new identity for themselves.'

L nods and sits back, clearly giving it some thought as we all look at him.

'What would you like?' Alice asks.

L shrugs. 'Call me some names and see what fits.'

'Okay, twat,' Alice says, making us all laugh as L gives her a high five. 'Alright, hang on. Hey, Lee!' she says in mock greeting.

'No!' Svetlana says. 'Liam, great to see you.'

'No, he's not a Liam,' Rachel says.

'Does it have to begin with L?' L asks.

'You can have anything,' Rachel says.

'Susan?' Alice asks. 'Mary?'

'Bubba?' Svetlana says.

'Roger?' Alice asks.

'Fortunes?' Another voice comes from the side, and we all turn to see an old woman in a black headscarf smiling at us with crooked teeth and a bent nose. 'Fortunes?' she asks in a sing-song voice, smiling and nodding. 'I tell fortunes for a small coin.'

'Tell us what his name is,' Alice says, nodding at L as we all laugh.

'A small coin first, young lady,' the old woman says, as Alice digs into a pocket.

'That's literally my last money.'

'Don't give it to her then,' Rachel says.

'L needs a name!' Alice says, handing it over and I watch as it disappears very quickly into the folds of the woman's cloak before she reaches out to touch L's hand.

'I can't give you a name my son, but I can say a great adventure awaits you!'

'Oh god, such baloney,' Rachel says. 'What's mine? Finding true love by any chance?'

'Would you know it if you found it?' the old woman snaps, with a sting to her words that makes Rachel flinch. 'Or will you keep running?'

'Hey! Play nice,' Svetlana says. 'I don't have a coin, but I want my fortune.'

'And I want dinner,' the old woman says. 'But without coin we both go without.'

'Rach, you got another coin?' Svetlana asks.

'I'm not giving her a coin after what she said!'

'Just give me a coin. I'll pay you back when we get money,' Svetlana says.

Rachel fishes into a pocket to dump a few on the table, and the old woman's hand shoots out to take the highest value.

'You don't hang around, do you,' Rachel says, as the old woman leans over to touch Svetlana's hand.

'And a great adventure awaits you too!'

'Seriously?' Rachel asks.

'But beware. Some will wish to take your beauty from you. Red hair. Dark eyes. Beware.'

'Ooh, that's good,' Svetlana says with a shiver.

'It's baloney,' Rachel says, as the old woman snatches another coin and places her hand over Alice's. 'Oi,' Rachel says, but Svetlana waves her to be quiet.

'Oh,' the old woman says, her eyes twinkling at Alice.

'Let me guess? A great adventure?' Rachel asks.

'A very great adventure,' the old woman whispers. 'You have power, young one. And a secret to share. A very deep secret.'

'Get off!' Alice says, pulling her hand away with a laugh, while also clearly uncomfortable.

'Okay, thank you, you've had enough coins,' Rachel says, as the old woman snatches another and reaches for me. 'No! Get off him!' Rachel snaps, all trace of humor gone. 'John, don't listen to anything she says! I said get off him!'

But the old woman grabs my hand and squeezes with hidden strength as her eyes grow wide. 'The one,' she whispers. 'The way. The one.'

'What?' I ask.

'I said don't listen!' Rachel says, trying to push the old woman off as we all get to our feet.

'What's going on?' the barkeep demands, striding over.

'Get this old woman off him!' Rachel orders.

'The one,' the old woman whispers at me. 'Seek it. Seek it, John! Seek the way.'

'L! Help me get her off,' Rachel says, as L grabs the woman to pull her away. 'That's the worst thing ever for a John! We're going right now.'

The old woman blinks at me, her hand outstretched, her eyes fixed and staring. Then she seems to shiver and shake it off, and pulls free of L. 'One steak pie and chips please, Gary,' she orders in a normal voice and toddles off as the barkeep nods happily.

'See! She's not real,' Rachel says, pulling me outside. 'John, I mean it. Don't let that sink in.'

'Why did she say that?' Alice asks.

'Cos she's a fraudster!' Rachel says. 'She's not even a fortune teller. Superman can't fly. Remember?'

'But she said seek it,' Svetlana says. 'Like the old man with the big moustache.'

'Yeah! She did,' L says.

'No! No no no,' Rachel says. 'Guys, stop. You don't know how damaging that is to someone predisposed to seeking a conspiracy. Seriously. It was garbage. I mean it! Alice, go and get the carriage. L and Svetlana will go with you,' Rachel says, waiting for them to leave before she turns on me. 'Now listen. You have done so well, John.'

I frown at her words.

'I'm not patronizing you. But you have done well. And I'm proud of you. Not just as your genre rep but as your friend, okay? But that was bollocks. Utter complete poo. Nothing she said was real. Don't let it take root. Come on. Nod at me. Say something.'

'Okay.'

'Okay? Okay what?'

'It's cool.'

She studies me for a long second and I try hard not to look at the strand of hair hanging down or become too aware of her hands on my arms holding me still.

'There is no van,' I say.

She nods and looks into my eyes. 'There is no van,' she tells me. 'You okay? I mean, we can go back to the city if you want.'

'No. I want to see the north shore.'

'What for?' she asks with a worried look. 'John, there are no docks.'

'I know. You said. But if you set out to do a thing you should do it. Besides, I'm having a great day and I think it's good for Alice.'

She stares at me and frowns gently.

'But are you okay?' I ask. 'She seemed to hit a nerve.'

'Nah. I just hate that stuff,' she says and turns away, but this time I reach out and take her arm and she turns back in surprise.

'You sure?' I ask.

She smiles and I see some of the tension leaving her eyes. 'I'm sure, but thank you for asking. That's nice of you.' She pats my hand as the carriage comes into view. 'Right then, mister. Last stretch to the north shore, and honestly, if we do end up in a flea-infested dump, I'm blaming you too.'

I smile and walk on with her, glad she's okay, and I take her advice and try to ignore what the old woman said. She's just someone in a costume saying random mysterious things to pay for her dinner and ale.

It doesn't mean anything.

There is no van.

But then why did she say *seek it?* Seek what? The way? What way? And why did she tell Alice she had a secret? And why did she ask Rachel if she'll keep running? Running from what?

But then she probably heard us earlier and figured Rachel doesn't like sex talk, which makes it an easy assumption. That's how fraudsters work. They spot an insecurity and exploit it.

Alice wears black and is a goth. She must have a secret.

L is a young man eager to please. He must be on an adventure.

Svetlana is beautiful. Someone must be jealous.

Rachel is prudish. She must run from love.

And me?

What am I?

What did she see?

She saw a brooding man, and I bet she's said that same thing to every Wick, Reacher, Bond and Bourne that ever went into that tavern.

We get into carriage and head off and I use reason to dismiss any lingering notions of the old woman's words.

But still.

Two people now told me to seek it.

But seek what?

CHAPTER TWENTY

We stay on the main track, heading north.

It gets colder too. I don't know how, seeing as we're on the same landmass within the same season, but I figure maybe we're passing into a micro-climate.

The geography and landscape changes, with heathland broken by rocky outcroppings and small hills of slate and stone. The land undulates. Rising and falling with an ever-increasing sense of true wilderness, which is only magnified when we don't see anyone else for a few hours.

It's still nice, and I sit up the front with Alice while the others stay covered and warm in the back, dozing lightly.

'You want to sleep?' I ask Alice.

'I'm good,' she says, handling the reins like she's been doing it her whole life. I think about what the old lady said, and Nietzsche and Freud before that, and how this might be the right time to broach a question about her past.

Except I don't. Not because she put invisible rules on me, but because the kid has obviously been through some bad times, and she needs to process that at her own pace, without pressure from me.

Plus, who the hell am I to try and help with such a thing? I'm a paranoid guy predisposed to mental health issues who is trained to kill other people.

'You're not worried, are you?' Alice asks, breaking my thoughts as I look at her. 'About the fortune teller. She was full of shit.'

I shake my head and we roll on, ever closer to the north shore.

'I mean. We've all got secrets,' Alice adds a few moments later.

I don't say anything. I watch the world go by and look at our horses, Stephen and King, who I think are both girl horses. But whatever.

'I really like Rachel,' Alice announces a bit later.

I nod to show I agree, and we keep going.

'And Svetty's so pretty.'

I nod again as Alice shoots me a look.

'And L's great fun. But Rachel, though. She's lovely.' She shoots me another look. I look back at her, wondering what her point is. She just laughs and we drive on. 'Do you remember your mom or dad?' she asks me.

'Nope,' I say. Realizing I don't know their names or anything about them. 'You?'

She shrugs. 'Kinda.'

A flash of something on her face. I don't press it.

'You said skills are teachable.'

I nod again.

'Can you teach me how to fight?'

I think about it for a second and try and understand *how* I would do that, or where I would start from.

'For defense,' she says, taking my silence as reluctance.

'Sure,' I say.

She grins at me. 'Can I ask a question? Have you ever killed anyone?'

'In my story? Yes.'

'How many?'

I shrug. 'Couple of dozen maybe.'

'Oh my god, seriously? What, with guns or by hand?'

'Both. But it's not real. I mean. No, Enders therapy says to us it is real, so it did happen, but I tell myself they weren't real people.'

She nods. Getting what I mean.

'You?' I ask.

'Have I killed someone?' she asks with a smile. 'No. Wish I had though,' she adds in a quieter voice.

It hangs in the air, but I don't pull the thread. We head north, and the air gets colder still.

'You know what, I'm freezing!' Alice says. 'Can you drive?'

I take over and she gets into the back to snuggle under the blankets on the same side as Rachel and Svetty, the three of them shoving closer to share body heat as L comes up front with me.

'You're not cold?' I ask, seeing he's still in his normal clothes.

He shakes his head. 'I like it. Oh hey, you smell that? That's the ocean.'

'How do you know that?' I ask, thinking he lived on spaceships.

'We went to worlds, man. Like lots of worlds, and I don't know. I just know that smell.'

I get it a few moments later, the scent of salt water growing stronger as we crest a long sloping hill to see the ocean ahead of us beyond more heathland and rocky scree.

'There it is,' L says. 'The north shore.'

'Are we there?' Alice asks from the back. 'I would get up but it's way too cold.'

'Not yet,' I say, and we drive down the other side of the hill for a long time as the track meanders and turns and snakes through the heathland and the ocean grows closer.

Then we hit the coast road and follow that as it rises with the shape of the land, growing steadily higher with the wind starting to bite, and I look out over the white chalk cliffs to the grey ocean and the white-topped waves.

We rise for a while, and I hear the others stir in the back, waking up and shifting position to see out. None of us talk, but then as cold as it is, the view is still breathtaking.

Especially when we reach the top of the hill and I ease back to stop the carriage, and there we sit. With the freezing wind blowing over us and nothing to see other than grassy heathland right up to the cliff edge. An unbroken line of it as far as I can see in both directions.

No docks.

No secrets.

No ships.

There is no van.

'We good for a moment?' I ask.

'Sure. Take your time,' Rachel says. I put the brake on and drop out onto the track. Patting Stephen's flank, feeling the warmth of her body. I go up front and smooth her nose. She seems to like it.

Then I head off the track onto the grassy heathland and keep walking to the edge of the cliff. Looking left. Looking right. Looking out to sea.

Nothing but waves.

Nothing but land.

Nothing anywhere.

I don't know what that means.

But I know it means nothing.

We are not characters now though, Mr Croker. We have life. We have existence. The question is, what will you do with yours?

I think about what Nietzsche said, and the robbery earlier and the things that have happened since I arrived here. Griff, the invisible man. The weird Fat George guy. The fight with Bond 12, and I know my mind is searching for a way to link everything so I can go *ah, that's the plot.*

Except there is no plot to life. No reason. We exist. End of . . . And so I come to a stop at the edge of the cliff and, like a child facing its life ahead, I wonder what I will be, and somehow, from everything, I think maybe the one thing I really need to be is kind.

Like Rachel was kind to me by doing this. And like L backed me up twice when he didn't have to. How Alice asked me if I was okay and looked like she really meant it. And how Svetty takes the time to explain things to Alice, to challenge her views without confrontation – and all of those things make me think of friendship, and how I forced a bond with Ibrahim and tried to latch on to people.

It makes me feel ashamed how I was in my story, and even in that wind my cheeks burn from thinking about it, and how I saw romantic gestures in a mere touch.

Don't be that guy.

Be a kind guy.

Be a thoughtful guy.

That's all. Just that. Go home to the city and find a job and accept what is.

I take a deep breath and let it go, and with it the need to find plot and reason, because Rachel was right. There are no docks and there is no van, and when I turn to go I startle at seeing them all a few feet behind me. Watching me closely.

'Dude, we thought you might jump,' L says. Alice whacks his arm.

'Don't tell him that!'

'What? We all thought it,' L says, as I smile and head back to them.

'Thank you,' I say. 'Come on, you look frozen. There's a place down the bottom of the cliff I saw. We can try there.'

'Someone's taking charge,' Svetlana says with a wink, or at least she tries to while her teeth chatter.

'Sorry. I meant it as a suggestion,' I say to Rachel.

'No, it's cool. It suits you,' she says with a smile, as her eyes find mine and she shivers under the blanket wrapped around her body. 'You're not cold?'

'I'm freezing!'

She laughs and stretches an arm out for me to get under her blanket. Svetlana does the same on the other side and I walk into the embrace, arms and blankets wrapping around me, then Alice squeezes in, and L, and it's weird and awkward and bizarre and literally impossible to walk all huddled together.

But it's also the nicest thing I think I have ever done, and we laugh all the way back to the carriage and set off down the hill to find the hotel.

CHAPTER TWENTY-ONE

We reach the hotel.

The once white walls now weathered and worn.

The once nice gardens now battered and torn.

A sign outside all broken and shorn.

THE OVERLOOK HOTEL
NORTH SHORE'S FINEST

'OKAY,' Rachel says slowly as we take in the once obviously grand, but now very rundown building. 'So? Anyone gonna say it?'

'What?' Svetlana asks.

'The Overlook Hotel,' Rachel says.

'What about it?' Svetlana asks.

'Dear god, did you ever read a book?' Rachel asks her.

'Nope. But I went to lots of parties and flew on private jets,' Svetlana replies with a sweet smile.

'It's from a famous story,' I tell the others.

'Everything here is from a famous story,' Alice says, as Rachel shrugs as though she has a point.

'And a movie,' I add. *The Shining?*

'All work and no play makes Jack a dull boy?' Rachel asks, to more blank looks. 'Oh god. Oh no. Seriously, we're not staying here,' she adds in alarm.

'Why?' I ask.

'Cos of that scene. The axe. The door. *Here's Johnny!* And, you know, you're called John.'

'I don't have an axe.'

'They'll probably have an axe in there.'

'Fine. I'll borrow their axe when I go mad.'

'Hey guys. FYI, we don't use the M.A.D. word here,' Alice says, mimicking Trixie or Bella's Californian drawl. 'Er, but seriously. I'm very cold and there's literally no other buildings anywhere.'

'Fine,' Rachel says. 'But I'm sleeping with John.'

'Whoa. Didn't need to know,' Alice says, as Svetty and L burst out laughing.

'Do I get a say in this?' I ask.

'No! I didn't mean *that.* I meant cos it's creepy as hell. Unless John turns into Johnny and does the door-chopping thing with the axe. Then I'm sleeping in the carriage . . . Okay, stop laughing! I said *not* like that. Don't make it weird.'

'You said it,' Svetlana says, as we head up the steps and through the door into a deserted, but thankfully much warmer interior. Albeit a very dated one, with a deep red carpet threaded with thick white lines, leading to a set of stairs to the reception and concierge desk, then dual stairs going up either side. Dark, stone-colored streaked marble everywhere, with golden lamps and dark wood side tables and dark leather chairs. All of it worn, faded, old – and very empty.

'Nobody home,' Rachel says quietly.

'The lights are on,' I say. 'And the heating is obviously working.'

We walk silently over the deep carpet, looking for staff or other guests and seeing neither. Then we reach the first flight of stairs and go up, our feet echoing under the vaulted roof until we reach the small concierge desk.

'Hello!' Rachel calls, her voice going unanswered as we all turn to look across the lobby to the doors we came in through. 'We can't leave the horses in that wind,' she adds.

'The horses have been taken to our stable, madam,' a voice says from behind, making us all yelp as we turn to see a guy with lacquered hair and a lacquered moustache standing behind the desk in a formal suit with a bow tie.

'Where did you come from?' Rachel asks, her hand on her chest.

'I was here,' he says in a strong accent, as I clock his name badge reads *M Gustave*.

'Okay. Er, Mr or Monsieur er, Gustave?' Rachel asks. The man smiles politely, but doesn't say which. 'Are you open?'

He looks left then right then back at Rachel. 'Oui.'

'Only it's very empty and we didn't know because . . .' Rachel starts to say, as Svetlana steps forward with her sweet smile.

'Five rooms please for one night.'

'I can't afford five rooms!' Rachel whispers.

'I thought you said this was on expenses,' Svetlana asks her.

'Lunch in the Village was on expenses. This isn't!'

'Okay. Just hang on,' Svetlana tells the concierge, then gathers us into a group. 'Rach! I can't believe you paid for all this.'

'I thought it would help you,' Rachel says with a stricken look. 'And I really wanted a day out,' she adds, looking more than a little embarrassed. 'No. It's fine. I've really enjoyed it, and I've saved a bit, but I didn't expect it to be an overnight thing in a big hotel.'

'Can't you claim it back?' Svetlana asks.

Rachel shakes her head. 'Everything's really tight now because of the number of people coming in. We're only meant to give you five days' basic input.'

'So this is your day off?' Alice asks.

Rachel nods. 'But honestly, it's good for you all to see it. I mean, this is what they *should* be doing with new arrivals, so they can see where they are.'

'Okay,' Svetlana says. 'We'll circle back to that. When do we get money?'

'Monday. You get your first allowance a week after arriving. It's not a lot though. I mean, enough for food, and then you get sent over to the employment office and they find you work.'

'Right. Monday. We all chip in and pay Rachel back. Agreed,' Svetlana says.

'Yes, ma'am,' L says.

'Of course,' I say.

'I get my allowance Monday too,' Alice says.

'Guys, no. That's not fair,' Rachel says.

'It's fine. We'll get John to tip a carriage over and rob someone on the way back,' Svetlana says. 'Right. Monsieur Gustave. We want a room each, with dinner and breakfast, and we need it cheap.'

'Oui, madam. But we do not have five rooms available.'

'Don't even try it. This place is deserted,' Svetlana says, as we all look at the concierge with his neat little moustache, and the way he smiles and looks past us to the empty doors that suddenly fill with people rushing through in weird livery uniforms with golden epaulettes shaped like wings, swigging from bottles and tankards.

'It is the Fiction Land Postal Service Annual Buffet,' M Gustave says.

'Up the Fiction Land Postal Service Annual Buffet!' someone in the big party shouts, as the others all cheer.

'Bugger. What are the chances of us being here on the same night as the Fiction Land Postal Service Annual Buffet?' Svetlana asks.

'Oui,' M Gustave says, with a polite shrug.

'What ho!' a handsome man calls as he bounds up the stairs. 'Posties? Where are your uniforms? We said mufti commences *after* checking in.'

'We're not posties,' Rachel says.

'Not posties!' the man says, as though such a thing cannot be true.

'They are not posties,' M Gustave says.

'But this is the night of the Fiction Land Postal Service Annual Buffet.'

'We didn't know,' Rachel says.

'You didn't know! By Jove. What a hoot! Hey, chaps. These folk aren't posties!' he calls down the stairs to the boozing, winged-epaulette-wearing mass of postal workers.

'Say what!'

'Not posties?'

'Why are they here?'

'Don't they know it's the Fiction Land Postal Service Annual Buffet?'

'Oh god. Hang on!' Alice says, as they all look at her. 'Is it the Fiction Land Postal Service Annual Buffet *tonight*?'

'Yes!' come the many chorused replies.

'Damn it!' Alice tells us. 'It's the Fiction Land Postal Service Annual Buffet *tonight*, and we're not posties!'

'I think we've booked all the rooms,' the postal man says.

'Oui. They have booked all the rooms,' M Gustave says.

'I think they've booked all the rooms,' Alice tells us.

'Oui,' M Gustave says.

'Yes!' the postal man says.

'Oh, I don't know,' Svetlana says with a slow smile at the postal man. 'I'm sure this handsome chap can help us out. In charge are you, by any chance?'

He smiles back with a twinkle in his eye and takes her hand in his to gently peck as he bows. 'At your service, madam. I'm Moist.'

'Me too.'

'Svetty!' Rachel says, as Alice bursts out laughing while grimacing and pulling a face at the same time.

Moist laughs and winks. 'Moist von Wiplig. Head of the Fiction Land Postal Service.'

'Is it your annual conference tonight by any chance?' Alice asks with a mock frown. 'What's it called again?'

Moist smiles in a way that shows he gets the joke, as his over-the-top persona eases back. 'I'm sure we can sort something out,' he says in a normal voice. 'From the city? What is it? Day out?'

'Something like that,' I say.

He looks at me as though recognizing something. 'I needed to be sure, too,' he says. 'That it's an island and there's no way off. And trust me. There isn't. That's why I joined this lot. I figured if anyone knew, they would.'

'Nothing then?' I ask. Figuring I should be suspicious at the fast connection he just made, but then I'm starting to realize Fiction Land is a very strange place full of very strange people.

He shakes his head. 'Nothing out there. But for what it's worth,' he adds in a conciliatory tone. 'I ended up quite liking my job. Anyway. Gustave! Jiggle things about, would you?'

'Hey. I'm L,' L says, holding his hand out. 'So er, John here used to be a parcel delivery guy and I was in charge of the mail run for my unit on the Killer Sun if it helps.'

'That'll do,' Moist says with a wink, then pulls back to throw his hands in the air. 'Splendid!' he calls, turning with a flourish to the other posties gathered in the lobby. 'I stand corrected! These other guests are new arrivals to Fiction Land, and guess what? They were posties!'

A roar goes up with cheering and whistles, as we smile and share looks before being swamped by posties swarming up to pass bottles and jugs into our hands.

'When in Rome,' Rachel says with a shrug, and we're swept along. Sipping booze and chatting to animated posties about routes and the best carts and sacks and how they're all *like totally underpaid* and how the whole of Fiction Land would grind to a halt if it wasn't for them.

But it's cool and they take us with them into the dining room to share their buffet and we join the posties, plucking plunder from platters to load on our plates as we find a table and enjoy the surreal experience.

And although it's weird and bizarre, it's no more weird and bizarre than waking up in a world inhabited by characters from unfinished books, or a day spent in a horse-drawn carriage with a stormtrooper rip-off, an angsty Alice, a sleepy Svetlana, and a reserved and reticent Rachel, going through Western World whorehouses where women search for lost husbands, or into the many muddled tropes of Middle Earth, a maze of a market, houses made of marble and places where old women earn meals by telling fortunes.

Nor is it as weird and bizarre as navigating to the north shore with a need to negate the nerves inside, only to find nothing but a cold north wind blowing on a neglected hotel nestled into the shoreline where we meet normally punctilious posties already pickled who permit us to pilfer and pinch their provisions.

And so, and now, after all of that, such a thing as this seems entirely normal, and so, and now, angsty Alice becomes amused and animated with mirth and joy, and L lessens the loneliness by leaning back and forth to laugh and loosens his tongue with jokes and japes, while Svetty becomes sensual and somewhat saucy by telling tales of her sordid story.

And then there's Rachel. Somewhat reserved and somewhat reticent, but clearly rebellious and perhaps a touch reckless in her attempts to reduce the receptors in my brain that seek plot by showing the reality of the north shore.

'I'm ravenous,' she says when she spots me watching her eat.

'You look relaxed,' I say.

She smiles. 'It's nice to rejoice in something,' she says with a laugh.

'What are we rejoicing in?'

'I'm just having a nice day. Even if we were robbed.'

'We weren't robbed. We rebuffed the robbery.'

'No. *You* rebuffed the robbery while we remained rooted in fear. Apart from L. And Alice who also tried to join in. And Svetty. Actually, I didn't even remain rooted in fear while you rebuffed the robbery by stopping them running in.'

'That's rather cool,' I say.

'It is, rather,' she replies with a twinkle in her eyes, then shifts a bit closer to talk more quietly over the music playing from somewhere and the general hubbub of many posties having a party. 'Why don't you ever ask?'

'Ask what?'

She frowns softly and searches my eyes. 'I thought it was arrogance at first, then I realized you're not arrogant at all, so I thought maybe you're so locked into your own plight that you couldn't think about anyone else.'

I take my turn to frown. Not getting what she means.

'It's impossible to read you sometimes. But I don't know. I think maybe you're content to wait and let the person tell you.'

I think I know what she means. 'I think I know what you mean,' I say. 'You mean your story.'

She frowns and smiles back at me with silent messages and expressions that carry meaning without words, and I remind myself they're not romantic gestures.

'It's weird, because I honestly think I could tell you and you'd not blink an eye,' she says.

'You won't know unless you try.'

She purses her lips with almost-mock thought, then pulls back a little. 'Not yet. But only because a great man once said *if you set out to do a thing you should do it*. And I don't think I'm ready. I mean, I might get halfway then stop. You know?'

I don't know, but I nod as though I do know.

'Yeah. You know,' she says with a smile. 'And besides, like you also said, we're having a great day, so why ruin it with *bloody* awful stories.'

A flash in her eye. Something dark and nasty. I see it and she knows I see it. But again, I don't pull the thread but leave it hanging until she draws it back and nods at me, then lays her hand on mine. 'Feels like the tables have turned and you're helping me through my issues now,' she adds with a laugh.

'You said we're friends,' I say, as she cocks her head over. 'And anyway,' I add with suspicious narrowing of my eyes as I take her hand in mine, *'I can see your secrets for a small coin.'*

She laughs, and the wine flows and the jokes roll around the table as we eat and drink and become merry until the night grows late, and our early start begins to show in our eyes and our yawns.

'Come on. I need sleep,' Rachel says, and although we're having a grand time, we admit that we too need sleep, and so we bid our new friends a good evening with many promises of free deliveries, and *if you ever need a postie the whole service is at your back*. Which is all very nice.

Sadly, Gustave isn't at the desk when we get back to it, so we look around and call out, then startle in fright when we realize he's right behind us again.

'How do you bloody do that?' Rachel asks, but he doesn't explain. Instead, he hands us three sets of keys.

'I'm afraid it is the best I can do, and they are small rooms on the top floor with shared bathrooms. We used them for staff.'

We take them in good spirits, glad at least of a warm dry place to sleep.

'Okay, so,' a rather drunk Svetlana says as she holds the keys. 'One for the boys,' she says, handing me a key. 'One for the girls,' she adds, holding one up. 'And one for the boss.' She hands the last one to Rachel.

'I would argue and say we should draw straws or something but honestly? I'm too tired and way too drunk,' Rachel says, as we start heading up the stairs. 'But if anyone does want a room, I'm happy to share.'

'With John by any chance?' Alice asks, and we all snort and laugh and giggle while Rachel overplays her outrage and blushes.

We reach the top floor, an area clearly reserved for staff with plain painted walls and narrower corridors.

A series of doors on the right. A bathroom at the end. Rows of windows on the left overlooking the sea. A nearly full moon bathing the ocean and the cliff and land in silvery light.

'Hey, what was that?' L asks, squinting at the windows.

'What?' Rachel asks, as Svetlana reaches the first door and misses putting the key in the lock by several inches.

'Wow. I am way more drunkener than I was thinking I was,' she says, trying and missing again.

'Man. I'm as bad as her,' L says, laughing at Svetty. 'Thought I saw lights.'

'Lights?' Rachel asks, turning to the windows as we all lurch closer, Alice bumping her nose against the frame with a yelp. 'That's not a light. That's the moon!'

'I meant down there,' L says, jabbing lower.

'How can we have a moon?' I ask, trying to think about spinning planets and the sun and not being real while also being really quite drunk.

Then I see it. A flash of light out to sea. Quick and gone in an instant.

'You see it!' L says.

'Yeah, I see it,' I say.

'I didn't see a thing,' Rachel says.

'I can't even see this stupid lock,' Svetlana says, still jabbing the key into the door.

'There was a light,' L says.

'There was,' I add. 'In the sea.'

'In the sea? Who'd want to be in the sea? It's too cold,' Rachel says with a shiver.

'Must be a boat,' L says.

'There are no boats,' I say, as the light flashes again. Small and fast, but distinct.

'Ooh, I saw it!' Rachel says. 'Well spotted, L! You've got good eyes.'

'They had us on guard duty *a lot*,' L says. 'And they'd test you to see if you saw things, and you'd get latrine duty if you missed it, or blammoed with a laser if it was something big.'

'What do you think it was?' I ask.

'Ha! Got it!' Svetlana says, as the door swings in and she falls through, with Alice and L bursting out laughing and rushing to help her.

'John! Nooo,' Rachel says, grabbing my arm and laughing.

'You think there's something out there?' I ask, feeling her pulling my arm.

'Yeah. Your van,' she says in a way that makes me smile and she pulls me into her with a gentle bump of drunken bodies. 'It'll be a buoy probably. You know. Rocks. Ships. Danger.'

'There's no ships to warn about rocks.'

'I dunno! Maybe someone took a boat out once and it smashed on rocks and they put a light on it to warn other people. I mean . . . we eat fish, and they must get fish from the sea.'

I realize she's right and feel a touch of shame at my brain lighting up with the prospect of a mystery, as the door to Svetty and Alice's room closes with the sound of L and the other two laughing inside, leaving us alone in the dark corridor and the moon bathing half Rachel's face in silver light. Giving depth and shadows to the contours of her nose and jaw and I look at that strand of hair hanging down and fight the urge to tuck it behind her ear.

She lifts my hand and I frown as she aims it to the side of her head to gently brush the strand, and my finger moves out to help tuck it behind her ear. My fingertip grazing the skin of her forehead. Her eyes staring into mine. I keep my hand there. Lightly. Gently. Softly. Her hands stays on mine. Not pulling it away, but then nor does she pull back, and we stay there for a while. Just that. Nothing more. I don't try and kiss her. I don't move a muscle other than my fingertips brushing the warm, dry skin of her cheek.

'I did something bad,' she whispers. 'In my story. And I'm an Ender like you. So to me it was real.'

I stay there. I don't talk. But my heart beats harder than in any fight I've ever had.

'Can I tell you one day?'

I dip my head a fraction.

'And you won't judge me?'

I remember what Freud said about how we impose rules on each other and set boundaries and expectations, and how we are often crushed or disappointed when the other person doesn't abide by our needs and wants.

'I don't know what it is,' I say, because I want to be honest and real, and I think kindness comes from being honest and not lying.

She nods. Seeming to understand what I mean.

'But I will listen,' I add.

She stares at me, then reaches in and stretches up to kiss my cheek. 'Thank you, John. I really mean that.'

She pulls back and we share expressions without words for another few seconds until she smiles. 'And honestly. No smashing doors down with an axe.'

She turns away as Svetty and Alice's door opens with L coming out laughing hard. 'I saw boobs! Best day ever,' he says as the other two roar with laughter, then he clocks us looking and throws his hands up. 'They were mine! My top rode up when we fell over the bed. Dude. I'm not a pervert.'

'He is! He touches his pee pee,' Svetty calls, setting us all off as Rachel pulls back, her hand sliding from mine, and I glance to the window and the silvery world outside, seeing no light because there is no van.

CHAPTER TWENTY-TWO

Monday morning.

THE DIFFERENCE in our ages shows at breakfast, with Alice and L full of energy, while Svetty, Rachel and I drink coffee and eat croissants with nothing more than grunts.

'And Moist said if I joined the postal service and did two years at ground level and passed exams I could apply for the accelerated promotion scheme,' Alice says.

'He said she's smart,' L adds.

'No, he said I was a smart-mouthed little shit with a quick mind who would clearly end up in prison like he did unless I had a plan. And he loved L! He said L could be a postal guard anytime.'

'Hang on, how did he get to be in charge of the postal service if he went to prison?' Rachel asks.

'Dunno. Said something about an old name. Whatever. He's so cool,' Alice says as we go back to grunting and drinking coffee, but I'm pleased for her, and L too. They both had a blast.

'How old are you?' I ask L.

'Nearly ten spans.'

'What's a span?' Alice asks.

'It's always either double or half a year,' Rachel says. 'Otherwise, the reader ends up having to do math for every character's age. So, if he's ten spans then he's probably twenty.'

'He looks twenty,' Svetty says.

'How old are you?' Alice asks her.

'I feel like a sixty right now,' Svetty mutters. 'I'm twenty-eight. Rach?'

'Thirty-two. John?'

'I don't know,' I admit, with the sudden realization that I know very little about myself. Not my age or birth month, or my mom or dad, or where I went to school, or even what unit of the military I was in.

Svetty studies me over her coffee cup. 'It's hard with guys,' she admits as Rachel nods. 'He could be anything from thirty to forty.'

'Go in the middle then?' Rachel suggests. 'Thirty-five?'

'Twenty-five,' I say.

'You wish!' Rachel says with a snort of laughter as Svetty shushes us and we go back to grunting and drinking coffee.

'We'd better make a move. Long way home,' Rachel eventually says, and we head to the empty concierge desk and turn this way and that until M Gustave clears his throat behind us.

'He's like a blooming magician,' Rachel mutters. 'We need to settle up and check out please.'

'There is no charge, madam,' M Gustave says, holding a hand up. 'Monsieur von Wiplig has covered your bill, courtesy of the Fiction Land Postal Service, and he has left his office details for Mademoiselle Alice and Monsieur Elle, and in this card are his personal contact details for Madame Svetlana, should she wish to join Monsieur Wiplig for dinner one evening.'

'Free oranges *and* a free hotel,' Rachel says with an impressed nod as Svetty thanks M Gustave and requests he pass a message back that she will, indeed, be in touch for dinner one evening.

Then we head for the door and brace ourselves for the cold north wind, but we step out to a still and frozen world, the ground covered in a layer of frost sparkling under the morning sun and Stephen and King waiting for us.

'I mean. I'm not complaining about the free hotel, but it's probably a bit fraudy or something putting it down to Postal expenses and using his position to try and date Svetty,' Rachel says.

'He's not,' Svetlana counters as we rush for the carriage. 'If he was doing that then he would have made dating him a condition of the free hotel and food, but this way shows generosity *without* any conditions. And that shows class. Anyway. I'm freezing. Night!' she says, running off to get in first and start burying herself under blankets.

'I'll drive,' Alice says.

'I'll come up front,' L says, clambering up, both of them wrapping blankets over their legs. 'I'll be your postal guard this morning, ma'am,' he adds in a mock deep voice, the pair of them full of beans as I get in back on the bench opposite Svetty with Rachel getting in next to her as we gather blankets.

'Actually, stuff this. Budge over,' Rachel says, scrunching into my side. 'Is this okay?' Rachel asks. 'I'm so cold.'

'I might see it as a romantic gesture,' I say, as I wrap my arm around her and we nestle into the seat.

'That's cos it is,' Rachel says. Then Alice releases the brake and we're off, once more trundling over the track, feeling the motion of the wheels and the vibration through the frame. Watching the glistening frost-covered world go by. The ocean flat and calm with barely a ripple.

Alice and L up front, chatting and laughing quietly. Svetlana already out of sight and no doubt snoring, and Rachel nestled into my side. Her head on my chest. My arm around her, and it's nice. It doesn't feel forced or weird.

I hear her breathing change as she falls asleep, but for a long time I stay awake, staring out at the passing world with a sense of calm inside. Then my eyes grow heavy, and I drift down to sleep, feeling the warmth of Rachel pouring into my body.

IT'S funny how a journey back is always shorter than a journey out, but I guess that's because of the unknown factor of finding the way there.

It's also funny that, for me at least, it seems to pass *too* quickly, and within a few hours we're in Middle Earth, exchanging Stephen and King for Terry and Pratchett.

We take food and drink with us and get back to chatting about this and that. Rachel doesn't try and cuddle into me again, but she smiles often and seeks eye contact, and this time I have to remind myself it *is* a romantic gesture.

We stop for a leg-stretch between Middle Earth and Western World, where the land changes from lush grassland to prairie scrub. We find bushes to pee behind, all of us feeling grimy from the travels and not being able to change our clothes, but the energy stays high and we crack open a flask of hot coffee bought from the kiosk in Young Olaf's Livery Yard & Horse Exchange and sit and chill at the side of the road. The sun high and warm. Neither too hot nor too cold.

'Okay, show me then,' Alice says, springing to her feet and facing me with her fists up and clenched.

'What, now?' I ask.

'Show her what?' Rachel asks.

'Croker's teaching me how to be a badass,' Alice says, punching out into the air. 'I got the moves. Ducking and weaving and blammo! An uppercut.'

'That's a hook,' I tell her.

'What's an uppercut then?'

'When you punch up.'

'What, like this?' she asks, punching into the sky.

'No,' I say, getting to my feet as I motion her in close then lower my stance, bringing my fists up into the guard. 'Hook, jab, cross and then uppercut,' I say, going through each slowly. 'But that's boxing, and it takes a long time to learn.'

'Well teach me something now then,' she says. 'Say someone tries to grab me.'

'Okay. Sure. Drop your hands. Be passive, like this,' I say adopting a casual neutral stance with my arms down. 'Most important is your feet. Widen your stance so you've got one foot back and one slightly forward. But do it discreetly if you feel danger. Say someone is acting weird but you don't want to telegraph your concerns.'

'I get that all the time,' Rachel says. 'When I'm walking back from work in winter and it's dark.'

'I think every woman gets it,' Svetlana says.

'Okay. So you see someone you're not sure of,' I say. 'Stay passive but stay alert. You can see people in your peripheral vision without staring at them. Or glance casually. But one foot back. One foot in front. You're centered and ready to either run back or go forward, or apply resistance is someone comes at you from in front or behind. L. Let me show them on you,' I say as L adopts the stance and just from that I can see he's had some training. I push on his chest to show how he doesn't fall back. Then he puts his feet together and I show how easy it is to unbalance him in that position.

'So cool,' Alice says as they push at each other. 'And then what? We high-kick! Ha! Karate chop!'

I laugh at the way she does it. 'Sure, you could try that.'

'No, but seriously. What should we do?' she asks.

'Okay, so the objective is to get away from danger. You don't want to stay and brawl. Bad things happen in fights. People fall down and crack skulls and break bones. Stay passive. Be aware. Then, if something happens – say the person tries to grab you, or comes in close, or you feel really threatened – you explode out with everything you have and aim for the attacker's eyes. Gouge, bite, scratch. Whatever you can do to make them flinch or fall back or turn so you can run. And scream too. Scream loud and shout the word *fire.* Shout it over and over. Don't shout *help*. Don't waste your breath. People get scared and go deaf in cities. But the fear of fire is ingrained. You shout that, and if anyone hears they *will* react.'

'And then *karate chop!*' Alice says, launching herself at L, who fends off and drops back as they playfight, and we drink coffee in a weird land.

By afternoon we hit Western World and exchange Terry and Pratchett for Ernest and Hemingway at Old Cobb's Livery Yard then we're back on the trail. Heading south with the summer heat building and the city looming in the distance.

There's a feeling between us. That special bond that grows when you travel with others or go through some adventure – it's a nice feeling, but we're also aware it's coming to an end.

'Well. We set out to do a thing, and we did it,' Rachel says, driving the horses up front with me as we hit the final stretch and the trail I walked out to that day, which was only a short while back, but it feels like weeks and I have to remind myself we've only been here a week.

'What happens next?' I ask.

'Well. When we get back I write your orientation up as complete, and you get assigned to the employment office who will find you some work until you decide what you want to do.'

'That's it then?' Svetty asks, as L and Alice fall quiet.

'You're only meant to get five days' orientation,' Rachel says.

'You get new people after us?' Svetty asks, and Rachel nods.

'When they come in, yeah. Or if no one from our genres comes in then we help the others out. General Crime and Detective Fiction are *always* swamped, and Fantasy Adventure are struggling to cope, and there's huge issues with this woke thing – the city doesn't know how to deal with LGBTQ fiction. At the moment they're putting them into drama, but they're demanding their own designated area and it's become this whole angry thing.'

We fall silent as we reach the edge of the city and soon we're passing buildings and sidewalks and people.

'But,' Rachel says after a moment, as she turns to look at me then at the others in the back. 'That's just my job, and what I do in my free time is my business. You know. Just saying, in case you ever wanted to hang out or.'

'I do,' Alice says too quickly, and it makes us laugh and turn to see her blushing but holding her chin up defiantly. 'I mean. If you do then, you know, that's cool.'

'No. I hate you all,' Svetlana says with an icy tone and an arched eyebrow, but with a glint in her eye that makes Alice laugh and lean over to hug her. Svetty grins. 'L can teach you how to be neat for when we live together.'

'Get off, you'll be married to Mr Wiplig,' Alice says.

'Er, excuse me! This girl doesn't do marriage! Not when there are wealthy single men to exploit for money so I can lose my dignity.'

'We're back to that!' L says with a laugh.

'Seriously though. We need to talk those views through,' Svetlana tells Alice.

'Okay,' Alice says.

'And you need to open up at this Enders therapy,' Svetlana adds as Alice's face drops. 'Don't let them cut your allowance.'

'I don't want to tell them anything.'

'Then don't. Just play the game and tell them *anything*.'

'But that's lying. Why should I lie?'

'It's different,' Svetlana says, as we all listen in. 'Okay, so lying to me is shitty, right? And I won't lie to you, because we're friends. But this isn't a friend, Alice. This is a system that has been designed by the city to force you into doing something with either the threat of sanctions, or the reward of money and greater freedoms if you comply. Now sure, you can be prideful and dig your heels in to make your point, but Rachel said the city is busy. They don't give a shit. You're just a name on a list. Fuck them. Fuck the city. Look after yourself. Get what *you* need. If that means playing the game, then play the game, because the greater reward is your own freedom to make your own choices.'

'Jesus,' Rachel says when Svetlana finishes. 'Everything you just said is so wrong, but I agree with every bit of it.'

'Hey. I only just got here,' Svetlana adds. 'But it's the same everywhere. Be loyal to your friends and the people that care for you, but more than anything, be loyal to yourself and that means making the right decisions for your welfare. You want out of Juvie Hall? You want to chill out with L and us and go for lunch in the Village? Then do what it takes to get the freedom needed to choose those things.'

Alice falls silent again. Troubled by the concept but clearly seeing the merit in everything Svetlana says. I also notice how she looks at the buildings we go by with an expression of dread at being back here, and the journey and our adventure being over.

'You got plans tonight?' I ask Rachel.

'I never have plans,' she quips, then shoots me a look. 'Why? You asking me on a date?' she asks, as Alice smiles but looks sad.

'I was thinking maybe we can drop the carriage off then go for a hot dog and float with these guys and help Alice get something together for Enders therapy. Alice? Last meal out before we take you back?'

'Yes!' Alice says, and I'm not the only one taking real pleasure in how her energy changes.

We get back into the city proper as the afternoon gives way to evening and we reach the final stables.

Anna's Livery Yard & Horse Exchange
Cheapest rates in F.L.
Modern carriages!

'SORRY WE'RE LATE BACK,' Rachel says as we're greeted outside by a man nodding politely.

'No problem,' he says, taking the reins.

'We just need to clear our rubbish out,' Rachel says as we start cleaning through the carriage.

'We'll do it. It's fine,' he says, waving us to go in a way that suggests he's in a hurry.

'Okay. Er, thank you,' Rachel says. 'Where do I pay the late fine?'

'No fine. It's cool. We don't want any trouble.'

'Trouble?' Rachel asks. 'What do you mean trouble? I'm a day late bringing it back.'

'Hey, don't look a gift horse and all that,' Svetty says quickly, as she smiles at the guy. 'Thank you!'

He nods and seems eager to go, glancing back to the offices as we gather our things and head off.

'You lucky sod,' Svetlana says with a smile at Rachel. 'No hotel bill, no late fine.'

'I know! Feels like my luck is finally changing,' she says. 'Right. We'll pop back to the office, and I'll sign you all as complete for orientation, then we'll get food. Good plan? But wow, though. I've never heard of them not fining someone for being late.'

'He looked all shifty,' L says. 'I bet he was on a promise.'

'Promise of what?' Alice asks.

'He means sex,' Svetlana says.

'Oh god, not sex chat again,' Rachel says.

'You and I are so going to talk about your prudishness,' Svetlana says, looping an arm through Rachel's as we walk through the busy city, onto Main Street and along past all the now-closed genre offices, all the way to ours.

HARD-BOILED & EROTICA
(& MISC. SCI-FI FANFIC OVERFLOW)

IT FEELS WEIRD INSIDE TOO. Smaller than I thought, and I can't believe it was only a week ago I came in here looking for Mascaponi. We take seats and I think about how my life has changed, the person I was and the person I am now, and our journey to the north shore.

'There is no van,' I say to myself, and Rachel smiles and touches my shoulder as she goes by to take a ledger from a shelf behind her desk.

'Well. I still think we need to explore the rest of Fiction Land just in case there *is* a van,' Alice says.

'Don't tell him that!' Rachel says with a laugh.

'Yeah. Don't tell me that. My receptors are firing,' I tell Alice.

'Yeah, you won't even think of your van when you and Rach get down to it,' Svetlana says, making us all laugh as Alice pulls a yucky face and Rach throws an empty paper cup at her while blushing again.

Which is when the door opens.

'Sorry! We're closed,' Rachel says.

'Yeah, I know you are,' a voice I recognize says, and I look over to see Detective Sam Shovel standing just inside the door with his hands in his pockets. His hat perched on the back of his head and his revolver on show, clipped to his belt. 'How you doing, kid?' he asks me.

'I'm okay,' I say as the energy in the room changes, and I look past him to see cops gathering outside across the street.

'Er, what's going on please?' Rachel asks, getting up from her desk.

'Well see,' Shovel says, shooting a tight smile at her. 'The boys said they wanted to come in mob-handed, seeing as he's a John that kept his skills.'

'What?' Rachel asks. We all get to our feet, which makes Shovel shoot me a look with another tight smile, and I spot the tension in his eyes.

'See, John. I figure if you wanted to, you'd get out the back door and run, and we'd probably have a hell of a job chasing you down and bringing you in, but here's the thing. Fiction Land ain't that big, and unless you want to grow a beard and change your name and live in a mud hut at the ass-end of Middle Earth, I suggest you let me take you in nice and easy.'

'I beg your pardon?' Rachel asks. 'For what?'

'How about it, John?' Shovel asks, eyeing me as he speaks.

'I said for what?' Rachel demands. 'John's been with us all week-end. He hasn't done anything.'

I look at her and realize why the guy at the livery yard seemed nervous. The cops had been there asking about me, which means they told them to contact the police when we got back. Then I look out the window again to the dozens of cops outside and realize that whatever it is, it must be serious.

'Are you arresting me?' I ask.

'Looks that way, kid.'

'Can you please tell me what's going on?' Rachel asks.

'Sure,' Shovel says without looking away from me. 'We need to speak to Mr Croker on account of him being the suspect in the murder of Jedediah Harper.'

'Murder?' Rachel asks with a gasp.

'Who's Jedediah?' Svetlana asks.

'The missing cowboy,' Alice says, as Shovel gives her a sharp look and I fight the urge to run. It must show on my face and in my stance, because the energy in the room becomes electric and I realize L is moving closer and Svetlana's hand is clamping on the back of a chair, ready to throw it, and I know from all those things that even though I could fight and get free and, like Shovel said, they'd struggle bringing me back in, it wouldn't just be me in the firing line.

It would be my friends too.

'I'll come in,' I say, and step forward with my hands together at the front.

'John?' Rachel says.

'I won't fight you,' I tell Shovel, as he tuts as though he's reluctant to put the handcuffs on my wrists and motions towards the door.

'John!' Rachel calls as I look back at her. She seems unsure of what to say, then swallows and blinks. 'Did you do it?' she asks, as they all look at me. Shovel too.

'No,' I say clearly, looking in her eyes, and we step out to a street full of cops and over to a solid-walled carriage marked with police livery. I go in, onto a plain wooden bench, and the last thing I see as the door closes is Rachel, L, Svetty and Alice watching me from the sidewalk – and Fat George smirking from a doorway further up the street.

CHAPTER TWENTY-THREE

Tuesday.

THEY PUT me in jail overnight.

The guy in the cell next to mine told me it's how they do things.

'It scares most people,' he said through the bars. 'They think this is what prison is like, so by the time the cops start interrogation they're ready to spill the beans.'

He sounded like he'd done this before, but he didn't look like a criminal. He was big. Easy six and a half feet, but he looked smart, and he spoke with authority while looking strangely relaxed. 'You a cop?' I asked him.

He shrugged. 'Used to be something like that.'

I wondered what that meant.

'Military cop,' he said. 'Been out a few years. Drifting mostly, but trouble always seems to find me, then I wind up here and they bust me straight into jail.'

'You just arrived?' I asked him, wondering why he was telling me all that.

He nodded. 'Woke up in a park yesterday with no recollection how I got there. But let me tell you something,' he said, as he leaned against the bars between our cells to stare down at me. 'I know Old Grayson poisoned that water supply, but drugging me and running me out to some weird town is only gonna piss me off, and trust me, you don't want Jim Treacher pissed off. And me busting a few of your phony cops up is just a taste of what I can do.'

I pictured him waking up in the park, still locked into his story and kicking off with what he thought were the local corrupt PD.

'Anyone told you where you are?' I asked him.

'Fiction Town?' he said, with a wry knowing smile.

'Fiction Land.'

'Sure,' he said, with a nod. 'Well. You tell Grayson I got his message loud and clear.'

'I don't work for Grayson.'

'The sheriff then.'

'I don't work for anyone.'

'So they just put you in the cell next to me for nothing?'

'No. They think I murdered a cowboy.'

'A cowboy?'

'From Western World.'

'Got it.'

He carried on with that smug weird smile, while leaning through the bars to show off his massive arms.

'You can go back to your bunk now,' I told him.

'Maybe I will. Or maybe I'll stare at you a while longer.'

I shrugged and closed my eyes.

'Grayson hired the best for me, huh? You're good. What were you? Delta? Ranger?'

'No idea.'

'More like deniable black ops. You got that look about you.'

'There is no look.'

'What?'

'The very nature of the work undertaken by black ops means the operators are selected because they *don't* have a look. That's the whole point, and you don't need to say *deniable* either. That's what black ops means.'

He carried on with the smug look, but I could see he suddenly wasn't so sure. I knew by then he was still locked into his character and *thought* he was a smart-ass ex-military cop, whereas he was just a product of a writer somewhere, who had no idea of the reality of such a thing.

It also made me frown, because I didn't know how I knew all of that stuff. But I knew I was right.

What exactly did my writer do in real life?

I pushed it to the back of my mind and focused on why I had been arrested, but truth be told, I had no idea what was going on.

I SLEEP a little and wake up when an old, uniformed guard brings food on metal trays with cups of water to pass through the serving slot in the bars.

'I know my rights. I want my phone call,' Jim Treacher says, and I can see he's trying to be cocky and self-assured but it's obvious the stress is getting to him.

'Simmer down. You're not being charged with anything. They got a genre rep coming in to get you out,' the guard says. 'You're damn lucky you can't fight for shit otherwise we'd keep you in.'

'I was drugged. You wanna try me now?' Treacher says, as the old man scoffs and walks off.

I eat the toast and beans and drink the water. I'm not hungry or thirsty, but I know I need energy to focus – and to get away if things go sideways. Then I remind myself that this isn't my story, and this isn't a plot. It's just a mix-up that can get straightened out.

'What's a genre rep?' Treacher asks, after watching me eat.

'Best they explain it,' I say, and hear the outer door opening as Pat comes through accompanied by two officers.

'Pat!' I say, getting to my feet. 'What's happening? Where's Rachel?'

'Hi, John,' she replies with a stiff smile. 'I'm actually here for him,' she adds, motioning the cell next to me as she goes by.

'Hey! You go and sit down,' one of the cops orders me.

I stop asking Pat because I can see how awkward she feels, but I don't go and sit down. I stay close to the bars and watch as they unlock the door to Treacher's cell and Pat goes in.

'Mr Treacher? My name is Pat. I'm going to take you out of here.'

Treacher stands up all cocky and big, but that fear is in his eyes clear as anything.

'What's going on?' he asks.

'I'll explain when we get to the office, but everything will be okay.'

'Grayson send you?'

'Let's just get you out shall we and you can tell me everything that's happened.'

'Yes, ma'am. You're my handler then, right?'

I watch them go and remember my first day and I how I said the same sort of things. Pat avoids looking at me as she goes past.

Then I'm alone with my head pressed to the bars, wondering what the hell is going on, and it's not until late morning that the door opens and a whole squad of officers armed with shields and sticks comes in.

'You're going to interrogation,' the one in charge tells me, as they position outside my cell door. 'You gonna cause us issues?'

'Nope.'

'Turn around,' he orders, and places cuffs on my wrists through the bars. Only then do they open the door, moving quickly to encircle me with shields and escorting me out of the cell block and along a corridor to an interrogation room.

'Hey kid,' Detective Sam Shovel says from the door, watching as I'm shackled to a metal loop on the desk. 'Sorry about the jewelry.'

I nod, but don't say anything as a uniformed cop shoves a chair hard against the back of my legs, forcing me to sit down.

'Take it easy!' Shovel snaps at the cop, then nods for them to clear out. 'I said I'd come get ya, John, but they're worried, see. The rumors about you in Diagonal Alley got all whipped up. Anyway. You're here now, huh? We just gotta wait for my colleague.'

He leans out the door as I figure the *colleague* will be some hard-ass ready to tag-team me with a *good cop, bad cop* routine. No doubt Sam Shovel will be trying to help me while the other one screams *they're gonna throw the book at you!*

I even picture what he'll look like, and summoning an image of an overweight cop, but broad and beefy, with a crew cut and hard eyes.

'Coming now,' Sam says, as I clock the smile he uses to greet the other detective which tells me it's someone he likes, then a second later the *colleague* bustles into the room.

All five foot two of her in a pale pink jacket over a white blouse and a pale pink skirt. Silver hair cut short, and a face lined with age.

'So sorry!' she says in a bright voice. 'Had to nip to the little girls' room. Ah, you must be John Croker? Pleasure, Mr Croker.' She holds a hand out, then tuts at seeing I'm shackled and moves in close to push her hand into mine. 'My name is Sally Wainwright. I work with Sam on matters of serious crime. Sam? Can we get these awful shackles off? I'm sure Mr Croker is no threat. You're not a threat, are you, Mr Croker?'

'No ma'am,' I say politely, still caught out by the older woman and her bright attitude and British voice.

'There you go, kid,' Sam says, using a key to unlock the cuffs as a uniformed cop brings in three mugs of coffee with a nervous glance at me.

'Right. Well. What a pickle, eh?' Miss Wainwright says as she sits down, patting her hands on a manila folder and smiling at me like a favorite aunt, and I feel the silence in the room becoming loaded with the need to fill it, but I don't. I sip my coffee and stay quiet.

'Told you,' Sam says after a moment, with a glance at Miss Wainwright.

'You did,' she says with an impressed look. 'The strong silent type indeed. What do you say about that, Mr Croker?'

I shrug. Not having anything to say about that.

'Detectives use silence as a tactic,' Miss Wainwright says with a wink. 'But it appears it's not a tactic you will succumb to. So how about we dispense with any mind games and get right down to it? What do you say, Mr Croker?'

'I'd appreciate that, ma'am.'

'Wonderful. And such nice manners too. Right. We're going to ask you some questions, Mr Croker. I might make some notes as we go along but that's only because I'm very old and I forget everything!'

I smile at the way she says it.

'Right. We're going to ask you some questions and I might make some notes because I forget everything!'

Sam snorts a quiet laugh and shakes his head and Miss Wainwright looks at us both in that way old people do to make sure we got the joke.

'Just a touch of humor, Mr Croker. Just a touch of humor,' she says. 'Okay. You arrived in Fiction Land on Monday last week?'

'Yes, ma'am.'

'You woke in the park and were directed to your genre office, Hard-Boiled & Erotica & misc. sci-fi fanfic, and there you met your genre reps Rachel and Pat. Correct?'

'Yes, ma'am.'

'And from your notes, we can see you are an Ender. Which, in Fiction Land, means we believe you were at the end of your story, which in turn creates the illusion that you are who you were written to be.'

I nod when she glances at me, and spot how Sam Shovel drinks his coffee and studies me over the desk.

'I was an Ender, Mr Croker, as was Sam here. So we do fully understand just how jarring that can be. I was an amateur sleuth in my story. Imagine Miss Marple or Jessica Fletcher. That sort of thing. But even after accepting my reality was not what I thought it was, I found I was still fascinated by crime. But enough about me. How are you finding it now?'

I pause at the open nature of the question and wonder if she means how am I finding Fiction Land, or how am I finding coming out of my previous reality.

'It's okay,' I say, figuring the answer can apply to both. 'It was difficult at first, but I think I'm accepting it now.'

Silence again.

I don't fill it.

Miss Wainwright smiles and goes back to reading the file.

'Your notes record that you have an obsession with seeking *the docks.*'

I don't like the way she says obsession, but I get what she means so I nod.

'What for?' she asks, peering up at me.

'It's where I ended in my story. I thought I had to get my van back to the depot to secure the bonus to pay for my niece's surgery, and my van was in the docks.'

'I see. Yes. And did you find it?'

I frown again, wondering if she means the docks or my van. 'I found a harbor, but no docks of the kind in my story.'

'And how did that make you feel?'

'Confused, initially. But I think it helped me accept the change.'

'And tell me about the fight in Diagonal Alley.'

'Yes, ma'am. Like I told Detective Shovel, I just got caught up in a scuffle.'

'A scuffle?'

'That's correct, ma'am. During which, unfortunately, I think a guy suffered a broken thumb.'

'I see,' she says, as if all of this is super interesting news. 'So, this *scuffle*. What caused it exactly?'

'I think it was a miscommunication. I saw a guy talking to my friend Alice who is only seventeen, and out of concern I checked she was okay, but things got out of hand.'

'And?'

'And that's how the scuffle happened. During which Mr Bond's thumb suffered an injury.' I glance at Shovel, remembering what he told me to say about *not* admitting to breaking Bond's thumb on purpose.

'I've asked you twice now, Mr Croker,' she says, with that bright smile. 'And twice you've avoided telling me how the fight started. Anyway. Moving on. Karaoke night was on Friday evening. Tell me about Saturday.'

'What about Saturday? You mean the cowboy?'

'Do you want to tell us what happened?'

'Sure,' I say, feeling unsettled about the way she spoke about the fight in Diagonal Alley. 'But I didn't kill him.'

Silence.

I sit back, thinking to wait it out, but it becomes too oppressive and I start to worry I'll look guilty if I don't explain things. 'I went for a walk,' I say, and spot the glint of victory in Miss Wainwright's eyes that I broke the silence first.

'What for?'

'Just for a walk. To see the city and get my bearings.'

'You sound defensive, Mr Croker. We're merely trying to ascertain your movements.'

'Like I said. I went for a walk and saw this cowboy guy. He was going in the same direction, and I saw him giving abuse to two gay guys with a kid, then he walks on and almost walks into this black guy and calls him a ni—'

'We don't use the N word here, Mr Croker.'

'I'm just telling you what he said. You want me to be accurate or not?'

'There's being accurate and there's being offensive. Please continue.'

I shift in my seat, feeling frustrated and goaded. 'So the cowboy starts on the black guy and he's going to attack him so I step in and –'

'Attack him?'

'Yes.'

'How did you know Mr Jedediah Harper was going to attack this person of color?'

'He pulled his fist back.'

'And?'

'And what? He was going to strike the black man. I mean the person of color.'

'How do you know that?'

'I just said. He pulled his fist back.'

'I heard you. But such an action does not telegraph an immediate threat of violence.'

'The guy moved in on the black – the person of color – while pulling his fist back. He was positioning to strike while shouting at the poor guy.'

'The poor guy?'

'The black man.'

'You mean the person of color. Who you automatically assume to be poor?'

'What?'

'Or did you mean feeble?'

'No! I don't know him. It was just instinct. The cowboy guy was –'

'Mr Harper.'

'What?'

'His name was Mr Harper. Jedediah Harper.'

'Okay. Harper was going along whistling at pretty women and

abusing two gay guys with a kid then he starts on the black guy, and I took his actions to be violent so I, you know, intervened.'

'Do you like intervening, Mr Croker?'

'No. I meant –'

'Moving on. You *intervened*, and then what? What did you do?'

'I got him off and the black guy had a go at me.'

'How did you get Mr Harper off?'

I bite the frustration down again. 'I grabbed his arm and delivered two blows to make him drop back.'

'Specifically, where did you hit him?'

I wince at where this is going. 'In the solar plexus, then in the throat. But it wasn't that hard.'

'Hard enough to cause bruising and induce swelling to his larynx and windpipe, which we noted during the postmortem. And bruising to his midsection.'

I hold my hands up. 'I didn't kill him. The black guy had a go at me, and I walked off.'

'Where to?'

'Out of town. I wanted to see the city edge and what else was there, so I just walked, then reached this hill and saw a sign for Western World and came back.'

'Whereupon you went into the Village with your genre rep. The girl Alice from your therapy group whom you felt the need to *save* from Jimmy, and your other arrivals group. Correct?'

'Yes.'

'How long was your walk into the countryside?'

I shrug. 'Hour maybe.'

'Did you see or speak to anyone else?'

'No.'

'Nobody at all?'

'I saw farms with people working in the fields, but they weren't close.'

'To summarize, Mr Croker. You had the fight in Diagonal Alley during which multiple people were injured –'

'I said we had a scuffle.'

'You keep calling it a scuffle, Mr Croker. Whereas I would suggest it was far more than a scuffle. Three bouncers suffered injuries. One had concussion. Another had a suspected fractured wrist and bruising to the ribs. Red Wheatley, also known as Ginger Ron suffered a broken nose, and three other males who rushed in to stop the fight were assaulted. Two requiring medical treatment – and of course one man sustained a broken thumb. Meaning you broke it.'

I glance at Shovel again who just stares back at me.

'My understanding, Mr Croker,' Miss Wainwright says, reading from the file, 'Is that *Croker forcefully and purposefully gripped Mr Secretan's thumb and yanked it hard, thereby causing it to break, this being while Mr Croker had Mr Secretan already immobilized over a table.*'

'Secretan?' I ask, not getting the name. 'I thought he was Jimmy or some James Bond rip-off.'

'James Bond is a fictional character created by Ian Fleming, Mr Croker. James Bond is not and never will be in Fiction Land. *Mr Secretan* came into Fiction Land having been written as a James Bond character, but on realizing he was the twelfth such living person he adopted the name Jimmy Secretan.'

She looks at me. I stare back.

'Did you break his thumb?'

I pause. Unsure how to answer. 'His thumb was broken during the scu . . . The incident.'

'Did you break his thumb, Mr Croker? Did you snap his thumb while pinning the chap over a table?'

'I er . . .' I glance at Shovel, who doesn't show a flicker of reaction. 'I mean.'

'And what about the other injuries? Were they all down to you?'

'The other injuries?'

'The broken noses and bruised ribs and fractured wrists,' she says, peering up like a teacher reading my homework. 'Some scuffle that was, eh? Sound more like a vicious brawl if you ask me.'

'No. It wasn't like that –' I start to say, but she cuts me off in that bright breezy tone.

'And from the statement, Mr Croker, it appears you walked into the Pigspot Tavern in Diagonal Alley, and after blocking the bar and being politely requested to leave you threatened everyone in there.'

'What?'

'Mr Croker then stated he didn't care if there were eight of us asking him to go because he wasn't an ordinary man and he could hurt us all.'

'It wasn't like that.'

'Did you say that?'

'No! I mean. Well. A bit of it but –'

'So you *didn't* say it, but you *did* say some of it. That right?'

'What? No. Hang on. I was in character.'

'You said finding the harbor helped you realize you were *not* in your story, and you were in the harbor *before* the violent incident in Diagonal Alley.'

'Right. Yes. No. I mean. You're confusing me.'

'There's nothing confusing about this, Mr Croker. Either you did or you did not threaten a bar full of people.'

'Okay. I said part of that, or something similar –'

'Something similar.'

'I reverted to type. In my story I had a habit of self-narrating. I did it then and spoke out loud.'

'So you *hadn't* accepted your story wasn't real then?'

'No! I had. I mean. I was on that journey. Or, like, I was trying to accept it. This feels wrong. You're twisting things.'

'I am not. I am asking simple questions. Did you break a man's thumb? Did you threaten a bar full of people?'

'Okay. Yes.'

'Yes, what?'

'I broke his thumb. I said those things, but the Harry Potter people were –'

'Harry Potter is also a fictional character, Mr Croker, who is not and never will be in Fiction Land.'

I shift in my seat from the growing frustration. 'The weird wizard people in the bar.'

'Weird wizard people? Have you got a hatred for other cultures, Mr Croker?'

'What? No! I mean. The wizard people. They're all in robes. That's weird.'

'By whose standards? By yours? Who are you to judge what is and what is not acceptable?'

'This is getting out of control.'

'There's only one thing out of control here, Mr Croker.'

'I wasn't out of control! The *people* in the bar were shoving into me from behind and I told them to quit.'

'Right. I see. So you were jostled in a busy bar during karaoke night *and then* threatened everyone. Is that right?'

'No.'

'No? But you just said you *did* make that threat. And you just said you *did* break Mr Secretan's thumb.'

'He was hitting on a seventeen-year-old!'

'Mr Secretan stated he was concerned a seventeen-year-old was in the bar and was trying to escort her home when you violently intervened.'

'He was hitting on her! He gave her booze and was being all sleazy. She's seventeen!'

'And that gave you justification to assault six people? Right after you threatened a bar full of people for jostling you? And let's move on to Saturday, shall we?'

'No! Not moving on.'

'Are you telling me how to conduct my questioning, Mr Croker? Do you have an issue with control? Or is it because I am a woman?'

I sit back with the realization that it *is* a good cop, bad cop thing. Or, to be more exact, a bad cop in the guise of a sweet old lady going for the jugular while Sam Shovel stays quiet and watches on.

'On Saturday, after being visited and warned about your conduct by Detective Shovel you *go for a walk* as you put it, and end up following Mr Jedediah Harper, and because he whistled at some women and had a disagreement with a person of color, you decided to punch him in the throat.'

'No.'

'You said he whistled at women. You said he had a disagreement with the person of color. You said you punched him in the throat.'

'Okay. Yes, but not like that. And he abused two gay guys. They had a kid. He called them queers.'

'According to you,' Miss Wainwright says in that chirpy way.

'He did!'

'We've had no complaints, Mr Croker. And how do you know they were gay?'

'They were hand in hand and one had a kid on his back.'

'And?'

'And what?'

'So you automatically decreed them to be homosexual because two men were touching each other with one carrying a child.'

'They sounded gay!'

'Oh, I see. They sounded gay. Did they dress gay too, Mr Croker? And these women that Mr Harper whistled at? Were they damsels in distress who couldn't possibly defend themselves, or could it perhaps be that either Mr Harper was simply whistling, as he was prone to do, or that he simply admired the beauty of someone else in a way that was culturally appropriate to someone from Mr Harper's genre and era? And let's talk about Mr Harper, shall we? Mr Harper was in the city to try and secure specialist education for his son, on advice from the school in Western World that suggested Mr Harper's son was academically gifted. Mr Harper had attended a meeting and gained a promise of funding if his son passed certain exams, and was on his way to a farmstead out of the city to collect his horse, seeing as livery charges in the city are very high and Mr Harper was friendly with the farmer and farm workers. Sadly, however, Mr Harper disappeared somewhere between leaving Mr Brian Joseph, that being the person of color, and the farm holding his horse. And from all accounts, Mr Harper and Mr Joseph parted on reasonable terms, having had a discussion about awareness and appropriate language usage, and after Mr Harper discovered that Mr Joseph taught at the specialist school he was trying to enroll his son into.'

Silence.

I swallow and clear my throat. 'I didn't kill Jedediah Harper.'

'But yet he was found dead on the exact same route you took out of the city.'

'I didn't kill him.'

'He died from a broken neck,' Sam Shovel says, speaking out for the first time. 'Doc said someone snapped his head over from behind.'

I look at Shovel then back to Wainwright.

'You ever kill a guy like that, John?' Shovel asks me.

'No.'

'No?' Shovel asks with a frown. 'But you've killed dozens of men.'

I realize they must have spoken to Alice, who asked me how many people I'd killed.

'They were in my story.'

'You're an Ender, John. Our stories are real to Enders,' Shovel says. 'Ask you again, you ever kill a guy like that?'

I clench my jaw and nod.

'From behind?' Shovel asks. 'You snapped someone's neck?'

I nod again.

'That takes some skill, so I'm told. And strength too.'

'I didn't kill Jedediah.'

'See, kid. I want to be believe you. Trust me, I do. I like you. You got a nice way about you. And I can see it too. The way you came in and saw this world like your story, that Alice had to be protected, and people of color and homosexual people are weak and should be protected, and pretty women can't defend themselves.'

'I'm not like that.'

'So that why you taught Alice, Svetlana and Rachel how to defend themselves?' Shovel asks.

'They asked me.'

'And this is during your trip, yes?' Miss Wainwright cuts in. 'To the north shore. Why were you going to the north shore, Mr Croker?'

I swallow again, sensing how this is all spiralling out of control. 'Just to see.'

'Checking for docks, I believe,' Miss Wainwright says, consulting her notes. 'According to your travelling companions, anyway. All of whom also observed you fight off several attackers during a highway robbery, the last of whom you had to be pulled from, because apparently you were about to kill him, even though he was already knocked out. That's according to the report from Captain Slackbladder, who also ordered you to attend the militia office in Middle Earth, which you failed to do.'

'I forgot.'

'Of course,' she says, with a look of genuine sympathy that only makes it all the more cutting. 'We're building up quite the picture of you, Mr Croker. An Ender who refused to accept he was no longer in his story, and even after a week was still searching for his docks and his van, and who had *intervened* with an ever-present white savior complex to defend and protect anyone he perceives to be weak and feeble. Who, as a result of which, has left a trail of injured people from one end of Fiction Land to the other.'

'I didn't kill Jedediah.'

'But you have killed, Mr Croker. You've bragged about killing dozens of men.'

'I didn't brag.'

'And you have done so in the same way that Mr Harper was murdered. By breaking the man's neck.'

'No.'

'No? You fought him, Mr Croker. You punched him in the throat while Mr Joseph had the situation under control. You broke Mr Secretan's thumb for trying to help Alice. You threatened a bar full of *weird wizards* after jostling you. You assaulted several bouncers trying to get you out. You almost killed a man *who was already knocked out* and then refused to comply with the lawful orders of Captain Slackbladder. Not to mention, Mr Croker, that you, *after saving dear seventeen-year-old Alice,* then took her on an overnight journey to the far side of Fiction Land without consent for an overnight visit, during which you plied her with booze and allowed her to drive a horse and carriage without a license, and then taught her how to fight.'

'It wasn't like that.'

'Which bit was not like that, Mr Croker?'

'None of it! You're twisting it all up. Those things happened, but not like that.'

'You mean to say your perception differs from those around you, yes? Which we have already established is a recurring problem of yours, given that as of yesterday you still believed you were in your story.'

'No!'

'Are you raising your voice at me, Mr Croker? Are you getting angry?'

'I'm frustrated.'

'Well. That's better than being dead like Mr Harper, isn't it? So tell me, Mr Croker. If you didn't kill Jedediah, who did?'

'How would I know? Ask that Fat George guy. He was smirking like he knew something when I got arrested.'

'Do you mean George Wheeler? Yes, he observed you being arrested and has openly stated he felt it was a good thing, seeing as you injured several of his friends.'

'I didn't kill Harper.'

'You have motive, Mr Croker. You were in the same place going in the same direction. You have the skills. You have the temper.'

'I didn't kill him! Ask Rachel and –'

'Your genre rep, Rachel Askew?'

'I don't know her last name.'

'Miss Askew, who aided and abetted taking a juvenile out of the city and getting her drunk and allowing her to drive a carriage. And who was seen behaving in a sexual manner towards you.'

'We didn't do anything!'

'It is forbidden for *any* genre rep to engage in *any* romantic activity with a new arrival.'

'We didn't do anything.'

'She slept on you in the carriage while a drunk unlicensed child was driving.'

'It was cold, and Alice wasn't drunk.'

'It was early morning after a very heavy drinking session. I would strongly suggest that Alice was still drunk.'

I sit back with a blast of air. 'I want a lawyer.'

'We are not in America, Mr Croker,' Miss Wainwright points out pleasantly.

'What are my rights?'

'You have the right to legal representation at the point of being charged. At the moment you are merely being questioned, Mr Croker. However, my strong advice is to admit the offence early and appeal for leniency in sentencing on the grounds of diminished responsibly due to being an Ender, and also due to being led astray by Miss Askew.'

'She did not lead me astray.'

'Prison is hard here, Mr Croker. We're not equipped to provide very good care to our prisoners at all. Especially not murderers, and especially not when the victim was a well-liked member of the Western World community.'

'He was a violent homophobic racist, but I didn't kill him.'

'Well now,' Miss Wainwright says, leaning forward with a glint in her eyes. 'I think you did, so it comes down to what one can prove and how convincing one can be to a jury.'

'Stop right there!' a voice bellows from the corridor outside.

'Damn,' Shovel whispers, as they both turn to the door slamming open and a tall, dark-haired man with a hawk-like face striding in.

'Release my client immediately!' he calls, in a voice loud enough to make me flinch. 'This is abuse of process! I should be present during questioning. Have they questioned you yet, dear boy?' he demands from me.

'They said I only get legal if I'm charged.'

'We said no such thing,' Miss Wainwright says with a gentle tut. 'And are well within our legal rights to ask questions. It is a murder, after all.'

'A murder my client did not commit!' the man booms as he towers over them, his hands animated and his whole body seeming to hum with energy.

'We got evidence,' Shovel says, sitting back in his chair to look up with a wry grin. 'We got a whole bunch of it.'

'Do you now?' the guy asks, drawing the words out as he braces on the table to lean in over them. 'I am very happy for you, but do allow me to counter, and raise your evidence with a witness.'

'What?' Shovel says, screwing his face up as he shoots a look at Wainwright. 'What witness? Where? Nobody saw the murder.'

'Indeed. But someone *did* see my client, Mr Croker, walk out of the city, and that someone kept my client, Mr Croker, in constant, uninterrupted view until he returned!' he adds with a loud flourish as he produces a sheet of paper that he slams onto the table and slides to face Wainwright and Shovel who both lean forward to read it.

I blink at the turn of events as the tall man shoots me a quick wink and drops his eyebrows as though to say *stay quiet.*

'Well look at that,' Shovel says, sitting back with his head tilted over.

'Yes. Look at that,' Wainwright adds and I note her tone isn't so bright and cheerful now.

'I believe my client is now free, yes?' the tall man asks quietly.

'Not free,' Wainwright says. 'But we will bail him pending further enquiries.'

'BAIL? He is exonerated! He is innocent. I have a witness!'

Wainwright and Shovel get up and leave the room with the tall man racing after them, shouting loudly at the injustice being perpetrated, and for a moment I think they've forgotten about me, until I peer out of the door to see the squad of shield-clutching officers in the corridor who must have been there the whole time. All of whom now look as confused as me.

'Can I go then?' I ask.

They shrug and look at each other until the tall man strides back into the corridor.

'Bailed! Can you believe it? And we've got a witness! A witness, Mr Croker,' he says, ushering me on through another door, past the shrugging, shield-clutching cops.

We go out through a charge desk to a sergeant rolling his eyes and pointing to an exit door, then out into the bright sunshine of a hot afternoon and the tall guy strides off while I blink and let my eyes adjust.

'In all truth, dear boy, I was expecting bail,' he says, then realizes I'm not at his side and darts back to take my arm and bundle me into a waiting carriage. 'Drive on, driver! I was saying, my dear boy, that I expected bail, but it never helps to admit anything to the Fiction Land police department. And especially not Wainwright. Shovel is a gumshoe, but he's generally honest enough, although I rather feel he's after a quiet life these days. On the wind-down to retirement, you see. But Wainwright! By Jove, when she gets the bit she doesn't let go. Like a blasted rottweiler she is. And did she put that act on? Eh? Sweet old lady? Favorite aunt? I bet she even took the shackles off. But know this, my boy. She would have ordered them on in the first place *and* she would have had that shield squad come and get you. She's a one. And it's lucky I got there when I did. She ties people up in knots and gets them to sign confessions on all sorts of things they have no idea about. But still! I got there in the nick of time, eh?'

The carriage bounces along and I listen to the guy speaking. He sounds British too, but not like Wainwright. He's educated and smart and full of energy. His legs bounce as he talks. He fidgets constantly, sitting back, then leaning forward and touching my arm to keep my attention, and 'I take in his dark trousers and dark formal jacket.

We turn into a street of houses, terraced but grand, with big front steps and big front doors, and the carriage has hardly come to a stop when he's urging me out and ushering me up some steps to a high-gloss black front door.

'Ah yes!' he booms, striding along the wood-panelled hallway after throwing his bowler hat towards a stand, where it misses and scoots across the floor. He doesn't stop to get it but rushes on into a room. 'Bailed! Just as I said. Where is he?' he asks, coming back to grasp my arm. 'Come along, dear boy.'

'Why am I here?' I ask as he propels me along.

'I told you! You need to listen.'

'You said I was bailed.'

'Yes! Bailed to here. With me.'

'What? I've got to stay here?'

'Indeed, you do,' he bellows as we go into the front room, or the parlor, or the sitting room, or whatever the hell front rooms are called in Victorian-style houses.

'Why am I here?' I ask, struggling to keep up as the tall man turns with a flourish.

'Because, my dear boy, I have been challenged to prove your innocence. And prove your innocence I shall! But there is more at stake here,' he adds with a sudden fierce whisper as he surges in close. 'Far more at stake,' he says, glaring into my eyes. 'And you are just what I've been waiting for.'

I glance at the dark shelves filled with books and the tables and lamps as I try and take it all in, and I think about the street name I saw on the way in, and the number on the door.

That being Baker Street, number 221B.

And I look into the dark blazing eyes of the man looming over me, who pushes a hand out to grasp mine in an iron grip. 'My apologies. In my haste I neglected to introduce myself. Sherrinford Hope at your service.'

CHAPTER TWENTY-FOUR

Tuesday evening.

WE GO FOR A WALK.

'Come come, Mr Croker, in the evening we stroll. It is the done thing. We have eaten our last meal and one should not rest after consumption. One grows fat and lazy by doing so. No, sir! We walk, sir! We walk off the ills of saturation and invigorate our minds and bodies.'

I didn't have a clue who Sherrinford Hope was when he introduced himself. I mean. I knew he was some kind of Sherlock Holmes copy from the way he spoke and acted and the Victorian house, but I didn't know that Sherrinford Hope was the original name for Sherlock Holmes.

Either way, it was just one more weird and bizarre thing in a whole series of weird and bizarre things that were getting weirder and more bizarre by the day.

'Take a seat,' Hope said in his parlor when he took me into his house and directed me to the end of a leather sofa while he rang a bell and waited for a maid to appear.

'Ah, Mrs Hudson! Tea for three please!'

'It's not Mrs Hudson,' the woman said with a roll of her eyes, as I wondered who else was coming for the third cup he'd ordered.

'Right, my dear boy!' Hope boomed as he sat back on another sofa with his arms stretched across the back. 'I should imagine you have questions!'

'Who was the witness?'

'Is that the most important question, Mr Croker? Indeed. A witness we have, but the question we *must* answer is *why* and *who*? Why, Mr Croker. And who.'

'You mean why was I arrested or why was Jedediah killed?'

I frowned as the woman came back carrying a tray with three cups next to the teapot.

'Am I serving?' she asked. Hope held a hand up to silence her and nodded at me to take another guess. 'Guess I am then,' she muttered, rattling the cups and stirring the teapot as I looked up at Hope.

'You mean *why* kill Jedediah to make it look like I did it?'

'Exactly,' he whispered softly. 'And then?' he prompted.

'The who.'

'Indeed. The *who,* Mr Croker. Are you serving that tea, Mrs Hudson, or stirring it to death?'

'My name is Maisy,' the maid told me, while pouring tea into the cups. 'Maisy Smith. Not Hudson.'

'Ah, but you are *my* Mrs Hudson,' Hope said, giving her a warm smile.

'I'm nobody's Mrs Hudson. I'm Maisy Smith. Right. There's your tea, Sherrinford, and there's yours, Mr Croker.'

'It's John,' I said taking the cup and saucer as she picked the third up and carried it over to a large, empty red chesterfield with several large pampas grass plants behind it, each with broad, creamy-colored heads.

'What the fuck,' I muttered, when a hand appeared from thin air to take the cup and saucer. Hope burst out laughing and even Maisy turned to wink and smile at me, and it took another second for my brain to discern what I was looking at.

Then I saw it.

A man in red clothes of the exact same hue as the red chesterfield and with a shock of white hair that blended perfectly with the pampas grass directly behind him. 'Griff?'

'Ha! What a hoot!' Hope cried out as he sank back in his chair. 'How's that for camouflage, eh? Meet your witness, Mr Croker.'

'Griff?' I asked in shock

'But . . .' I said, floundering for a second, too caught out to think straight. 'No. I lost him. I knew he was following me, and I confronted him and this lady told me off. But he didn't follow me after that.'

'You didn't *see* him follow you after that, you mean,' Hope said, as Maisy smiled again and walked out. 'Griff *let* you see him, Mr Croker. I'd instructed him to test your surveillance skills, and by all accounts they are really quite reasonable. But once you had confronted him, Griff then worked properly and tracked you out of town all the way to the hill where you stopped.'

I shook my head, trying to think where he could have been hiding. 'How? Where was he? Where were you?' I asked him.

'You can't see me,' he said, sipping his tea, and now I could see him it was obvious he was there. But I'd had no clue a moment ago.

'Needless to say. Thank your lucky stars Griff *was* following you,' Hope said, and seemed to pause as I duly, and no doubt ponderously, reached the next question. 'You're going to ask *why was Griff following me*, yes?' Hope said.

I nodded and drank some of the tea. It was nice.

'Griff works for me, Mr Croker, and sometimes also for Annie Holmes, which I'd rather he didn't,' Hope said stiffly.

'She's pretty,' Griff said. 'She sees me.'

Hope grunted. 'I asked Griff to follow you. He's been doing it since you arrived.'

'Why?'

'Let's just say I take a keen interest in all Enders, and particularly those that retain any real-world skills.'

He didn't answer the question, but the way he said it made it feel like he *did* answer the question.

'What happens now?' I asked.

'I need to think,' he said quietly, and that was it. He never said another word but sat and looked miserable and stared at nothing until Maisy came and got me.

'I'll show you to your room.'

'I'm staying here?'

'Sherrinford said you're bailed to this address,' Maisy said, as she led me up the stairs 'That means you have to sleep here, Mr Croker. Mr Hope signed an agreement to that effect. It's all part of the bail conditions. But he we are. All yours. Bathroom is opposite. The bed is quite comfy, and I took the liberty of getting you a few bits. Toothbrush and a change of clothes. I'll let you wash and call you for tea.'

'I just had tea.'

'No, I mean tea. Evening tea?' she asked, as I looked blank. 'Dinner, Mr Croker. We call dinner tea.'

'Why not just call it dinner?'

'Where's the fun in that?' she asked with a smile, and headed off.

I washed and changed and felt a bit better, seeing as I'd been in the same clothes since Sunday morning. I'd asked about my friends and Hope said they were all unhurt. Then Maisy came and got me, and I went down to eat pork chops and mashed potato and green peas all covered in gravy. Which I thought was the most British thing I had ever eaten until Maisy cleared the dishes away and plonked a steaming bowl of gooey mess in front of me.

'Spotted dick,' she said.

'What is?'

'That is.'

'That is?'

'Yes. And custard. Sherry loves a spotted dick, Mr Croker.'

'Do you like dick, Mr Croker?' Hope asked from the other end of the table, without a flicker of humor in either of their faces.

'I don't know.'

'Ooh, try it,' Maisy urged. 'You might like it. You look like a man that enjoys some dick.'

Truth be told, I think I *was* a dick man. Spotted dick and custard is good.

I don't know if it was the food, or his blood sugar levels or what it was, but Hope perked up as soon as he ate.

'Come come, Mr Croker, in the evening we stroll. It is the done thing!'

WE WALK through Little Victoria with folk nodding and greeting Hope as we go by, and more than a few asking if I'm his new Watson.

'Griff saw your carriage coming back,' Hope says as we reach the main road running in from the edge of the city. 'He followed it to the livery yard and saw them call the police, then by the time he reached the genre office you were being arrested.'

'They kept me overnight,' I say, as Hope shrugs. 'I mean, I'm grateful you got me out, but why wait till the next day?'

'Because it was too late for me to do anything, but first thing the following morning I made contact with your fellow travellers and –'

'You spoke to Rachel?' I ask as he walks off towards a collection of stores, restaurants, and coffee shops. 'Was she okay?'

'Refine your question, Mr Croker.'

'What?'

'By *okay* do you mean was she alive and unhurt? Then yes. She was. By *okay* do you mean was she emotionally stable? I would suggest she was. But by *okay* do you mean she wasn't upset or confused, or indeed somewhat angry and fearful, then I would also suggest that no, she was not okay.'

I frown at the long answer and rush to keep up as he comes to a sudden stop. 'What is she scared of?' I ask.

'Losing her job, Mr Croker. She's been accused of taking a juvenile out of the city without consent, plying her with alcohol and letting her drive a carriage without a license, *in addition* to breaching the Code of Ethical Standards for Genre Reps by entering into a romantic dalliance with you.'

'We didn't do anything.'

'You cuddled, Mr Croker, which by any definition is substantially more than *we didn't do anything*.'

I get a pang of guilt and regret inside when he says that.

'What can I do?'

'About that? Nothing,' he says, as though it's of no concern.

'So, what then?' I ask as he stands on the sidewalk and stares across to the eateries and stores across the way. 'I mean, What do we do?'

'That is the question, isn't it,' he says quietly, tapping his cane against his leg. 'There's more to it all. I'm sure of it.'

'More to what? Jedediah being murdered? You said it was so I'd get framed.'

'More,' he whispers. 'A lot more I suspect. Coffee?'

He strides off across the road to a café. 'Two coffees. And a plate of those lemon sponge fingers!'

We take a seat on bamboo chairs surrounded by green plants as I peer around for Griff pretending to be a lamp or something.

'He's not here,' Hope tells me and waits until the coffee and cakes are served and takes a sip with a nod of pleasure. 'I do like a coffee before bedtime. Keeps me awake.'

'Isn't that a bad thing?'

'Not if you don't want to sleep. But tell me, Mr Croker. What do you make of it all?'

'What?'

'It. All,' he says, motioning to the world around him before lurching forward to grab the plate of cakes. 'Have a lemon sponge finger. They're very nice.'

'You mean the murder?' I ask while eating one. 'I don't know. I had one fight at the karaoke night but that's not enough to set someone up for murder.'

'And by all accounts you foiled a robbery.'

'That was miles away, and the murder must have been before that.'

'Was it?' he asks. 'The cowboy's body was not found until Monday morning, by which time you were at the north shore.'

I shake my head. 'It doesn't feel right. The highway robbers didn't know who I was, *and* I took their leader down. Why would they back-track to the city and find a cowboy I argued with? Makes no sense.'

'Leave the sense-making to me, old chap. And do go on. What else?'

'What else what?'

'Whatever your instincts are telling you.'

I frown at his nonsensical way of speaking. 'Like I said. I don't know. I mean, I was locked into my story, and I thought, so, okay, let's be sure there are no docks and then I can get on.'

'I see,' he says, and leans forward a few inches. 'But tell me. Was it the docks you were really looking for at the north shore?'

'Yeah, what else?'

'What else. What else indeed. What else *could* there be?' he says, with a quick flash of a smile. 'Haha! I can see it in your eyes, Croker!'

'See what?'

'The same level of utter disbelief that I feel,' he says. Then, in a sudden ferocious whisper, 'Fiction Land? What is that? Where are we? Who made it? How do we exist? We were characters in unfinished books? And we're meant to just accept that, are we? But yet we do,' he adds, with a bewildered expression as he looks around the café at the other patrons at their tables, and the waiters rushing between them, then outside to the people walking by or crossing the road. Some stopping to chat or nodding in greeting. Horses and carriages going by. The drivers yelling to one another. 'They accept it, Croker. They accept it like it's the most normal thing that could happen.'

'What choice do they have?' I ask him.

He gives me a sad smile and takes a lemon sponge finger before sitting back. 'They don't,' he admits, and eats it in two big bites. He eats angry too. Working his jaws as though rushing to swallow it. 'But then they do. We all do. But then we don't, do we?'

'What?' I ask, once again lost.

'My apologies. They have a choice. We all do. But they *don't* have a choice because they refuse to see the choice or do anything about it. But see, you and I, Croker. We think differently. We *know* it isn't right, or at least it doesn't *feel* right, so we challenge it. I did the same thing on my first week here. I stole a horse and took it around the entire island.'

'The whole island?'

'The whole of the thing, Croker. In one giant circle. Or not a circle, as the island isn't round. But yes, you get the point. And what did I find?'

'No docks.'

'No docks,' he says, with a knowing nod. 'Well. No. Technically, I found quite a few docks, or harbors, or pontoons, or other structures used for the mooring of fishing boats. But that's all there was, Croker.

Just fishing boats. And none of them were big either, and certainly not the type you'd want to use to cross a big sea.'

I sip my coffee and let him talk, figuring that's the easiest option.

'Then, I went back to the old harbor, you know the one?'

I nod. 'The Jack Sparrows.'

'There were no Jack Sparrows back then. They came later. Back then we had Long John Gold, and Captain Steel and Captain Wickham and more pirate captains than at a dinner party of captains on national captains' day.'

I frown because I never met anyone like that when I went to the harbor.

'They disappeared,' he says quietly, seeing my expression, and he leans closer. 'I'd been around the island and couldn't see a way off. No airstrip. No commercial harbor. No docks. And I told Captain Steel that. He laughed at me. They all did. They said *go home. There's nothing out there. Accept what you have and live with it.* But I sensed something about them. They shared glances. There was an energy. An aura, if you will. And that same night. That same night, Croker. They took a ship out of the harbor and were never seen again.'

He sits back and drums his fingers on the armrests of his chair. 'Of course, there's no way of knowing what happened to them.'

'Was there a storm?'

'No, but there was a strong wind and I'm told the currents around the island form eddies and strange suctions that pose dangers if you go too far out.'

'What causes them?'

'Reefs. Shallow depressions. Ledges. Either way, my take on it is that they tried to leave, or they went further out and they either made it to somewhere else, or a calamity befell them, or perhaps a greater force prevented them from returning.'

'That's a lot of guesses.'

He nods darkly. 'Indeed. Too many. But you see my point? Yes? You didn't just go to the north shore looking for the docks from your story. You went because you needed to see it for yourself – that this really is an island, that this really is happening.'

I shrug and drink the coffee. 'It is an island, and it is happening.'

'Exactly,' he says, as though he just proved some profound point.

'We are on an island, Croker. An island,' he says, leaning closer again. 'An island rapidly filling with people.'

I hold still. Not making the connection he wants me to make.

'And they're all locked into it,' he adds, motioning them around us. 'They believe in it. But like we said, what choice do they have? So they accept it. It's easier to do so. They get jobs. Places to live. They fornicate and breed and yet more arrive, so we open more genre offices and train more genre reps and create more jobs and they fornicate and they breed, so we create more places. Western World. Middle Earth, and I've no doubt we'll soon have an area dedicated to LGBTQ, and if that happens then the hardcore sci-fi lot will demand *their* own space . . . Which creates more jobs and more demand, and more people will come, and they will fornicate and breed. But, as I saw, and as you said, we are on an island.'

I stare into his dark eyes and eat another lemon sponge finger.

'That, Croker,' he says, nodding at it.

'What about it?' I ask, with my mouth full.

He rolls his eyes, as though I'd just missed the point of his whole poetic speech. 'Where does it bloody come from?'

'The waiter brought it over.'

'Where did the waiter get it from?'

'I don't know. The storeroom?'

'And how did it get there?'

'From a delivery service?'

'And where did the delivery service get it from?'

'From a baker?'

'You stubborn shit, Croker! Where did the baker get the ingredients from?'

'From a wholesaler?'

'John!'

'Okay, I get it.'

'Finally,' he snaps, sitting back to rub his nose.

'Whoever is behind it all likes lemon sponge fingers.'

'You insufferable shit!'

'I'm joking!' I say as I eat another sponge finger.

'Where does the bloody food come from, Croker? We're on a fucking island!'

I blink at him cussing that way and shrug again. 'I saw farms when we went to the north shore. And Rachel said in orientation they grow everything.'

He gives me a withering look. 'We grow coffee, do we? And bananas? And oranges, and apples, and grapes, some for eating, some for making into wine, and we grow hops for beer, and we make glass bottles to put the beer into and we make bamboo chairs and bamboo tables and we grow wheat for flour and lemons to make sponge fingers? And we grow enough sugar and crops to feed everyone, and all our horses, with the exact amount of produce they need. On an island – inhabited by people half developed as Batman or Harley bloody Quinn, or morose teenage dystopian shits with bouncing bosoms and big-armed jocks – or more crime scene investigators and FBI agents and coroners than you can shake a stick at, nearly all of whom know nothing about actual crime scene investigations, or, more importantly, anything about farming or manufacture, so pray do let me ask you again. Where does the food come from?'

'Is that rhetorical? It's just I don't know you and –'

'It's not bloody rhetorical! It's a question. Where does it all come from?'

'I don't know.'

'I know you don't know. And I don't know either. But that's what we *need* to know. That's the link, right there. There's no point stealing a boat and trying to sail away. We don't know how to sail, and something tells me those pirate captains did not make it out. Which means being discreet.'

I pick up the last sponge finger and bite into it as he gives me a look. 'Sorry. Did you want it?'

'Not with your gob all over it. But see, Croker. I can't help but think they're worried.'

'Who?'

'*They*, as in the general term used in reference to the generic baddies of the story.'

'Is this another story?'

'I hope that sponge finger gives you the shits. No. It isn't a story. Or is it? I don't know! It could be. Who knows anything? My point is, though, that I can't help but think they're worried . . . because of *you*.'

'Me?'

'You retained your skills, Croker. And you persuaded other people to go with you and search the island within a week of arriving. You'd already been into the harbor asking questions and by that night in Diagonal Alley you'd got the weird wizard shits picking a fight with you.'

'I said they were weird wizard shits!'

'Dirty little robe-wearing bastards,' Hope says with distaste. 'The point is, they started on you, and I can't help but think they were trying to give you something else to worry about. To make you stop being you. Griff was there, Croker. He saw the whole thing. He said they swarmed you in the bar. Why? And Griff saw the fight outside. He said some of the wizards were running over to the other Bonds to make them aware, so they'd help Jimmy Secretan. Why do that? There have been rumors for years that the wizards and Bonds compete with certain criminal activities. They wouldn't assist each other. But they did.'

'Hang on. If this is all an illusion or controlled by someone else, why would they let criminals operate in the city?'

'Because crime *creates* the illusion of free will. It gives people something to fear and berate the police about. Then, after Diagonal Alley, you went north. Tell me about the highway robbery.'

'They used a cart to block the road on the pretense of a recent accident with someone hurt. It's a common tactic.'

'Did they see you earlier?'

I think back. 'At the Wayside Inn. The leader even nodded at me as he left. Wait – you think that wasn't a robbery?'

'Perhaps. Or perhaps it was an assassination *disguised* as a robbery. Which failed, so on your return you are duly arrested for murder, with credible witnesses willing to testify that you had already assaulted the murder victim.'

'But we've got Griff saying I *didn't* do it.'

'But they'll tie him up in knots under cross-examination. At best, Griff has bought us some time, because they *will* charge you with murder, and you *will* stand trial for it. That's if you're still alive by then.'

I sit back and take it all in as he does the same.

'Where does the food come from. That's what we need to know, because one way or another they will find a way to take you down. They can't have people with your level of skill here, Croker. You're not cowed by them. Your physicality is greater than theirs.'

I frown at him with the next question forming in my head, and again he beats me to it before I even open my mouth.

'What's in it for me?' he asks. I nod, and that dark look crosses his features again. 'The truth, Croker. I want the truth of it all. It claws at my insides not knowing.'

'So why didn't you do this before? You went round the island. You stole a horse. You questioned people. Why can't you find out where the food comes from?'

'I had to stop,' he says, with a look of discomfort.

'Why?'

'Why?' he asks, stretching his legs out to tug his waistcoat and shirt up while twisting in his seat to show me his naked lower back. 'That's bloody why.'

I peer closer and spot the tail end of a thick scar running up the side of his back then see a few more crisscrossing higher up.

'Someone broke into my room in the dead of night and did this with a knife. They made it look like a robbery, but it was no robbery,' he says, turning back to tuck his shirt in. 'It was a warning. So that's why. You help me and I help you.'

He thrusts a hand out while glaring at me with that seething intensity, and as weird as it all is, I don't detect any dishonesty in him. He isn't doing this for charity or for money. He wants something. He wants me to protect him. And in return, I'll help him find out where the food comes from.

Which, in my head, means finding the docks.

Because maybe there is a van after all.

I shake his hand, and the irony is not lost on me that I'm a John agreeing to work for a Sherlock.

CHAPTER TWENTY-FIVE

Wednesday morning.

'BE DISCREET,' I tell myself, remembering what Hope said.

'Discretion is everything, Croker. We need to find out without looking like we are, indeed, finding out!'

It was the coffee. And probably the high sugar content in the plate of lemon sponge fingers we polished off, but either way, Hope was *wired* when we got back to his place.

'And let me tell you why discretion is so important,' he said, and called me over to a table to show me a file of press cuttings.

'We have newspapers here?' I asked.

'No, I wrote them all myself,' he said, giving me a look. 'Yes! We have several newspapers, which is also a tool used to create the illusion of free will.'

'How?'

'Because having newspapers giving opposite views to everything and whipping people into a frenzy over the price of bloody jam stops them asking the bigger questions.'

'Like where the jam comes from,' I said.

He gave me a side-eye. 'I can't tell if you're being facetious. Nevertheless,' he added, slapping a hand on the press cuttings, 'listen to this one. *City News reports the tragic loss of recently arrived Abacus Finch, a promising citizen who was said to have retained skills as an experienced lawyer and investigator. Finch went missing while hiking out of the city and is thought to have been attacked by a bear.'*

'We have bears here?'

'Yes. Obviously. They wouldn't say a mythical creature ate Mr Finch, would they?'

'Is that why the price of jam is so high?'

'I'm not going to dignify that comment with a reply. Needless to say, although it was before my time, it's obvious from the wording that Finch was asking questions. And listen to this one.

NATKISS READYGREEN, TEEN DYSTOPIAN GENRE, SADLY DIED YESTERDAY AFTER FALLING UNDER THE WHEELS OF A HEAVY CART TRANSPORTING BARRELS OF BEER. NATKISS, WHO HAD BEEN IN F.L. LESS THAN A WEEK, HAD PREVIOUSLY MADE HEADLINES AFTER ASSAULTING FOUR POLICE OFFICERS WHILE VIOLENTLY DEMONSTRATING IN THE VILLAGE

. . . I was here for that one. It was a week after my robbery. Natkiss was wild, Croker. She could fight, and she was fast. They tried securing her in Juvie Hall but she got out and went on a rampage through the Village, demanding to know the truth. I remember it! Then look. She's run over and killed. And what about this one –

THE FICTION LAND GAZETTE IS HEARTBROKEN TO REPORT THE TRAGIC DEATHS OF THREE POLICE OFFICERS, KILLED WHILE TRYING TO ARREST HARRY CALLAWAY. CALLAWAY, WHO HAD ARRIVED ONLY FIVE DAYS PREVIOUSLY, HAD REFUSED TO ENGAGE WITH ORIENTATION AND THERAPY AND HAD BROKEN INTO THE CITY POLICE HEADQUARTERS AND TAKEN DETECTIVE SALLY WAINWRIGHT HOSTAGE. THE MOTIVE IS UNCLEAR AT THIS TIME, BUT OUR THOUGHTS AND PRAYERS ARE WITH THE FAMILIES OF OUR FALLEN HEROES. DETECTIVE WAINWRIGHT WAS SAID TO BE UNINJURED.

Does the name resonate with you? Harry Calloway was a copy of Harry Callahan. As in *Dirty Harry*, and by all accounts he was very tough and very determined. And there's more. Johnny McClane committed suicide. Wan Bolo fell off the cliff after stealing a horse and reaching the north shore. Dick Reckard drowned. Not to mention the missing pirate captains. And more recently Jack Spiller – he was a Reacher. Merry Pason. Mr Maple. All of them died within a week or two of arriving, Croker. All of them refused to accept what they saw. And that's just in the city. I should think Western World and Middle Earth have their own editions, covering the same sorts of things.'

'Why didn't they just warn them off like they did with you?'

'Because I heeded the warning, Croker. They, clearly, did not. And some, I'll warrant, were too explosive to even attempt to warn, and were executed very quickly. Do you see, dear boy? That is why discretion is so very vital. Whatever we do, and however we do it, we *must,* at all times, be discreet.'

'OKAY. DISCREET,' I remind myself as I cross the road, while figuring that even I would struggle to fight a bear.

I walk into the supermarket, grab a basket and start perusing the aisles like any old regular shopper. I find it comes naturally to me. Which means I must have been a spy, or had training to do this sort of thing.

Either way, I keep my cover as a browsing shopper and start picking packets and jars up.

The pamphlets and guides we read in orientation said that everything is produced in Fiction Land, and that thanks to a complex network of diversification, whatever that means, we are able to enjoy an ever-increasing range of foods and supplies.

But then Hope was also right about something else. I think of Svetty and L and Alice, and even myself and John Candle. None of us know anything about farming, or mass-manufacture or processing, and although I can't say *all,* I would guess most authors who create characters are not skilled in those things either.

But then Hope also said to let him do the smart thinking while I do the legwork on his behalf.

Which makes me remember what Rachel said, that Johns are predisposed to find plots and seek conspiracies – and I gotta be honest, the receptors in my brain are lighting up from everything Hope has told me. Thinking that makes me want to talk to Rachel, but I don't know if that's allowed, or if it will cause her trouble.

I miss the others too, L and Svetty, and I hope Alice is okay and hasn't suffered because of what happened. And in turn, that makes me remember the other thing Hope said. That Griff will fall apart under cross-examination, which means I really need to find a way out of this murder rap, and fast.

I put my mind back to the task at hand and absorb myself into the role of the dutiful shopper, out perusing and purchasing ingredients to make dinner for my family. But a sudden thought strikes me as I hold a jar of plum tomatoes.

Just where do these delicious plum tomatoes come from?

'Say, I was wondering if you could help me,' I say to a bosomy young woman with very blonde hair stacking shelves. 'Do you know where this comes from?'

'Huh?' she says, looking at the jar. 'Back there on that shelf.'

'No. Ha! Sorry. I mean *where*. As in where do the tomatoes come from?'

'I dunno. They probably make them in a factory.'

'Sorry, what?'

'What?'

'I think tomatoes are grown on plants. They're not made.'

'Yeah? That's so cool. What, in the wild?' she asks.

'Er, no, I'm guessing they're probably on some kind of irrigated set-up in a growing house.'

'Wow,' she says with wide eyes. 'Mindblown! I did not know that. What about potatoes?'

'What about them?' I ask.

'Are they grown on plants?'

'What? No! They're grown in the ground. In earth.'

'What, like the dirt?'

'Yes.'

'That's disgusting.'

'No, they wash them. Or actually, I think the dirt helps preserve them and you're meant to wash them before you cook them.'

'Mate. You're like a genius,' she says, without any sense of mockery. 'And hot. You wanna go out?'

'I'm sorry, what?'

'For a drink. Or for sex.'

'For a drink *or* sex? Not both then?'

'Oh god! Mindblown again. Wow. You're like a professor.'

I stare into her beautiful blue eyes, so very empty of anything remotely connected to intelligence, and smile politely. 'I'm married.'

'Is she smart too? I'll do a three-way.'

'Okay! Bye then!'

'Bring your wife!'

'No.'

'Or your husband. Is he a hot professor?'

'No!'

I leave the supermarket and find another, and once more browse the shelves, adopting my persona. This time, I select my target with greater care and aim for an older-looking guy in a shirt and tie.

'Say, excuse me. Are you a manager?' I ask.

'Hi! Yes, I am! How can I help?'

'I'm new. Just arrived a week ago and I was just wondering about the produce here.'

'Welcome to Fiction Land!' he says, grasping my hand to shake earnestly. 'I'm Glynn.'

'Er, John.'

'Great to meet you, John. I love this question! Come with me. Come on!'

'Wait. What?' I ask, as he walks to the end of the aisle by the checkouts.

'We got a newbie, guys!' he yells out, clapping his hands. 'Newbie alert! Everyone, this is John! He looks like a Wick. Are you a Wick?'

'No! I'm a er, a Croker.'

'John Croker!' Glynn shouts before I can stop him. 'Everyone say *Hi John Croker*.'

They do it, too. The whole damn store. Every shopper and every worker.

'Say hi to everyone at Cloud Ten Store, John Croker!'

'Er, Hi!' I say, with a wince.

'And John Croker wants to know where our food and goods come from?' Glynn says with that big shit-eating grin. 'Well, John. I can tell you it's all grown right here in Fiction Land! Everything we could ever need, which is why we are so darned lucky and happy to be here.'

'Great! Well, thank you,' I say and try to slide away, but he grabs my arm and pulls me back as the staff and shoppers all smile and wave.

'Tell you what, John. Why don't I give you *the special tour*! How about that? We normally reserve it for school parties, but heck! Let's go wild!'

'AND HE DID IT?' Hope asks me with a look of horror as I tell him what happened back in his parlor. 'He gave you a tour? Of the store? In front of everyone?'

'Yes.'

'Which is after the bosomy woman asked for a three-way.'

'Yes. No! How did you know about that?'

'I see you,' Griff says, making me jump as he steps out from the wallpaper.

'What part of discretion did you fail to understand, Croker?' Hope asks me.

'I tried!'

'Just how is being offered a three-way and being introduced to every single person in a supermarket *and* using your real name after asking *where does the bloody food come from* in any way match trying to be discreet?'

'I didn't ask for the three-way! I asked where tomatoes came from, and she thought they were made.'

'I had a three-way once,' Maisy mutters as she pours the tea.

'Sorry, what?' I ask, glancing from Hope to her then over to Griff merging with the wall.

'Why did you ask her in the first place?' Hope demands. 'Griff said there was a delivery cart unloading at the side! Why didn't you follow that? Or infiltrate the supply network. Dear god. And you told him your actual name! Your actual name! Discretion, Croker. I said discretion! Did you not hear me reading out that very long list of people killed?'

'Yes! Bears. Jam. Catpiss fell off a cliff. I heard you.'

'Oh dear,' Hope says, with a dramatic final throwing of his hands before slumping back in his chair. 'Well. We might as well put a big sign outside saying *we are actively trying to find a way off this island*.'

'Righto. Tea's ready,' Maisy says. 'I'll go and make a start on that sign for you, Sherry.'

'Aren't you going to stop her?' I ask when she walks out.

'She's fine. Mrs Hudson loves arts and crafts.'

'It's Maisy!' Maisy shouts from the hallway as I try and find Griff.

'Good god, Croker. He's right beside you,' Hope snaps as I slowly turn to see Griff sitting on the sofa next to me with a big grin.

'This is so fucked up,' I mutter.

'Isn't it just,' Hope says darkly. 'And now I'm getting a depression. I can feel it coming on.'

'Maybe I'm not so good at the spying thing.'

'Really? What gave it away?'

'Why don't you try?'

'Because I am routinely followed. And if I so much as ask the origins of a teabag I have no doubt something terrible will befall me. We need someone natural, Croker. Someone who can ask a question without it being obvious *what* they're asking.'

I think of Svetty asking the orange seller about the north shore, and then the concierge at the hotel and how she flattered Moist into giving us some rooms. 'I might know a woman who can help.'

'I am assuming by the fact you have suggested her that you think her trustworthy?'

'Yes. I think she is.'

'Fine. Fetch her.'

'Fetch her?'

'Summon her! Collect. Retrieve. Seek. Piss off outside and go and bloody find her while I wallow in self-pity. And do not have sex with her on the way back you bloody cad!'

'I haven't had sex with anyone!'

'What. Not ever? Oh, good lord, you're not a virgin, are you? Whatever. Stop talking. Go and find this femme fatale and don't say a blasted word about anything until she's back here. Not a word, Croker. Not one single word!'

'DAMMIT, CROKER!' he yells from the same chair a few hours later as we crowd into the parlor. 'What part of being discreet confused you this time?'

'Well,' I say. 'What happened was . . .'

CHAPTER TWENTY-SIX

What happened was that I set out to find my van.

No.

Wrong mission.

I had to get Svetty to help us.

The first problem, though, was finding her.

I went to the rooms we'd been assigned. But they were empty.

I went to the genre offices. They were empty too, other than a mouse sitting on a desk twitching his whiskers.

I tried the fifties diner. But there was no sign of Svetty.

Next, I tried the Village. It was busy as hell, but I couldn't find her there either.

'Ah, Croker!' Nietzsche said over a game of chess with Freud. 'Been framed for any more murders?'

'Quietly, Nietzsche,' Freud whispered. 'The Village has ears, old chap.'

'I didn't do it,' I told them.

'And even if you did, I'm sure there'd be a reason,' Freud added in a quiet voice. 'Just go carefully, Mr Croker. Anyway. Regards to Hope. Oh, and do tell him bridge night has been moved to this evening.'

I said goodbye and started my search again.

But I could not find her in the house.

And I could not find her with the mouse.

I could not find her here or there.

I could not find her anywhere.

'Good lord, Croker,' Freud said, as I passed them again. 'They're in the arrivals park! Not the greatest spy, are you?'

I walked briskly from the Village to the arrivals park to see Svetlana holding a clipboard.

Except she wasn't alone.

'Hey,' I said, as I walked over to them.

'Croker!' Alice cried out, running over to give me a hug.

'Dude. What happened?' L asked. 'They questioned us for hours!'

'Literally all night,' Svetlana added.

'All of you?' I asked.

'All of us,' Rachel said from my side. 'I'm glad you're okay though.'

'We heard there's a witness,' Alice said, as a guy woke up on a nearby bench.

'ZOMBIES, RUN!'

'Jesus. Another one?' Svetlana asked. 'How many unfinished zombie books *are* there?'

'Seriously. He's like the tenth one already,' Alice told me, as Pat walked over to the guy.

'Why are you here?' I asked, seeing they all had clipboards.

'New scheme,' Rachel said. 'Oh god, there's another one already,' she added, as a curvaceous woman in very thin and very tight leather called out as she rose from a bench.

'Fair maidens and gallant sires! Hast thou seen my horse? He is as white as snow and as fast as the wind!'

'Fantasy erotica?' Svetlana suggested.

'Got to be,' Alice said.

'My turn!' L said, already running off. 'Alas, fair lady! Allow me to assist you!'

'L! You come right back after dropping her off,' Rachel called.

'You were saying why you're here,' I prompted.

'They're developing a New Arrivals Taskforce,' Rachel said. 'Who will deal exclusively with new arrivals and vet them for skills,' she added, giving me a look. 'And guess who's heading it up? The charming Miss Wainwright. But in the meantime, we get to form an

Arrivals Committee. Which is also a way of punishing us for our *infractions*.'

'I was kidnapped, apparently,' Alice said.

'John! Good to see you,' I heard John Candle call, and turned to see him walking over with his hand held out. 'Heard about the er, *situation*. Hope it all works out for you.'

'Thanks,' I said, as he turned away as though dismissing me. 'Patricia? I've returned from the last arrival. Shall I take the north end of the park? I think I've got the run of things to carry on.'

'Sure,' Pat said, eyeing our little group with a nod to Rachel. 'I'll come up with you.'

'See you later, John,' I said.

'Ah. It's actually Simon now,' John Candle said he walked off. 'Simon Smith.'

'What the hell happened to him?' I asked.

'He's embraced this shit,' Svetlana said.

'He's changed his name so people don't think he's a Wick,' Rachel explained.

'Are you really living with Sherlock Holmes?' Alice asked. 'That must be nuts. Is he like, *ah, my dear Croker. Shall we hunt for clues?*'

'He's called Sherrinford Hope, and he's one smart guy, although he cusses a lot. But in British which doesn't sound quite so rude.'

'Bloody hell!' Svetlana said in a British accent. 'Wish I could jolly bloody meet him what what!'

'Yeah. On that,' I said.

'Ooh, what?' Alice asked as they crowded in.

'What's happening, dude?' L asked as he jogged back over.

'Guys. Maybe we shouldn't ask,' Rachel told the others. 'But seriously, is it about the case?'

'No, I mean, I just needed to talk to Svetty.'

'You need me?' Svetlana asked, then nodded as though she understood. 'I've got it. Who is he?'

'Who?' I asked.

'The man you need seducing.'

'There isn't one.'

'Oh! Is it a woman? No, okay. I can roll with that.'

'There's no woman either,' I said.

'Then who am I seducing?'

'Nobody!'

'Then what do you need Svetty for?' L asked.

'Cos she can do more than just seduce people.'

'Like what?' Svetlana asked, as though such a thing couldn't possibly be true.

'You know. Like ask questions.'

'What questions?' she asked me.

'I'm good at asking questions,' Alice said. '*Where's the toilet?* See. How natural was that?'

'No! I mean, like discreetly. Hope said it has to be discreet. I mean like how Svetty did with the orange seller. And the concierge. And Moist.'

'Me too! Ha! Never gets old,' Svetty said, sharing a high five with Alice.

'John, what questions?' Rachel asked me.

'I can't say! I mean, I tried myself. But this woman offered me a three-way with my husband and –'

'Whoa. What now?' Rachel said.

'No! I mean. She said my wife first.'

'You're married?' Rachel asked.

'No!'

'I'm in,' L said. 'Is she in Middle Earth?'

'No. A supermarket.'

'Why was a woman asking you for a three-way in a supermarket?' Rachel asked.

'Cos I asked her where the tomatoes came from!'

'What!' Rachel said.

'And so I explained and she thought I was this hot professor and it all went wrong, so then I went to this other place to ask them where the food comes from and met literally the nicest manager ever who introduced me to the whole shop while I was trying to be a spy but I gave him my real name and he took me on the special tour and was like *so this is John Croker. John wants to know where our food comes from!* but he did give me a really cool badge.'

'You have a badge?' L asked.

'Yeah,' I said, showing them the badge.

'So cool,' Alice said. 'I want a badge.'

'It is a cool badge, actually,' Rachel said.

'See! And Hope made me take it off. He was all like, *you're a bloody shit spy, Croker! I told you to be discreet! What part of that didn't you understand? Now go and get Svetty so she can find out where the food comes from! But don't tell her a single bloody word!*'

'Okay,' Svetlana said slowly. 'Starting to see his point a bit, John.'

'What?' I asked.

'Yeah, bless,' Alice said.

'What?' I asked again.

'You literally just outlined the entire plan,' Alice said.

'I did not!'

'Why does it matter where the food comes from?' L asked.

'Oh god! We're on an island,' Alice said. 'Of course! How can we grow or manufacture everything we need?'

'What? No! You're not meant to know,' I said.

'But how is that connected to this murdered cowboy?' Alice asked, with a thoughtful expression. 'Unless they're worried about John because he kept his skills and keeps looking for his docks. Yes! John did that! He went to the harbor and asked around then the wizards picked that fight with him. They must have been trying to warn you off or something. But then you fought back and they realized you were skilled, so they sent Detective Shovel to your room to scare you. But that didn't work so they set the robbery up to take you out. But even that didn't work, so then they set up him for murder! And now I bet Hope realizes that the only way off this island, and for Croker to avoid going to prison, is by finding out where all of our supplies come from. What? Why are you all staring at me?'

'AND THAT'S WHAT HAPPENED,' I tell Hope, as his dark eyes stare over to Alice sitting next to L on the big red chesterfield.

'What? Why are you all staring at me again?' Alice asks in her torn tights and unlaced DM boots and baggy black T-shirt, her dark eyes made darker by thick makeup.

'That is remarkable deductive reasoning, young lady. I am

assuming you are a Holmes?' Hope asks, as Rachel, Svetty, and I all share looks.

'I didn't even consider that,' Rachel says. 'I figured she was an Alice in Wonderland.'

'Maybe she's both,' Svetty says, as we all look at Alice holding her chin up defiantly. 'Are you?' Svetty asks.

'What difference does it make?' Alice asks, clearly uncomfortable at her backstory being probed. But then she's not the only one, and I glance at Rachel, figuring both of them are hiding whatever they did in their previous lives.

'Ooh! It's been a while since we've had a party, Sherry,' Maisy says, bustling in with the tea tray.

'We've never had a party, Mrs Hudson.'

'She's called Maisy,' I tell the others. 'Not Mrs Hudson.'

'Tea all around is it?' Maisy asks. 'And what about tea? Are they staying for tea, Sherry?'

'She means dinner,' I explain.

'I'd thought we'd have either bangers and mash or toad in the hole,' Maisy says, as the others look at me again.

'No idea,' I say. 'But you should try the dick.'

'Dick?' Rachel asks.

'I like dick,' Svetlana says.

'It's spotted,' I say.

'Yeah, not so keen on those ones,' Svetlana adds.

'What about you, Griff? Stopping for tea?' Maisy asks, holding a cup of tea out to a potted plant.

'What the fuck!' I say as Griff appears, smiling and taking the cup. 'How does he do that?'

'Actually, Maisy, thank you for the kind offer, but we won't be stopping,' Rachel says, in a way that makes us all look over to see her glaring at Hope. 'The reason we are here, Mr Hope, is not to encourage this fantasy but to put an immediate end to it.'

'Rach, no,' Alice says, with a degree of alarm. 'We said we'd help Croker find out about the food thing.'

'We didn't, Alice. *You* did, and we are not doing anything about the *food thing*, because there is no *food thing*. And you, Mr Hope, should know better. What on earth possessed you to tell a newly arrived John such a ridiculous conspiracy theory? He hasn't even finished therapy!'

'Miss Askew. I understand your concerns. Truly, I do,' Hope says. 'But this is not a conspiracy theory.'

'He's got evidence,' I tell Rachel. 'Show her the evidence. The jam man and the woman that pissed down the cliff.'

'What!?' Rachel asks me.

'People died. Mr Hope said people asked questions before and got killed for it.'

'That's another conspiracy theory, John! People die here all the time. It's a big city full of thousands of people on a big island full of, I don't know, *lots* of people.'

'No. He said one got run over . . . And another one fell off a cliff.'

'A woman got trampled by a horse outside my office the week before you arrived. Was she murdered? How about the man that fell down the stairs in my block when I first moved in? Did someone push him?'

'I don't know. Maybe.'

'Listen to yourself. There is no van.'

'I'm not looking for my van, Rachel. I'm looking for the . . . the food thing.'

'There is no food thing. You're looking for a plot, John. And there is no plot either. I thought we'd got past this. We went to the north shore. You saw it for yourself. There's nothing out there.'

'No, hang on,' Alice cuts in. 'What about when they tried to kill us.'

'An assassination attempt,' Hope says.

'It was a highway robbery,' Rachel snaps at him. 'They happen all the time out in the countryside. And the army captain even said they were getting more frequent.'

'What about the wizards then!' Alice says.

'The wizards are awful! Everyone knows that. They hated us holding karaoke night in Diagonal Alley. If they hadn't picked a fight with John, it would have been someone else. And that only happened because that creep was giving you alcohol. And that wasn't a conspiracy either, before you start. It was a stupid fight.'

'Then pray tell, Miss Askew, why was Croker arrested for the murder?' Hope asks, as Alice nods eagerly.

'They're trying to stitch him up,' Alice says. 'Because John was asking questions.'

'Right,' Rachel says firmly, pushing her teacup and saucer back onto the tray. 'If I walked outside and punched the first person I saw, who then later gets murdered, I would absolutely, and quite rightly, be considered a suspect. Yes?'

'That's not the same!' Alice says.

'Yes?' Rachel asks over her.

'Yes,' Hope says, giving her the point.

'John was in a physical confrontation with that cowboy. Of course he'll be considered a suspect. There'd be something wrong if he wasn't. Alice, no! I mean it. Mr Hope, do not put anymore stupid ideas in John's head. We grow our own food here. We produce what we need on the island. There is no way off.'

'Rach! Come on,' Alice says. 'It's fucking bullshit and you know it.'

'Language!'

'No! I'm meant to believe I was a character in a book and now we're here and that's it? What is that?'

'It's our reality!' Rachel tells her, before turning back to Hope. 'I will not let Alice get involved.'

'But Alice *is already* involved, Miss Askew. As are you all,' Hope replies.

'Svetty! L!' Alice says. 'Back me up.'

'Honey,' Svetlana says with a soft smile. 'Maybe Rachel is right.'

'She's not! L. You saw that robbery.'

'I mean. Yeah,' he says. 'But it seemed like a robbery. I mean. If they were going to kill us why not have crossbows or swords ready? Or guns maybe.'

'Thank you,' Rachel says, shooting Hope a look before turning back to me. 'John. You need to stop this. Okay? No! Hang on. Let me finish. This isn't just you now. You can do what you want. But if you start doing stupid things then Alice will too.'

'What the fuck! I'm not six!' Alice snaps.

'John! I mean it,' Rachel says, as Alice gets ready to explode. 'She is seventeen and already struggling. Do not put her into more trouble. Do you understand me?'

'Okay,' I say, the force of her voice making me suddenly perceive that maybe she's right.

'Miss Askew,' Hope says in a deep voice, leaning forward to steeple his fingers. 'Why are we here? What for? Don't you want to know? Of course you do! You hired the carriage and took John to the north shore because you feel the same thing that we all feel, that this isn't all there is. I tried to ask questions when I arrived and was cut with a knife for my troubles, and others fared worse than I. You're a genre rep. You should know this.'

'You're damn right I am. And that means I know people like Holmes and Johns and Reachers and Bournes, and all the other mystery-solving characters, are predisposed to find mysteries to *flipping well* solve! I don't know what happened to you or why you got cut. But there is no conspiracy. We'd know if there was. Someone would leak it. And even if by some weird miracle there was, I still wouldn't put Alice in danger like that. I'd even applied for her to live with me, which we can't do now because I took her out of the city and gave her alcohol! Now she's got to stay in Juvie Hall. Do you see my point? There are consequences to our actions.'

'Yeah, let's talk about Juvie Hall?' Alice cuts in. 'They have six-year-old kids crying themselves to sleep in pitch-black rooms while the matrons and orderlies play cards and laugh in the staff room. And do you know what happens when I get back? They make me sign in then they check my pockets for contraband. And the matron makes me breathe out so she can sniff my breath. It's fucking gross. Then I have to use a shared bathroom, which is timed, then into my room by 9 p.m. Lights out at 9.15.'

'Sounds like a prison,' Svetty says.

'Yeah? Well get this. That was *before* getting in trouble. Now I'm back by 8 p.m. and not allowed to talk to anyone. I mean literally no one is allowed to speak to me. And it's bed and lights out by 8.30. Rach, come on! Do you know what it feels like having to go back there?'

'What do you want me to do?!' Rachel asks her. 'I said I'd let you live with me, but they won't allow it.'

'Then let me help Croker find a way off this island!'

'No!'

'Rach!'

'I said no, Alice! It's out of the question.'

'You're not my fucking mom!'

'Okay!' Svetty calls. 'That's enough, Alice. Rachel cares deeply for you! You're just frustrated. Enough! Don't shout over me. You need to cool off. And for what's it worth, I think Rach is right. You need to back off, Mr Hope. Don't get John in more trouble. John, just let it go.'

I think to argue, but like I said, I can already see the shift in perception and how quick I was to latch onto a plot. 'Okay,' I say.

'Just see the therapy through,' Rachel says, reaching over to squeeze my hand. 'You have to stay here under your bail conditions but promise me you won't go hunting or trying to find things out. Let's get this murder thing out the way, okay? And I'll try and make another appeal or something for Alice to live with me. Alice?'

Alice shrugs. Clearly pissed as hell, but Svetty nudges her and the kid nods at Rachel.

'Okay. Good,' Rachel says. 'Right. Lovely tea. Thank you very much, but it's getting late, and we need to get Alice back.'

They start rising. I get up with them. 'I'll walk with you. I need some things from my old room.'

We start heading for the door, the others all saying goodbye to Hope.

He nods once but stays silent and brooding and we walk out, while I tell myself there is no van.

CHAPTER TWENTY-SEVEN

Wednesday evening.

WE SET off through Little Victoria to walk Alice back to Juvie Hall.

'I can't face going back there,' Alice says as we approach the doors.

'Just stick with it,' Rachel says, giving her a hug. 'We'll figure something out. I promise.'

The kid nods, and I swear I see tears in her eyes that she blinks away furiously.

'Go on. And don't get angry. Keep your head down,' Rachel says.

Alice nods as the big wooden door swings open, a hard-faced woman in a white uniform glaring out.

'In,' she orders.

'I'm coming,' Alice says, before turning back to us. 'Can I work in the arrivals park again tomorrow?'

'Now, Alice!' the matron snaps angrily.

'Problem here?' a deep voice asks, as a gnarly guy looms over the matron. 'Get inside, Alice.'

'Don't talk to her like that!' Rachel says.

'Who the hell are you?' the guy demands.

'She's the one that kidnapped Alice and got her drunk,' the Matron says as they both give Rachel a filthy look, which in turn makes me stiffen until Svetty gently touches my arm.

'Don't make it worse for her,' she whispers. 'Go on, Alice. We'll see you tomorrow. We'll go for pancakes in the Village for breakfast.'

'I think she's had enough junk food. Have you seen her thighs?' the Matron sneers as Alice goes past with a stricken look.

'How dare you!' Rachel snaps.

'Hey. Not cool,' L says.

'Don't body shame her!' Svetlana says. 'She's seventeen! She's still developing.'

'Don't stand there gawping!' the man snaps at Alice. 'Wash. Bed. Now!'

'I'm going!' Alice mutters, heading off.

'Do not backchat me!' the guy snarls.

'Or?' I ask, as a silence descends and Alice pauses to look back.

'Is that a threat?' he asks.

'No. A threat would be that if one hair on her head is mistreated, I'll come back and break every bone in your body. That would be a threat,' I pause to read his name badge, 'Gavin.'

'You'll be reported for that,' Gavin says with a grin, but I can see the uncertainty in his eyes.

'I didn't hear anything,' L says.

'Not a word,' Svetty says, beaming him a big smile. 'Night, Alice!'

I spot the smile on Alice's face as she turns and disappears inside.

'We're meant to be making things better, not worse,' Rachel says.

'So, we had this section head during training,' L says. 'C36. He got off on making our lives hell and it went on for years. We were kids. I was like eight or whatever, and we all thought it was normal. Anyway. So we graduate, right? We get assigned roles and we all go off to fight in wars to try and get rid of the damned Fedis. But then this one night we all meet up for a drink in mess hall. And we're all grown up and we see C36, and he comes over and he's trying to be like *you little maggots! I made you into soldiers. I'm the only reason you got through the training*. And we're like, dude.'

'And?' Rachel asks when he trails off.

'Oh, we totally kicked the shit out of him and told him he ever beats another recruit again we'd airlock him. Seriously. Best day ever.

You gotta stand up to bullies like that. It's like the system empowers them to be that way, so it becomes normalized. You want my take on it? Croker did the right thing.'

'Thanks,' I tell him. 'I was worried I'd made it worse.'

'Oh dude, you totally have,' L says. 'They'll make her life hell. Fuckers like that always do.'

'But you just said Croker did the right thing,' Svetty says.

'Yeah. Damn right. I bet she's back there right now smiling at them all cocky, knowing Croker just scared the shit out of Gavin. I'm telling you. Hope is like a shield you can pull around to deflect some of the bad shit. Not all of it, and she needs to get the hell out of there because it ain't healthy living like that. But I think right now, she knows we've got her back. And that means something.'

We walk in silence, absorbing the rare insight from L.

'You coming up?' Svetlana asks Rachel when we reach our block.

'No. I'd better get back home,' she says, and I hold back while Svetlana and L head inside.

'Listen. Thank you,' I tell Rachel after they've gone.

'What for?'

'You know. What you said back there.'

'I said it for Alice, John.'

'I know. But. Yeah. That's what I meant,' I say quickly, as a faint smile touches her lips.

'Yeah, and I did it for you too,' she admits, with an exaggerated eye-roll. 'You're my friend, John. And friends look out for each other.'

'We're still friends then? I figured you'd run a mile.'

'No,' she says simply, looking me in the eyes. 'You're a decent man, John. Kind. Loyal. Calm. Jesus, I've never met someone so calm. It just radiates from you and it's good for Alice to be around that.' She pauses for a second. 'And me,' she adds, with a touch of raw honesty.

I look at her, not getting why anyone would want to spend time with a crazy guy constantly looking for plots and conspiracies.

'You'll be okay,' she says, maybe reading my thoughts or seeing my expression. 'And, I dunno. Maybe this bit of excitement has been good for me. But only that bit!' she adds with a laugh as she bumps my side. 'No more. Promise me!'

'Okay, okay. I promise.'

She stays close. Staring up into my eyes. 'Anyway. I'd better go. I'd invite you to mine for coffee but . . .'

'It's fine. I've got a three-way waiting for me.'

'Idiot,' she says, hitting my arm again. 'No, but seriously, you haven't, have you?'

'No! Honestly. That's not my thing.'

I spot that look in her eyes again. The fleeting glimpse of panic, or something going unsaid.

'You okay?' I ask.

She opens her mouth to speak, then blinks and smiles as the moment passes. 'Fine. Just tired.'

'Sure. I'd better get back, but hey, er, thanks again. It means a lot having you in my life.'

She smiles. 'Night, John.'

'Night,' I say and turn away, but she catches my arm and turns me back to kiss my cheek.

'And that was another romantic gesture,' she says, and rushes off while my heart beats a little weirdly.

'Such sweet romance,' a voice says, and I turn to see Jimmy Secretan walking slowly towards me.

'How's the thumb?' I ask, spotting the dressing still on it.

His face hardens with spite, but he forces a smile. 'Worth it for the trouble you're in, old boy,' he says, playing up his educated British accent.

'What you doing here anyway? You stalking me?'

'No. Her,' he says, as I take a step towards him. 'Still no sense of humor then, Croker,' he says with a laugh. 'I'm just out for a stroll and happened to see you lovebirds sharing a magical moment.'

I grunt, itching for a reason to take him apart, but he gives me a charming smile and strolls by.

'Oh, but I should make one suggestion,' he says lightly. 'Do ask Lola about her story, won't you. Oh, darn it. Did I say Lola? I meant Rachel. Goodnight, Croker. I am sure we shall see each other very soon.'

I wait for him to disappear to make sure he doesn't follow Rachel, then turn and head inside, figuring that whatever Rachel's story was is her own business and she'll either tell me when she's ready, or never at all if she wants.

I like her the same either way.

I head into my old room and start gathering my belongings, when I hear a knock and turn to see John Candle in the doorway. 'John,' I say with a nod.

'It's Simon.'

'Simon. Right.'

'You're back?' he asks.

'Just getting some things.'

He nods slowly. 'And er, noticed you're growing a beard.'

'What, this?' I ask, rubbing my stubble as I clock his is the same. 'I didn't have my wash kit to shave.'

'So, you're *not* growing a beard?'

'What? No. I'm not. Why?'

'I'm trying to lose the whole *John* thing, and you know, what happened with you and the cowboy, and I thought I'd grow a beard, but if you grow a beard then –'

'Relax, John. I'll shave when I get back.'

'It's Simon.'

'Simon. Whatever. Don't worry. It'll be gone by tomorrow.'

He nods again. 'You don't like it here then?' he asks.

'Like it here? Like what, exactly?'

'There's a lot of opportunity in the city, John.'

I frown at the way he says it and how he's dressed now. Svetlana was right. He's really buying into this place.

'Maybe finish your Enders therapy and then, you know, you could apply for some work. I've been talking to the guys at social services and we're thinking about developing ongoing group therapy sessions led by the user but, you know, *for* the user. I think something like that could really help you.'

'Sure. I'll keep it in mind,' I say, thinking he'll go, but he lingers and watches me packing my things into a bag.

'Acceptance is the key, John.'

'Sure. Acceptance,' I reply. Understanding what he's trying to say but not liking the patronizing tone. 'But, you know, most people just go along with it cos there's no other choice.'

'So, what? You're the man to change it? *John Croker on another mission.* That it, John? The receptors firing, are they? You don't think maybe you got hooked up with the wrong people and they're feeding your paranoia?'

'I like you, Candle. But keep going and I won't.'

'This isn't a book, John! Saying shit like that doesn't work in real life.'

'Okay, *Simon,*' I say, and motion for him to move over, and for a second he looks ready to try again but sighs and moves over a step to let me get by.

'Take it easy, Croker.'

'You too, Candle.'

'Smith.'

'Good choice,' I say, and head down and out into the warm night air and home to Little Victoria.

CHAPTER TWENTY-EIGHT

Thursday morning.

'HOPE NOT JOINING US FOR BREAKFAST?' I ask Maisy the following morning.

'He's still in his dark mood,' she says, while taking the tops off my two soft boiled eggs, held within their cups. 'I've cut your soldiers all ready for you,' she adds, smiling at my little pieces of toast all in a smart line, ready to launch an attack on the runny yolks. 'Sherry does like his soldiers all neat.'

'Thank you,' I reply, and start to tuck in as she leaves. Then I stop and stare around the suspiciously empty room, looking for Griff. I even lean over and use one of my soldiers to attack the air over the seats next to me in case he's there.

Then I jab under the table and get up to swipe at the ferns and run my hand along the dado rail, before going to back to my chair and lowering down onto two legs and a lap already sitting there.

'What the fuck!' I launch back up.

'Can't see me,' he says, dipping a soldier in my one of my eggs.

'Get off my eggs.'

'Can't see me!' he says, then growls when I try and take my eggs and soldiers away.

'Fine! Keep the damn eggs.' I gulp my coffee down before heading for the door. 'I spat in both of them.'

He just stares at me like he knows I didn't because he was watching me the whole time. 'They'll see you,' Griff says.

'Who will?' I ask as he slowly dips one my soldiers into my eggs. 'Griff. Who will see me?'

He doesn't reply, just stares and eats the eggy toast. I roll my eyes and head out to warm summer morning. The street already bustling with people going by and the road filled with delivery wagons and carriages.

I pause to watch a heavy cart pulled by two enormous draft horses and figure maybe I can get to work on the delivery networks today. Rachel and the others have to work in the park, but I don't. Maybe I should simply follow a delivery cart back to wherever it comes from. That doesn't involve talking to people – and it uses skills I actually have.

A plan made, so I head off to the Village for some pancakes and coffee, and to see if Alice is okay, and maybe get a nice smile from Rachel.

I think back to the carriage ride on that frosty morning and the two of us cuddled up under the blankets. Her body pressing into mine. The scent of her hair. The warmth of her.

'STOP!' a voice yells, as I start crossing the road.

'Sorry!' I call out to the driver of a wagon, thinking he was about to run me over.

'I didn't shout, mate,' he says, nodding past me to two cops running towards me.

'STAND STILL!' one of them yells.

'You're nicked, mate!' the other shouts, already pulling handcuffs from his belt as the other one draws his baton.

I start backstepping while lifting my hands to show them empty palms. 'What's going on?'

'Just stand still!' the one with the cuffs orders.

'What for?' I ask, still going backwards.

'HE'S OVER HERE!' the one with the baton shouts, as I hear yells and turn to see two more cops running from a side street.

'What for?'

'You know what for!' one of them shouts, pointing his baton at me. 'On your knees! Hands on your head.'

'What? No!'

'You've gone and killed someone else, you bleedin' psycho,' the other one says.

'I haven't killed anyone!'

'STOP MOVING!' one of the cops coming from the right shouts. 'GET DOWN NOW!'

'ON YER KNEES!'

'HANDS ON YOUR HEAD!'

'You're nicked for murder. Get the wagon here!'

'I didn't kill anyone!' I shout, as two more uniformed police run into view. All of them young and fit and clearly ready to fight.

'How many?' I hear the cart driver mutter, and turn to see a wagon pulling into the road, more cops jumping from the back of it with shields and batons.

I back up again, not liking it one bit and not wanting to get arrested again. Wainwright is clearly gunning for me. Rachel and the others aren't here this time, but still, resisting won't get me anywhere. I need to go with it and trust Hope will step in again. I come to a stop and lift my hands.

'Said on yer knees!' one of them yells, as they start encircling me. But I shake my head. I won't fight, but like hell am I getting on my knees for them.

'Are you resisting?' another one shouts.

'He's resisting!'

'STOP RESISTING!' they all start shouting.

'He ain't doing anything,' the cart driver calls, as more people stop and look. 'He's just stood there!'

'LAST CHANCE!' the closest cop yells, face full of fury as he draws his stick back. 'On. Your. Fucking. Knees!'

I look at him, then at the others, and keep my hands still. It all goes silent. Very, very silent.

'Cunt,' the cop snaps, and surges in swinging, and it takes every ounce of control *not* to react or block or counter, and let him hit me with an explosion of pain to the back of my head.

'OI!' the cart driver yells. 'You can't do that!'

The cop lashes out again. Hitting me on the shoulder as another cop strikes my back, then another comes in aiming for my legs. Cart drivers and people walking by shout in alarm, but the cops with shields order them back, while sprinting along the road to join in.

I take the blows with grunts and tell myself they'll stop and cuff me. Except they don't. The one who first struck me lashes out with a face full of spite and hits me across the back of the head again. And I don't know, I guess that's my limit, because when he does it again I catch the baton mid-strike and look at him in a way that makes the blood drain from his face.

'Go on, son!' the cart driver yells, and I rip the baton free to step back and go low, hitting a shin with a loud crack, then I lift and turn and strike a kneecap, then flip the body over my hip, sending him bowling into the others. All of it within a second or two and all fluid, then I'm moving out to drive my knee into the first cop's groin then backstepping into position, to drive my knee into his face. 'Run, mate!' the driver yells, snatching my attention to the shield cops coming in fast, and flicks his reins to move into the cops' path, buying me a second to run.

I go fast into an alley, but I don't know the twists and turns of the city, and all around me I hear police whistles and shouts.

A second or two later I sprint across a road, with cops giving chase. I try to outrun them, but another police carriage comes into view ahead, making me take a left into a side road with more cops chasing.

I spill out onto Main Street and run past the genre offices, just opening for the day, the reps turning to see me running full tilt with dozens of cops chasing and yelling after me.

I try and think which way to go and figure I'll need a horse to get out of the city, but I don't know how to ride a horse, and a carriage will be too slow.

Then more cops are coming out from roads and alleys, blocking me off, and I have no choice but to take the main road and sprint into the village. The place is already packed with people out for breakfast and coffee, and I have to stop as the police close in on all sides with shields and batons.

The first one comes in fast with his shield presented to the front, and in that instant, I know it's a standard four-foot clear polycarbonate riot shield with two loops on the reverse designed for the user's arm to slot in and a handle to hold, so the user can keep one arm free to use their baton. Which this cop has ready in his hand – and I wonder where, on an island filled with unskilled, unfinished characters, they design and make professional, industry standard shields and batons. Then I look at the cops' boots. Modern stitched leather with reinforced toecaps. Did they make those here too?

I see all of that within a second, then he's on me and punching out with the shield to press me back while pulling the baton back ready to strike, and again I don't know how I know it, but I know this is a standard drilled move, presenting the shield *to give the assailant* something to attack. I can feel the urge to kick or punch it. It's big and flat and oppressive and coming at me.

But I also know the power of any strike I deliver will be spread across the shield, which in turn will do its job and protect the cop behind – all so he can bring that nasty baton down hard on my skull.

So I don't kick or punch it.

I let it come at me, and at the very last second I reach down to grip the lower edge and heave it up and out, knowing the cop won't be expecting it, nor will he be able to counter the sudden leverage gained. He cries out, leaning back to stop the top of the shield from slamming into his head. I reverse my thrust, ripping the shield forward to slide the hooks off his arms, and suddenly he doesn't have the shield anymore.

I do.

Two more coming from the right.

I could use the shield to fight them.

But I don't.

Instead, I drop it face down and kick it fast so the slick front slides over the smooth paving slabs under their tread.

Their feet snag on the grip hooks, and they both go down in a tangle of arms and clattering shields as I hear the fast feet of someone heavy behind me. I step to the left and grip the side of the cop's shield as he passes, wrenching to make him spin and fall over the two still trying to get up.

'DUCK!' someone shouts.

I don't need to duck. I know the next cop is swinging a baton at my head. I can see him in the reflection of the store window in front of me, so I lean away, catch the baton mid-swing, and yank hard on seeing the baton is attached by a lanyard to the cop's wrist.

He sails off his feet, joining the others already on the ground, and I turn to make ready for the rest coming at me. Dozens of them, all getting in a circle ready to charge at once, and I figure I'm about to get one hell of beating.

'IF ONE BATON TOUCHES MY CLIENT, I WILL HAVE THAT OFFICER'S JOB!' Hope's voice fills the Village as he strides into view with his coat tails flapping about his legs and his cane in his hand. 'Mr Croker is surrendering peaceably. Everyone here is witnessing that!'

'Okay, okay. Let's cool it,' Sam Shovel says, coming in from the other side with his hands in his pockets and his hat perched on the back of his head. 'But the kid's still gotta come in.'

'What for?' I ask.

'You'll have to go with them, John,' Hope tells me. 'But I'll be at the station to meet you.'

'What for?' I ask again, the tension clear in my voice.

'Well kid, same as last time,' Shovel says. 'There's been another murder, see, and you were the last one seen arguing with the victim *again.*'

'Who?!' I ask, as a cop cuffs wrists too tight and too hard.

'Take him away, boys. And Hope, we'll see you at the station. Oh, and I'd better say the words, I guess. John Croker, I am arresting you for the murder of Simon Smith, otherwise known as John Candle . . .'

CHAPTER TWENTY-NINE

I get a beating in the wagon then another one when we arrive at the police station.

They avoid my face, but they also keep my hands cuffed to my back, so all I can do is roll with the kicks.

Then I'm straight into the same interrogation room and once again shackled to the table.

'Mr Croker. Such a pleasure,' Wainwright says, as she comes in with Shovel, and this time they *don't* take the shackles off.

'Where's Hope?'

'I'd say you have none,' Wainwright quips. 'Just a bit of humor, Mr Croker. Just a bit of humor.'

'I don't think this is very funny,' I tell her.

'Oh, I quite agree. Murder is not very funny at all,' she says, every single trace of humor vanishing as she speaks. 'You murdered John Candle.'

'I didn't kill anyone. I liked John.'

'You killed John Candle because he tried to stop your *rampage*.'

'My what?'

'This angry violence you keep displaying. Demanding to know where the food comes from. Threatening supermarket managers. He tried to reason with you. He tried to speak to as a friend, and you flipped into another homicidal rage.'

'Kid. We got you bang to rights,' Shovel says. 'There's nobody else with motive. And there's no sign of forced entry to the block. You were there. You argued. You're angry. You won't let go of your story. Mascaponi or whatever the hell it was. Scaring shopworkers. Demanding to know where the food comes from. We got a pattern of behavior on you, see.'

Wainwright smiles and takes her turn. 'And Orderly Gavin Pilbow from the City Juvenile Hall said you threatened to break every bone in his body, which was witnessed by the Matron. Hmmm? What do you say about that, Mr Croker? You might as well admit it and see if you can get a reduced sentence.'

'Do yourself a solid, kid. You're bang to rights. Two murders. Both with the same M.O. You argued and assaulted Jedediah Harper before murdering him, then the same again with Simon Smith. Even your own friends have provided testimony against you.'

I know that's a lie designed to make me confess. 'Go to hell. That shit isn't working this time.'

'Oh, I think you misunderstand what's happening here,' Wainwright says with another wry smile. 'It doesn't have to work, Mr Croker.'

I frown at her. Not getting what she means.

'You see, John,' she says, leaning over the desk as though telling me a secret. 'This is our city and we have our own way of doing things. And in this city, there won't be an armada of FBI agents pretending to be UPS drivers, or whatever happened in your frankly terrible story. There is no cavalry, John. We are the cavalry, and you know what that means, don't you?'

'It means you're the bad guy, kid,' Shovel says.

'The monster in our midst,' Wainwright says, with a shiver of delight. 'And the whole city saw you beating those brave, dedicated police officers today. Hmmm? What do you say about that, John?'

I don't say anything. I sit silently and take it in.

'And when *we* decide,' Wainwright continues, 'and at a time that suits us, we'll end you.'

I smile and lean closer like it's my turn to tell a secret. 'Good luck with that,' I whisper, and see the twinkle in her old eyes as she leans closer still.

'You are a brave one, aren't you. But maybe we should see how brave your friends are.'

I tense against the shackles, making Shovel flinch, but Wainwright grins in delight at getting under my skin.

Wainwright nods for them to go and they get up and walk right on out, leaving me cuffed to the table until another squad of officers comes and takes me to the cells.

I get roughed up again. Then I'm in the cell, nursing my painful limbs and body, and time passes. I wait for Hope to come and tell me what's going on.

Except Hope doesn't come, and through the opaque glass in the cell block I see daylight fade.

Then the officers come back and take me up to the charge room. I figure I'll get charged with murder and sent to whatever prison they have here until the trial.

But again, that doesn't happen. Instead, they bail me out, and ten minutes later I'm on the street with the charge room door slamming in my face. I might not be a very good spy, but even I know that people don't get bail for two murders.

CHAPTER THIRTY

It's fully dark when I head through the city towards Little Victoria. I think about calling in on Rachel, but dragging her further into whatever mess this is just doesn't feel right.

Where was Hope? Why didn't he come to the station?

And why would someone kill John Candle? I can't help but think I caused it by blundering into the supermarkets and asking stupid questions about where the food comes from. But killing someone in response to that feels excessive. And why John Candle? We arrived here together but we're not buddies, and he didn't go to the north shore with us.

And was that a confession of sorts when Wainwright said *maybe we should see how brave your friends are*?

Or is my brain *still* trying to find a plot? Are these all coincidences, or are they connected? And if they are, then why bail me again? Why let me out when they could have staged an accident and killed me in the station.

It's confusing, and I know I'm not so good at figuring this stuff out, so I keep going past Rachel's block and rush into Little Victoria to get Hope's view on it all and ask why the hell he didn't show up at the police station.

Then, at the same time as I recall Wainwright saying *maybe we should see how brave your friends are,* it hits me *why* Hope never showed up.

She said something else too. She said they'll end me when it suits them.

I might not be a good spy but I know a show of power when I see it, and I start running through the streets. Passing couples strolling in the evening air. Carriages pulled by horses in a weird fucked-up place that shouldn't exist. That isn't real. But that *is* real because I can see it and I'm here.

I start to question my own reasoning, which brings doubt to the jolt of fear I felt a moment ago. It makes me slow to a walk with a rush of embarrassment that burns my cheeks, because I'd done it again. Seized on a nugget of thought and turned it into a plot. Rachel was right. There is no plot. There is no van.

I've got to stop doing this. Even John Candle said acceptance is the key – and he's a John like me.

But they killed him.

And they'll go for my friends.

I start running – and again, within thirty seconds, I'm slowing down and wondering what the hell I'm doing.

But Hope never turned up, and he believes in this whole plot more than I do. The guy has been here for years, secretly observing, just waiting for someone to come along and push back against the authorities. And he didn't just turn up in the Village when I was fighting the cops. The guy *ran* in, shouting at them to stop.

Which means he would definitely come to the station and help me.

So why didn't he?

Maybe we should see how brave your friends are.

I run again.

I stop.

Indecision cripples me.

Confusion slows me.

I reach his house and go up the stone steps to the glossy black door to bang the heavy metal knocker, and only then do I notice it's shaped like a magnifying glass. The sight of it makes me smile and I figure it's Hope's way of telling the city he's still here and watching it all.

Watching and waiting.

The door swings in and I step through, my mouth already forming the words to say thank you to Maisy.

Except she's not there.

Nobody is.

I stare at the empty hallway then back to the door, figuring maybe it was unlocked and the energy transferred from the knocker caused it to open. But I heard it unlock.

Did I?

And why hasn't Maisy come yet? She always runs for the door while shouting *hang on!* to whoever is calling.

It doesn't feel right, but then I'm too wired to know what *does* feel right.

'Maisy?' I call out, but get no response. 'Hope? You home?'

A scuff from my right. Griff emerging from behind the door. Easing forward from dark into light. His eyes wide and wild, and such is his expression it sends a chill through my body.

'They can't see me,' he whispers in a voice filled with fear as I spot the smear of blood on the inside door handle and look down to Griff's hands. Both of them covered in blood.

I move fast from the hallway into the parlor and grunt at the sight of the bodies. Hope on his back. Stabbed repeatedly in the chest. Maisy's lifeless body sprawled across the red chesterfield.

I press my fingers into her neck. Searching for a pulse.

Nothing.

I turn her head to face me. Her eyes are open. Her body cool but not cold. She's without rigor, and the blood in the room glistens wet and vibrantly red. I touch a pool of it, detecting trace warmth.

Death was recent. Within the last hour.

Maybe less.

I don't know how I know that.

I cross to Hope's side and check for signs of life.

Nothing.

But then I spot the way he's lying, with his right arm stretched out. Something about it. Something about the angle and the way it's reaching behind one of the big potted plants behind the chesterfield. I lean over to see his hand covered in blood, his fingers still pressing against the white wooden skirting and my heart lurches at the sight.

Hope was a smart guy. Even in his last few seconds of life he's told me exactly what I need to do by leaving one word written in blood.

Wizards

THE CONFUSION VANISHES.

The indecision disappears.

I run out the room to see the front door open and Griff gone from sight. Then I'm out and running through the streets of Little Victoria.

A few moments later I stride into Diagonal Alley and aim for the doors to Pigspot Tavern.

Wizards inside.

I told the orderly that if he touched one hair on Alice's head, I'd start breaking bones.

But I don't think they were listening.

So maybe I need to start breaking some bones.

I go inside.

'Eight of them and only one of me. An ordinary man wouldn't stand a chance. But then I'm not an ordinary man.'

They laughed the last time I said that.

They don't laugh now.

'Stop him!' Fat George yells. They surge towards me and I start breaking bones.

I snap the wrist of a wizard trying to punch me from the left. He goes down as Ginger Ron swings a pool cue at my head. I step in fast, arms raised to break the wood. Then I grab the thick base of the cue from his hands and bring it down onto someone's skull before pivoting and driving it hard into a shin, breaking the bone with a loud crack.

Then I'm up and jabbing it into the belly of a fat wizard who gasps and sags and pukes Cheetos as he drops, by which point Ginger Ron has rearmed himself with a broomstick and comes in swinging. I dance back and grab a weird metal ball fitted with wings from a shelf.

'Not the Quidditch ball!' many wizards shout in alarm.

I throw it anyway.

And break Ginger Ron's big fat ginger nose again.

A few moments later, and with the Pigshit Inn or whatever it's called carpeted in the broken bodies of weird freaks in torn and bloodied dressing gowns, I advance on Fat George, rapidly backstepping towards the bar.

'You'd better bloody well bugger off!' he yells.

'That's very British,' I tell him. 'Do you like dick too?'

'Whoa. Dude. Homophobic,' Ginger Ron shouts, clutching his re-broken nose. 'We're accepting of all sexual orientations here.'

'Spotted dick. It's British. Maisy made it with custard.'

'Oh,' Fat George says weakly, backing into the bar with a look of pure panic and blinking behind his round glasses. 'It's just. You know. We're kind of associated with the whole toxic gender thing.'

'Not touching it,' I say as I come to a stop, towering over him. 'You, however, I will touch. But not sexually. This isn't a sexual thing. This is purely a rampage of violence because you killed my friends.'

He cries out as I reach down to grab one of his fat ankles and heave him over the bar so his upper body is dangling upside down.

'We didn't kill them!' he screams, thrashing as I grab a tankard of beer from the bar top and pour it over his upside-down face. He coughs and gags while trying to scream in fear of drowning, and flaps his hands like he's ready to talk. 'We didn't! I promise.'

'Who?'

He hesitates.

I pour more beer over his face then punch him hard in his belly while he hangs upside down, making him puke and choke on his own vomit until I reach down to grip his hair and heave him up.

'Who?'

'We only watched the house! I promise!'

'Hope's house? Who killed him? Who killed John Candle? Who killed Maisy?'

'I don't know!'

I grab a finger and snap it hard, then pour more beer over his thrashing head.

'Bloody hell, mate!' Ginger Ron says in horror at the torture, prompting me to drop Fat George and stride over to grab his arms, prizing them away from his face to give my knee access to his already-broken nose. I strike him hard, then do it again until his screams cut off and he drops. Either dead or unconscious. Then I'm back to Fat George.

'Okay, okay!' he cries out. 'It was Shovel! He told us to follow Hope and tell them when he got home.'

'And?'

'And what?'

I hit him in the belly.

He pukes and sobs then finally draws enough air to speak again. 'He went to the station. Hope did. He kept yelling at them to let him in to help you. They got nasty and a cop started hitting Hope with his baton. Hope went home and we told Shovel, and some other people came.'

'Who?'

'I don't know! I swear it. They had masks on. I heard Hope's maid scream and we left. That's all we do. We follow people or pick fights to put the arrivals off asking questions. But they never said you could fight! I swear! We're low level. We don't kill. We just deal drugs and do thieving. Please, put me down.'

I pour another tankard of beer over his head then slam him up and down a few times.

'You helped kill my friends,' I say and grab another one of his fat fingers to snap.

'We didn't do it!'

'You were part of it!' I reply, and snap another finger. Then another and another as the wizards look on in horror at the monster in their midst.

'Mate. You need to go,' a female voice says, and I spin around to see Fanny off to one side stealing drinks while her buddies get beaten.

'You murdered my friends,' I reply, thinking to kill the lot of them.

'Nah. We didn't. We just followed them.'

'That's the same thing!'

'It ain't though, is it,' she snaps at me in a harsh English accent. 'And Hope weren't the only one we had to follow.'

I blink at what she means.

'They'll do 'em all,' Fanny says with a strange look.

'Fanny! Shut the fuck up!' Fat George yells. 'They'll fucking kill us, you stupid bitch!'

'I'll kill you,' I say, and he looks at me in fresh terror.

'Fuck 'em!' Fanny says. 'It's getting shit here. I hate it. We're meant to be a cool gang doing drugs and stuff, now we just work for Wainwright. Seriously. Go save your mates then get to the tower.'

'What tower?'

'Really? The big bloody tower!' she adds, as I still look blank. 'Literally the only tower in Fiction Land.'

'Middle Earth?'

'Bingo,' she says without a trace of humor.

'Why? What's in there?'

She shrugs and steals another drink then belches loudly. 'Dunno. But all this shit runs from there.'

I turn to go.

'Here. Hang on. I did hear a name,' she says, as I pause by the door. 'Someone called Mascaponi . . .'

CHAPTER THIRTY-ONE

Mascaponi.

I stagger back at hearing the name and lurch through Diagonal Alley.

Mascaponi.

A life I left behind.

Twice.

My brain lights up, the receptors fizzing with glee as too many thoughts run through my head at the same time, and I come to a stop. Shaking my head while knowing I have to focus on the mission at hand and prioritize the immediate objective.

Which is to save my friends.

Wainwright said it herself. *Maybe we should see how brave your friends are.*

And Fanny just said Hope wasn't the only one they followed.

She also said Mascaponi.

But I can't think of that now.

My friends are my mission.

I look up, my mind clear and any trace of indecision once more gone as I set off, running through the city into the quieter residential parts, plotting the route in my head. My old block is closest. I'll go for L and Svetty, and tell them to get to Rachel's while I go for Alice.

I reach my old block, expecting to find bad guys to fight as I go through the street door, but the foyer is empty. So are the stairs that I take two at a time until I'm bursting onto our landing and in through the door to the communal kitchen.

'John!' Svetlana says, blinking at me in surprise from the table, her hands clasping a glass of wine. L looks over while stirring spaghetti into a pan of boiling water.

'What the fuck, dude! They said you killed Candle. We thought you were in jail.'

'They let me out, but the wizards said they're going to kill you.'

'Sorry, what?' Svetlana asks in shock.

'We have to go,' I say, urging them to move.

'Dude. I just put the pasta in,' L says.

'And I've just opened a bottle,' Svetlana says.

'Guys! We have to go! They are going to kill you.'

'Okay. I mean. Yeah. Sure, I guess,' L says, shooting a look to Svetlana.

'You sure there, Croker?' she asks.

'Yes!'

'I mean. You know,' she says, motioning the lack of anyone trying to kill them.

'So? Am I cooking this pasta then or what?' L asks.

'They've already killed Hope and Maisy!' I tell them both. 'I got released and went back and they'd both been stabbed. Wainwright told me they were going for my friends.'

'They see you!' A shout from outside. I go to the window to see Griff on the street.

'They must be near. We gotta go,' I say, as L runs into his room to grab his helmet and Svetlana grabs her glass of wine, then thinks better of it and ditches it to take the bottle instead.

'It's expensive!' she says as we start down the stairs.

'Get to Rachel's. I'll go for Alice.' I shoot a look back to see they're not entirely convinced that this should be happening. But I have to accept that they're at least willing to go along with it until I can get them all out of here.

'L, you keep them safe for me,' I say when we get outside.

'Yeah. Course, buddy,' he says, as I set off with a rush of shame at sounding so stupid and wanting them to believe me.

But I don't have time for that.

I have to get to Alice.

Then I'm at Juvie Hall, aiming for the big wooden door, and just manage to stop myself from hammering on it. All that will do is tell someone inside there is an issue.

Instead, I bite the frustration down, knock normally and wait. Willing someone to open it.

'Hello!' I call out in a friendly tone. 'Anyone home?'

'Hang on!' a voice inside snaps, coming closer. 'Out of hours. We don't take visitors.'

'Not a visitor! I just found a wallet outside for Gavin? He works here. It's got money inside. I thought I'd better hand it in.'

'Bloody idiot,' the woman mutters as bolts and locks get unfastened, and only when the first crack shows do I hit the door with force, sending the nasty matron back with a cry.

'Remember me?' I growl as I push my way in. 'Take me to Alice.'

'There are children here! You can't just force your way in.'

'Alice. Now!' I get in her face as she tuts darkly, giving me a foul look, then turns and starts off along a corridor. Passing doors with small windows giving glimpses of darkened interiors and small figures sleeping on rows of beds or in bunks.

The sound of crying comes from both sides. The pitiful noise plucks at my heart. 'Why aren't you comforting them? Where are the staff?'

'There's only a couple of us,' she snaps, 'and we can't run to every snivelling child. They need to learn.'

I blink at the brutality of her words and tone as she shoots me a look.

'You think it's good for a kid if you keep running to them? You obviously don't have any.'

'I know kindness when I see it.'

'Kindness doesn't provide adequate funding in an already overpopulated city.'

I hear voices ahead coming from around a corner. 'Get to bed!' Gavin orders. Loud and deep.

'Fuck you!' Alice replies, making me speed up.

'Alice, I swear to god! If you wake everyone up . . .'

'Leave me alone then and I won't.'

'Get inside your room!'

'No! I said I'm leaving. Don't touch me! GET OFF ME!'

I start running as the matron shouts in warning, and round the corner to see gnarly Gavin gripping Alice's upper arm, trying to force her back into a dark room.

'You selfish little bitch! GET INSIDE NOW!' He shunts her hard, making her lose balance and stumble, as he carries on manhandling and shoving and grabbing roughly. Hurting her.

'I warned you,' I say, as the matron shouts again from behind me, making Gavin and Alice both snap their heads over.

'Croker!' Alice says, as Gavin lets go and steps towards me.

'You can't be here!' he starts to say, reaching out stop me as I grab his wrist and yank it down hard enough to dislocate the shoulder with a loud crunch.

He drops instantly, gasping in pain and shock as I reach Alice and help her up.

'We gotta go,' I say.

'You don't have tell me twice,' she says, already running out of her door to throw herself at Gavin. Punching his head and kicking his legs. 'Don't ever touch me again, you fucking cunt!'

'Alice!'

'Fuck you! FUCK YOU!' she screams as I get an arm around her waist to pull her back. 'And you're another evil bitch!' she yells at the matron, who stares back with a look of resigned distaste, as though this is just another evening like any other.

'Where are you going?' she asks, as I set off with my arm still holding Alice back from getting at Gavin.

'Off this fucking island!' Alice shouts.

'There's nothing out there, Alice. This isn't healthy. And you,' the matron says, shaking her head at me, 'you're just going to get her killed.'

'It won't be us that gets killed. You tell them that,' I call as we walk off. Then I let Alice go and we run for the door and out into the night air. 'Are you okay?' I ask her. 'Did he hurt you?'

'Just grabbed me. I'm fine. What happened though? They said you killed John Candle.'

'I didn't.'

'I know you didn't!'

'But they got to Hope and Maisy.'

'Oh god. No,' she says with a look of horror as we rush along the street. 'Are they . . .?'

I nod grimly. 'Both stabbed. I found the bodies in the parlor.'

'That's why they let you go,' she says. I shoot her a look. 'But what made you come for me?'

'The wizards,' I say, as she frowns. 'They said they followed Hope and suggested you guys would be next. Svetty and L are going to Rachel's. But they said we've got to get to the Tower in Middle Earth and . . .'

'And what? Croker? What did they say?'

'They said they heard a name. Mascaponi.'

'What the actual . . .' she says, breathing hard as we jog through the dark city streets. 'The lady from your story? You sure it was the right name?'

'The wizard lady said it. Let's worry about that later. We need to get you all out of here first.'

'I think we need to worry about all of it at the same time,' she says, before yelping when I grab her wrist and speed up to a run.

'Jesus, John,' Rachel says with a groan, yanking the door to her first-floor apartment open. 'Come on. Get inside.'

'We gotta go.'

'John! Come inside,' she says, and we traipse into her living room to see Svetlana still holding the bottle of wine.

'Dude! You're okay,' L says, rushing to Alice. 'Hey, who did that?' he asks in alarm, seeing the vivid welts on her arm.

'Gavin the orderly, but Croker broke his shoulder.'

'Jesus, John!' Rachel says.

'He was attacking Alice.'

'Attacking?' Rachel asks me, with a very questioning expression.

'Yes! He was grabbing her.'

'Grabbing? Grabbing is different to attacking.'

'Okay. No. So he wasn't like, *attacking* me,' Alice says, as Rachel gives me a furious look. 'But I said I wanted to leave, and he said I couldn't, and he grabbed and pushed me into my room.'

'They're not allowed to let you out at night,' Rachel says, rubbing her nose with another groan. 'Oh god, John. What did you do?'

'Gavin was being a fucking prick,' Alice says. 'And Hope is dead, and Maisy, and the wizards said they were going to kill us next, and they said –'

'Slow down!' Rachel cuts in. 'L and Svetty said Hope is dead. And Maisy. They're dead, yes?'

'What the hell. Yes!' Alice says.

'I'm asking John.'

'Yes,' I say. 'I got released from the station and went back and they were both stabbed in the parlor.'

'John Candle was stabbed too,' Rachel says, in a way that makes me want to immediately deny killing anyone.

'Croker didn't kill them,' Alice says.

'Sure,' Rachel says.

'Rach. Jesus. No,' Alice says. 'Don't even think that! Croker went to the wizards. They said they were told to follow us.'

'Alice. Just,' Rachel says, holding her hand up to cut her off. 'Okay. John. I'm going to ask you to leave, please.'

'Hey. Whoa,' L says.

'Rach!' Alice says.

'John. I know you care for Alice, but you need to leave her alone now,' Rachel says, as I take my turn to lift a hand to speak.

'They will kill all of you.'

'Who will, John?'

'Wainwright. Shovel.'

'They're the police. Why would they kill anyone?'

'Because I'm asking questions.'

'You're telling me they'll kill what, five, six people because one guy asked where the food comes from.'

'They killed Hope and Maisy!' Alice says.

'Somebody did,' Rachel says. Alice's mouth drops open, clearly stunned at the unspoken accusation.

I look to Svetlana, and she looks as torn and confused as I feel. L the same.

'John. You know I like you,' Rachel says. 'I haven't felt *that* way about someone since I got here, but this isn't healthy . . . And if it was just me? I don't know. But it's not. Alice is a child.'

'I'm seventeen,' Alice says quietly.

'Please. Just go,' Rachel tells me.

'I didn't kill them.'

'John!'

'I can't go! They'll kill you. How can I make you believe me?'

'I don't know! But I can't just take your word for it, John. The cowboy. John Candle. Hope. Maisy. You had access to all of them.'

'But I didn't! And Fanny said Mascaponi is in the tower.'

'What?' Rachel asks, as I realize how I sound.

'John went to them,' Alice says. 'They told him we're all at risk.'

'Right. You just walked in, and they told you.'

'Well. No. I mean. I made them tell me.'

She closes her eyes and gives a slow nod as though that's everything she needed to hear. 'Mascaponi. Okay, John. Sure.'

'Oh my god, Rachel. What's wrong with you?' Alice asks. 'And why aren't you defending Croker?' she asks Svetlana and L. 'Okay. Right,' she says, holding a hand up to emphasize a point. 'Number one. People do not get bailed for two murders. That literally doesn't happen. But they let Croker go? And he goes home and finds two more bodies that he can be framed for? In the house he is living in? Which means they let him go *for that reason*. No? Not enough? Okay then, how about this one. Number two. Croker saved us in the robbery. We all saw that. We all saw the robbers were armed, but Croker wasn't. And even when he took them out, he didn't take their knives off them. He took that blackjack thing and used that. And all those cops who attacked him – he fought them all off without killing any of them. And I just saw him *literally* break Gavin's shoulder with one hand. But he's meant to have repeatedly stabbed John Candle and Hope and Maisy. With a knife. Croker doesn't need a knife!'

'She's got a point,' L says, as Svetlana nods.

'Number three,' Alice says. 'Hope said they attacked him when he arrived for poking around. Why would he say that? And why would he help Croker if none of this were true *while knowing* they'd probably kill him? Number four.'

'Alice,' Rachel says.

'Number four! I guarantee you those cops were waiting in the street when they tried to arrest him for the murder of John Candle. Why not just go to his house and do it? And they beat him. And I bet the only reason they did that was to make Croker fight back so they could show the city how bad he is. *Look at this bad man attacking our brave police officers. He must be seriously deranged.* And they made it happen in the Village.'

'It felt like I was being forced that way,' I say.

'See! But it backfired, because the people in the Village weren't cheering for the cops. Which probably made Wainwright realize there are more people questioning it all, which is why she then went for another double murder to really sell the fact that Croker is a psycho. He's been set up! The whole thing is a set up. Rach. Come on!'

'God, you are a Holmes,' Svetlana says. 'How the hell did you work all that out?'

'Rach?' L asks, giving her a pained look. 'That kinda made sense.'

'They see you!'

A voice from outside. I cross to the window to see Griff once more in the street below.

'We gotta go,' I say.

'Who is that?' Rachel asks, joining me to look down. 'Griff? What's he doing here?'

'He saw them kill Hope and Maisy,' I say.

'He's a witness then!' Alice says.

'Griff is autistic!' Rachel says.

'Oh my god! What is wrong with you?' Alice asks her. 'You're like one of those flat-earthers shown the planet from space. *No! That's made up. I still think it's flat.*'

'We have to go!' I say, heading for the door as L grabs his helmet and Svetty grabs her bottle of wine.

'Honestly! It was really expensive.'

'Guys!' Rachel says. 'No. I mean it. I said no! This ends now.'

'THEY SEE YOU!'

'Shut up, Griff!' Rachel snaps again, as we rush back to the window to see people in black running along the road towards this block and Griff flapping his arms in panic before running away.

'Stuff this,' Svetlana says, grabbing Rachel's hand to drag her along. 'You can say we kidnapped you if it goes wrong.'

Rachel tuts, but I notice she doesn't hold back or fight free, and we rush down the stairs towards the front door.

'Wait,' Rachel says, shaking her head as she gets to the front. 'We'll go out the back.'

She leads us through a rear door into a dark yard and along an alley that twists and turns until we can see her block from further up the street. We hunker down and creep out, peeking at the figures in black who stop outside Rachel's block and motion each other with hand signals before drawing knives and starting the breach. Surging in silently, and Rachel gasps when, a moment later, she sees figures inside her apartment.

I touch her shoulder and motion that we need to get further away. She nods and we run on through narrow alleys, then across the wider main road, hiding when carriages or people go by.

'You smell that?' L whispers as we start drawing closer to the city center. 'What is that? Smoke?'

The smell gets stronger the closer we go, and within a few minutes we're hiding in the mouth of another alley. Rachel's face now shows the horror we all feel.

Horror at the sight of the fire opposite us.

The fire surrounded by fire crews using horse-drawn carriages, trying to douse the flames soaring out of the Pigspot Tavern in Diagonal Alley.

But the fire isn't the reason for the horror we feel.

It's the bodies of the wizards being laid outside.

Fat George. Ginger Ron. More of them in a line. Most of them still smouldering.

And the one last one being lowered to the ground.

The body of Fanny.

The one who told me to find Mascaponi in the tower.

CHAPTER THIRTY-TWO

Saturday morning.

WE FEEL the wagon going over the Middle Earth drawbridge and watch the market setting up for the day.

'I still can't believe we're doing this,' Rachel's muffled voice says. 'Worst plan ever.'

'Er, no. Best plan ever,' Alice's equally muffled voice says as I turn to look at her.

'You're looking at me,' L tells me.

'I thought you were Alice.'

'I'm Alice,' Alice says from opposite me.

'This whole time I thought he was Alice,' I tell Rachel on my other side.

'Why you telling me?' Svetty asks.

'I thought you were Rachel!'

'I'm here!' Rachel says, sitting next to Alice on the opposite side. 'Is that why you've been playing footsie with Svetty?'

'I thought she was you!'

'Which is why this is the worst plan ever!' Rachel says as we all turn our red-helmeted heads to look at her.

SHE SAID the same thing just before dawn this morning as we ran out into the arrivals park dressed in red rip-off Stormtrooper outfits.

Or, as L corrected us, standard issue Thunder Soldier uniforms. Which we obtained after breaking into the Fiction Land Uniform Trade Store.

But then we had no choice.

John Candle, Sherrinford Hope, and Maisy had all been killed, along with a whole bunch of wizards from Diagonal Alley.

In the arrivals park we slumped on benches and waited for some people to walk through, then made a show of waking up and being all surprised.

'But we can't all be from the same book, can we?' Svetty asked.

'It does happen sometimes,' Rachel said. 'If there are multiple main characters that are deemed to be of equal value then they all arrive. Especially with things like military units.'

And so it was with us.

We woke up pretending to be Thunder Soldiers from The Killer Sun and duly headed to the Middle Earth genre office.

'Morning, guys!' a woman greeted us as we filed in. Rachel told us later she's called Claudette. 'So, welcome to Fiction Land. Lots going on today. Apparently there's a murderous fugitive on the loose! Killed loads of people and burned a bar down. But yes! Welcome. Honestly, it's normally really nice. Oh, but er, why are you here?' Claudette asked with a look of confusion.

'We are Thunder Soldiers looking for The Killer Sun!' Rachel said, in the worst pretend deep voice ever.

'Right,' Claudette said. 'Okay. So, someone has sent you to the wrong office. Go back out and head down Main Street to Sci-Fi Space Opera, and if that's closed then try Hard-Boiled & Erotica & misc. sci-fi fanfic overflow. But ask for Pat. Rachel is the other woman there but she's been a bit off the ball lately. Especially what with her banging the murderous fugitive.'

'What!' Rachel said.

'Er, we mean, why would we go there?' Svetty cut in, stepping in front of Rachel.

'You're sci-fi, guys. This is the Middle Earth office. For fantasy.'

'Sorry!' Alice said. 'Our fault. Our goblin overlords have had us working literally non-stop.'

'Sorry? Did you say goblins?' Claudette asked, as Alice shot a look at L.

'That's right!' L said. 'Er, because of the orc uprising. Yeah. Crazy times. They P180d us on a requisition to train with the er, sandworm riders.'

'On Arrakis,' Alice added. 'Due to the Elvish war against the, er . . .'

'The Witchers?' L asked.

'The Witchers!' Alice said. 'Cos er, well. I mean, I was the chosen one and L was the secret heir and we had to fight the evil overlord while er, you know, being totally reluctant heroes.'

'Jesus. Couldn't your writer stick to a genre?' Claudette asked as we all mumbled in agreement.

'No! Er, what do you mean!' Rachel then said in her mock deep voice. 'What is this *writer* thing you speak of? We are but simple characters in a story and know nothing of this *writer*.'

'Wow,' Claudette said. 'Guess we know who the idiot in the group dynamic is then.'

'What the fudge!' Rachel said.

'Anyway. Fine. Whatever. Hang on here and we'll get you on the train to Middle Earth. They can sort you out when you get there.'

'There's a train?' I asked when she walked off.

'Not a choo-choo train,' Rachel said. 'She means a train of carriages that go direct from the city to Middle Earth every morning, but er, what did she blooming say about me being off the ball? I am so on the ball.'

THE WAGON STOPS and we get out, stretching our legs and backs, still in our helmets.

'Thank god,' one of the other passengers says, shooting us a look as the other new arrivals all murmur in agreement. All of them dressed according to various fantasy tropes.

'Good morning and welcome to Middle Earth!' a voice calls, and an Arabic-looking fellow strides from a building with a big smile. 'I'm Gene. I was written as a genie. Desert trope. Ali Baba slash Aladdin slash Indiana Jones. Come in! Come in! Please. Help yourself to a beverage. And there's fresh fruit to refresh your energies after your journey. Oh. Hello!' he says, seeing us. 'And who told you to come here? I think you might belong back in the city.'

'Yeah, send them back,' the passenger who moaned about us says, as the rest nod and mutter. 'They literally never stop bickering.'

'We don't bicker,' Svetty says.

'Er, we kinda do,' Alice says.

'No, but it's not bickering. It's just chit chat,' Rachel says, as we all start bickering again.

'Okay! Let's get you back on that wagon to the city, shall we,' Gene says with a bright smile as he starts ushering us to the door.

'No, we're fantasy,' Rachel says.

'You're definitely not,' Gene says.

'We really are! We had the things on our Death Star and –'

'Killer Sun,' L whispers.

'Killer Sun!' Rachel says. 'The ugly things. Oh god. From *Lord of the Rings*. The baddies?'

'Orcs?' Gene asks.

'Orcs!' Rachel says, clicking a polymer gloved hand at him. 'We had orcs.'

'I'm an orc,' a hairy guy says, holding his hand up.

'Okay. And that's a great starting point,' Gene says to everyone. 'Because we're none of us orcs, or trolls, or er, plastic Lego people.'

'Thunder Soldiers,' L tells him.

'Or those. What we are . . . Are *people,*' Gene says with a nod at everyone.

'Um. But so . . . I mean. I *identify* as an orc,' the orc says.

'Right. Yes. Which is totally your right,' Gene says. 'But you are a *person*.'

'Yes. An orc person,' the orc says.

'No. A person person. Everyone sit down and we'll all introduce ourselves. Shall I go first? I'm Gene. And like I said, I was a genie and written as a spirit or a form of immortal being to cast wishes. But now I realize that was just a story and I am a *person*. Okay? Who's next?'

'Hi everyone. I'm Gary. I'm an orc.'

'Not an orc, Gary.'

'What's the issue?' Svetty asks. 'Let him be an orc.'

'He can't be an orc,' Rachel says. 'Genre reps *have* to tell people coming in that they're people.'

'How do you know that?' Gene asks her.

'I er, overhead Claudette saying some rules back in the city,' Rachel says as Gene nods and looks away. 'She seemed off the ball, personally.'

'Sorry, what?' Gene asks.

'No. I'm just saying,' Rachel says. 'Not very professional at all,' she adds in a sing song voice. 'Unlike the rep who trained her. Apparently. So I heard. I mean. I just arrived like everyone else.'

'D9 was our HR advisor on the Killer Sun,' L says as Gene nods as though understanding.

'Okay! So who's next?'

'Er, is that me?' a woman asks, standing. 'Hi everyone. My name is Jodo Hamhock and I'm a bobbit from Bobbitshire.'

'Not a bobbit, Jodo. A *person*,' Gene says.

'If Gary's an orc, then I'm a bobbit.'

'Gary isn't an orc. Gary is a person.'

'I'm an orc! My mom was an orc. My dad was an orc. My granny was an orc, but I think my grandfather was like, half troll?'

'Hey! I'm half troll,' a very big woman calls with a wave. 'I'm Tina.'

'No. You're a person,' Gene says.

'Ooh, where you from, Tina?' Gary asks.

'Trollshire.'

'I'm from Bobbitshire,' Jodo says with a wave.

'Orcville,' Gary says.

'Guys!' Gene calls.

'Come on, guys!' Rachel calls at the same time as Gene shoots her another look.

'I really don't need any help, D9,' Gene says.

'Really doesn't look that way, Gene,' Rachel says. 'Kinda losing the group there, bud.'

'You there!' A slender young man calls to Gene and gets to his feet. 'The Elven do not associate with *scum*,' he says with a disgusted look at Gary, Jodo, and Tina.

'You're not Elven. You're a person,' Gene says as the smile starts to look forced.

'If he's an orc, and she's a bobbit and that thing is a troll then I am Elven.'

'Don't call Tina a thing!' Alice shouts.

'Why, are you half troll also?' the slender man asks with a sneer.

'You cheeky fucker!' Alice shouts.

'Yo, bro! You take that back!' L shouts with his chest puffed out.

'Young Elven. Know the Wizards of Narmiang stand with your kind,' a robe-wearing bearded guy shouts while, I lean over to tap Rachel's shoulder.

'Hey. Great plan,' I whisper.

'Can't see me,' Griff says from inside the suit.

'What the fuck, Griff! How are you here?'

'He's always been here,' Svetty says.

'He was in the wagon with us,' Alice says.

'Fuck,' I whimper, 'which one of you is Rachel?'

'Rachel?' Gene asks with a frown.

'He meant D9,' Rachel says. 'Rachel is er, his pet name for me? Because we're lovers?'

'Fuck me. I was going to say nice distraction,' I tell Rachel.

'Eh?'

'With getting it all whipped up so we could sneak out,' I say, and she looks at me blankly for second before giving a sudden thumbs-up.

'Totally the plan. Er, right then. Let's sneak out. Guys! We're sneaking out now.'

'Don't tell everyone!' I say.

'Are you sneaking out?' Gene asks.

'No!' Rachel scoffs. 'L! Stop picking a fight. We're going.'

'You can't go yet,' Gene says.

'Oh my god, Gene. We're not going anywhere,' Rachel says while backing up for the door.

'You know I can see you, right?' Gene says.

'Look over there!' Rachel shouts, then turns and runs as we all share looks and follow her out. 'Okay. Great execution, guys,' Rachel says as we get outside. 'I don't think Gene saw a thing. Ha! And Claudette said I wasn't on the ball. Screw you, Claude. Sooo? We all fit? Great! Let's go and sneak into that tower!'

CHAPTER THIRTY-THREE

We disappear into the rat-run alleys and winding lanes of inner-city Middle Earth.

'You okay?' I ask Rachel. 'You seem a bit strung out.'

'I'm fine, dude,' L says, as I realize I've asked the wrong person again. 'But wow. What a night huh?'

'Yeah. For sure,' I say, and drop back to Rachel. 'Hey, you okay? You seem a bit tense.'

'I drank a bottle of wine while running around the city in high heels. Which equates to a sore head *and* sore ankles,' Svetlana says.

'Er, sorry to hear that,' I say and drop back again. 'Rach?'

'Can't see me.'

'Fuck my life.' I go back again. 'Rach?'

'She's up front,' Alice says, motioning to the first Thunder Soldier in our group, marching with purpose.

I stride past them to the figure at the front. 'Rach? Is that you?'

'No. It's someone else wearing a red plastic outfit for fun,' Rachel's muffled voice says.

I fall in at her side and suddenly feel a bit foolish asking if she's okay when I know she clearly isn't, and that thought renders me silent as I realize there's not a lot I can say.

'I'm sorry,' I tell her. She shoots me a look. I mean, she turns her plastic head, which in my mind equates to giving me a look.

'It's not your fault,' she eventually says.

'I think it is.'

'Okay. It *is* your fault, but, you know, it's happening. So.' She turns to look at me again and I hear a long sigh. 'Don't look so sad. It's fine,' she says, reaching out to pat my hard plastic arm.

'How can you tell I look sad?'

'Cos your big red head is all droopy. Look. It was always going to happen. So. Now it's happening.'

We walk on.

'I mean, you coming to Fiction Land and asking around. That's the bit that was going to happen. It wouldn't have been any different if you'd had another genre rep, or other arrival buddies. You'd still have asked, and the wizards would still have picked a fight, and somehow you'd still have gone to the north shore and yada yada yada. But it's fine! We're all fine! Let's just get in that tower and . . . Speaking of which, what exactly are we doing in the tower?'

'I don't know,' I tell them. 'The wizards didn't say. Fanny just said go to the tower.'

'Seriously?' Svetlana asks, craning her head to look up at the massive tower looming over the whole city. 'That's a very big tower.'

'It has to be connected to the supply network somehow,' Alice says, as all of our plastic heads turn to look at hers. 'I keep thinking it through. The island is big, right? But it's also finite. Which means that *if* they are bringing extra things in, then it must service the whole island. Which means all of the towns. The city. Western World. Middle Earth.'

'How does that help us?' Rachel asks.

'I don't know. But at least we have an idea of what to look for. The delivery system. Or the supply network. The logistics of it. Something like that. We'll just have to scope it out. But then what choice have we got? Oh, and FYI, this is *still* way better than Juvie Hall.'

'Were you a Holmes then, Alice?' Svetlana asks as we walk on. 'Hope said you were. And you're smart like a Holmes.'

'Holmes wasn't smart,' Alice says. 'Conan Doyle was. He wrote Holmes. The character is made-up. And honestly? There's like a billion detective books, so writing a mystery plot clearly isn't hard.'

'Yeah, but they solve them so fast,' Svetlana says.

'But they don't,' Alice says. 'The author spends months agonizing over a laptop in Starbucks while stuffing croissants up their ass and being all stupid in a cardigan, and then just writes it that way. But hey, why don't we ask Rachel what her sad backstory is.'

'What?' Rachel asks.

'Go on. You're always asking me. Tell us yours.'

'I didn't ask. Svetty did,' Rachel says. 'What is this, Alice?'

'No seriously. Isn't this the part of the book where we share our sad backstories? Yeah? Give the reader some insight into our tragic pasts so they feel compelled to believe in us. So, come on. What's yours? Are you here just to undermine Croker every step of the way?'

'Hey!' Rachel snaps.

'What? You're the hot insider who falls for the hero and switches teams, but has to constantly remind the reader of the perils by opposing anything the hero wants to do.'

'Wow,' Rachel says, coming to a stop with her gloved hands on her plastic hips.

'Am I wrong?' Alice asks.

'Harsh, dude,' L says.

'Said the loyal sidekick,' Alice says.

'Alice!' Svetty snaps.

'Said the hot sidekick,' Alice says, as they all start trying to talk at her at once and get two middle fingers in response.

'Alright. So what character are you then?' Rachel asks, in a clear attempt to try and play Alice at her own game. Which the rest of know won't end well because Alice is just too damn smart.

'Duh. I'm Velma from *Scooby-Doo*. I'm the fat troll with the bright ideas.'

'Alice!' Svetty says. 'Where's this coming from? You're not fat at all.'

'But!' Alice says over them all. 'At least I'm fucking loyal.'

'Okay, okay,' Rachel says, nodding her big plastic head. 'I know exactly what this is. You're stroppy because I didn't immediately believe John and . . . And jump into his arms or swoon from being saved. This isn't a book, Alice. We're not characters anymore.'

'We're dressed as Thunder Soldiers in Middle Earth!'

'I know! But it's not a book, is it? This is real or isn't real. Damn it! I don't know what this is. Okay! I said it. I don't know. I don't know anything. And I'm sorry I didn't immediately believe in John, but I don't know him, Alice! Life makes you guarded and, and . . . And it makes you not trust people. And it makes you keep asking people *why are you doing that? What for? What's in it for you?* Okay? I'm sorry. And I care for you, which is why I was so worried.'

'I didn't ask for you to care for me.'

'Alice!' Svetlana snaps.

'I didn't!' Alice says, as Rachel's hand comes up to cut her off.

'No! just shut up. We're here, Alice. Isn't that enough? We're dressed like idiots and we're doing this thing with Croker. What more do you want? That we hold hands and skip along merrily?'

'No!'

'What then?'

'I don't know!' Alice says, a whine creeping into her voice.

'Yo. So. Er,' L says with a shrug, holding his hands out. 'And I don't want to touch on nothing traumatic, Alice. But I don't think you're used to being in a close-knit group like this. You know? It's how tight units operate for the most part. They fall out and fall in and snap and bitch, and that's okay as long we all know we got each other's backs when it comes to it. You're pissy at Rach. That's cool. Say it. Deal with it. Shake hands. Hug it out. Whatever. Get over it and move on. That shit is toxic to a team. It's okay to have different views, but this ain't Twitter. Don't fall out and start making death threats over something stupid. Hey! I'm serious. Get in there and hug it out. Go on now!'

Rachel makes the first move. Lifting her plastic arms and motioning for Alice to step in, the pair of them clunking heads and chests and knees while trying to rub each other's back until they hear the snorts coming from L, which sets Svetty off.

'L! You dick,' Alice says, trying to swipe him.

'Oh, come on! You look so stupid! You can't hug in armor,' he says, as Alice bundles into him, sending them both knocking into Svetty, all of them laughing while Griff shakes his clenched fists in a sign of excitement.

'I see you!'

It vents the bad energy and eases the tension. Not all the way, but enough for us to keep walking round the next corner, where we come to a stop at the sight of the base of the tower ahead of us.

'OKAY. Wasn't what I was expecting,' Svetlana says. 'Was hoping for more of a five-star luxury hotel vibe. But this? Well. It's something between a casino at the cheap end of Las Vegas and a Walmart crossed with a convention center.'

'Nicely described for the reader,' Alice says, earning a middle finger from Svetty, like a big sister putting the gobby sibling in her place.

'Which entrance?' Rachel asks, as I realize the tower has a very wide base with lots of entrances at equal distance from each other.

'Closest one I guess,' I say and start towards the nearest entrance. A set of glass doors built into the stone wall. 'The Babel Entrance.' I read the plaque over the doors with a smile. 'Nice.'

'What's that mean?' Svetlana asks.

'From *Senlin Ascends*,' Rachel tells her and the others, who all shrug. 'The book? The Tower of Babel? Oh my god! Have you read anything?'

'Um. I read makeup ingredients to make sure they're not tested on animals,' Svetlana says.

'You don't need to read. They have the cruelty-free symbol,' Alice says.

'Yeah! I read that.'

I snort a laugh as we reach the doors to see two signs stuck to the glass.

L.S A.C. (Babel Entrance)
D.S A.C. (Dark Tower Entrance)

'WHAT THE WHAT NOW?' Rachel asks, looking around as we all shrug again. Not knowing what it means.

'Something to do with air-con maybe?' Svetlana says, as I take the lead and head inside to a tiled floor and bland walls filled with signs for emergency exits and upcoming events.

GET YOUR TICKETS FOR THE ANNUAL STEPHEN KING WEEK!

Elves Are Kindly Reminded That Racism Against Trolls, Orcs Or Any Other Self-Determined Race Will Not Be Tolerated.

'ELVES ARE KINDA DICKS THEN,' L says.

'Looks that way,' Alice says.

'Bit like you then,' L quips, earning another swipe from Alice.

'Yeah, and er, who does this Stephen King think he is, huh?' Svetlana says with a scoff, as we all look at her. 'He gets a whole week? What did this King guy ever do?'

'Wow,' Rachel says. 'No words.'

'Man. I'm from space and even I know who Stephen King is,' L says.

'I see him!' Griff says, and we all spin around expecting to see Stephen King.

'I think Griff means he knows who King is too?' I say as Griff nods at me.

'I was hoping to see a directory,' Alice says, looking around at the walls. 'There's always a business listing on the wall at this stage of the plot. You know, like *ACME Evil Fuckers. Floor 13.* That sort of thing.'

'Again. We're not in a movie or a book,' Rachel says.

'Again. We're dressed as Thunder Soldiers in a big tower reading signs telling elves not to be wankers. But! I do deduce, by my awesome deducing skills, that this is not the main entrance, but rather a side entrance. Which means we need the main entrance, to find the business listing thing on the wall.'

'Wow. Look at Croker go,' Svetty says, as I start striding off. 'He's like *I've got a mission!*'

I turn back with a sheepish grin, then realize they can't see it. 'I have a sheepish grin,' I tell them.

'Better than having a grinning sheep,' Rachel says, as we head off through another set of doors and along a dark and foreboding corridor.

'Why does this corridor feel dark and foreboding?' Svetlana asks.

'It's cos we're in Act Three,' Alice says, earning looks. 'You know. The buildup to the final part of the book?'

'Stop that! We're not in a book,' Rachel says. 'It's just a long corridor. See. The doors are right there . . . We'll just go straight through and . . . holy sugar plum fairies!'

We bundle inside and come to dead stop at the sight of a large room packed with people dressed in linen pajamas of earthen colors underneath flowing hooded robes, and others in orange or red flight jumpsuits.

Most of them are holding plastic beakers of drinks and clutching paper plates as they queue and shuffle alongside a long buffet table laden with shrimp and cheeses on sticks and sausage rolls and chicken nuggets. Bowls of rice next to big platters of untouched salad alongside nearly empty metal trays of French fries.

And as one, those people all turn to look at the six of us coming through the big double doors that slam back into the walls with a bang.

The six of us all dressed in the red plastic armored uniforms of Thunder Soldiers – and in that same instant, we look up to the big sign stretching across the end wall of the convention room.

WELCOME TO THE LIGHT SIDE ANNUAL CONVENTION!

'Oh! That's what L.S A.C. means,' Svetlana says as we all turn to look at her. 'But er, what's the Light Side?'

'I know what they are,' L says in a very deep growling voice as we all turn to look at him. 'FEDIS!'

'Stormtroopers!' the linen-wearing, paper-plate-holding people all shout.

'For the last time! I am a Thunder Soldier!' L shouts.

'Oh poop!' Rachel says.

But it's too late and L's striding out into a room full of his sworn enemies. Not that they're *all* Fedis. Seeing as Fedis were from his story. But they are Cedis. And Dedis. And Gedis with a hard g, and Bedis, and lots more Edis – most of whom turn to face L, while a few tubby ones take advantage of the distraction to queue-jump, running past the salad bowl to get at the chicken nuggets.

'Er, excuse me!' a stocky middle-aged woman with short blonde hair and a name badge saying KAREN, LIGHT SIDE ORGANIZER on the front shouts angrily. 'What in the force do you think you are doing? We meet later in the soft-play zone!'

Not that L is listening. But that's fair enough. I wouldn't listen to stocky Karen either, and L runs past with his fists up, yelling, 'Let's brawl bitches!'

'They see me!' Griff shouts, and sets off with his fists raised.

'Griff!?' Rachel says, as we both chase after them, as do Svetty and Alice, and, seeing as our faces are covered by the helmets, the Fedi, Bedi, Dedi, Cedi, hard-g Gedi and Edis duly assume that we're all running to fight them.

Which of course prompts a reaction, with many Fedi, Bedi, Dedi, Cedi, hard-g Gedis and Edis all grabbing whatever food they can from their paper plates and platters to launch a barrage of shrimpy, chicken-nuggety, cheesy sticks and sausage rolls at us – although, again, I do notice none of them try to grab the salad.

And as the first gooey missiles strike our shiny red helmets, L runs into a group of strange, robe-wearing folk with his arms outstretched, sweeping the lot of them over the buffet table, the whole thing collapsing and many tubby Edis all shouting in great consternation, which only seems to inflame the situation, as even more angry Edis then grab food to throw, and beakers too. And cutlery – although it is disposable bamboo stuff.

I run in and start pulling Edis out of the big bundling mess to get at L, then blink at the surreal sight of Griff sailing past me shouting *I SEE YOU,* before impacting into another group of Edis, sending them into the already big, bundling mass floundering on the now-broken buffet table.

Then I see Rachel, or at least I think it's Rachel, grabbing at an Edi to pull them away as another Edi pushes her, which then prompts either Svetty or Alice to push *that* Edi, which, obviously, sparks a chain reaction, after which it becomes a big messy brawl and I lose track of who is who from our side and focus on grabbing at anyone in a red helmet.

'Retreat!' L yells, covered in food as someone throws ice cream at his helmet.

'Dude! Not the ice cream,' a tubby Edi yells at the thrower, but I can see L is right and that we need to retreat due to the overwhelming size of the opposing force. We form a cohort and start forcing a way to the exit doors while getting pelted with food and plates and shoes and beakers. All of them jeering and screaming abuse.

'Fuck you, Dark Side!'

'Vader bitches!'

'Sick Sith fucks!'

The jeering magnifies as we retreat, and as much as this isn't my fight, it still galls me to be retreating while being heckled. Especially when they start chanting *'E.D.I. . . .E.D.I. . . .E.D.I. . . .'*

'Why are they making it sound like USA?' Svetlana asks.

'Not touching it,' I reply, as we hit the doors and once more come to a dead stop at the sight that greets us.

'Holy sugar plum fairies!' Rachel says as we take in another convention room much the same as the last, with a sign at one end.

WELCOME TO THE DARK SIDE ANNUAL CONVENTION!

'Why would they hold them at the same time?' Svetlana asks, as we take in the long buffet table giving service to people dressed in dark pajamas and dark hooded robes, and many, many others all in the same hardened polymer uniforms as us. But in blue, or green, or yellow, and even a few in pink.

'Pink?' Alice asks.

'Dude. I'm telling you. The Dark Side doesn't discriminate,' L says. 'Everyone is welcome. And by welcome, I mean kidnapped and brainwashed as children.'

And as one, those people queuing, and the ones that have already harvested the buffet – and this time I do notice a healthy mix of proteins, complex carbs and greens – all turn to look at the six of us covered in crap coming through the big double doors . . .and then the chanting leering jeering Edis behind us.

'Motherfuckers,' says a big figure in a very cool-looking black and white polymer uniform, before calling out in a parade-ground voice, 'Units! Make ready!'

They're disciplined, I'll give them that. As one, the lot of them stand or turn and grab food with their gloved hands as a stocky dark-robe-wearing woman with a name badge saying KAREN, DARK SIDE ORGANIZER strides out. 'Er, excuse me! Buffet first, *then* we meet in soft play.'

'Fuck off, Karen!' come the many voices from the Dark Side.

'UNITS ADVANCE!' the black and white soldier shouts, and as one they set off in a synchronized march, holding their missiles ready.

'INCOMING!' an Edi in the other room shouts. 'PREPARE FOR INVASION!'

'Karen! Stop this,' Light Side Karen yells from the other room.

'Excuse me!' Dark Side Karen yells back, and they both put their hands on their hips and start blaming each other. 'I want to see your manager!' Dark Side Karen yells as Light Side Karen throws herself to the floor twenty feet away.

'She attacked me!' she yells, as Dark Side Karen throws herself over a chair.

'She beat me!' she yells, the two of them thrashing on the ground as both sides pause for the most fleeting of seconds to shake heads and tut before once more crying out and marching at their sworn enemies.

I start to move, to grab my team and bug out, because we're not here for this.

This isn't our fight.

We need to find Mascaponi and get the hell out of Fiction Land before Wainwright tracks us down.

That's what we should be doing.

Except, like I said, it didn't feel right having to retreat like that, and I guess the time spent with L has formed a bond with his side. And maybe it is the Dark Side, but as he said, they don't discriminate.

And that means something to me, so I look L in the eye.

'Why are you looking at me?' Svetlana asks.

'Fuck it!'

'I'm here,' L says, as I turn to look at him. Man to man. Buddy to buddy. Brothers in arms.

'You wanna do this?' I ask him.

'More than I want to have sex. I mean, you know, I really want to have sex so if the offer for that is there, I'd probably skip this. No? No offers?'

'I see you,' Griff says, holding a hand up.

'Yo buddy. Flattered and no judgement,' L says. 'And I'm not saying never. But my first time?'

'Are we fighting these fiddlesticks or what?' Rachel asks, and we all turn to look at her. 'I have repressed anger. Don't judge me,' she adds, grabbing two fistfuls of chicken nuggets from a table. 'DARK SIDE CHARGE!' she yells, sparking the rest of them to start running as L and I grab food and join in with Svetty and Alice and Griff.

Cos why not.

'DARK SIDE! DARK SIDE!'

The chanting fills the air a short while later as we stand victorious over our broken and scattered foe, their light-colored robes now covered in gooey crap.

It wasn't just food either – things escalated from food to fists, and there's more than fat lips and bloody noses, and honestly? I'm not pointing fingers but I'm pretty sure it was either Rachel or Griff who threw the first actual punch – all while the two Karens rolled about in their respective rooms screaming for attention. And managers.

'EVERYONE STAND STILL!' a loud voice shouts from one end, and we all turn to see Detective Shovel framed in a doorway with his hat perched on his head and a whole lot of city cops at his back. 'We're hunting six fugitives on the run from the city dressed as Stormtroopers—'

'Er, excuse me!' Dark Side Karen shouts, her hands back on her hips. 'We are not Stormtroopers! We are a collective of Rain Warriors, Cloud Beaters and Sun Destroyers.'

'And Daisy Pullers,' someone else shouts.

'And Thunder Soldiers,' L calls, as yet more shout their derivative names.

'Whatever,' Shovel shouts, waving a hand to shut them up. 'But see. These guys have murdered a Sherlock Holmes and several wizards already.'

'Poop,' Rachel mutters, as the big black and white soldier turns to look at us.

'We didn't kill anyone,' I tell him. Man to man. A bond between us since we fought together side by side.

'Fair enough,' she says in a surprisingly feminine voice. 'Shuffle in,' she orders the closest soldiers, who all start crowding in towards her, blocking us from Shovel's view.

We start to back off towards the closest set of double doors in a low lumbering loping run.

'Are they wearing red by any chance?' Light Side Karen calls, and we all glance over to see her pointing at us. 'Because those six are trying to sneak out.'

'They see me!' Griff says with a flap of his hands as we start running.

'STOP THEM!' Shovel yells as the cops start pouring into the room.

'Stop them stopping them!' the black and white lady soldier yells as the Dark Side all surge forward to block and impede the cops. 'May the force not be with you!' she yells as we reach the doors and get into another long, foreboding corridor and run along in our red plastic suits, all covered in rice and shrimp sauce, but not salad.

'We need the main entrance!' Alice says, just before we bundle out into a central atrium giving access to the many convention rooms. People around us in all manner of dress sucking Slurpees and playing arcade games, while yet more lounge on benches or peruse the merchandise stalls.

'It's like the worst Comic Con ever,' Svetlana says as we twist and turn, trying to see a way to the main entrance through the crowds and hanging signs. 'Cops!' she adds in a frantic whisper, as I look over to see two city cops running from the corridor we came through.

We dart off into the crowd and start weaving through and around the stalls.

'We need a directory,' Alice says, with her head up, searching the walls.

'There!' Rachel calls, seeing a large list on the wall behind the information desks at the far end.

'STOP!'

We spin back to see Shovel striding at the head of an entourage of cops coming from the atrium.

'So close,' Svetlana says. 'Elevators!' she yells, pointing over to three sets of elevators doors. We burst away, all of us hitting buttons and stepping back with groans of dismay, seeing the little arrows above the elevators indicting they are all at the top floor.

'There's no way out, Croker!' Shovel shouts, as the cops barge people aside and yell at everyone else to move.

'Come on! Come on!' Rachel urges the elevators as I glance back to see Shovel and his guys sweeping in. 'Bum! We're not gonna make it!'

'We are,' I say, and stride out to meet Shovel and his cops.

'You coming quietly?' Shovel asks.

'Nope.'

'Good,' he says, and flaps a hand to send his guys at me as I surge forward to meet the first one with a clothes-line arm to his neck, flipping him over and dumping him on the floor. The next swings a baton at my head, but the suit protects me. I lean back and strike the outside of his elbow with an open palm. A crunch of bone. He screams and drops the baton. I snatch it up and twist to hit the shin of the next one coming at me, then rise and take another down with a strike to his knee, and as he drops I hear a ping behind me.

'CROKER!' L yells.

I speed up. Hitting left and right in a blur of motion to strike arms and legs. Sending cops off yelping and crying out as I risk a peek to see L rushing them into the elevator while Rachel hits a button on the inside.

'John!' she shouts, but I wait for the ping and the doors to start closing then strike even faster, buying time to sprint away and get inside with a middle finger up at Shovel as the doors close.

The six of us stand gasping for air, still dripping food, while cheesy music plays from speakers above us.

'Did you see the directory?' I ask, looking at Alice.

'No,' she says from my other side.

'Which floor did you select?' I ask, looking at Rachel.

'Twenty. Top floor,' she says from behind me.

'What the fuck!'

'Dude. How can you not tell us apart?' L asks.

'You all look the same!'

'We're totally different sizes!' L says. 'Rachel's slim. Svetlana has big boobs, Griff is small and lean. I'm stocky and . . . Alice is that one.'

'Oh wow,' Alice says into the awkward silence follows as we all wince. 'I'm *that one*. You mean the fat one then, yeah?'

'What? No! You're not fat,' L says. 'I just mean, you know, you're *bigger* than they are.'

'L!' Svetty snaps.

'Wow. Body shaming much?' Rachel says at the same time.

'I never said fat!' L says, as Alice gives him a withering shake of her head.

The elevator stops. The doors ping open, and she lifts a hand to cut L off and steps out. We follow behind her to see we're at the back of a long queue stretching along a corridor and, as one, we all lean out to see two big doors ahead and a sign over the top written in flaming font.

THE EYE OF SAURON

FICTION LAND'S #1 NIGHTCLUB

'IT'S ONLY JUST AFTERNOON,' Rachel says. 'Why are people queuing for a nightclub?'

'Not everyone is as wholesome as you,' Svetlana says.

'Or as fat as me,' Alice says.

'I never said fat!' L says, as the people ahead of us in the queue start giving us strange looks.

I look for another way out, but other than the elevators the nightclub is the only entrance. 'Come on,' I tell the others, and rush past the end of the queue to immediate shouts.

'Hey! There's a queue, buddy!'

'Oi, get back!'

It gets worse, with pretty much everyone yelling at the six of us rushing past in our food-coated plastic uniforms as two big hairy guys who look like Gary the Orc step out from the doors.

'No queue-jumpers,' one of them says as they block our path, at the same time as the elevator doors ping open behind us with more cops spilling out.

'STOP THEM!' Shovel orders, leading the charge.

I turn to go forward. The bouncers step in to stop me and both go flying back through the doors as we rush inside to thumping music and flashing lights. People gyrating on tiered dance floors while bartenders rush to serve drinks.

'Ooh, I like it,' Svetlana says, swinging her hips. 'We should come back one night.'

'We're being chased by the cops!' Rachel says.

'Yes. I know! I meant after that.'

'I don't think there is an after that,' Rachel says.

'Bouncers!' L shouts over the music as we spot more hairy orc and big troll guys dressed in bouncer black shirts rushing towards us as the cops burst in through the doors behind.

Again, I search for a way out, but there's only a raised walkway bordered by a long low railing, giving a view of the dance floors. The bouncers are all coming from there, but the alternative is back through the cops, and a quick glance shows me a few are now drawing pistols.

Which leaves me no choice.

'L, bring up the rear,' I shout, setting off with Rachel behind me, the others in a line and L at the back, and aim for the walkway and the incoming line of bouncers.

I hold my hands up in surrender when the first one comes at me, then lash out with a throat punch and step in with an elbow to his head. He drops.

I take three steps with the others behind me, and the next one surges in with a big swinging haymaker. I duck and pivot and bring my fist into the back of his knee, making him drop as I send him head-first into a column.

Two steps this time, and the next one comes in fast. I feint left then lunge back in with a leg sweep and a fist to the nose to finish him off as another bouncer grabs me in a bear hug from the rear and lifts me clean off my feet. I drive the backs of my heels into his shins and grope for squishy parts of his groin, and squeezing and twisting and raking his bones at the same time as slamming my skull into his face.

He cries out and lets go. I drop to all fours and back-kick his gut, sending him into the next one coming, then surge up, using the dropping guy as a springboard to launch myself into the next. Grabbing his arm and pulling down to flip him over on the floor as a foot sails by, narrowly missing my face, and more bouncers steam in.

Rachel shouts and throws herself at one and I see Svetty and Alice running in, while Griff and L throw trays and chairs at the cops to keep them back.

A yell of pain and I snap my head over to see a bouncer hitting Rachel in her plastic head, sending her flying back into Svetty and Alice, and the risk magnifies significantly in that second.

The cops coming in with guns drawn on one side.

The bouncers on the other.

Rachel, Svetty and Alice now down.

And one thing is clear.

This isn't a food fight.

I move fast as the bouncer who hit Rachel pulls his foot back to kick her while she's down. I rip him off his feet, sending him over the railing and down to land hard on the dance floor, his arm snapping under his weight as revellers scream out in panic.

I don't hesitate but keep in motion to grab the next bouncer and twist hard, snapping his wrist, then driving my knee into the back of his elbow before I yank back to dislocate his shoulder. He drops with a scream, and I grab Rachel's hand and help get them all up and moving with L driving them on from the back.

The music still plays. The lights still strobe, and we run fast along the walkway to an emergency exit as a shot rings out behind us. The sound of it almost lost within the music, but the bullet strikes the wall and gouges plaster out as it ricochets.

We duck and run and get through the doors and keep going, past the toilets and offices and storerooms to another door at the far end and through to a concrete stairwell.

With no other direction to go, we start down, all of us grunting and gasping and running for our lives as we hear the cops hit the door above us, one leaning over to shoot down the middle section.

We cry out and cling to the wall and keep going down, past level eighteen as another shot's fired, the round hitting nearby.

'Oh my god. They're actually trying to kill us,' Rachel says.

'Now do you believe me?' I ask. 'Alice! Figure something out,' I say as we go past the doors to level seventeen.

'Don't ask me!' she gasps.

'You're the Holmes.'

'You can't put it on me! And I wasn't just a Holmes. I was an Alice in Wonderland,' she says, before crying out as more shots hit the middle section, pinging off walls.

'You were both?' Rachel asks.

'Yes!' Alice shouts as the gunfire continues. 'And a teen angst thing,' she adds as Svetlana yelps from a bullet hitting too close. 'It was fucked-up. Honestly. Like all these genres warped together. You wanna hear it? I mean. We're obviously gonna die and this is obviously the right point in the plot to share my sad backstory.'

'We're not in a book!' Rachel says. 'But whatever. What was it?'

'My mom and dad were serial killers.'

'What the shit?' Svetlana asks.

'Dude!' L says.

'Seriously. They were these strict Christians running a guest-house in this normal town, but they were like totally embarrassed by their fat goth daughter, who, as it turns out, was the great-great-great grandkid of Holmes or something. Anyway. I found a secret passage that led to this underground network of weird tunnels and a fetish snuff club where the punters dressed as characters from Alice in Wonderland. And I ended up finding the bodies and getting caught, but I escaped after stabbing the Mad Hatter, who turned out to be my dad. So yeah. That's why I never shared it. I mean. Poor old Gretchen and her gay husband woes and sad Thor 46 really don't want to hear about that . . . Holy fuck! Go back! Go back go back!'

'What?' I ask, as she flaps her hands out and starts off back up to the last light.

'There's no number,' she says from outside the door on the next landing up. 'We need to go in here.'

'They'll know which door we went through,' I say.

'Croker! Just trust me. We have to go this way!'

I grunt and go for it, battering through the door first with the others coming in behind me to another utility corridor. A cleaning closet nearby. I get inside and grab a thick wooden mop to jam through the handle to the stairwell, then start running for the door at the far end and into an executive reception area. 'No way,' Alice says. 'Ha! Knew it.'

'Knew what?' Svetlana asks.

'There was no number for this level,' Alice says. 'We went past fourteen then straight to twelve. Which means this is level thirteen . . . And look at that,' she says with a nod at the sign on the wall behind the reception desk.

ACME LOGISTIC & SUPPLY SYSTEMS

'WELL DONE,' I tell her. 'I think we just found what we're looking for.'

'Okay, what do we do now?' Rachel asks.

'I don't know!' Alice says. 'We need to find someone and ask them.'

'There's someone inside here,' Svetlana says, seeing through a slim glass pane in an office door. 'There is! They're having a meeting.'

'That'll do,' I say, rushing over and through the door to see a large oval conference table filled with people in dull office clothes, all startling and flinching in surprise.

'Who the hell are you!' the closest man asks, getting to his feet to block us off. 'You need to get out!' he says, then drops from a headbutt as the rest cry out in panic. But I don't slow my momentum and get to the next person along, another guy, grabbing his right hand as he tries to squirm free, while others shout in alarm.

'What is this place?' I ask him, knowing we only have a few moments before the cops get inside.

'Get off me!' he yells, so I break his wrist, slam his face down onto the conference table, and move on to the next person.

'What is this place?' I demand, grabbing the back of his hair.

'Croker!' Alice says, rushing to my side as the others block the door to stop the office dwellers from escaping. 'Let me ask.'

I nod and step to the side so Alice can face the guy I'm holding, and the people in the room.

'We want off the island,' she says. 'How do we get off?'

None of them respond. She nods at me. I slam the guy's face into the table and let him slide off, then rush to grab the next, who screams and panics and drops to his knees.

'He won't stop!' Alice shouts at them. 'Tell us how to get off!'

'There is no way off!' the guy on his knees says, as I wrap an arm around his neck and lift him to his feet. 'Please! I'm begging you. I'm married.'

'Yeah, and I'm fat apparently,' Alice says.

'Dude! I never said fat.'

'Not now!' Rachel snaps. 'Just tell us how to get off this flipping island!'

'I just said there is no way!' the guy I'm holding says with a gasp as he squirms and weeps.

'Then pray tell me, kind sir,' Alice says, in a dangerously low voice. 'Where does the bloody food come from?'

A ripple of energy pulses through the others. A change in the air.

'Yeah,' Alice says, nodding her red plastic head. 'I felt that little pulse of fear. Kill him, Croker.'

I lift the guy higher and tense as though ready to snap his neck.

'No!' he screams.

'Things only come in, I'm afraid,' a calm voice says, and we all turn to another door at the other end of the room and a man standing there drying his hands with a paper towel while giving us a wry smile. 'I take it that's you, Alice?'

Alice nods and finally reaches up to pull her helmet off, freeing her sweaty head and flushed cheeks.

'Ah, and so that must be Croker.'

I reach up to prize the helmet up, thankful to be able to breathe easier as the guy looks over with a charming smile at the others. 'Miss Askew. Miss Graphite, and L, of course.'

They take their helmets off, their backs still to the other door.

'I think you can let him go now, Croker,' the man says. I glance to Alice. She nods. I let the guy go. He slumps and crawls off.

'Moist,' I say with a nod.

'Me too,' Svetty murmurs. 'But from sweat this time. These suits. They're sweaty,' she adds.

'Oh,' Alice says with a slow nod at Moist. 'That's clever. The head of the postal service runs the secret supply network. What a plot twist.'

'Alice, we're not in a story and those cops had real guns,' Rachel says. 'Whatever! Let's just get the hell out of here.'

'Er, well,' Alice says while tilting her hand side to side. 'We're kinda meant to let Moist make some long speech about how he arrived and couldn't settle into his new life and he just knew there was something else going on, so he decided to find out, and spent years working his way up to the top of the postal service, which gave him access to every delivery network and supply hub in Fiction Land, and ultimately to this very place, and all so he could also get free. But the question is . . .' she pauses as Moist smiles and nods with a prompt for her to keep going. 'Does Mr von Wiplig still want to escape, or is he happy here now?'

Moist stares at her. His eyes twinkling. A challenge in the air between them. Both clearly very intelligent. But then Moist is older and more experienced, which I would think gives him the edge.

'Or do we set Croker on you?' Alice asks, playing her ace and proving she truly is a Holmes. 'Either way. We're leaving this island.'

'Nobody gets off,' Moist tells her. Holding her eye contact. 'It's a one-way system. I tried. And you were right. That's why I worked my way up into this organization. To get off, but it's impossible.'

'Now now, Mr Wiplig,' Alice says. 'The only way to achieve the impossible is to believe it is possible.'

'I just said it's impossible.'

'Why, I am sure it is, but sometimes I've believed as many as six impossible things before breakfast . . . And anyway. You didn't have a John Croker. We do.'

'Funny thing that,' he says as the cops start shooting the door to get through. 'Someone else mentioned your name, Croker.'

I frown at him. Not knowing what he means.

'We intercepted a message from someone called Mascaponi.'

'I told you!' I say, turning to look at Rachel.

'You can gloat later. What message?' Rachel asks Moist. 'And where from?'

'Tell you what,' he says, with a sudden and very wolfish grin. 'Get me off this island and I'll tell you. Deal?'

'I'll take those terms,' Alice says with a wink, as she nods for Moist to turn around. He does with a yelp, staggering back at the sight of Griff standing right behind him holding a police baton up and ready to strike.

'You didn't see me,' Griff says. His helmet off and his shock of blond hair poking up.

'You people are very odd,' Moist says, as he heads to the door he came through.

'This book is very odd,' Alice replies.

'This isn't a book!' Rachel mutters. 'Whatever. Let's just get out of here.'

CHAPTER THIRTY-FOUR

Tunnels.

WE GO through an executive bathroom to a back corridor and eventually to a door leading to a much smaller staircase.

'You spoke to Mascaponi?' I ask as we start rushing down, but Moist just shakes his head.

'I said we intercepted a message. And I also said I'll tell you when you get me off this island.'

I notice Alice giving him a studied look before she glances at me, but there isn't time to ask or stop and speak, and that feeling of urgency only magnifies when we hear voices shouting from the top of the stairwell.

'The cops are coming!' L shouts from the back as we speed up, but the stairs are narrow and steep, making it harder to descend safely.

'Where are we going?' I ask, as Moist snatches a breath and waves for us to keep going down. I count the landings off, figuring we'll hit the ground floor and exit through some secret back doorway.

Except we don't do that.

'Keep going,' Moist says, and runs down the next flight, urging us to follow him. 'Everyone in that meeting saw me help you. They'll kill me too,' he gasps.

I don't get his intentions, and truthfully, I don't trust him, but right now we don't have any other option, so we keep going down until he slows and comes to a stop with one more flight to go.

'Okay, let me do the talking,' he says, sucking air and trying to compose himself. A shout from the stairs above us. Moist straightens and inhales deeply before setting off down the last flight. As he strides out of the landing through a natural arch there's a remarkable transformation, from a breathless guy running in panic to his normal confident and charming self.

'Hi guys!' he calls cheerily, as we follow him out into a huge underground cavern filled with workers unloading boxes, barrels and produce from the backs of horse-drawn wagons. 'Everyone okay? What's in those barrels? Are they beer? My office please. Ha! That got you all laughing. Right, back to work while I show these newbies around, eh?'

The chat works, and although the workers cast strange looks at us, they don't question it as we rush between two sets of wagons and cross into another cavern stacked with more goods.

'Jesus,' Rachel says as she looks around. 'It's true then?'

'Yes,' Moist says as we rush on. 'The island can't produce anywhere near enough food, and certainly can't make enough clothes and equipment. I'm amazed more people don't question it. But then people don't care, do they? As long as they can eat and drink what they want who cares where it comes from. Or how many people die bringing it to them.'

'People die?' Svetlana asks.

'This is an illicit underground network. Of course people die. Either through accidents, or because they talk about something when they shouldn't. Not to mention the people who arrive and start asking questions,' Moist says with a nod at me.

'STOP THEM!'

'Damn it,' Moist says as we start running again. 'They'll execute us on the spot down here. That way. Quickly!'

We veer off through another arch, past workers pushing carts and stacking boxes and goods, who look up in surprise as we run through. 'Back to work, chaps!' Moist shouts.

'STOP THEM!' A roar from behind. 'OR GET SHOT!'

'Whoa. That's not fair!' Rachel says as the workers around us share looks, then a gunshot rings out followed by a man screaming in pain.

'YOU WILL BE SHOT! STOP THEM!'

That does it, and the closest worker grabs a crate of oranges to launch at us, as L moves fast to stop them hitting Svetlana, grabbing the crate to throw back.

'John!' Rachel shouts as a guy rushes us from the front, leading the charge of the other workers. I surge past Moist and twist around the guy to get behind, grabbing his head and wrenching with an explosion of violence. Killing him outright as the others falter, suddenly not so confident.

'Go!' Moist says, his voice breaking with tension, and I see he looks sickened by the murder as we run on. 'They were right about you then,' he says.

'Who were?' I ask, as bullets strike the walls and sacks of food around us.

'No time,' he says, and runs through the last arch to a row of horses being watered while attached to their now-empty wagons.

We run for the front to see four horses attached to a large flatbed wagon, and Moist yells for the worker tending the beasts to move out the way as he vaults onto the back of the wagon.

'Can any of you drive?' he asks.

I wrench Alice up and push her onto the front.

'She's a kid!' Moist says.

'Just get down!' I yell to those behind, as Alice gets onto the driver's bench and grabs the reins.

She yells out with a flick of her arms, and we all fall back from the sudden lurch as the horses burst forward.

I stay behind Alice, using my body to protect her from stray bullets, and spotting the muzzle flashes from pistols as the cops surge alongside the horses and wagons.

'Get after them!' Shovel yells, while I curse myself for the tactical error of not cutting the reins and straps on the wagons as we ran.

It only takes seconds for the cops to and a whole score of workers to get onto wagons and set off behind us, building to a run with pistols banging and flashing and bullets going wide, striking walls as we plunge into a tunnel. Alice builds speed, the wagon rattling noisily with everyone clinging on in the back.

'How far?' Alice shouts. 'Moist! I need to know how far?'

'What?' he asks, lifting his head with a frantic look.

'The horses!' Alice shouts. 'How hard can I work them? What's the distance?'

'I don't know!'

'Think!' I tell him.

'We're going to the north shore,' he blurts.

'That's miles away!' Alice shouts in alarm.

'It's not!' Moist says. 'The road above twists and bends. This is perfectly straight. It's a lot faster. Like half the normal road time, and there's a mid-station to change horses.'

'Got it,' Alice shouts, driving the horses faster, and we all feel the increase in speed. For a moment, I gain confidence that we're outstripping the next wagon, then I hear shouts and look back to see it's gaining fast, with six horses thundering at the front.

'Is six faster than four?' I ask.

'Are you seriously asking me that?' Alice asks, casting me a quick look. 'Yes! They've got less weight to pull. Are they gaining?'

'Yep.'

She turns to see the wagon behind riding through the next pool of light and clocks the speed. 'We won't make it. They'll catch up before we reach that mid-station.'

'Look for things to throw,' I tell the others.

'Don't you dare throw anything at those horses!' Svetlana says, as we start grabbing at the few sacks and boxes left on the wagon.

'They're gaining!' L shouts, and we look back to see the wagon full of cops getting closer with every pool of light it passes through.

'Why aren't they shooting?' Rachel asks.

'In case they hit one of our horses,' Alice shouts over her shoulder. 'They're going too fast to stop if we crash.'

I look ahead to our horses, then back to the wagon behind us and clock more wagons behind that one.

'How far to the mid-station?' I ask Moist.

'I don't know! I don't come down here very often, and I don't ride this bloody fast through the tunnels either!'

'Guess then,' I say, as he flaps his hands.

'Maybe five minutes.'

'They'll reach us before that,' Alice says as we pass through the shadows into the light, and behind us the wagon gains each time. Getting closer and closer until it's only a dozen meters behind.

Another minute or so and they'll be close enough to take aimed shots with their pistols and start picking us off.

Which means there's no alternative.

'Alice. Slow down,' I order. 'But do it gradually. Let them think they're gaining.'

She shoots me a look and clearly thinks to argue, but curses and gently eases the reins to reduce the speed a touch.

'John, what are you doing?' Rachel asks. 'Moist said they'll execute us.'

'Steady, Alice,' I say, ignoring Rachel as I clock the wagon of cops getting closer in the next pool of light. 'Okay, slow down again . . . And when I say, you go as fast as you can and do not stop.'

'Why? What are you doing?' she asks, as she eases the speed and I hold one foot on the driver's bench and the other on the front lip of the wagon and keep my eyes fixed on the dark and empty space behind us.

The wagon comes into view, and Svetlana cries out at how close it is. Just mere meters away, with the cops showing surprise at how close they are and starting to draw pistols.

'Now, Alice! GO GO GO!' I yell.

Alice flicks the reins and the horses pull away, and I sprint down the length of our wagon and make the leap. Sailing through the air to land sprawled across the back of one of the leading horses, but the motion jolts me off, making me slide into the gap between the beasts with my feet trying to find a grip on tracers and lines and buckles.

For a second everyone on my wagon is staring back in shock, with Alice turned and screaming out as the cops shout, but in that second I nod at L and can see he knows what to do.

'GO, ALICE!' he yells. 'GO NOW!'

Their wagon pulls away while I slip and trip and get onto the back of the first horse and up into a crouch as I fix the cops with a look, and glance at the backs of the horses between me and them.

'What's he doing?' one of them asks with a look of horror as I surge up to leap from the first horse to the second. The cop shouts in alarm and lifts his pistol to fire at me.

I land awkwardly, but somehow keep my momentum and leap for the last horse, almost slipping as I throw myself as hard as possible over the driver's bench into the back of the wagon full of cops and, as one, they draw batons and start lashing into my body.

Which, as it turns out, doesn't really feel the blows due to hardened polymer armor I am currently wearing.

'Fuck!' one of them shouts when I grin. 'Hit his head!'

I catch his baton and take his advice, hitting his head with a nasty thunk that makes him drop instantly. Then I'm up and swinging my baton out in a messy close-quarters brawl. Jabbing throats and breaking arms. Snapping legs. Busting knees and elbows. Smashing teeth from mouths.

Then some fool draws a gun and fires at me, sending a round through my armor and winging my stomach. I cry out, driving my elbow into his solar plexus and snatching the gun free, then turn and fire into his head. Killing him instantly as another cop scrabbles for his dropped gun. I shoot him dead, and the next, and the next after that.

Then I aim at the driver, who screams and throws himself from the side, only to get killed by the wheels.

I was only going to tell him to slow down.

Which happens anyway as the horses, without the driver yelling and flicking reins, start easing their pace and I look behind to see Shovel in the next wagon along. Too cowardly to come up into this one and risk his own life.

We lock eyes for a second.

Me standing over the bodies of his dead corrupt cops.

Him standing in the back of his with more corrupt cops, and yet more behind him in other wagons.

Then I plunge into the next set of shadows and quickly grab the reins to gee the horses on. Speeding them up until I see a different flicker of light ahead and a sign whizzing by.

Slow!
Mid-station Ahead!

I PULL the reins to slow the horses then hunt through the bodies for a knife, finding one on a cop's belt. I jump down and cut through lines, gunfire opening up and sending me running on foot.

'He's stopped the wagon!' the driver of the next carriage shouts.

'GET IT MOVED!' Shovel yells.

I run fast into the shadows and see light ahead. But different from the lanterns. Brighter. Fuller.

Another large cavern with room enough for four wagons to stop abreast. Shouts ahead. Something happening. I keep running and snatch a glimpse of workers arguing with Moist, trying to stop him taking a fresh empty wagon.

'I said no! Not without authorization!' a burly woman yells at Moist.

'We don't have time for this!' Rachel snaps.

'And you can fuck off,' the woman yells at her, as Rachel pulls her helmet on and headbutts her hard, sending her flying back into the others.

'Oh my god that really hurt!' Rachel says, as Moist and the others start clambering onto the wagon. 'I literally can't see! My eyes are watering!'

I sprint to her side and scoop her up into my arms to throw into the wagon.

We set off with shouts coming from the tunnel, yelling at the workers to stop us. One grabs the back and almost gets in, only for Svetty to kick at his hands and make him fall off.

Another frantic moment comes to pass as the cops get line of sight and any hesitation they had before vanishes as they start firing pistols, a volley of bullets slamming into the wagon.

L screams out, shot in the arm, and drops with a gasp as I get to the front and launch Alice behind me. 'Get down!' I yell at her, then flick the reins and shout for the horses to go.

We get into the next tunnel and into the dark pools, and I glance back to see cops loading into the wagons.

'I cut some of the lines,' L says with a grin, as I look back to see horses walking free of harnesses and cops yelling at workers to get more wagons brought forward.

It's bought us time. A few minutes maybe. But still not enough, so I yell at the horses and flick the reins to keep them moving fast.

'Croker! Not so hard,' Alice yells, clambering over the side to take the reins from me.

'Keep them moving,' I order her, and jump into the back to help L strip his upper armor off. 'Through and through,' I say with relief at seeing the bullet passed clean through his upper arm.

'We need to bind the wound,' Svetlana says, pushing me aside and tearing at L's shirt to get a strip free to wrap around the bleeding injury. 'You were so brave,' she tells him, bending down to kiss his forehead.

'How brave?' he asks with a wink.

'You dirty man,' Svetlana says, with a laugh to break the tension.

'Rach? You okay?' I ask, crabbing over to check on her.

'Can't see me.'

'Fuck's sake! Griff?' I ask seeing two of them with their helmets on.

'How can you not tell them apart?' L asks as I get over to Rachel.

'You okay?'

'No,' she says as I help pull the helmet off to see her nose bleeding. 'I didn't think it would hurt in the helmet.'

'Guys! Lovely chat and all that,' Alice shouts from the front. 'How far away are we?'

'Not far,' Moist says. 'It's only a few minutes from what I recall, but please know, I only saw it a few times.'

'Saw what?' I ask.

'And you said we need the north shore,' Alice calls. 'We're nowhere near the north shore.'

Moist looks momentarily lost for words, like he's afraid to tell us. 'Lights ahead!' Alice shouts as we all turn and clamber to the front to see the tunnel ending.

'Moist! You need to start talking,' I tell him. 'Where do we go from here?'

He looks stricken as the light grows stronger and we punch through the tunnel mouth to another enormous cavern with a strange pattern of light bouncing off the ceiling in a way that is familiar yet strange at the same time. Stacks of shelving filled with goods line the area, creating aisles and walkways, and the whole thing reminds me of a warehouse.

I spot wagons ahead in a long line, all facing away, then glance over to the right and see another tunnel stretching off into the darkness with more horses and wagons going into it, and figure that must be the way back.

With no choice – the roadway isn't wide enough to go around – we stop behind the last wagon and jump down. Moist nods at us to follow him past the line, all the way to the front where workers are pushing carts of goods in from another section and others are loading the wagons ready to go back out.

'Hello chaps! All well?' Moist calls as he breezes past them, clearly trying to use the same charm as last time. 'What's in those barrels? Beer is it? My office please!' he adds with a laugh.

Except they don't laugh back this time.

Something about his manner.

His nerves.

A touch of mania perhaps.

Enough to make a big guy with a surly face step in front while holding a clipboard. 'Who are they?' he asks bluntly, nodding at us.

'They're escapers. I'm showing them the way out. Is that alright is it, Bogmire?' Moist says with a wink and a smile, but Bogmire doesn't wink or smile back.

'Newbies don't come straight here. 'Specially not straight off the wagon from the city.'

'Wow,' L says as he nods at Bogmire. 'I see what you mean, Moist. Are they all like this? Okay. Svetty, mark that down as a training issue please,' L orders. 'We've got an obvious lack of discipline with clear disrespect shown to ranking officers. What's your name? What's this man's name, Moist?'

'Bogmire,' Moist says.

'Bogmire, *sir*,' L prompts, with a show of forced patience.

'Apologies. This is Bogmire, sir,' Moist says as the other workers sharpen their focus.

'Bogmire. What are you? Section head?' L asks.

'Foreman,' Bogmire says gruffly, and L freezes in such a way that it seems to suck the air from the room.

'Did you mean fore*person, sir*? I'm sure you said *foreperson, sir*. As I am equally sure you read your interdepartmental training manual on the correct use of non-discriminatory language within the workplace. And I am also sure, *Bogmire,* that you read the memo informing that specialists were being brought in due to the inadequacies of the current supervisors and middle managers, namely, vis-à-vis the sacks of shit currently employed as fore*persons*. And seeing as we are a secret clandestine operation that doesn't give written warnings but instead uses unmarked graves that we fill with those sacks of shit to give warning to those that come after, you know what will happen if you ever use the phrase *foreman* again. But if you are in any doubt, *Bogmire,* it will go something like this. *Say. Whatever happened to that Bogmire? Bogmire you say? Well he got executed for being a gobby, sullen, surly, lazy, rude, ill-disciplined IGNORANT SLOUCHING MESSY PIECE OF SHIT! NOW STAND UP STRAIGHT! CHEST OUT! BUTT IN! CHIN UP! DO NOT EYEBALL ME YOU FILTHY MAGGOT!'*

Bogmire does it too. They all do, and even I bring my feet together and push my chest out.

'Right then,' L calls out, hands behind his back as he views them all with obvious distaste. 'I am sure, as a working unit, we can overcome any current *training issues* and develop a cohesive and productive team *without* the need to FUCKING SHOOT THE LOT OF YOU AND START AGAIN!'

Silence.

'Is that clear?' L enquires softly, cocking his head over as though to listen, while we all mutter *yes, sir* at varying volumes, which only makes L wince and clear his throat. 'Try again shall we. Is that clear?'

'Yes, sir!' come the many voices all at once.

'Wonderful!' L says with a bright smile. 'Carry on then, chaps. And Mr Moist, let's continue the tour, shall we.'

'Right this way, sir!' Moist says, snapping out a salute that makes Bogmire salute, which in turn makes everyone else try and salute.

'Add salute training courses to the list please, Svetty,' L says as we go by.

'Er, should I actually be writing this down?' Svetty whispers.

'Just pretend,' Rachel says, and Svetlana pretends to write on her hand as we hear a distant yell coming from the tunnel where we exited.

'Do not run,' L says as we force ourselves to walk until we're through into the next part of the warehouse cavern. 'Now run!' he says, and we set off as Alice shoots a look of awe at L.

'Oh my god, L! That was incredible!' she says, holding her hand up for a high five. He blushes at the compliment and gives a cheeky grin.

'Where are we going?' I ask Moist, as I clock that shimmer of light on the ceiling again.

He pauses and swallows and veers off through another arch, then comes to a stop behind a wall of boxes, and as we peek through I realize what was causing the shimmer.

'And that,' Moist whispers, 'is the only way off the island.'

'A submarine.' Svetlana gasps at the sight of a copper-colored submarine moored at the edge of an underground quay in an even more enormous pool of water.

'Cool plot twist,' Alice says. 'The lights! The north shore. It was that! That's why we couldn't see anything *on* the water. It was *under* the surface.'

'That's the approach warning,' Moist whispers. 'The light, I mean. We're not given a schedule and we don't know when it will come. And it's not manned either. When it docks, a hatch opens in the front for workers to get the goods out to be sent to either Middle Earth, Western World, or the city.'

'Why are you still here?' Alice asks. 'I'd have been on that thing like a shot.'

'Because anyone who hides inside and tries to leave comes back dead inside the hold. That's why I haven't left. And that's why I told you there's no way out.'

'But you brought me here,' I reply, giving him a look. 'Why?'

'Because of the message we intercepted,' a voice says from behind. An old voice but one full of humor, and I tense at the first sound of it, knowing exactly who it is.

I close my eyes and exhale slowly as I turn to see Wainwright standing in the arch, next to Shovel and lots of city cops all aiming their guns at us.

'We got the drop on you, kid,' Shovel says.

'And another plot twist,' Alice says.

'This isn't a book!' Rachel says.

'Well. I think we've seen enough, Mr Moist,' L says in his officer voice. 'We'll see our own way out from here. Good day!'

'Sorry, L. It won't work this time,' Moist says, in a way that makes us all look at him. Something in his tone. In his manner. In his eyes as he shrugs with an expression of regret.

'Well done, Moist,' Wainwright says, as he starts walking over to the other group.

'Holy sugar plum fairies! I did not see that coming,' Rachel says.

'Classic double-cross,' Alice says.

'Are you being serious?' Svetlana calls after him.

'Fraid so,' Moist says, turning to walk backwards with his hands out in apology.

'Wow. And you can forget that dinner date, buster,' Svetlana says.

'Which will, I am sure, becomes one of my life's very great regrets,' Moist says. 'But I did tell you there really is no way off this island.'

'You mean other than in that submarine,' Alice says.

'I wasn't lying. Anyone who goes in that vessel comes back dead,' Moist says.

'You don't think we've tried?' Shovel asks. 'We sent messengers in peace, and they still come back with more holes than when they left. Waddya think you'd do, Croker? Huh? You think you can just breeze in here and find a way out?'

'Yes.'

'We tried!' Shovel snaps over me, jabbing his revolver in my direction. 'We tried, kid. There ain't no way out, see. This is all there is. And we gotta make the best of it, which is why we stop damn fools like you poking your noses in. It upsets people. It makes 'em question things they got no right to question. And what happens? They get dead! That's what happens. So we keep a lid on it. We get the goods and we dish them out and people are happy.'

'They're not happy. They're brainwashed,' I say.

'Better than dead, kid!'

'Is it?'

'You know what? You're gonna find out. Send me a postcard from hell,' Shovel says, lifting his gun.

'Buy us time,' I whisper at Alice next to me.

'Whoa, whoa, whoa,' Alice says, flapping a hand at him. 'None of that makes sense.'

'What?' Shovel asks, scowling at her.

'Literally nothing that you just said makes any sense. Come on! Seriously? Is that it? That's the plot? We're going with the whole *greater good* thing, are we? No fucking way!'

'Will you stop it with the plot thing!' Rachel snaps. 'And stop swearing!'

'No. Right,' Alice says, holding a hand up to cut everyone else. 'You're telling me you've got a whole secret underground operation running to keep the flow of goods coming into the island, hidden from the people living here. That makes no sense. You could do it all in the open and nobody would care. Moist was right. People don't give a shit as long as they can stuff their faces and buy more crap. No. Seriously. I want the proper end-of-story baddie epilogue with the real reasons.'

'There ain't no more reasons, kid!'

'Not from you,' Alice says, ignoring him as she looks at Wainwright. 'I want the real boss to tell me what's going on.'

'I rather think your friend is right, my dear. This isn't a story. And there is no plot, so therefore there is no final explaining speech,' Wainwright says.

'Go on,' Alice urges her quietly. 'I can see you want to. Oh, but you can't, can you? You can't tell us because the people on your side would know the truth.'

'She's stalling for time,' Wainwright says.

'Am I? Shoot me then,' Alice says, still looking at Wainwright. 'But er, guys? After we're full of more holes than we arrived with, perhaps you need to have a good sit-down chat with Ms Wainwright here about the real reasons for doing all of this.'

'What's she on about?' Shovel asks, flicking his eyes to Wainwright.

'She's not on about anything. She's a very silly girl clutching at straws. Just shoot them already.'

'And you're a very old woman running this secret club because someone offered you a way out,' Alice says. 'What was it? Do five years and we'll set you free? But nobody can find out? Something like that? And what happens when you've done your time? You kill all the others and someone else takes over? Oh shit! Moist! Ha! That's it. Moist is the protégé! He's your replacement. Wow. I really do have deductive superpowers.'

'What the hell she talking about?' Shovel asks, shooting a look to Moist.

'Nothing!' Moist snaps at the same time as Wainwright, which only makes them look more guilty.

'Kill them,' Wainwright orders.

'Keep going,' I mouth.

'Kill us, and she'll kill you straight after,' Alice calls. 'Guys, listen to me. This is why Wainwright got so worked up over Croker. He started asking questions, so she got the wizards to pick a fight, hoping to put him off, but without realizing Croker kept his skills. And then what happens? He convinces people to go looking at the north shore with him on the exact same night the next delivery was due.'

'We don't know when the shipments come in!' Shovel says, trying to shout her down.

'But she does! And so does Moist, which is why he was at the Overlook Hotel to keep an eye out for the approach signal.'

'Baloney!' Moist says. 'It was the Fiction Land Postal Service Annual Buffet!'

'Which you planned in advance! Because you knew Wainwright's tenure was coming to an end. Which means you don't trust her either. You wanted to make sure she wasn't skipping out early and dropping you in the shit.'

'Dear me. That is a terrible plot,' Wainwright says, but I can see the uncertainty in Shovel's eyes, and it's clear the cops follow his orders, not Wainwright's.

'So, knowing we were on our way to the north shore, you staged a robbery to kill us,' Alice says. 'And when that failed you framed him for murder. Only for Hope – who had been quietly waiting for his chance to get back at you – to step in with a witness and get Croker bailed. And then Hope sends Croker off to start asking questions and you have a massive overreaction and kill John Candle. Which was mistake number one, because I am damn sure you meant to kill Croker, seeing as that creep Jimmy Secretan saw Croker going into the block. But you used it to your advantage and set Croker up again, and this time you arranged for a bunch of cops to attack him in the street, to provoke him into running into the Village, so you could show the whole city just dangerous he is.'

I flick my eyes from Wainwright to Shovel and can see Alice is scoring hits, but more importantly, she's buying time.

'Which is mistake number two,' Alice continues. 'Because you had Croker in custody. You should have killed him, but you let him go? What the actual fuck?'

'I said it was a bad idea' Shovel says.

'I mean, who came up with that plan?' Alice asks. *'I know, we'll release Croker again and, in the meantime, kill all of his friends and pretend he did it. Cos, duh. That really worked the first time with Jedediah Harper.* Genius, guys. Really well done.'

'Just shoot them already!' Wainwright snaps, but Shovel doesn't relay the order and Alice rushes on.

'Come on! Tell me I'm wrong,' Alice urges them.

'That was actually my idea,' Moist says with a smile.

'Shoot them!' Wainwright orders.

'No, credit where credit is due,' Moist says. 'Alice is quite correct with most of her deductive reasoning. But the whole point of letting Croker go again was knowing he would find Hope's body and go for the wizards. Within whom we'd planted the name Croker so desperately needed to hear.'

'Mascaponi,' I say, before I can stop the name coming out.

'Which we knew from Rachel's very detailed records,' Moist says. 'And of course, knowing how skilled Croker was, we let him do the work for us and round his friends up and bring them to the tower, where I just happened to be waiting,' he finishes off with a splay of his hands. 'And you know the rest. I bring you all the way to here where there truly is no escape.'

'Is that really it?' Alice asks, holding eye contact with Moist. 'Or did you use Croker to reach here after being ordered to stay back by Wainwright? Yeah. That's more like it. I can see it in your eyes. You were told to stay away, and you needed a reason for being here, so you used Croker. Why, Moist? Tell me why?'

He stays silent. His eyes fixed on hers. Shovel frowning and Wainwright tensed, having already given orders to kill us that are going unheeded.

'Someone else?' Alice murmurs, clearly trying to work it out.

'Give me a gun!' Wainwright orders.

'She was going to take you with her!' Alice says with realization. 'It's not just one ticket out, it's two. You're going with her, but you don't trust her, so you got Croker to make sure you reached here! Who are you worried she'll take instead? It can't be Shovel. He's just a lackey.'

'I'm not a goddamn lackey!' Shovel snaps.

'Well,' Moist says with a tilt of his head.

'Oh shit! Ha! I just worked it out!' Alice says.

'Give me that gun!' Wainwright orders Shovel.

'You give her that gun she'll shoot you with it,' Alice shouts. 'Because she's taking Secretan.'

'My, my. What a clever little thing you are, Miss Holmes,' a British voice says in a charming tone, as a figure emerges from the shadows off to one side, giving a slow clap. 'How very astute.'

The energy changes instantly. Even Moist tenses and shoots a dark look at the sight of Jimmy Secretan strolling towards us, stopping close by to adjust his sleeves with that nasty little smile.

'Jimmy,' Alice says. 'Now that is a plot twist.'

'Isn't it just,' Jimmy says. 'Hello, Lola. You're looking very pretty,' he says to Rachel. 'Have you told them yet? No?'

'What the hell is he doing here?' Moist demands.

'Now listen here, Moist,' Jimmy says. 'I did what you wouldn't, or couldn't, do. So I think the second place is mine, is it not?'

'Wainwright ordered you to kill Croker, not Candle,' Moist says.

'I know! But see, I do love stabbing people. It's a thing of mine. That's why I did poor sweet Maisy in when I was only meant to kill Hope, and that's also why I stabbed all those wizards before I set them on fire. Call it a compulsion if you will – I'm sure I can get treatment for it in the real world. Or even better, perhaps my services will be useful to the powers that be. Who knows?'

'It's my space,' Moist snaps, glaring at Wainwright. 'You promised me!'

'Dear Moist. As Jimmy said, you wouldn't kill for me,' Wainwright says.

'The kid was right?' Shovel asks.

'Oh can it, Sam. You wouldn't last five minutes in the real world,' Wainwright says. 'This is your home, and you get to take over the police department when I'm gone. All you have to do is give Jimmy a gun and let him finish this.'

'You're leaving me behind?' Moist demands.

'You won't kill, Moist!' she snaps. 'You lack the guts to do what's needed. Shovel was right. The people here can't know about this. They need to stay locked into their pathetic lives, and *you* need to make sure they get the food they need. I'm leaving. You're in charge. Enjoy the power!'

'I am so confused,' Svetlana says. 'Who are the bad guys?'

'All of them,' Alice says, waving a hand across from Wainwright to Moist, standing next to Shovel with the cops behind them, then over to Secretan off to one side. 'What happened was that Wainwright ran this whole operation on the promise of a way out. She never told Shovel, but she *did* tell Moist – and Secretan has been doing her dirty work and killing people, and he also wants to leave, so she *played* Moist and promised *Secretan* to take him with her on that submarine. Which is why Moist pretended to switch sides. So he'd get to here with Croker.'

'Right,' Svetlana says slowly. 'Erotica is so much simpler.'

'Isn't it just,' Secretan says. 'Just ask Lola Love. Oh, I am sorry, I mean Rachel Askew.'

'Oh shit! Were you from Erotica?' Svetlana asks her. 'I thought you were Hard-Boiled.'

'Just drop it, please,' Rachel says, shooting an imploring look at Jimmy.

'We are what we are, Lola,' Jimmy says with his hands out.

'Rachel! My name is Rachel. Please, Jimmy. You've caught us. You've won. Don't humiliate me before you kill us.'

'Sorry Lola, but that thing departs very soon. And I plan to be on it,' Jimmy says, drawing a gun from his waistband.

'Wait!' I snap, knowing I have to buy more time. 'I need to know.'

'Know what?' Moist asks.

'Your backstory,' I say to Rachel, seeing the look of horror mixed with fear in her eyes and an expression like I just slapped her.

'John, please,' she whispers.

'Oh this is priceless! She really hasn't told him,' Jimmy says in delight.

'You know mine. You know L's and Svetty's, and even Alice told hers,' I tell Rachel.

'John,' she whispers, imploring me to stop.

'Croker? Maybe leave it,' Svetty says, seeing Rachel's discomfort.

'No. I want to know. If we're seeing each other then I want to know. We are seeing each other, aren't we? I mean, *I see you*,' I tell her as she frowns. 'But we don't have much time!'

'Enough of this!' Wainwright snaps. 'That submarine is leaving in five minutes. Shoot them, Jimmy.'

'Gladly,' Jimmy murmurs, lifting the pistol.

'Now!' I shout at Rachel. 'Fuck's sake. NOW!'

'FINE! I was a porn star! Happy now? I held the gangbang world record.'

Silence.

Absolute silence.

'Whoa,' Shovel murmurs.

'Good lord,' Wainwright says.

A hundred questions whirl in my head as I turn to see Griff standing behind Shovel with a baton raised in the air – which is why I told Alice to buy us time.

Which is why I shouted at Rachel.

For Griff to get in position after pouring lantern oil over the crates of goods stacked nearby at the edge of the quay.

'I see you,' Griff tells me. His shock of blond hair poking up and his eyes wide.

'I see you too, buddy. NOW, L!'

It all happens at once.

The lantern oil ignites with a whump of fire and flame, at the same time as L shouts and turns to dive at Svetty, Alice, and Rachel with his arms out. Taking them down in a heap like he did in the convention center.

And in that same second, Griff shouts and swings the baton into the side of Shovel's head, sending him flying into Wainwright as Moist shouts and leaps at Jimmy – who tries to fire at me as he twists to get away and misses, the shot pinging off a wall.

Then Moist is down and brawling with Jimmy, and Wainwright is screaming as Shovel's blood pours over her face.

And me?

I do what I do best.

Thirty of them.

One of me.

An ordinary man wouldn't stand a chance.

But then I'm not an ordinary man.

I move fast and duck as I run to snatch Shovel's fallen revolver, coming up to drive the butt into a cop's nose. Busting it with a crunch of bone and a spray of blood. He reels back, giving me space to get a round through his head. Then I twist, getting another round into a guy on my right as I duck low, move, and come up to shoot another one down. Two more after that.

Five killed in as many seconds.

I ditch the pistol as another cop swings his arm to shoot at me, and pivot to grab his wrist, bringing his aim onto his buddy with his own reflex pulling the trigger to shoot him dead. I stamp on the side of his knee and wrench his gun free to put a round through him, then drop down to avoid someone shooting me. The bullet goes overhead as I land on my back and double-tap to the chest. Then a twitch of aim, and I gun two more down with two shots each.

Ten killed.

Twenty left.

I roll fast and spring up to stay within the press of bodies, using close quarters to make them confused and hesitant for fear of shooting each other. A neck snapped. A knife snatched from a belt. A stab to a throat. Another into an eye. Another step and I stab into a groin to open the artery, then throw the knife into another.

Fifteen killed.

Halfway.

And the air fills with smoke from the rapidly spreading fire, casting glows of orange on the walls and glinting off the shiny copper submarine.

But the advantage I gained wanes fast as the cops rally, realizing they will all die unless they put me down. They start firing, fast and panicked. I dive to the side and roll and take another one down with a leg entanglement, rolling over him to turn his gun in his own hand to shoot him through the head – then I carry the roll on, using his body as a shield, feeling the rounds slam into him. Fired by his own colleagues.

I get my arm free and aim to fire, but the pistol jams and I see two cops getting the drop on me as L swings his helmet into one of them from behind, dropping him instantly, as Alice jumps on the back of the other and starts punching his ears.

I heave the dead cop off me and get to my feet to see Rachel and Svetty and Griff using their helmets to swing at cops. Then Rachel grabs a fallen gun and shoots one dead before yelling at Alice to get off, and then shoots that cop as another one gets a round, skimming my shoulder. I grunt and turn to get the blade of my hand into his throat. He chokes and gags and drops the gun. I snatch it as it falls and shoot him dead.

Twenty down.

Ten left.

Nine. Eight. Seven. Six.

The smoke gets thicker. The fires spread fast, and the last five cops turn and flee. I spin round to see Wainwright on her feet, trying to get away as Rachel goes after her, grabbing her hair from behind and dragging her over to throw in the water next to the submarine.

'That's for making me tell them what I did!' she yells at Wainwright, floundering in the freezing water.

A shout nearby. A gunshot rings out and Moist and Secretan finally separate, Secretan springing to his feet while Moist clutches his belly.

'Told you old boy, you lack the guts to kill,' Secretan says, lifting the gun to aim down.

'But I don't,' I say, and he twists in horror to see me behind him. He tries to shoot me dead, but I move in fast and use a double-handed slap to knock the gun from his hand. He shouts in rage, but I see the fear in his eyes and hold off for a second, enjoying the spectacle of him realizing he can't fight me, while knowing there's nowhere else to go.

But he's also cunning and he holds a hand up in surrender. 'Okay, okay. You win, Croker. You're the better man.'

He rubs his side as though in pain and whips out a switchblade, lunging at me. I sidestep and kidney punch him. He gasps and tries it again. I sidestep and kidney punch him again. He almost drops but swings back to try one more time.

I sidestep and kidney punch him.

He drops the knife.

I break his wrist.

His elbow.

His shoulder.

He drops to his knees. His mouth gaping like a fish.

'Who would win in a fight between Bond and Wick?' I ask him. 'Well. Now we know.'

I put my foot to his chest and gently push out, sending him over the edge of the quay into the water after Wainwright.

'It's moving!' L shouts, making us snap over to see the submarine pulling slowly away from the quayside.

'How?' I ask.

'It's automated,' Moist gasps, clutching his belly. 'Get on board! Quickly now. You'll die if you stay here.'

The others start moving as I stride off, then I stop and rush back to grab Moist and heave him up to his feet, half-carrying half-dragging him over the walkway onto the submarine just before the access plank drops away into water. We aim for the big hatch at the front. The others are already going inside and waving at me to rush as the hatch lid starts to close.

I run, with smoke billowing around me and fiery embers drifting down as the fire spreads from cavern to cavern and from tunnel to tunnel. Destroying everything in its path and all the food meant for the island.

'Croker!' L shouts, urging me to run faster, and I cry out and speed up, to launch Moist through the gap, before diving and rolling through as the hatch clangs shut with a sound of pressurized sealing.

Darkness.

Pitch black.

Only the sounds of our breathing.

Our gasping.

A light comes on.

Instant and bright.

A large storeroom.

All of us inside on the floor.

'We all here?' I ask, counting them off. Only counting five. 'Where's Griff? GRIFF!'

'I see you,' he says, from behind me.

'Buddy! Don't do that,' I say as I draw air, then rush over to Moist as the others do the same and crowd in.

'Why did you save him?' Alice asks. 'He was on their side.'

'He helped us,' Svetlana says. 'He went for Jimmy.'

'Yeah, only cos Jimmy stitched him up!' Alice says.

'Whatever. Jesus. That island would make anyone go nuts,' Svetlana says, getting to Moist's side. 'Let me see,' she says, gently pulling one of his hands away, as more blood spurts out. 'That's an internal organ or an artery,' she says, clamping her hands down hard enough to make him grunt in agony.

'Is it bad?' Alice asks.

I nod back at her. Knowing a wound like that, unless treated very fast, is fatal within minutes. 'Listen, Moist. I know it hurts. But we need answers,' I say, leaning over him. 'What's at the other end?'

'Croker!' Svetlana says, pulling me back.

'That's a fatal wound,' I tell her. 'We need answers.'

'I don't care! We're not monsters,' she snaps, pushing me away.

'I am,' I growl, and Svetlana slaps me hard across the face.

'You back off right now!' she yells, unafraid of me and who I am and what I can do, but then we've got that bond between us, and any one of them has that right to tell me to back down.

I ease away with a pulse of shame as she turns away to take Moist's hand in hers while soothing his forehead. 'It's okay. You'll be okay.'

He tries to smile as though he's knows she's lying, but coughs with a dribble of blood coming from his mouth.

'Well now. That's not very attractive, is it,' she says and wipes the blood free.

'I need to tell you,' he whispers.

'Ssshhh. You don't have to speak. Just breathe. Tell us when we get you off,' Svetlana says.

'Are you gonna get me off, are you?' he asks with a grin, and coughs again.

'After dinner and dancing, but before I spend all of your money.'

He smiles again. 'I'd like that,' he whispers. 'You're very beautiful. On the inside too. That's rare.'

Svetlana smiles as the tears roll down her cheeks and Moist grunts from the pain as his eyes grow heavy and the blood still pulses out too thick and too fast.

'I lied,' he whispers. Growing weaker by the second. 'We didn't plant that message . . .' he trails off to cough with more blood coming out as I get in closer.

'What message?'

'Mascaponi,' he whispers.

'What about her? Is she behind this?'

He shakes his head while laboring for air. 'It's not like that. That's why it scared Wainwright so much.' He stops again and I have to suppress the urge to drive my finger into the bullet hole in his belly to sharpen his focus. 'Pocket,' he whispers.

Svetlana frowns and pushes her hands into his pockets to find a piece of paper folded into a square.

'It was pinned to the wall in here,' Moist says. 'I'm sorry. But I never killed anyone. I just wanted to get out.'

'I know,' Svetlana says, holding his hand as his life force drains quickly.

He tries to smile but spasms from a last dying stab of pain before his body relaxes as his mind shuts his system down, readying for the final few seconds of life, and he blinks up at Svetlana framed with the light behind her head. 'You're an angel.'

The submarine starts to descend with strange noises all around us and a feeling of plummeting, and with a final gasp, Moist's head rolls lifelessly to the side.

None of us moves for a long minute. We sit where we are, listening to the submarine and feeling the motion.

Then Rachel reaches out to take the letter from Svetlana's bloodied hand and starts opening it, taking care not to tear the blood-soaked paper.

'Rachel,' I say. 'About what you said.'

'Not now,' she says in a blunt tone, not looking at me.

'I was just buying time and trying to tell Griff to –'

'Said not now,' she mutters and opens the letter to spread on the floor as we all look at the handwritten words that started this whole thing off and made Wainwright so scared.

Send Croker.
We need him
Mascaponi

WE ALL READ it and one by one, they all look at me and the weight of expectation hangs in the air.

But I have no answers to give.

None at all.

All I know is that I have to find Mascaponi.

CHAPTER THIRTY-FIVE

We travel for a long time. Hours pass by.

'How did you work it all out?' Svetlana asks Alice.

'I didn't. I mean, Croker told me to buy time so I just started gabbling and it all came out,' she explains, then falls back into thoughtful silence.

And the hours pass by.

A clunk.

A clang.

A feeling inside of the submarine rising.

The lights go out, plunging us into darkness.

We hold hands and listen to the noises that seem so sinister in the pitch black.

Hissing.

The sound of the hatch unsealing.

It cracks open.

Weak light seeps in that grows stronger as the hatch opens.

'Don't shoot!' I call, standing up first to present myself with my hands in the air.

Nobody there.

Nobody at all.

Only another underground dockside. A narrow platform and nothing else. No doors. No tunnels.

We clamber out of the submarine and help each other over the gap, still in our red Thunder Soldier uniforms.

'There's a ladder,' L says, nodding further down the platform.

'Wait,' Alice says, as I go first and start climbing. We look at her and I see the expression of deep worry on her face. 'We might not all make it.'

We all frown. Not understanding what she means.

'We can't all be main characters, and this feels like the end, so whatever is up there might not be for all of us.'

'This isn't a book, Alice,' Rachel says, taking her hand. 'It'll be okay.'

'And you'll be fine,' Svetlana tells Alice. 'Like you said, I'm just the hot sidekick.'

'I didn't –' Alice starts to say.

'Joke,' Svetlana says. 'Relax. What will be will be. Go on, Croker. We need to see what's up there.'

I look at Rachel, wanting to say things in case Alice is right and we don't all make it to, or get through and survive, whatever is above us. But it's not the right time or place and she offers a pained smile and nods at me to go.

I start climbing. L brings up the rear.

'There's a hatch,' I call down from the top.

I open the hatch.

Sunlight blinds me, a wall of strong dry heat making me gasp.

I shield my eyes and clamber out onto sand and turn to help the others out one by one.

All of us blinded by the sun.

All of us shielding our eyes and taking time to adjust.

And when we do, when we can see properly, we stare out to rolling dunes of sand stretching off in every direction.

'Er, guys?' Svetlana says, and as one we all turn to blink at the giant billboard behind us.

The once white wood now weathered and worn.

The once nice words now battered and torn.

Words that we all read.

Welcome to Story Land!
Where You Are More Than What You Were

'HOLY SUGAR PLUM FAIRIES,' Rachel says. 'Now that's a plot twist.'

'Thank god,' Alice says as we all look at her. 'There's obviously a sequel. That's why we're all still here.'

I look at her, then at L and Svetlana and Alice, and frown when I realize I can't see Griff. 'Griff? GRIFF?!'

'I see you,' he says from behind me.

'How the fuck!'

'How can you not see him?' L asks.

'You need your eyes testing, Croker,' Svetlana says, as we try and absorb something too big to think about. Not immediately, after what we've just been through, anyway.

But there is something else we *can* talk about.

'Sooo, about this gangbang book,' Svetlana says as we all look at Rachel.

'I'm more shocked that you swore,' Alice says.

'Nope!' Rachel says, striding off. 'Not talking about it. Literally never. Don't even ask.'

'That's not fair! I told you about my serial killer parents,' Alice says, rushing after her.

'Which is, perhaps, the most surreal conversation I have ever heard,' I mutter to myself, then turn to see Griff smiling with his shock of blond hair standing up.

'I see you,' he says.

'I see you too, buddy. I see you too.'

FADE TO BLACK.

ABOUT THE AUTHOR

RR Haywood is a Washington Post, Wall Street Journal, Amazon and Audible bestselling author with multimillion downloads.

Celebrated for his contributions to the self-published science fiction and fantasy genres, Haywood has captivated readers with his gripping storytelling and an ability to combine compelling characters, intense plotlines, and a perfect balance of horror and humour. Haywood's work has earned him a devoted fanbase, making him one of the most downloaded indie authors in the UK.

ALSO BY RR HAYWOOD

FICTION LAND

"Imagine John Wick wakes up in a city full of characters from novels – that's Fiction Land."

Not many men get to start over.

John Croker did and left his old life behind – until crooks stole his delivery van. No van means no pay, which means his niece doesn't get the life-saving operation she needs, and so in desperation, John uses the skills of his former life one last time… That is until he dies and wakes up in Fiction Land. A city occupied by characters from unfinished novels.

But the world around him doesn't feel right, and when he starts asking questions, the authorities soon take extreme measures to stop him finding the truth about Fiction Land.

EXTRACTED SERIES

EXTRACTED

EXECUTED

EXTINCT

Blockbuster Time-Travel

#1 Amazon US

#1 Amazon UK

#1 Audible US & UK

Washington Post & Wall Street Journal Bestseller

In 2061, a young scientist invents a time machine to fix a tragedy in his past. But his good intentions turn catastrophic when an early test reveals something unexpected: the end of the world.

A desperate plan is formed. Recruit three heroes, ordinary humans capable of extraordinary things, and change the future.

Safa Patel is an elite police officer, on duty when Downing Street comes under terrorist attack. As armed men storm through the breach, she dispatches them all.

'Mad' Harry Madden is a legend of the Second World War. Not only did he complete an impossible mission—to plant charges on a heavily defended submarine base—but he also escaped with his life.

Ben Ryder is just an insurance investigator. But as a young man he witnessed a gang assaulting a woman and her child. He went to their rescue, and killed all five.

Can these three heroes, extracted from their timelines at the point of death, save the world?

THE CODE SERIES

THE WORLDSHIP HUMILITY

THE ELFOR DROP

THE ELFOR ONE

#1 Audible bestselling smash hit narrated by Colin Morgan

#1 Amazon bestselling Science-Fiction

"A rollicking, action packed space adventure..."

"Best read of the year!"

"An original and exceptionally entertaining book."

"A beautifully written and humorous adventure."

Sam, an airlock operative, is bored. Living in space should be full of adventure, except it isn't, and he fills his time hacking 3-D movie posters.

Petty thief Yasmine Dufont grew up in the lawless lower levels of the ship, surrounded by violence and squalor, and now she wants out. She wants to escape to the luxury of the Ab-Spa, where they eat real food instead of rats and synth cubes.

Meanwhile, the sleek-hulled, unmanned Gagarin has come back from the ever-continuing search for a new home. Nearly all hope is lost that a new planet will ever be found, until the Gagarin returns with a code of information that suggests a habitable planet has been found. This news should be shared with the whole fleet, but a few rogue captains want to colonise it for themselves.

When Yasmine inadvertently steals the code, she and Sam become caught up in a dangerous game of murder, corruption, political wrangling and...porridge, with sex-addicted Detective Zhang Woo hot on their heels, his own life at risk if he fails to get the code back.

THE UNDEAD SERIES

THE UK's #1 Horror Series

Available on Amazon & Audible

"The Best Series Ever..."

The Undead. The First Seven Days

The Undead. The Second Week.

The Undead Day Fifteen.

The Undead Day Sixteen.

The Undead Day Seventeen

The Undead Day Eighteen

The Undead Day Nineteen

The Undead Day Twenty

The Undead Day Twenty-One

The Undead Twenty-Two

The Undead Twenty-Three: The Fort

The Undead Twenty-Four: Equilibrium

The Undead Twenty-Five: The Heat

Blood on the Floor

An Undead novel

Blood at the Premiere

An Undead novel

The Camping Shop

An Undead novella

<u>A Town Called Discovery</u>

<u>The #1 Amazon & Audible Time Travel Thriller</u>

A man falls from the sky. He has no memory.

What lies ahead are a series of tests. Each more brutal than the last, and if he gets through them all, he might just reach A Town Called Discovery.

<u>THE FOUR WORLDS OF BERTIE CAVENDISH</u>

A rip-roaring multiverse time-travel crossover starring:

THE UNDEAD

EXTRACTED.

A TOWN CALLED DISCOVERY

and featuring

THE WORLDSHIP HUMILITY

www.rrhaywood.com

Find me on Facebook:

https://www.facebook.com/RRHaywood/

Find me on Twitter:

https://twitter.com/RRHaywood

Find me on TikTok

https://www.tiktok.com/@rr.haywood

Find me on Instagram

https://www.instagram.com/rrhaywood_/

Find me on YouTube

https://www.youtube.com/channel/UCm1elw5vXMlG4NFfl7oZXEQ

Printed in Great Britain
by Amazon